Darkness in the Shadow
By
J. Jay Ross

COVER PHOTO USED WITH PERMISSION FROM:
CATHERINE GRAY

For hundreds other beautiful photographs you can reach
her @
cagray44@hotmail.com

For
Mary

MAY 2010

Early Morning Somewhere in the Southern Nevada Desert

Jason raised his head as far as he could. He could feel the fresh scab from the gash pulling at the uncut skin near his left eye, the trickle of warm blood was next, and then the cooling effect as the blood began to assume room temperature and coagulate. *It was cool in here*, that was his first thought as he came to.

His next thought was of Carrie; where was she, and Dusty. *What happened to them?* It was then he heard a scrape, nothing more than a boot or a glove or something heavy against sand covered rock in an enclosed space, but it was a familiar sound anyway. He was in the cave. Had to be.

Lifting his head any further than a few inches brought on white light blinding pain and sharp chest aches. He probably had a broken rib, or at least a deep bruise; breathing became difficult for him when he tried to lift his pounding cranium. Another drop of fresh blood oozed from the dried wound above his eye and he moved his hand to wipe it, that's when Jason discovered that his hands were bound behind him. His legs were tied together too.

After lowering his head back down to the rough surface of what felt like granite, the pain subsided a little, his next thoughts were how did he get here and where the hell was he? He knew that he was probably in the cave, the temperature was cool and there was no light-at least any that he could see from under the little crack in his blindfold near the bridge of his nose-and there was an echo of his breathing. A familiar smell of ammonia meant rats or bats and that meant cave or mine. It had to be the cave. But how far back in? A few hundred yards? A few feet?

Another shuffling noise, he couldn't tell how far away because in places like the one he imagined himself to be in, sound travels differently than in open air. The blood dropped from his forehead and he could almost hear it splatter to the rock in front of his face. He closed his eyes as he tested the strength of the binds on his hands. They must have been from some kind of hemp instead of nylon, because the more he struggled, the more the strands cut into his wrist. He paused for a moment when he thought he heard a sniffle.

"Carrie?"

No answer.

"Dusty?"

"Airplane Man?" It was a whisper.

"Dusty are you alright?" Jason moved his head towards the shaking murmur.

"Do you know where your sister is?"

"Cassie?"

"Yes."

"She's sleeping next to me, but she's very cold. Her skin is like night-cold. Her eyes are looking at me, but she doesn't see me."

Jason felt a rush of relief over the fact that Dusty wasn't blindfolded, but then he realized what the boy was saying. If he was right, Carrie was dead.

FIRST CHAPTER
Fallcast, Nevada
December 2009

She brushed past him as he entered the store. Dusty, dirty, sweaty. That was her first thoughts as she recoiled after their shoulders touched. Carrie tried not to look obvious as she cringed away from the man but he turned just as her eyes rolled.

"Sorry…"

"Excuse me…"

Carrie opened the door and stepped outside into the cold. She rubbed her shoulders in the traditional way to express a chill and pulled her collar higher to her chin. She looked to her left towards the street, the town center and then right towards home, she chose home.

Carrie Marie Dodson was not a young girl anymore. At twenty-nine she had spent her last dozen years in anonymity, hidden from the real things in life that made a young person into an adult. She had kept to herself for many reasons, but her father and brother weren't able to shelter her anymore, weren't able to hide or protect her from the things she wanted to try, the things she wanted to feel and experience for herself.

Brown hair, long and naturally silky; golden hazel eyes that sparkled like amber in the sunlight, almost glowing in the moonlight. With her imposing Native American Indian dark features, she was raving, her face was extremely feminine but it pouted. Her beauty was part of the reason she was kept from the mean, cruel world by family. A prisoner of love? Somewhat, but there were other reasons, not all of which were pure intentions.

She was told it was her fault she had to be locked away. She was told that her growing body and looks would tempt men to hold her and take her from her family while she was beguiled by their-the men's-charms.

Carrie kept walking as the cold bit her nose and cheeks. She sniffed as the breeze picked up and wafted down the street, touching everything with a grip of frozen death if it stayed too long in one spot. December was here in Fallcast, Nevada.

The high desert was ruthless when it came heat in the summer; in Fallcast, which some say is closer to Hell than Satan himself, the summers ran around 115 degrees; the winter dropped the mercury down below the zero mark frequently. Those who braved the heat in the streets usually were dead in days, the ones who were homeless and just off the train in the winter were frozen to the ground like the castings of those souls found in the Pompeii ruins.

Since the railhead passed through the town of 2,500 people, the population fluctuated when the freighters passed through, slowing to a stop to allow for the several spurs to be utilized. There wasn't much of the town but three mills, mining for borate was the only thing that kept life breathing here, and the railcars were shuffled off towards the main mill site of Dowards, the biggest one of all.

Those who favored themselves hobos would leap from the boxcars or empty container rail stock. Few would survive the harsh conditions if they stayed, and the graveyard three miles outside of town was half filled with the relatives of townsfolk, the other half with simple granite makers with numbers instead of names. At least they were buried.

In the early eighteen hundreds the town was formed, but now it was the end of 2009. The storefronts looked much like they did one hundred and fifty years ago; the wood facades were still made from lumber harvested by the once prolific trees around the town. Now the trees were gone, little more than sagebrush and juniper remained.

The town was first founded by miners looking for gold and coal, but eventually it was found out to be rich in salt. Salt minerals called borate, borax, boron and a number of other things.

Borate or borax salt minerals were made famous with the Twenty Mule Team, hauling mined borax from Boron, California to the country for soap during 1883-1889 through Furnace Creek in Death Valley. The ore can be found only in low humidity and low rainfall areas, since the salts dissolve in water.

The original mines were shaft mines, named so after the countless shafts cut vertically and horizontally into the crust of the earth along lines of sediment where the mineral was buried; another reason for the lack of tall trees, the miles of shafts were buttressed with timbers cut from the small forest, which disappeared around 1910, forcing the sawmill to close along with it, cutting the population from 12,000 to 9,000. Firewood and building materials were imported from then on.

Eventually around the turn of the century, steam powered shovels and large dump-trucks allowed for open-pit mining or strip mining as it is called by environmentalists. Strip mining is essentially that, the ground is stripped layer by layer to access the minerals and the filtered rock was deposited on and around the mine in a wall fifty to eighty feet high in some places. When the "pit" opened and the shafts died off around 1921, more than 6,500 more souls left for better jobs elsewhere.

The only big mine left in operation is the open-pit now nicknamed *Nattie*, after the famed mule, a swing teamer of the famous 20 Mule Team in 1999 at Death Valley Days. The pit is one mile long and half that wide, with a gradual decline downwards of over two hundred feet and growing deeper with each passing month. It is owned by the Dowards Mineral Works, the Dowards being one of the first families of borate mining in Fallcast. The second largest belonged to the Dodsons. Speculation centered around who was here first.

The Dowards were the actual founders or Fallcast. After the need to expand operations, a call went out to the mining towns around the country, mostly along the west coast where experienced miners had gathered for decades. Miners pulled up roots and families and headed out into the high desert town from places like Virginia City, Sacramento, Yuba, and east from places like Gold Hill and Tonopah.

The eldest Doward, Henry, died of consumption in 1854. His son Martin followed five years later. It ended up with Henry's oldest of three daughters running the operation of seven shafts and four saloons herself.

Harriet Doward was not a pretty woman, her face and body were marked with years of hard work and exposure to harsh elements, but she still wed an educated young man named Bradley Dodson in 1895. The talk was that Bradley just wanted part of the Doward fortune and was granted that when his dearly beloved died of cancer in 1910.

They had two sons and one daughter, the latter of which herself perished in the winter of 1925. The family branched out and one son Neville, kept running Dowards Mining and Minerals; the other Baxter Neil Dodson, became a drunk philanderer and was forced by the old fashioned shotgun wedding to marry one of his nightly squeezes. Baxter died of cirrhosis three years later, not before nearly beating his young son Bernard to death on more than one occasion.

Bernard Dodson grew to age eighteen and married his high school sweetheart JoAnn Dooley, and they had a son named Terrence Randolph Dodson. Carrie Marie's father. Terry Dodson had two more children; one was Thomas (Tommy) Joseph before Carrie and one after named Dusty Howard.

CHAPTER TWO
Wednesday December 9th, 2009

Jason was still staring at the door the young woman walked out of. He'd heard of the girl, many of the miners talked about her, especially the older ones who had been here a little while. She was a sight to behold in the flesh. Her perfume, or shampoo or whatever she scented herself with was still wafting around him. It was sweet; it had a tang of citrus like orange or lemon with a redolence of berry, maybe blueberry or huckleberry.

Jason David Parmenter was born in 1977 to a wealthy family in Colorado. He had grown to be a good, hard-working man; a smart young boy that sprouted from a short five foot six in his freshman year in high school to his current six foot three frame in his sophomore. His blond hair, sapphire blue eyes and dimpled chin made for a champion against others when it came to having dates for prom or just a night on the town at *Dairy Queen*. His sinuous body was exemplified by large helpings of muscle where it counted.

His job brought him here to Fallcast, forty miles (as the crow flies) north west of Vegas. He came by air, Jason owned his own Cessna 182RG and had all the accoutrements of a private pilot, including an instrument rating and had logged thousands of hours flying for Monolith Minerals-his employer-alone.

"She's gone now, you want something?" Heather Baylee asked.

Heather was a nicer looking woman. *Nicer* than most seventy year olds; her hair had gone from blond to silver when she was fifty-five, her skin beheld the age of a lifetime in the desert outdoors, wrinkled and weathered. She and her husband Eldred (Ed) Sr. had owned the Baylee

Hardware and Mercantile since taking over from the previous owners thirty years ago.

"Pardon?" Jason was still staring at the double wooden doors with glass windows out into the street.

"Miss Dodson. She's 'bout halfway home by now. You want something?"

"Uh yeah." Jason turned to meet the woman behind the counter eye to eye. He shook the sight of the girl from his mind and thought fast about why he had entered the store in the first place.

"Mr. Parmenter, I got customers waiting…"

"Oh. Sorry." He turned to the only customer in the place, a seven year old boy with a licorice whip in his hand. "Sorry." He turned back to Heather, "I…I need to know if that fuel has come in yet."

"Fuel? *ED!*" She startled Jason. "He'll be right with ya okay? What you got Charlie?"

The boy pushed ahead of Jason, and laid a dollar on the somewhat dusty counter.

Jason stepped back and let the boy buy his candy. "Thanks."

He slid back into the oblivion of the store. The front of the store in its old fashioned way told of its interior. The walls were lined on both sides with shelves from about four feet off the ground to the ceiling, which was about twelve feet. The counter ran the length on both sides of the building with access behind them via a wooden hatch.

A thin steel rail on the floor and one suspended from the dividers every ten feet carried a ladder on wheels, to allow the clerks into the cupboards above. Each of the three by three cubbyholes was filled with memorabilia. Antique pharmacy bottles, toys, and old coffee cans from about the time they started tinning the black drink.

The store itself was about the length of a football field and wide as one. The floor was made of wooden slats that creaked in different pitches when stepped on, rubbed

11

smooth from shoes worn by customers over the past one hundred years the place was open and small holes in the floor had been patched with leather strips and square nails.

There were actually two halves to the store; the front, which held the reach in coolers that kept veggies and fruit cool, with flaps of plastic added in the seventies to keep the electric bill down. These ran every four or five feet along the counters on both sides, tall racks in between displayed post cards with pictures of the town and other ghost towns, old privies and funny birthday cards. One rack had homemade coonskin caps; another had wooden Daniel Boone cap pistols and rifles.

Halfway down on the unused *Ritty Register* side of the store or the south wall, was the butchering section. In front of a huge steel walk-in cooler door was a display cooler with cuts of local and trucked in beef, lamb, chicken and venison. Seafood, according to a sign on the wall behind the counter, was available on request. It was kept frozen in the back.

A porcelain scale with stainless table and large readout facing the customers, a giant roll of butcher paper sat next to it and a paper tape dispenser alongside. On the wall above a wooden cutting table three foot wide and six foot long made from stainless steel with an assembled sugar maple top were arranged a half dozen knives and a large pair of scissors for trimming and slicing meat into perfect steaks or chicken into friable portions.

In the walk-in was the old roof racks used for rolling in beef carcasses, now primarily filled once a year with the bodies of dead deer. Baylee still prided himself in aging and carving the venison for his customers who brought in their own game.

The center of the floor between the counters up front was lined down the middle with a two sided rack and had openings every fifteen feet. Staples such as flour, sugar, salt, etc. were kept on one side in five, twenty and sixty pound bags. The other side displayed home furnishings like plates, utensils, cups and mugs.

Under these were more cubicle storage that held larger sacks of dog food, it seemed to Jason it was mandatory that every person in town owned a dog, the chews made from sows ears and horse hoof clippings for man's best friend. Assorted odds and ends were placed on other areas on these racks also, just about everything you needed to maintain a normal life, like cereals and canned goods and other items for those who are cut off from a Wal-Mart or a Costco. Fact is, the hardware store carried more than seemed practical to life in the middle of nowhere.

Directly across from the cash register against the wall was a shelf; four foot across and six feet high filled with what the sign on the top of it said was VIDEO RENTALS. Mostly VHS tapes that were worn from use, the boxes were a little faded from sitting near the front window and door. A small selection of DVD's was available, but not many new releases-actually only three were new and they came from lost and found at the nearby hotel.

Next, the front area also had souvenirs for the passing tourist such as bins filled with common gems and crystal rocks supposedly collected from around the area (mostly purchased from bulk trinket shop suppliers in China) and candy. Loads of candies from the favorites like rock sugar candy on a string to the infamous horehound, a cure-all back in its day. Chocolates, jelly-beans, licorices, hard candies, saltwater taffy and homemade beef jerky filled dozens of other tubs and halved whisky barrels.

The back half of the store was the actual hardware. Shovels, axes, sledgehammers, picks and a few gold-panning pans lined the walls and shelves. Bulk rotating gondolas of nails in just about every size from brad to railroad spike; screws, nuts, bolts, washers and dozens of spools of wire with over a dozen different gauges.

Horseshoes were hand-made off to the right side of the store where an opening allowed the farrier to go in and outside to size up the horse marched directly to the place. He did business with his customers through a Dutch door, which was kept closed this time of year.

Boxes of mining samples were marked and set around the place, most of which were too old to assay but were used as a place to sit while waiting for an order to be wrapped up or to get your feet measured the old fashioned way with a real Brannock Device for buying a new pair of work-boots or shoes.

There were lassos, tack of every kind for the horseman; gloves of at least a dozen different type of leather from pigskin to cows hide. There were jeans and coveralls, wool socks and waders for working in harsh weather, heavy Carhartt work jackets and even heavy wool shirts.

But instead of racks in the center of the back of the store, an old potbelly stove sat. Four iron feet supported a rounded four foot pot with a leaky smokestack leading up through a hole in the ceiling with creosote and tar running down it from a quick patch job above.

Around the stove was arranged eight wooden and pegged back chairs with wire holding most of the legs on, a wood box for holding kindling and a few pieces of wedged firewood on one side, three cuspidors made of brass that had lost their sheen and a half of an old Second World War practice bomb filled with sand for an ashtray surrounded the relic centerpiece. Most of the time, the chairs were occupied by the *Old Timers*, they sat around and spit Beechnut or Redman tobacco juice at the spittoons and usually ended up hitting the stove with a gurgle and a hiss instead.

The Old Timers were a group of about six to eight men from town, locals and natives of the area, who were chased from the Salt Lick-the local diner-because of a limited amount of seats. They were for the most part harmless, three of them had been in WWII; two more in Vietnam and the rest were farmers from around the outskirts of town. They ranged in ages from seventy-five the youngest, to eighty-three the oldest; and they all were a little rowdy and loud at one time or another. They sought refuge in the winter around the potbelly stove in the back of the hardware store.

Eldred fought modern times as much as possible, but both up front and here in back, he'd purchased two Dell Vostro 460 Mini Towers. He had them installed during the spring to help manage inventory, keep track of outstanding debts owed by frequent customers, find hard to locate products that aren't available in the store, plus write checks and balance the books. It took three months before Eldred, also known by his wife as Ed, to figure it out.

Heather at more than one time or another regretted talking him into buying the machines since he spent more time surfing the net than sweeping or doing the simple things he used to. Now he kept up on the news, watched futurities live via streaming video and *Twittered*, whatever that was. But her job was also easier now, her arthritis had been aching badly from writing out accounts and checks last winter and the new system let her keep track of video rentals and expenses like never before.

Jason moved into the back of the store just as Ed was coming in from the storage room behind the back wall counter. He had ordered three, fifty gallon barrels of *Avgas*-aviation fuel-for his plane two weeks ago and was promised it would only take a week to get here from Las Vegas.

15

"Hey Ed. Any news of that shipment of Avgas?" He asked like a child who wanted a toy badly enough to be kind.

"Hey young feller. Nope. Three barrels was it?" He immediately went to his terminal and began typing. "Yep, here it is."

"I need to get to the air soon sir."

"Leavin' us behind are ya?" Ed smiled his gapped tooth grin.

Ed was about three years younger than Heather, but he looked ten years older. His shoulders slumped forward in a frightening manner; his hair was all but gone, a few wisps around the ears and liver-spot stained bald dome made him look like Mr. Burns from the *Simpsons* cartoon show.

He had kind and laughing eyes though, blue and grey, with bushy white eyebrows that could be mistaken for bird's nests built by small sparrows. He typed with his two index fingers as rapidly as Jason used all five on each hand. Ed liked to sound technologically advanced as his new computer was, "Hate to see ya flyin' off too soon. Google says the weather's gonna change."

Jason shook his head in frustration and said, "No, I have to survey some of the area west of here near the border. The Jeep the mine lent me is great, but the roads are pretty bad about the five thousand foot level."

After a few seconds and squinting at the 17 inch flat screen monitor Ed looked up with a smile as Jason approached the counter, "Seems the barrels are on a freight truck bound for Tonopah, then they'll be here in four or five days. Next Tuesday'll be my best bet."

Jason pursed his lips, "Tuesday. I guess I could use the mine Jeep till then."

"Or maybe ask that fine Dodson girl out for a ride to the mine dumps!" One of the old timers said with a burst of laughter afterwards, followed by the three others sitting

16

around the potbelly altar of fire. "That's if her daddy don't kill you first!" More guffaws.

Jason smiled and nodded his head at the old men, he respected them, they had served their time in the world and now needed something to do to bide their remaining years. Although it wasn't such a bad idea. Jason had overheard Carrie once refer to the spot in which these codgers sat around as *God's waiting room.*

Jason had seen Carrie around town his last few weeks here. She was quiet and kept to herself, even when he nodded and smiled at her. She never smiled back, or even nodded for that matter, but what he didn't know is at times she glanced over her shoulder back at him as they passed, sometimes even with a smile of warmth.

"I wish I had time for stuff like that." Jason replied with a smile.

"Listen boy, you take that Ol' crate out in weather like this and your fuel lines'll freeze before you get a thousand feet off the ground." One old man called Timber said.

"She's not that old and besides, I've flown her in weather colder than this."

"I'll bet. But back in the big one called *Two* I had charge of this Ol' Piper trainer that would freeze up while taxiing to the strip in Nome. Better just wait till spring, if you're smart enough…"

Jason nodded his acknowledgement of the old timer's wisdom but also smiled in a sarcastic way. If this guy knew about the new Cessna technology and advanced systems, he would die of heart failure. But he just said, "I'll keep it in mind."

"Spring is for the young, youngster." The one called Jerrycan said, "Best be getting' home to *Coloraydo* for the winter. You're not cut out for pogonip here."

Jason would love to do just that. He would love to get the hell out of this Hell and back home to Denver, but he had a contract to fulfill and yet to get close enough to his objective. He needed his plane for that and it was sitting in a rusty orange and black Quonset hut at the airstrip with an empty fuel tank.

He thanked Ed and walked back towards the front of the store where an older woman was buying some corn and tomatoes. Jason stopped at the video rental shelf and ran his eyes over the titles for the umpteenth time since he'd arrived in Fallcast.

The DVD's were mostly romantic comedies, but there was hardly anything remotely *romantic* about them anymore. They were acted by young up and comers who used the F word more than an entire class of thirteen year old boys in middle school. Fart jokes and other scenes of degradation including some with children actors just didn't make sense. The romance scenes were filled with sometimes graphic nudity and sexual innuendo that seemed inappropriate for pillow talk or even something that would make a real woman feel respected.

His eyes focused on Chuck Norris in a movie called *Invasion USA* or a chick flick, *A Walk to Remember*. He settled for the latter, it was a good movie and even warmed his heart, in such a cold environment. Besides, he had seen the Chuck Norris flick at least a dozen or more times. And-this was a reach-but the girl on the cover of the DVD, Mandy Moore, reminded him of Carrie Dodson. Not the eyes of course, but the smile she had while looking down in a pose on the cover. It was a peaceful smile, love and trust.

Jason knew he'd never meet a girl like that, either the character from the movie or ever have a chance at dating Carrie. Rumors flew about the Dodsons and Jason didn't have time for drama or being beaten within an inch of his life. The Dodsons were known for their brutality.

He took the DVD to Heather and she nodded at him, "Got it." She would enter his name into the computer later; she was busy gossiping with the old woman with the tomatoes and corn.

Once on the street Jason made the left handed turn from the steps of the mercantile towards the Sand and Juniper, the hotel he was staying at. He pulled the collar of his North Face Redpoint jacket up close to his ears and retrieved a wool cap from his pocket. After adjusting the roll in the cap to double cover his ears, Jason snuggled the DVD under his arm and jammed his hands into his pockets then started walking towards the hotel.

Carrie Marie was a few hundred yards from her domicile, her own home. It became hers when the trouble began a few years back. It was ten in the morning on December ninth, and the pogonip was indeed in full bloom.

Pogonip is the Shoshone Indian word for cloud. Ice fog is the more common name given to it east of the Rockies, but with western tradition and even stronger Indian influences in the west, pogonip has a story to its own. First referred to by indigenous tribes as *White Death*, because it was feared that the ice crystals would be inhaled into the lungs, freezing them.

As the temperature dropped below zero each night, passing clouds would descend and freeze. The result was large ice crystals falling and latching on to trees, car antennae, sagebrush, practically anything; giving it an eerie white painted or flocked look. Unlike snow, which was heavier and collected on the ground, pogonip was thin and remained stuck to vertical objects. Carrie's cyclone front gate as well as the rest of the chain link around her house was frosty white.

She was thinking about the man Jason, the one the *Old Timers* at the mercantile referred to as the *Outsider*. He was an odd boy, close to her age, and every time she walked passed him he would look in her direction and offer a smile to her, as her own body tingled a little.

She would of course deflect his advances for two reasons, one: if her father or older brother saw her or found out about her return flirt, she would be in for another confrontation and two: she was never allowed to talk to boys from the age of ten till the big trouble began three years ago. Although she was on her own now, she still had trouble speaking to men, especially one she was attracted to, sort of.

Home schooled and kept under close watch by her father, and then eventually by her brother, Carrie was never allowed to experience the things that turned a young girl's heart to mush-young boys.

She was scared of saying anything to the *Outsider* because she didn't want him to think she was an idiot. Her schooling was not exactly the best; she could hardly read the Sears-Roebuck catalogue or the comics in Sunday's paper at age eighteen. It took her ten years of self-schooling to be where she is now. The *Outsider* was a smart man, he could fly an airplane after all, and she felt as if she were just wasting her time even thinking about the newcomer. But he was so cute and her tummy made funny movements when they were near each other.

After letting herself in, Carrie took her parka off and tossed it onto the chair by the door, then walked by the full length mirror on her way down the hall towards the bathroom. She took a deep breath and looked at her body, clothed in a blue turtleneck, blue jeans and calf-high leather boots. It took a second, but she built up the nerve to look at her face. Carrie was raised to fear her reflection. Her father told her it was a sin to look at oneself in vanity.

A tear formed, in the last three years Carrie has been able to read books forbidden by her father and brother; see movies at the Windemere Theater downtown, rent movies and play them on the temperamental VCR she bought at the Fallcast Thrift Outlet. She has learned more about life outside Fallcast from the internet at the library in the last six years than she was allowed to in the last sixteen.

The tear slowly ran the length of her cheek and dropped from the edge of her chin to her sweater, leaving a little spot of dark on the blue. She shook her head and walked away from the mirror.

Years of being told she was not what a good man wanted, days of frustration not understanding the feelings she had inside for the boys she would see at church on Sunday when she turned thirteen-it all welled up in her. Then at eighteen, when she sprouted to her five foot nine inch frame and developed grace through books she snuck from the mercantile shelves-yes, she admitted to herself, she was a thief-Carrie Marie would have never known what it was to be like a real young girl.

After spending hours on a subject of captivity by a young girl whose parents sexually abused her while chaining her to a cage in the basement of the house they lived in for eight years, Carrie was thankful that her father and brother went the other way, even though it was the opposite extreme.

Carrie felt love, if it weren't for the big trouble she would have never lived love, or maybe, just maybe, she would have. But you can't pretend the past never happened.

CHAPTER THREE
December 9th

Jason walked the last twenty paces to his room located at the back of the T shaped Sand and Juniper Hotel. Just a few blocks from the Baylee Hardware and Mercantile, it had been home for the weary and homesick geologist since November 29th.

As usual, Jason waved to the clerk Mary in the office. She ran the hotel with her husband and was the all-day watch. A TV mounted above the coffee and pastry table in the glass enclosed lobby kept her stationed at the front desk. She watched TV all day, mostly the *SOAP Channel* on the satellite and occasionally she would tune to watch the noon news broadcast from Vegas.

The hotel sat on a mine dump or tailing pile from the original Doward Mill site. The berm of crushed ore and rock became such a burden to the mine that they simply moved the buildings to the other side of the hill. The place sat about eight feet higher than the street level because of this and there was a little climb up railroad tie steps to get to the parking lot level if you were on foot.

The original hotel was constructed in 1921 after the mill moved, but subsequently burned down in 1938 after a raucous New Year's Eve party that went terribly bad. The namesake was a three story Grand Hotel type of its time; but like most buildings in the twenties, was all wood and had no sprinkler system; the city's water mains were frozen from the seasonal cold, so the hydrants didn't function and twenty-five people died in the fire that completely leveled the structure. Even the glasses and beer mugs in the bar were reduced to flat pools of debris.

Some chunks of glass and brass can still be found in the pile of rubbish at the bottom and the back of the tailing hump where it was all pushed by dozers to clear the site for a reconstruction that never occurred.

The lot sat empty until a man passing through town thought it would be a good idea for a new place for travelers to stay. He bought the land and erected The Sand and Juniper II Hotel in 1964 and the place remains basically as it was then, save a few minor changes. A pool was added in 1969, individual air conditioning units were added to each room in 1973, and the southeast part of the T was built a year after that.

The building, when originally completed, had an L shape. The main leg jutted from the hill behind the dumps towards the street, the office in the top of the L. The seven rooms went south to the hillside and jutted to the west with another five rooms. During the mining boom for uranium in the seventies, the hotel was booked solid with miners, assayers, geologists and Bureau of Land Management surveyors. All were using the Sand and Juniper as a base of operations and bunkhouse for one of the biggest dirt digging operations in Nevada history.

When the uranium hunt went bust, the crowds left the hotel in near shambles. But the traveler who built S&J II (as he called it), decided that if another boom happens, he'd be prepared. So he commenced the construction of the other side of the hotel adding seven rooms behind the original seven, and another five plus a semi-modern laundry room to the southwest portion of the L, making it a T. The one holdback-the rooms that were built to the back of the original building had no back window, and the existing windows on the older section had to be bricked closed. The only rooms with more than one window besides the office were the ones located in the back of the T on both sides. Jason requested one of these rooms, he felt less confined in a room with two windows, even though the view was of a hill directly behind the hotel.

In 1999 the traveler who wanted to build a hotel and now the owner of the largest hotel in forty-seven miles by air, James Carl, became mayor of Fallcast. He's now serving his third term of four years. He had to sell his interest in the place (officially) to Mary and Jack Taylor, who now run it.

The primary occupiers of the whitewashed S&J II Hotel are miners, geologists, and surveyors; although not in as great as numbers as there was when nuclear energy was going to save the world. Ten of the twenty-four rooms were rented to the transient specialists; the other rooms sat empty most of the time year-round since the highway was rerouted through a different canyon towards Vegas and the main flow of tourists all but stopped coming.

There was still the occasional rock-hound and gold prospector who got compulsion to hunt for the yellow rock from a magazine somewhere, folks who like to travel off the beaten path and every year during Death Valley Days, folks would meander through and stop to get a glimpse of an old mining town that still had occupants, then continue on their way through to California; sort of like the Salton Sea still attracts lookie-loos to see what the hubbub was all about. One last link to the past was the dirt wash-boarded road that led west over the mountains to the Golden State

Jason took his key from his pocket, the old fashioned kind on the elongated green diamond plastic tag with the hotel name and a direction IF FOUND DROP IN ANY MAILBOX-POSTAGE GUARANTEED.

The lock was well worn and the key jiggled in the slot easily. The tumblers lined up and then Jason turned the knob and reached inside feeling for the light switch with his hand. The drapes were open when he left this morning around five a.m., but the maid always draws them shut when she cleans the room around eleven. These were thick curtains, and they blocked out any incoming sunlight, since this room was on the back side of the T, Jason had a window in the bathroom but the bathroom door was closed-as usual-so the room was as dark as a photo lab.

The lights flickered on, the hotel had installed CFL lamps in all of the rooms to save energy in 2006 and the cold room affected the performance of the fluorescent bulbs for the first few minutes. Another energy saver was performed by the maids (there were two full timers), they would shut the heat down to 55 degrees in each room after they made it up. This kept the pipes from freezing in the bathroom, but the weekly renters would sit and shiver for the ten minutes it took to warm the room up. Two rooms were kept at 68 degrees though, that would be the two rooms that might be rented each night. The hotel staff didn't want newcomers to think they were chintzy.

Jason dropped his key on the round table by the window and threw the drapes fully open, giving him a view of the rest of the hotel to his right, the pool in the center of the parking lot-which was drained and covered this time of the year of course-and the town below the tailings. It was a good view, and you could even see the far runway of the airfield from here plus the top of the hanger that he kept his plane in.

Each room was basically the same, two beds-queen size and a nightstand between them; a round table for eating or writing on, even though there was a writing desk next to the TV, that table had no room for anything but papers and keys. A lamp suspended by a thick chain from the ceiling over the round table, a lamp mounted on the wall between the beds, another light in the little alcove between the bathroom and kitchenette.

The bathroom was smaller than one in any normal travel trailer; a toilet, shower and sink plus a wall mounted hair dryer and one cup coffeemaker. Just across from the bathroom door-about three feet-was the kitchenette. It boasted a two burner hotplate, a three cubic foot refrigerator, a one tub sink and microwave. Most weekly renters ate out.

The TV was chained to the "writing table" and the satellite box was chained to the TV. The remote for both was mounted to the nightstand with a thin cable also, making it impossible not to get up to change the channel if you were sitting at the round table.

Jason took his jacket off and shook it; he just felt the chill in his bones might be cleared up a little if he jiggled the thing. He went immediately to the bathroom and used it then returned to the room and flipped the cover on the cooler/heater under the window and pressed the HEAT button, and then cranked the thermostat all the way to 99.

He knew it wouldn't heat the room any faster, but the psychological temperance it gave him made his chattering teeth stop. Next he inspected the new phone in the room for messages, the hotel had installed a new system at the end of October and voicemail was now available for guests (for an extra fee). No messages.

Jason sat on the edge of the bed for a moment and thought about what to do next.

He could go to Vegas and pick up a couple of barrels himself, if he could find a pick-up truck. But he didn't want to shell out the $280.00 a barrel himself, it would take months before he would get reimbursed for it. And then Dave might make him pay for the fuel that will eventually be delivered to Fallcast, since he couldn't take it back in his plane.

He wanted to get airborne and do his surveys for three or four days, that would increase his chances of leaving here for good; a final report on the strata in the upper elevations that was only accessible by small aircraft like his Cessna or a helicopter had to be made. But just after he arrived back in November, the fuel promised him by his company had yet to arrive; the delay was starting to gnaw at his insides. He had barely enough fuel to turn the motor over every two or three days, just to keep the oil and other fluids from solidifying.

He sighed and looked out the window, hoping deep inside that a flat-fueler like those at large airports would break down out front and he could barter the driver for some Avgas. Maybe let the driver stay in his room. Fantasy. Fantasies were bad when you were desperate to get the hell out of the town you were stuck in.

Thinking along those lines, he remembered the DVD he had rented at the mercantile. He stood and retrieved the case from his jacket pocket, the inside one. He had placed it there when he was fishing for his key in his pants pockets.

Jason then pulled his laptop, an older Dell with an excellent optic drive, out of his briefcase and plugged the patch-cord into the TV receptacles provided on the front of the newer model Panasonic. It took a few seconds for the computer to warm up, the room was still about sixty-five and climbing, and he opened the disk drive and inserted the DVD into it. Using the remote for the laptop, he back-stepped to the bed and laid back with his shoes on the spread.

After setting the TV via remote to the right setting he crossed his hands across his chest and watched as the movie began. In fifteen minutes, he was asleep.

The wind picked up outside and Carrie remembered when she was little how the howling frightened her. Her father would come into her room and light a fire in the fireplace, but that was hardly good enough. The house they lived in, the old one that her father still occupies on the other side of town; was built in 1917. Wood slats over two by four frames with just plywood covering the walls and no insulation in between but old newspapers made for a chilly winter.

Carrie thought about how when the wind blew hard enough, the wallpaper covering the plywood would flap up and down against the wall. The wind would make a horrific noise as it slipped through the cracks and crevices of the old house, sometimes it sounded like a ghost in those old movies, other times it made a sound much like a child screaming in pain. A sound Carrie knew well.

Even though she wasn't sexually assaulted by her father or brother, and even though they were actually trying to keep her safe, *spare the rod and spoil the child* was not a philosophy practiced in the Dodson home. Punishment was swift and painful. Sometimes, her father would practice psychological punishment at the same time by telling a young Carrie to go out to the willows down the road and fetch a switch. The same switch that meted out her penance.

Life was not all that bad; she was well fed and clothed. Although she was a prisoner of her house five to six days a week, she was still allowed to play out front as long as someone was home; and she did attend the Fallcast Catholic Congregation of TFP every Sunday in the basement of City Hall.

She loved church not only because she got out of the house, but it was time to learn things she couldn't get at home. Her reading improved tremendously while reading the Bible-which was all she was allowed to read at home besides certain sections of the Sears-Roebuck for clothes she was allowed to pick out on her own once a year-and she was taught about Jesus and the sacrifices he made to absolve mankind of his sins. She thought Jesus was the best example everyone should set for themselves.

Since most of all her relatives lived within a ten mile radius of Fallcast, holidays were especially a treat. She could help with the cooking with her aunt, until her aunt's death in 1987. She could garden and plant flowers in the spring and harvest produce in the fall with her cousin Michael who went to Kuwait in 2001 and never returned.

Carrie sighed as she looked out the window of her home; she saw two figures making their way up the walk towards the house. She was alone, inside and almost out. Everyone she liked was gone or was not what she needed for proper mental stimulation-a phrase she saw on the computer at the library one day.

A knock came to the door and Carrie stood and smiled. She walked over and opened it, standing on the old wooden porch was a young a boy and an older woman. The boy was preteen in age, his hair was nearly blond with a cowlick that rivaled Alfalfa's. He had piercing dark eyes like his father's, but the structural features of his face and especially his jaw said he was of Native American Indian descent. He looked like a light haired mirror image of Carrie.

"Hi Meg." Carrie said as she nodded in the woman's direction. She then looked to the young boy who was cowering behind Meg. "Hi Dusty."

"Dustin." The boy corrected from behind the other woman.

"Dustin." Carrie revised. "C'mon in."

She opened the screen door against the wind and the pair scampered inside before a gust would slam it shut on them. Megan Cooke was a pretty young woman; the same age as Carrie, her short dark brown hair left her face exposed, pale like a China doll. Her lips were thin and set back into a permanent smile, her thin features from chest to toes spoke little of her figure, but she had one she hid under oversized clothes. Meg's eyes were just a little off-brown and barely hazel, but they could look at a person with great intensity.

"Damn cold Cass." Meg called Carrie by her nickname, only a couple of people were allowed to do so. "Gonna bring a big snowfall in the passes again."

When the snow fell hard in the winter, the town was cut off for a few weeks till the state could get snowplows up there to the seven thousand foot level to clear the only way in and out of town by paved road.

"Hope not." Carrie replied and she took the jacket off the boy and led him towards the kitchen. "Hot chocolate Dustin?"

The boy looked at her with a smile then stepped away from her. "Okay?"

"Sure." Carrie replied.

"Cass?" He was the only family member allowed to call her that, "Are you my mommy?"

Carrie teared up, just like every day this scene plays out when Dusty comes back from the babysitter. She wiped a tear away and said, "No honey, I'm your sister."

The movie had several minutes left when Josh woke to Jonathan Foreman singing *Only Hope* during the wedding sequence. He had napped for the length of the film, nearly two hours, but he felt exhausted and wanted just to remain in bed. Then the phone rang.

It made him jump, since it was so close to his head on the nightstand, after a few seconds of recovery he reached over and picked it up on the third ring.

"Hello?"

"Did you get to do any flying today?"

"Hello to you too Dave."

Dave Selnick was Jason's boss back at Monolith Minerals in Colorado.

"Sorry. Been a long day here, we've been trying to figure out this gold market."

"No. I haven't. Thanks to our logistics department, the fuel still hasn't arrived and won't be here till the next railcar comes in on Tuesday."

There was a long pause on the other end; Jason knew Dave was trying to figure out a way to pin the mistake on him.

Instead he asked, "How about assay samples?"

"Got so many ground samples I'm going to need a push start to the end of the runway."

"Anything in particular?"

"No. Preliminary shows little or no *color*. But I think I've found something more interesting, there's a rumor here that one of the old abandoned shafts was rich with lithium, but they didn't have a proper way to extract it."

"Lithium?"

More silence.

"Wow!" The receiver rattled.

"Don't get your hopes up too high boss. These folks are a nice bunch; well most of them, but the head geologist at the mine says it's probably a fluke or misread data at the local assay office, which by the way is closing in a week for the holidays. And speaking of the holidays…"

A chuckle came from Dave, "I know, I know. Look, when the fuel gets there give her a few days over the passes and get me that strata report-complete with photos-and we'll get you home. You still don't care about Christmas?"

"Working the holidays doesn't bother me."

"It will. Is the mountain good enough?"

"There's a lot of runoff, lots of erosion, so the layers are visible. Should be able to get some great close ups. But you'll have to send some proper stuff in to get up there; it's at least a six mile hike straight up."

"Mm."

"Dave, there's a lot of alkali deposits here."

"We're not looking for the brass ring now; we need to find out if the investment into a gold mine is feasible. That's all. Lithium is skyrocketing as fast as gold and besides, the Chinese are kicking our collective butts on the stuff. Gold, right?"

"Yes sir."

"Don't sound so dejected. Isn't there a whorehouse or something in that town that can cheer you up? I heard Nevada has lots of 'em."

"Dave..."

"In a town that small there has to be some kindly widow or something that'll take you in and warm you up."

"I'm not in the mood for this."

"Alright. Listen, I'll call and see if I can get you some fuel faster. Damn it all to hell, why don't you have extra tanks on that thing?"

"Because my boss promised me that the big blue cans of gas would be waiting here for me..."

"Yeah, well don't trust him-that's all I'll say."

"Thanks."

"Hey, maybe you could borrow the lab from the assayer for a day or two and run your own analysis."

"Folks around here aren't too friendly. It's kinda like those movies where the good guy is kept at a distance from the locals because they have something to hide."

"As long as the good guy doesn't piss off the mine owner, I'm fine with that."

"Yeah, well in those movies, the good guy ends up having to blow up the town to escape..."

"Maybe you should try renting a romantic comedy."

"Thanks."

"Look, I know things ended badly for you and Lindsay. I'm sorry and I know this trip came too fast after the separation, but I need my top man on this."

Jason held his breath at the mention of *her* name. He shook the vision of her from his mind and whispered, "I've got to go."

"Okay buddy. Listen, as soon as you get in the air this will be done and over with. Then you can get home to open your presents from your grandparents. They probably bought you a glider this time."

"Bye, Dave."

Jason hung up without hearing the terminating goodbye on the other side. He was even more frustrated now than before. He hated the way his boss beat around the bush for things and he hated the way Dave was always saying '*Listen*'. He was on the phone with him, why wouldn't he listen, it's not like he didn't have a choice or stopped listening when Dave talked. But he was always saying things like *listen*.

By now the credits on the movie had rolled and the DVD went back to the menu, playing the same music over and over while Mandy Moore was leaning back in Shane West's arms.

"It was easy for you honey, you died…" He said to the TV screen.

Loneliness was a terrible thing to get over in the middle of nowhere, the breakup just a few months before he left Colorado made it even worse. It had been years since he was alone, or at least had no-one to talk to on the phone, at no-one that would constantly say *Listen*. He knew he had to stop renting romance movies, but they made him feel better. Feeling better by feeling miserable. At least he slept through this one.

The heater under the window clicked on and Jason built up the energy to get up and take a hot shower. He'd been in the mountains since early in the morning and now he was hungry, and lonely.

He stripped his clothes off after closing the drapes to the room, tossing the dirty, smelly clothes to the growing laundry pile in the corner of the room. Even the maids refused to move that or touch it. Geology was a dirty job, without Avgas.

Carrie finished off her mug of hot chocolate and watched as Dusty chased the tiny marshmallows around with his tongue in his. Her sadness for the moment had subsided, after all it was three times a week that she had to endure his confusion. She could never get a good job, going out day after day leaving him with Meg for more than a few hours-whom she had to introduce to Dusty each time-then have to explain the thing over to the boy again when he came home.

She looked out the window from her kitchen to the backyard and the swing-set. The wind was blowing hard and every now and again a gust would push the wooden benched swing up to window level, then it would drop back down on its chain and sashay back and forth in the residual breeze.

She heard huge gulps and the mug hit the wooden table.

"Done!" Dusty said with a chocolate moustache over his satisfied smiling face.

"Bout time. What do you want for dinner tonight?"

Carrie stood and walked to the fridge, what her father had always called the *icebox*, and opened the freezer side. "We have beef or chicken."

"Is beef the cow?"

"Was."

"Oh." The boy pondered this for a minute and then smiled, "Let's have Ginger!"

Ginger was the name of one of the lead characters in his favorite animated movie *Chicken Run*. Dusty sometimes associated things that way, it was easier for him to remember things like the cow, several of which grazed on the front lawn once in a while, so Carrie one day yelled out to the owner as he herded them off, "I'm going to make steaks out of them next time!" and Dusty immediately took to comparing live cattle with the red meat in the freezer.

"Chicken it is." She was always trying to get him to remember the actual name.

She removed the butcher paper wrapped hen and placed it on a plate that was in the drying rack next to the sink. She set the plate in the microwave and pushed 5 minutes at 30% power. She didn't have a fancy one that had a defrost setting.

As the plate and the butchered bird in its package twirled around in the microwave, Carrie let her mind drift to the store earlier today, when she was in ordering a new jacket for Dusty. The man. The *Outsider*. He *intrigued* her.

She saw that word one day at the theater on a poster, "Intriguing!" So she went to the library and looked it up on the computer. From then on she thought of the stranger with the airplane as intriguing. Her inside tickled a little when his face took form in her mind.

He was young, close to her age at least and he lived outside of here. And he was kind of cute.

Jason was stung as he entered the shower stream. He had the water on a little too hot, but after a few seconds his body adjusted. The day started at four-thirty for him, the alarm clock, the cold shower-it seems the water only gets hot after seven a.m.-and the revelation when he reached the hangar that the Avgas had not yet arrived.

He paced the Quonset hut for a few minutes then decided he was going to try and get up the mountains southwest or town in the Jeep Wagoneer that the Doward Mine and Mill Company loaned him. He just had to get the photos of the strata, which is the layering that occurs between periods of time and is played out in almost storybook form to a geologist when the stratum layers are exposed by earthquake, landslide or erosion. Used to identify many minerals and geologic activity, the photos will only be a step towards actually determining the content of the mountainside.

Teams will be sent up to do sampling, core samples will be taken with drilling rigs; dozens of people will become involved, but first things first. He needed photos to go with his assessment report.

The road up the first few miles was alright to travel on in terms of a four wheeled drive vehicle, but then lack of maintenance and washouts rutted the trail. A small dusting of snow made the road less visible and Jason nearly ran off of it twice. After making a thirty point Y turn (most Y turns consist of three) he managed to get the Jeep facing downhill. He tried to walk up as far as he could, but the road was long and winding and he figured he'd have at least seven miles to go to get to the area that had the slide.

The slide area is what he wanted. It was fresh, about five or six years old at most and had uncovered at least a million years of volcanic and erosive evidence. He had to get to that area, and he needed his plane. So, sweating in the near sub-freezing conditions, he turned and headed back to town to ask old man Baylee about his gas delivery.

Jason turned the water hotter as the progression of his body's adapting to it. Then at the mercantile he saw her, again. He had seen the girl around town a few times, once in the company of a young boy, another time or two in various locations like in front of library alone or in front of the closed movie theater.

She was no supermodel, no over the top reason to look at her other than her eyes. Her eyes were golden greenish or light brown. They stood out like a gold nugget at the bottom of a blue mountain stream. After being mesmerized by her eyes he noticed something else, she *was* attractive. She had this air about her that said *I'm quiet and shy and I like to be romanced.*

Well, that's the way Jason saw it anyway. There was just something about her that made him want to get to know her even more. Maybe a date? No. He had heard the rumors about her father and brother beating a man half to death who was simply seen walking the girl home one night.

Maybe it was the challenge?

Maybe it…

The room went dark. The exhaust fan-affectionately called a *fart fan*-stopped turning and this startled Jason, who fumbled with his balance as he searched for the knob to turn off the shower. He managed to scald himself one more time before finally getting the water to ice cold and then off.

He stood there dripping, his left arm against the wall and head down, eyes closed; listening to the dripping sound of the water falling from his head to the porcelain tub and the gurgling sound of the day's last insult being sucked down the drain.

"Perfect. Just… perfect." He didn't even have the energy to swear.

He slowly slid the curtain from one side of the tub to the other and looked around. There was a little light coming from between the cracks of the heavy draperies. The DVD player was still playing, but only through the speakers and screen of his laptop, the TV was out as was the heater. The heater…

By the time Jason got out of the shower and was completely dry, the wind had blown the room cold, not ice cold, but it was on its way there. Without power there was no heat. Jason wondered aloud to himself colorfully why the hotel had no generator as he walked from the dressing area to the window, banging his shin on the wood frame for the second unused bed.

Tears formed at the back of his eyes, half pain-half frustration, so he laughed it off in a maniacally sad deep belly laugh. He threw back the curtains in anger and looked towards the front of the hotel towards the office. It was a little distance, but he could see the TV still on in there.

"If that don't put the icing on my day."

He put his jacket on hastily, jammed his feet into his boots and did a simple wrap around the top of them with the laces to keep from tripping on them and stomped out the door towards the office.

The wind was cold, very cold as it bit at his face. He had to close his eyes and turn his back towards the room door to keep from being blasted by a cloud of sand that rose from the abandoned field across the street from the hotel; and when he saw his door he realized he forgot his key on the round table. He stopped walking backwards. A smile came to his face then he turned towards the office and continued his trudge, less angry than before. He had given up.

"Good afternoon Mr. Parmenter. A little windy today." Mary said without taking her eyes off *The Young and Restless*.

"Yes. I suppose that's what caused the power outage?" He said, hiding his lack of happiness at the moment.

"Oh yeah." She looked down from the TV screen and into Jason's eyes. "Jack went down to McPherson's to get some diesel."

"The office and rooms are on different circuits?" Jason asked, knowing the answer.

"The rooms draw too much power and we need the extra one for our computers here and our home," Mary indicated the place they lived behind the office door with a nod. The two room one bath home came with the place, "of course he forgot to fill the tank on the big generator after the last outage."

"Of course." Sarcasm was not too far off.

"If you would like, the Salt Lick has a warm place to sit. Or there's the Horseshoe."

Jason pondered whether he wanted to sit at the bar or eat. "That's it? How long till Jack gets the power back on?"

"Well, he usually takes an hour or so because he and Jimmy Mac spend so little time with each other anymore…" She drifted off, Jason got the hint. "Or you could also hang out down at Baylee's. They usually have a good fire going and Ed has a big generator."

Jason wondered how long he could keep his cool with the ornery old timers sitting around the stove spitting tobacco juice all over the place and telling war stories. "Thanks."

He turned and walked out without asking for a replacement key. The battery would run down on his computer soon enough and he was in no mood to go back to his room. He headed for the Horseshoe Club.

Carrie was searching the pantry for a canned vegetable to go with the chicken when the power went out. The microwave stopped of course, so she walked over carefully using the kitchen table as her guide and opened the door to the little oven. She had a bar-b-que in the backyard and could cook the chicken there if was defrosted enough…

She picked the paper up and squeezed. Nope. Hard as a rock still. She thought a second about filling a sink with warm water and soaking it in there, but Dusty interrupted her.

"The power fell again."

"Out. The power is out again." She corrected him gently.

"Out." He said with a smile. "I'm hungry."

Carrie pursed her lips. She was in no mood for three hundred *I'm hungrys* until the chicken defrosted enough to cook. She walked to the counter and picked up her pocketbook then counted the bills. Twenty-four dollars till the end of the month. A sad feeling bit her hard, Christmas was just around the corner and she had only bought a few presents with the money she had left from the state. More was coming in a few weeks, until then she would make sacrifices.

Dusty walked to Carrie and pulled at the hem of her turtleneck. "I'm cold."

The Horseshoe Club was like any other small town bar. Or *bars*, Jason mused. There were four in town and two in the sticks by the farms. Those were usually filled with the farmers and field workers. Six bars and two churches. A usual combination and ratio.

The bar itself was normal in all ways as a small town bar. There were deer heads mounted on the walls about every ten or twelve feet, a stuffed jackalope, three huge elk and one moose about the size of Jason's Cessna. The little brass plaque under it read: ***Fred "Timber" George 1967 Alaska***

The redolence of stale beer in the form of a yeasty smell hit him first. Then fusty and fresh cigarette smoke, cigar aromas and sweaty men. The music coming from the jukebox was pure country gold; Hank Williams singing about crying into his drink; the sound of glasses clattering and chatter from the packed place drowned out everything else.

Everyone in town knew this was the place to go in a power outage. Jason reasoned with himself for a minute before approaching the bar, would he stay and drink till he was drunk or just wait a few hours till Jack got back and fired up the generator at the hotel? He didn't know. It was kind of nice to be in a crowd though, and everyone was having fun.

Jason was on his second beer when a man of about thirty walked in and sat down three stools from him. He knew this guy; the customer was wearing old worn coveralls, a white T shirt and a tattered U.S. Army cold weather jacket. He smelled of old booze and no baths. His facial features revealed a man who drank too much, his skin was red and blotchy and eyes glazed nearly yellow, the color of his hair. His thin torso made the jacket on him look more like an army tent and his bony hands held out a ten dollar bill for the bartender.

"Tommy Dodson." The bearded barkeep said with a hint of distaste. "I told you, you ain't welcome here anymore after the last visit. You cost us three hundred dollars in damage!"

"You can take that crap and…" Tommy began, but a hand on his shoulder stopped him.

"He's with me Ron." A gruff and low voice rumbled behind Tommy in the shadows.

Ron, the bartender, nodded and emphatically moved towards the reach-in cooler to retrieve two Budweisers. He sat them on the bar and quickly moved to the other side, where he began nodding his head into a conversation that had started without him.

The man with the gravelly voice slid in quietly next to Tommy and placed his callused hands around the beer bottle. He spoke quietly; Jason had already determined to leave the moment he saw Tommy.

"Tom… I told you to stay away from these places."

"Sorry dad. But it was a bust ass day at work and I needed a…"

"Not bad enough to end up in the hoosegow."

The older man looked around and saw that Jason was looking out of the corner of his eye towards them so he fixed his gaze on the spy for a few seconds before re-engaging his son. Jason downed his beer so fast his cheeks bulged from not being able to swallow fast enough; beer dribbled from his lips to his chin as he set a fiver on the wooden bar and walked towards the door.

Jason pushed through the doors and out onto the cold street. He had heard stories of the famous Dodson family. Criminals, fighters, troublemakers, *murderers*. As in most small towns, talk is cheap, but he didn't want to prove any gossip true with his own neck. He shuffled his feet towards the Salt Lick. Maybe dinner and bed would do him some good. At least he knew where the Dodsons were.

As he trudged against wind towards the end of the street where the restaurant was, Jason felt the image of old man Dodson haunt his mind. The man was well into his fifties. He had a greying beard that needed trimming with a dark tobacco stain under the lip. His eyes were like pieces of dark coal, Jason couldn't even tell the real color of them. He walked with a purpose, deliberate and sure of each step. He was very confident in himself, and it was displayed for everyone to see as he walked, sat and ordered drinks. His large arms bulging from under the rolled up sleeves on his Pendleton shirt emphasized his strength, he stood about six-two and weighed around two hundred pounds. No fat.

He was a man with the world full of trouble on his shoulders, a man who spent his life weighed down by the injustice and trivial laws that plagued the not so tall pillar of the community. A man who had a vision of himself as a patriarch of Fallcast, but in reality was nothing more than owner of large tracts of land, and the second largest mine and mill in Fallcast.

Jason also sensed in the man a soul on the verge of goodness. A person who was tired of his past exploits and in a way, wanting to make amends to those he wronged, a man who carried a burden of guilt over something bad that happened a long time ago. He had that in his gait too, a walk of a man who was sorry for something, the way he held his head and the way his shoulders sagged.

The distance between the Horseshoe and the Salt Lick was nearly a mile, but with a good tailwind provided by nature, Jason had closed the gap in record time. A freighter was coming in from the mountains and the engines were covered in snow. That, Jason thought, was a bad sign. Snow on the cars meant snow on the ground and snow on the ground meant he wouldn't be able to photograph the higher elevations. More delays.

The boxcars and containers clanked and sputtered their steel on steel sounds as the rolling stock passed him; heading the other way towards the many spurs and the shoofly that eventually became permanent around the old Boxing mill site. The mill was set to expand in the early seventies, but when America "ran out of oil", the mill owners pulled up and moved out. The Boxing family had no representative left in Fallcast; still, the family name is visible on the side of the fading grey-white wooden building. The railroad now uses the *shoofly* or temporary bypass on the street side of the old mill site, as a parking spot where the engineers pull off for mandatory rest.

There was something eerie about the cars tonight. Something maybe about the foot or so of white glistening blue snow that was blowing off fast and making a fake little snowstorm in town. It was in the sound of the wheels as they trudged along the steel road. It was the protest of the diesel engines as power was added to get the locomotive up the small incline towards the back side of town where the warehouses were. Spooky, or as Jason's mother called it-ominous.

He had seen a dozen trains come in during his stay here in Fallcast, but this one seemed out of place. Maybe he was tired; maybe he needed a good meal and some real sleep. Maybe he just needed to get out of town.

The rolling stock banged together and apart as the engine made the small but steep grade and more snow fell off the roofs and onto the tracks behind the last car. No longer a caboose, just a red flashing light on the final stock. Called FRED for Flashing Rear End Device, the little red light and electronic package was known as the *F-ing* Railroad Device by many old fashioned hobo types and the men who manned the often romanticized and glorified cabooses that were replaced by the little box.

The box was powered by battery or a small turbine generator run by air in the brake line that hooked to the device. It monitored brake pressure and/or accidental separation at the end of the long trains and sent the info back to the engineer via the HTD computer, known affectionately as *Wilma*. Replacing most if not all of the famous trailing car stock by the mid 1980's. The caboose was dead. Another era gone, another machine replacing the job of several men. Hail progress, Jason thought.

The little red light winked at Jason as it passed him on towards the center of town and the mills, an omen for sure.

CHAPTER FOUR
Evening of December 9th

The Salt Lick was another average in the style of diners that graced small town America in the fifties. An old converted triple-wide mobile home with the corrugated steel shroud around the bottom to hide the axles and wheels; a terrible job of chopping the tongue off with a cutting torch was evident from the slagged edges at the base just under one of the large windows looking out.

There were about six windows in all; all very large and looked out upon the street which everyone called Main, but was actually named Sluicebox Avenue. Sluicebox was the primary street coming in from Highway 201, the one that used to run to the western side of Vegas.

The door was only big enough for one person to enter at a time, and there was only enough room at the front counter for ten people to sit. After Vietnam, a newer extension was built behind the trailer into the hillside and made the kitchen large enough for a couple of bigger fryers, a huge grill and other amenities like a walk-in and shelved storage in the back.

This also allowed five tables and three booths to be installed towards the back, increasing the capacity to just over 50 diners. The food hadn't changed much since it was opened in 1952, even with the new appliances, but the atmosphere did. Each year meant a new type of theme inside and most of last year's theme remained in smaller portions to the east rear sides on the walls.

Old Tonka trucks from 1949 sat on shelves near the ceiling next to Lionel Trains and rolling stock in S gauge, even an old Radio Flyer wagon was bolted to the wall and a century old bicycle hung from rafters; Applebee's would be proud of the antiquity of some relics. Then as you looked closer to the front of the diner, the flair became more modern; 'tins' advertised beer and sodas of every kind, roller skates and hockey skates went from ancient to new age. There was even a shelf with memorabilia from the space shuttle program and of course, what southern Nevada town wouldn't have a shelf or two reserved for Area 51 trinkets and posters.

One poster read "WELCOME TO AREA 51 NOW YOU DON'T EXIST EITHER!" another one displayed aliens walking around men dressed in black suits and waving with the caption "FUTURE UFO SIGHTINGS BY APPOINTMENT ONLY!"

Jason stepped inside and the atmosphere seemed claustrophobic. Every table was filled to capacity, every booth had an extra body sitting at the edge, the counter was full and even one boy sat at his father's feet at the end of that. Seems everyone else of the 2,500 population who couldn't make it to the Horseshoe, ended up here.

He started to turn when Gloria the waitress tapped him on the shoulder.

"Hi cutie. Gonna have a booth ready in about three minutes, you interested?" She winked.

Jason met Gloria his first night in town two weeks ago. He was hungry and looking for a bite to eat after discovering that there was no fuel for him at the airport. He was testy, angry and wanted to slap someone around- namely a guy called Dave-so he stomped in here to get a bite. As the door creaked to a close Gloria appeared with a menu and a sly smile for him.

She wasn't old or butt ugly, but she was way too forward for his liking. She had nearly over-fondled him on the way to the seat that day. He had been in here several times afterwards and each time Gloria caught up with him and sat him in her section so she could make flashy eyes at him.

Blonde, or at least on the outside, with brown eyes that sparkled in the dim café lights; short, about five foot five, and not too overweight. Gloria looked to be about one forty or fifty, but most of it was in her top half. Yes, she admitted loudly one day to another customer, *they* were fake.

She was dressed in her usual work attire, a light blue dress that went to the knees, a soft round collar with just a little V opening that revealed ample cleavage. A white apron over the top that made the whole getup look similar to what Shirley Booth wore in *Hazel*.

"I thought you had the early shift?" Jason asked quietly.

"I did honey, but when the power goes out the people jam in here and the tips get pretty heavy, especially when folks don't want to leave. Some feel guilty about taking the tables up for more than an hour or so, so they fork over a little more cash."

"Oh. I'll wait if that's okay."

"Sure sugar. These folks over there are ready to leave, since they're staying at the S&J."

Jake craned his neck towards the south window to see if he could get a glimpse of the hotel, "The power's back on?"

Gloria lowered her voice and put her hand to her mouth, "Nope. But when I saw you comin' I told them it would be any minute now." She tee-heed at her little indiscretion.

Jason smiled as mischievously as he could manage without it looking as phony as he felt doing it and winked at her. *No sense in ticking her off…*

It took about five minutes, but the family of four finally scooted out of the corner booth by the east window. Gloria nodded and thanked them as they passed her on their way to the cash register to pay for the meals. She seated Jason facing the back, giving him a pinch on the butt as he started to sit down. He spun his head as he slid a little farther in towards the center of the seat and she just winked at him.

"Coffee, honey?"

Jason checked his watch, it was a little after five. He didn't want to be up all night with the caffeine high. "Please."

"Thought so, caught a little whiff of beer on your breath." She winked again and spun on a heel, shaking her backside as she went towards the waitress station for java.

After she disappeared behind the walled area where the soft drink dispenser and coffee makers were kept, he surveyed the room. He knew about four of five faces, mostly from the mine, some from mercantile and maybe one or two from the hotel. These were the ones who, like Jason, took advantage of the continental breakfast that Mary put out every morning in the office of the Sage and Juniper.

Everyone was bundled up for the cold wind, except maybe a tourist or two who thought like many easterners that the desert was always warm. Fooled them. The high desert can be one hundred degrees some days and eighty at night then a couple of days later be forty during the day and below zero just before the sun rises.

A seemingly very happy Gloria nearly danced her way back to Jason's booth and sat a cup in front of him, and then poured fresh hot coffee into it from a pot that looked to be in need of retirement or burial.

"Eatin'?"

"Sure. How about the ham steak and eggs, over easy with sourdough."

The ham steak was the size of the plate it came on and still had the bone in the middle. Grilled to perfection, the pork was the best Jason had ever tasted. When he inquired how it was cooked, Gloria rolled her eyes and said, *"Don't ask..."*

The day had drug on as long as possible and now Jason worried that the night might follow. The wind had died down some, so every time the door to the café opened the blast of cold air was no less of a shock on the patrons, especially those at the counter who stared at the incoming folks as they entered. There was a steady stream. Some came in and found out about the wait and left, others found a seat on one of the three couches by the register to endure for a table or escape the frigid conditions outside.

Jason was pondering the alternatives to his plight and more or less, lack of flight, no rhyme intended. If he had owned a Cessna 172 like his father or a 152 like his grandfather, he might be able to substitute 80/87 octane motor gasoline and get the hell out of here. But the 182 like many of the newer made general aviation aircraft were not the same under the cowling. It wasn't a question of combustion in the engine, more rather Mogas or motor gasoline has a higher vapor rate in newer aircraft systems, meaning a vapor lock in a fuel line can allow the engine to die in flight or on the crucial takeoff. That would be bad.

Making his thoughts worthless is the inclusion of ethanol into auto gasoline this time of year by states to decrease pollution, ethanol in any form is a no-no in aluminum or aircraft engines. If any alcohol enhanced fuel is ever used in an aircraft engine of any type these days, the user is in violation of FAA regulations dating back to the 1960's.

He did find one drum of Jet A fuel in the back of the hanger his company had rented, used by the forest service during the summer in their firefighting helicopters, but once again it was useless to him; Jet A was made from kerosene and won't work in piston engines.

Conclusion: no Avgas-no go. All it would take is about fifty gallons to get him to the next airport for a fill up, two more stops, then off to home. Trapped. No sense in worrying about it much more than he was, it wasn't doing anyone any good. Besides, he could hold out till Tuesday. A few more land based trips up the mountain towards the slide area that he wanted to film might get him some better samples; there was a lot of erosion in the area.

After his third cup of coffee, *so much for going easy on it*, he had to go pee. Jason had eaten his eggs and ham and was snacking on his sourdough toast with grape jam when he could ignore the urge any longer. He stood and nodded towards the restroom door as he passed a smiling Gloria on his way.

"Give it a shake for me honey." She whispered at him as he passed.

Three cups of coffee on top of the beers he had at the Horseshoe took its time draining. The bathroom was as busy as the eating area; men were standing in line to use the stalls, many wanting to avoid any roadside stops on the way over the passes out of town, Jason was still working out his problem in his head and thinking of the poor travelers. With one at 6,500 feet heading towards Vegas and the other at 7,200 feet heading north towards Reno and the snow Jason had seen earlier on the railcars-which didn't use the passes, but its own rail bed running along the backside of the mountains-indicated that the roads might close up anyway.

Half these travelers were probably making a wasted trip to the summits where a flashing sign would tell them PASS IS CLOSED DUE TO WEATHER CONDITIONS TUNE TO 1600 AM FOR MORE INFORMATION. Then a recording would say the same thing in a pleasant female voice over the radio, '*The 201 pass over Klondike (north or Shepherds to the south) is closed due to severe snow accumulations. Be advised that chains may be required when these roads open. Passes are subject to closure without prior warning due to severe weather. Shelter can be found until the roads are cleared in Fallcast.*' Then the message would repeat.

Pass closures were rare due to the lack of snow this far south in the Nevada desert, but not uncommon to happen more than once or twice a year. On a side note, more than thirty people had died since 1942 on Highway 201, the usual cause of death was exposure, once again folks never think about being trapped in the snow in the desert and many die unprepared to stay the night in a car if it happens. Some die from carbon monoxide poisoning while idling their car in the snow drifts.

Jason finished his business and stood in line to wash his hands. After a few nods at other gentlemen as he left the restroom, he stepped slowly back to his table. Then he saw them.

Someone was sitting at his table. One was wearing a green ball cap, probably John Deere, with a ponytail hanging out the back. The other was a boy around the age of twelve or thirteen. The boy was playing with the silverware and the person who had their back to Jason was looking at a menu. Gloria didn't even have the decency to clear off his plate yet.

Jason curled his lips and started to walk out. He'd had enough for one day and was going to skip out on the bill. He'd pay later. Gloria caught him just as he turned for the front door.

She whispered so the newcomer wouldn't hear her, "Sorry honey. The boy was starving and cold. I couldn't let him stand by this door any longer. I figured you wouldn't mind sharing…" She smiled convincingly.

Jason took a deep breath and looked over the invader's shoulders to the street outside. It was still dark as tar, which meant the power was still out and Jack hadn't started the generator up yet. The usually neon-glowing sign that read "SAGE AND JUNIPER- ALWAYS READY ALWAYS A VACANCY" was dark as the night.

"I'll make it up to you sugar. How 'bout no charge for the coffee?" She smiled a little less convinced.

Jason sighed through his nose and nodded. As he did the person with their back to him turned towards him. It wasn't a he, but a she and to be more specific, it was Carrie Dodson. The beauty he had bumped into earlier in the day at the mercantile. She smiled a very uneasy grin, she too wasn't seemingly happy about the arrangement. Jason smiled back.

Turn around and go. Pay your bill and just go. Power or no power, whatever is at the hotel is better than what will come of you sitting down with her. Jason's mind was waving its arms in front of his face to get his attention. *This is a bad idea, and things will not be good after this.* Jason walked over and sat down.

I know I'm going to regret this. He told himself. He was right.

"Hello Mr.?" The young girl opened as he shuffled his butt to the opposite side of the booth, his back to the window.

"Parmenter, Jason. You can call me Jason." He eased.

"I'm…"

"Carrie Dodson." He interjected.

Jason had never heard of a son of hers, he was a little let down that such a young girl had such an older child, but now a days in small towns like these…

She blushed and lowered her head, "Yes, well I guess everyone knows me. This is Dustin he's my…"

"Dusty." The boy protested towards his sister, then looked to Jason. "Call me Dusty."

"Brother." Carrie finished.

Jason's ears pricked up when he heard brother. Even though he would probably be beaten within an inch of his life if he was ever caught holding this young woman's hand, the fact the boy was not her son but her brother made some kind of tingle up Jason's spine. He nodded at the boy with a friendly wink.

"You're the guy working for Dowards mine."

"Yes and no. I work for a company that was hired by the mine to do some exploration."

"Exploration?"

"Yes. Geology samples and an overall assess of the area and its attributes."

Carrie looked down. She hated that she was so dumb. Jason saw this, he back-stepped with a smile. Sometimes he overinflated what his job entailed and he knew he had gone over this young girl's head.

"I study rocks." He said with a huge sheepish smile.

"Cool!" Dusty said as he twirled a fork on the table.

"You're the guy with the airplane then."

At the word airplane, Dusty looked up from the table with his eyes wide and his mouth open. "You have an airport?"

Carrie tapped him on the back and said, "Airplane."

"Airplane?" Dusty said without skipping a beat.

"Yes. And no fuel. Might as well be a fish with no water, huh?"

Carrie looked down at her hands again. She smiled. Her full M shaped brownish-red lips formed the perfect semi-circle as the dimples on each side sunk in. Her cheeks flushed and Jason thought for a moment he was staring at an angel. She had the most beautiful smile he had ever seen on any woman before, a natural warm smile that said she would never hurt anyone, that she was indeed capable of tenderness and compassion. All that from just a smile. He hoped.

Something about her made things seem trivial. He had been around her only a few times; never this close, and now he could be himself. He wanted to anyways. Jason knew that a romance was out, that even thinking about dating a local girl with connections to the family that owns a good portion of the town was a reason to get beat up by said family.

He had seen miners in other towns, small towns like this one, get involved with relatives of businesses and in the end some of the infracting miners were bullied out of town or worse, in one instance, ended up in jail.

But things were not balanced for him right now. He was lonely, alone for weeks without very stimulating conversation and he hadn't been with a woman since Lindsay. He was a little let down about that too. He didn't need sex, but he sure needed some intimacy, he had always been that way.

"How long before you get some?"

Jason was still thinking about Carrie and missed the direction of her question.

"*Some* what?" He flushed with a thump of panic in his voice.

She flushed. "Gas, uh fuel, for your plane…"

"Oh." Now he looked at the table, "Next Tuesday. I hope."

A huge gust of wind rattled the windows and shook the trailer half of the restaurant, the chatter died down and most of the customers looked out the windows. The large panes of glass, some old enough not to even be tempered, flexed in and out. There were some oohs and aaahs that followed and then the distant sound of what many played off to be a Dumpster rolling over a few blocks away.

Carrie took the quiet opportunity to drink some water and look at Jason while he surveyed the bowing window glass behind him. He was definitely a good looking man, strong shoulders visible even through his thick sweater. A nice light green heavy knit, and the sleeves were pulled just a little back from his wrists to mid-forearm. As he turned she could see muscles tense in his neck, he didn't have a thick stem like the boys who played football; his was more toned and subtle, until he moved it.

His hair was cut like someone who always kept it short enough to stay out of his eyes, the perfect little pomp that turned from left to right in a feathered look. The blondish brown color said he spent a lot of time out of doors, in the sun. Matching eyebrows and a little set of wrinkles made him look like he was always thinking about something. Must be something big too, he was always concentrating. Until he saw her, every time she caught his stare he was looking at her, his brow lines disappeared and he seemed to walk a little straighter, a little more focused. She knew he liked her, she knew he'd be trouble for her. And then there was Dusty.

Feelings were feelings. But she had to protect her little brother, and Mr. Pilot was out of this foul berg as soon as he got his gas and she knew that. But there was nothing wrong with having a little crush and maybe they could have a moment or two together where she would experience a taste of love-nothing physical, she couldn't do anything like that-but maybe a kiss from the handsome stranger who would be gone on the next breeze north.

He turned back from the window and caught her staring at him. Her eyes went south again. He smiled and the lines of thought on his forehead faded into oblivion then he lifted his coffee and took the last sip.

He coughed a little and spoke, "That sounded like something bad out there."

Carrie raised her eyes to his and for a second each felt a tingle, on cue the front door burst open and in stepped Darrin Parker. Deputy Darrin Parker, aka *Parks*. Brown hair and quarterback good looks with blue eyes, a baby-faced man who tried to hide it with a silly looking frown, Parks was really a pussycat. Dressed in the standard tan slacks with a black strip down the leg, a black Tuffy jacket that ended just above his Sam Brown gun belt. A dark automatic, probably a Smith & Wesson M&P 40 .40 caliber Jason assumed, poked up just below his elbow on his right side.

The cop was tall, over six three and had a toothpick in the corner of his mouth, swishing it back and forth. His hands were covered in tight black gloves with bulged knuckles meaning he was wearing sap-gloves. Little raises in the leather there meant the knuckles had been filled a with sand or lead shot, and were used for busting bad guy's jaws.

Parks gave the crowd on both sides of the diner a once over and cleared his throat.

"Ladies and gentlemen!" The room came to a pause, "There has been an accident on 201 a few hundred yards from here west. A boxcar derailed and tumbled into the roadway, the contents of the car spilled over the roadway and down the embankment blocking both the highway and the lower access roads."

There were rumbles of concern amongst some of the diners.

Parks continued, "Now we've been told that the contents are not deadly, but they are hazardous; some kind of stuff for the mine." He took a dramatic breath.

The rest of the folks who were here seeking shelter from the wind or the power outage silently held theirs too. Jason knew it couldn't be good news, if it was the deputy would've just spilled the beans right away-no pun intended-and gone to the counter for his complimentary cup of coffee. There was going to be another inconvenience in his life as soon as the deputy told everyone what the big to do was about. A gust of wind rose as a background crescendo.

"The road access to the lower parts of town is closed." He pursed his lips for effect as he raised his brows and pulled up on his Sam Brown belt, the leather creaking as it strained against his muscles.

After a few low grumbles, the toothpick in Parks mouth pointed nearly straight down. Not the response he had hoped for, so he continued, "That means if you're staying at the Best Western or Sand Tides, you are stuck on this side of town until we get the mess cleaned up."

Now the response was more to his liking since half of the patrons were staying at those places, and a few more were on their way out of town heading towards the mountains, south towards Vegas. There were questions shouted back at the officer.

"Can I get around it? I have to be in Sin City by noon tomorrow."

"No." Parks raised his voice, "Let me be clear! The road is closed. Those of you headed south on 201, then you're stuck here. I think the Sand and Juniper has extra rooms."

Another customer raised his hand and spoke at the same time, "What about us *Darrin*? Can we get home?"

Jason couldn't tell what annoyed Deputy Parker the most, the question or the way the man said "*Darrin*". Parker took a deep breath and the toothpick went straight north.

"The access road," Raising his voice so he didn't have to repeat himself again, "is closed also. The spill went all the way down the embankment and covered the road and the side ditches.

"The nature of the chemical makes it unsafe to walk around, unsafe to wade through it, unsafe to be near. So, there will be no one walking along the road home." He took another deep breath; this one was loud enough to make even the densest townie understand the gravity of the situation. "Any *more* questions?"

Patrons looked back and forth amongst each other and some shook their heads back at the deputy.

"Parks?" A female voice rose above the murmur. It was Carrie.

Deputy Parker spun on his combat booted heel towards the table she and Jason shared with Dusty. Dusty was busy playing with the silverware, Jason was trying to scoot low enough into the seat to hide his face. Parker's face went into a scowl.

"Miss Dodson?"

"Where do we go?"

Parks looked to his sides cautiously, Jason knew immediately that the tall cop wanted to say '*At my place if you wish…*', but his duty and probably the fact that the elder Dodson would be uncomfortable with this made the now nervous looking man turn his head to address the room again, "The Sand and Juniper usually can accommodate a few extra guests. Miss Dodson, you can probably talk to Jack and Mary and they'll put you up in their guest bedroom. Dusty too."

Dusty raised his head at his name and while looking at Jason said out loud without looking at the deputy, "Dustin, my name's *Dustin*."

"Dustin."

There were a few chuckles at the expense of the deputy. Parks took his cue and walked to the counter for his reward without looking around. Gloria made goo-goo eyes at him and poured coffee into a Styrofoam cup. He smiled at her and dropped a dollar on the counter and walked back out without another word.

The chatter rose to a din. Jason had his chin in the cup of his right hand and was still staring at the back of Carrie's head as she turned towards him. "Can I stay with you? I know you're staying at the S&J."

Every now and then the earth stumbles on its axis and things shift suddenly; Jason's hand slipped from his chin as it dropped open and it struck the coffee cup in front of him, that struck the water glass and it tipped, spilling its contents over the table. Dusty began playing with the little pool with his napkin.

"Yo…sawha?" As it came out of Jason's mouth, *Say what?*

She laughed. "Just kidding. Mary'll put us up." Her smile was back.

She was kidding, in a way. Carrie wanted to see his reaction. He liked her too.

"I m-mean," He stuttered, "y-you could, but…"

Carrie dropped her big smile. "Dusty?"

Jason's insides gurgled. "No! Oh, no not all I just… it's just that…"

A small smile. "Relax. I was really kidding. We've only just met."

Jason kept talking, "I have to get up early and…"

"Are you *planing*?" Dusty asked.

"Flying? No. Planing is a sailing term."

"Are you sailing?"

Jason laughed and touched the boy's soft cheek, "No. I'm driving." He looked back up to meet Carrie's eyes, "Really early."

Carrie's golden-browns flashed light then a little darker. "I was kidding." Then she took Jason's hand, the one that was wiping up the spilled water with a wad of napkins, "But you're a nice guy. I know now I could've counted on you."

Jason was about to change his tune and offer her and her brother a bed in his room when Dusty tapped his hand. "Can I go flying with you tomorrow?"

Jason looked from Carrie to Dusty and thought for a brief second. A ride in the plane for this boy could mean a conversation with his sister. Maybe a little time just to chat with someone who didn't want to talk about mineral contents or assay reports. He took a chance.

"I'm not able to tomorrow, but I'll tell you what. If your sister says it's okay, we can go next week when my fuel gets here."

"Cool!"

How much farther would she allow him to go? "Dusty, we'll have to wait and see okay?"

"Awe."

The boy's head dropped a little, he started fidgeting with the fork again; this time stabbing the water soaked napkins with it. Carrie hated to disappoint him, but she let this thing-this flirting-get too far. Sure, she would like to get to know Jason a little better and a trip with him would be fun, but where would it end, how would it end? Her brother, the older one, would object and he'd been known to go a little too far when he didn't get his way.

"Power's on." Gloria had walked over to the table while Jason and Carrie were engaged with one another.

"Thanks."

Gloria watched as Jason and the Dodson siblings left the restaurant, she sighed as she fumbled with the tip coins in her apron pocket. She knew the couple had less chance than she and Jason did. Things involving Carrie Marie Dodson and others never went well. Never.

The wind had died down again. Jason looked over his shoulder towards the southwest end of town down the highway. Red and blue lights flashed, dozens of them, cars blocked the road as far away from the shoofly as three or four blocks. He could see a couple of deputies standing outside of their cars, two cars that were pointed in a V, blocking the road. The deputies were standing with their hands in their Tuffy jacket pockets; tan stocking caps covered their heads.

There were three fire engines, two from the county firehouse on the north side of town, one from the mine emergency response unit on the other. Jason could see a large black object in the center of all the attention with firemen wearing Scott Airpacks and Nomex suits foaming the area around it.

As the wind died, folks began to gather around the lower areas to get a glimpse.

He looked down to his left, the downside of the hill that most of the town was built on and another mine engine and a half dozen firefighters hosing the area down also. There were three firemen wearing hazmat suits pulling gear out of side lockers on the mine fire truck.

Most of the city's emergency response crews were either at home or at the Horseshoe Club and when the town siren mounted on the roof of the firehouse sounded (few heard it north of town because of the wind) they were separated from their equipment by the wreck. The firehouse was on the north end of town. Three fire engines sat in their bays at the firehouse with no volunteers close enough to run them. It would take another half hour for the crews on the north end of town to get there. The paging units each one carried or kept close by was set off by a radio signal at the courthouse, one of the few buildings that took a while to get the generators running.

A comedy of errors, Jason thought. Fortunately no one was hurt, and there was no fire.

"I guess coming in for a cup of coffee and dessert is out. Huh?" Carrie said quietly.

Her back was to Jason as she walked about two steps ahead of him; she had to keep up with Dusty, who seemed to be energized by the late evening walk. He kicked at stones and trash along the road, then ran up the hill that used to be mine tailings, towards the hotel parking lot.

Jason slowed even more after her remark, "Pardon?"

She turned without stopping and smiled at him. Her eyes betrayed her seriousness, they sparkled in the moonlight-the quarter moon had made its appearance over the mountain top, giving a little glow to objects that sat in darkness without the power to run the sodium streetlights. Jason stopped and smiled back at her, it was if he understood what she was asking in a roundabout way.

Carrie looked up towards the office of the S&J, Dusty was half way there; he knew where to go. She looked back down at the ground at Jason's feet and inhaled slowly, "I like you. I mean for company, you know? You're smart and I don't get enough of that kind of conversation. All the guys around here wanna talk about mining or how many deer they poached last fall."

"Uh, thanks?" Jason was unsure now of what she was going to say next.

"How long are you going to be here? I mean, before you have to leave permanently?"

"Two weeks, maybe three at the most." Jason kicked at a white stone at his feet. He classified it as Dolomite.

Carrie lowered her head in a shy way, and then thought out loud, "That's past Christmas."

"Yeah. Probably. If the fuel arrives next week like it's supposed to."

"Don't you have family? No one to spend the holidays with?" Carrie's insides began a little Irish jig.

"My grandparents I guess, but they're not expecting me this year; my folks are dead and my... *ex*-girlfriend, well... never mind."

Carrie ears perked up a little. "Ex?"

"Yeah. We broke up a couple of months ago. This close to getting hitched..." Jason made a very small space between his index finger and thumb out in front of Carrie.

"So you won't be home for the holidays?" She tried not to smile too broadly.

"No. I'm not really into the whole thing anyways, I'm away most of the year doing research and hunting down claim stakes. Then the rest of the time I spend writing reports and filing counter claims or doing errands for my company."

Carrie shuffled her feet a little slower. She noticed that Dusty was already inside the office and Mary was pouring him some hot chocolate from the coffee maker. She wanted a few more minutes with Jason, for no other reason than she enjoyed his voice, his manner of talking to her like she was just as smart as he was, or vice versa.

"Doesn't sound like being a geologist is much fun." She said after a brief silence.

"Oh no. Don't get me wrong; there are moments of sheer pleasure when I get to *do* geology. But most of what I told you is not really geology but the toils of working for a company that doesn't hire many people, and they use me more than I should allow. I love studying old rocks." He smiled a gullible look at her. She giggled.

"Why not just do that then?"

Slam! Right in his face. A question he could never answer right out loud. Lindsay asked the same question as she was attempting to not let the door hit her on the bum on the way out the first time she left him.

Jason took a small breath and looked into Carrie's eyes and said, "If you figure that out about me, tell me won't you?"

They had reached the pinnacle of the parking lot, to the immediate left of the couple was the glass enclosed office, Dusty was already parked in front of the TV watching *CSI* and Mary was setting up the ingredients for a fresh pot of coffee. Carrie paused and turned towards Jason, standing about three feet away.

"See ya, I guess?"

Jason felt a lump in his throat. This was like asking that girl to prom so long ago, the eternity it took for her to answer.

"Hello?" Carrie lowered her eyes to meet his. Jason was drifting off into the past with a ragged sailboat.

"Oh jeez. Sorry. Yes. I would like that very much." He shrugged his shoulders as if to imply he was tired.

"Goodnight Mr. Parmenter."

"Goodnight Miss Dodson."

Both turned towards their respective directions and didn't look back at each other.

Jason was busy unplugging his computer and cursing under his breath for leaving it on when the power went out. If the generator fluctuated in voltage on the job in any way it could have damaged the components. Modern electronic gadgets were not meant to run with generated power without special filters.

The lights were on in the bathroom when he opened his door, the lamp next to the bed also and the TV. In sort of frantic dash around he managed to turn off all but the lamp next to the bed, he didn't know why, maybe it was because he didn't want the stupid generator running out of fuel before dawn. Then again it didn't matter. He had a back-up plan.

The wind had died so any noises at all were noticed and just as Jason was checking his cell-phone alarm for the wake-up time, he heard a shuffling noise outside the back window. The walls on this side of the hotel were cinderblock, which more or less telegraphed the cold through to the indoors, but the window in the bathroom was a single pane with cracks around the caulking separating the outside from inside and any movement in the gravel out back could be heard also.

A few moments later, a knock came to the door. The rapping sound was light, small knuckled, Jason thought. He stood and walked up to the door and peeked out the spyhole. It was Carrie. He gulped back a quick sigh of surprise as he turned the deadbolt without looking at it. He opened the door and nodded at the young girl.

"Miss Dodson?"

"I'm sorry to bother you…"

Jason stepped back as if to allow her in his room, "Please."

"No. I… can't. Mrs., uh…Mary sent me over. She wanted me to tell you that the power was not a permanent thing tonight and she couldn't guarantee your five o'clock wake up call."

"No worries. I use my own alarm clock as a failsafe."

Carrie looked down. Jason knew she wanted to say something else, he was cheering her on in his mind to come on out and say it. She cleared her throat.

"I'm sorry if I bothered you at dinner. Gloria thought it would be a good idea for me to keep you company and all."

Gloria? I thought she was hounding after me…Jason thought. "Gloria? I… she always seemed to make passes at me; I didn't realize she put us together. It's alright anyways."

Carrie giggled. "Oh no. Gloria's married. She's been with a guy named Joe Lampoc for over fifteen years now. No. I think she just looks like she's flirting." A few more giggles.

"*Nice.*" Sarcasm escaped Jason's mouth.

"I mean, would it be okay if we were at dinner and all? I don't want people thinking that you and I are well… you know…" Jason could see her color turn in the darkness.

"I enjoyed it."

"You did?" Her eyes lit up like golden urns filled with fire.

"Yes. You're the first person here in this… town that treated me like a human. I would like to see you again, I mean like lunch or breakfast or something."

"You would?" She started to shake a little. Carrie rubbed her shoulders to pretend it was the cold bothering her, but since the wind died it was actually warm. "Tomorrow? Could Dusty come?"

Jason smiled, "Of course. I like him; he seems to be interested in what I do."

"He likes what everyone is always doing." Carrie tried to change the subject and say goodnight again. "I should be…"

"Your family won't mind?"

This hit Carrie hard. She knew there was always talk around town about her and she also knew it centered on the way she was raised by her father and her brother. She also knew of the rumors that her father and brother beat anyone senseless that gave her a flirty look. Her face turned down as she looked at the door mat.

"My father and brother are not supposed to be within 100 yards of me at any time."

Now it was Jason's turn to be struck by lightning, "Pardon?"

"It's all legal and that. But if you're afraid…" She let the corners of her mouth turn up into a dimpled coy dare as she teased his eyes with hers.

Jason thought to himself that he should say no politely and close the door before this went any further. The incident at the bar, the talk around the pot belly stove at the mercantile was a warning, a lesson in what was to come of a relationship formed between the geologist who was just passing through and the local who was thought of as forbidden by the others in town. Carrie picked up on his hesitation.

"That's it isn't it?" The smile faded to a frown then a pout and finally turned to a look like she was about to cry. Her golden eyes that were moments ago shimmering like iron pyrite in a clear mountain stream were now flickering red and black. "Damn those two!"

Carrie spun on a heal and kicked a bit of dust from the gravel parking lot as she used her right foot to propel her away from Jason's door. Her strides were long and fast, her tall legs made that possible.

66

"Carrie! Wait!" There was a note of desperation and fear in his voice.

She stopped and lowered her head, more out of shame, but she was hurt and felt like moving on back to the comfort of the office and TV and then the spare bedroom where she could close her eyes and cry into her pillow while her little brother dreamed away. There was a moment of silence; Carrie began to move forward again, she was tired of waiting and she was also infuriated that her family kept her from a relationship.

"I'm sorry." Jason began, "Yes, I am a little daunted by your family, but I'm also afraid that I might get too close."

This made her stop cold. A shiver ran down her back; *did he say get too close?* Carrie turned slowly, dramatically not on purpose, and looked sluggishly from the ground at her feet up to Jason's eyes.

"*Too* close?"

Jason looked left then right to make sure there was no Dodson-other than Carrie-or ears that might report back to a Dodson. He cleared his throat and in a voice just loud enough for her to hear he said, "I told you I just broke up with someone. I've been very alone these last few weeks, hell. These last two months. I'm dying to talk to someone at my level, someone who isn't afraid of small talk and long chats about life in general…" He left her to decide.

Carrie let this all run through her system. *At my level-he considers me an equal?* No one has ever done that.

"No expectations?" She finally said.

"Only friendship." He smiled; this was his best one tonight.

Now it was Carrie's turn to look both ways before talking. She stepped closer to Jason at his door and whispered, "I've been alone too. But not for months, for years. I've never had a boyfriend or someone who talks to me like an equal. They're all afraid of my family. I need a friend too, but I can't have a… lover."

Jason blushed now. "Lover? I doubt things will go that far. But I would like to get to know you better. Hear your side of the story as it were…"

"Other than the pitiful rumors that run the streets of this town like the feral dogs?"

A *big* smile. *Best* yet.

Carrie mimicked Jason's smile and took another step forward unexpectedly and Jason shuddered for second, wondering whether or not to retreat inside. He stood his ground and nearly blinked when she offered her hand out to him. He took it and shook it slowly while not breaking eye contact with her. Her hand was warm; it did something to his insides to touch her like this, like she was Eve at the infamous tree, enticing him to consume of the forbidden fruit.

"How about breakfast?" She asked quietly as their hands moved up and down.

"I won't be here for that. I'll probably be up on Power Peak looking for a road to the summit."

"When will you be back?"

"One?"

"Lunch at one. Is the Salt Lick okay?"

"Sure."

Carrie took a deep breath and let it out like a relaxed sigh. "Goodnight."

Jason nearly copied her with the breath thing and had to struggle to say, "Goodnight."

He watched as she ambled her way back towards the office. She looked once over her shoulder and threw him a flirty smile, then looked back to her destination and doubled her steps till she reached the heavy glass doors. She paused, like she was going to look back again, but instead she opened the door and slipped inside.

Jason closed the door to his room and looked around. He couldn't seem to focus on why she had come to see him in the first place. Oh yeah, the alarm. He sat down on the edge of the bed and fiddled with the buttons of his cell phone till the time was set right. Then he kicked off his shoes and lay back against the pillow, which was propped up to the headboard. Maybe he had a friend here, now. Maybe things would be better for him and the wait for his fuel not so tedious if he had someone to talk to.

Four hundred yards away Carrie was tucking the sheets she had gotten from Mary for the guest bed. Dusty was spinning around in the small chair by the window, pretending he was an airplane. She had felt a twinge in her psyche all of a sudden.

Why had she been so forward? She never approached a man like Jason before. It was as if she had to do it, like it was fate or something. She smiled at the thought of her and the new guy eating lunch together at the diner. Then her smile dissolved.

At the diner. The place where nearly all of the rumors were started in this town about her, between the diner and the old farts at the mercantile, things were going to get out of hand. All of a sudden, the new found pleasure of a man taking interest in her, the feeling that she was being treated like an equal by a stranger instead of the guilded property of her father and brother, it all faded. Things would get out of hand. Someone might get hurt. Tears filled her eyes.

CHAPTER FIVE
Thursday December 10th, 2009

Jason was finishing up on some collections when he sat down for a break. His satchel was full of enough samples to build a small mud-house, he thought, just by the weight. He pulled a bottle of spring water from his backpack and took three long swallows as he felt the sweat rolling from his neck to his lower back right down the center along the spine. He took out his earphones for the IPod Shuffle that was clipped to his collar.

Sometimes Jason based his day on how many songs he listened to on the little thing as he walked. He knew basically that most of the songs on there were an average of three and a half minutes and he had counted 48 songs since he turned the machine on back at the Jeep.

He had been in the sun for over three hours now according to his watch, even though it was only around fifty degrees, the sun was still warm and climbing up hillsides and steep ravines looking for color or signs that might interest his employer also added to the heat buildup.

His mind was not on the rocks. He had seen thousands of samples of quartz, feldspar, serpentine both green and gold, biotite, magnetite and muscovite from the metamorphic classes. He had stepped over hundreds of traps and felsite sample of the igneous and many miles of sedimentary deposits. This was a heavily volcanic area thousands of years ago and a treasure trove of minerals for study.

Jason had a hard time concentrating on stones and sticks because Carrie Dodson was on his mind. The young beauty that knocked at his hotel room door last night in a hidden attempt to ask him out-so it seemed. It looked that way, she had a simple message that could have easily been delivered by its originator, Mary; but there was a look of anticipation over another subject and she finally got around to spilling it to him.

Not that he didn't want to hide from her, but he knew that seeing a local girl while here on a temporary basis raises suspicions amongst the brood, mainly against her supposed maniac father and homicidal brother.

But, she said, they were under court orders to stay away from her. Like candy in the window. A challenge, but a dramatic one, in return he could see Carrie and spend time with her and her little brother who is full of all kinds of energy, energy Jason wish he had now as he nears his mid-thirties. Jason loved being around children, his ex-girlfriend's nephew was a handful, but he loved to fly with Jason and Lindsay as much as possible and her niece was a doll. She loved to dress up and play princess and ask for Jason's hand in marriage when he rescued her from the evil queen.

Dusty was no problem. He already seemed fascinated by the fact Jason was a pilot and that he had a plane. He felt the inner need to get that kid into the air and tool him around the mountains.

But, Jason had a sad thought; there was something about the boy that wasn't right. He seemed... slow. Maybe it was just the lack of exposure to kids in the last few months, but Dusty seemed a little different than other kids his age; Jason figured him to be about eleven or twelve. Maybe a few days around Jason would make him happy, happy kids meant happy adults. Happy adults were more often than not willing to open up about themselves. He wanted Dusty to be happy, to have a blast and he knew exactly what a kid like Dusty needed, but the problem again was the fuel.

As soon as it came in and the day was clear enough he would ask Carrie if they would like to go flying with him. Carrie didn't seem to be the type that scared easily, and Dusty-well all he had to do was ask and he knew the boy would be first in line.

Another slug of water from the bottle and he took off his cap and wiped his brow with the cool bottle then replaced it in its spot in the backpack. Then Jason pulled the earplugs of each ear and ran his index finger in each ear to scratch it and squeegee out any sweat. He took a deep breath and looked around; the ground always seemed more interesting when he was a kid. It took four years of college and three more struggling to get where he is now to come to dislike geology. It was okay, but it just wasn't the same as when he did it as a hobby when he was a boy. Deadlines, reports, on the road for weeks at a time and selling his soul for his bosses all added to the despair of the work he once enjoyed.

He heard a quail chirp a few yards away and Jason turned towards it and smiled. The outdoors was so much better than the *in* variety; out here you were one with the world. His thoughts drifted again to Carrie. He had a daydream as he listened to the breeze collide with the craggy rocks above him.

Maybe Carrie wanted out of this small town less than fifty miles from Las Vegas, but a million miles from nowhere. She wanted to hop into the little blue and white Cessna and fly off to Colorado with Jason. Dusty would be in the back seat looking out the window at the flat desert and small towns below, excited to be within a few hours of the big city. Roller-skating, cinemas, fast food joints, satellite TVs; all the things a kid could ask for were there for the taking. A few stops for fuel along the way and there they were. Home.

Reality came back in the form of a hawk gliding overhead. Its scream tore the image of the new couple from his mind and set him back on a mountainside in southwestern Nevada. Jason took another breath and stood upright, stretching his back. He resumed his step and look, step and look routine. Just another hour and he would head back down the road-if you could call it that-and lunch with Miss Dodson. That made him tingle.

Carrie. Yes, she made him feel young again and he thought he could live better now. All that in Colorado was behind him; Lindsay and her boyfriend, the dreams they had about the future and the way things fell to pieces in just a week.

Jason sighed as he made for a break in the rocks along a sheer wall inside of two small gullies that had large sheets of bedrock in basalt. Fractures were filled with small animal nests and sediment from ages of erosion. Jason slid down the shallowest side and came to a thump in the soft sand of a little dry streambed. Runoff over the last few hundred years had eroded the base of the rock into a half-arch shape with little bowls at the bottom;, trapped in the small pockets was a collection of minerals untouched by human hands. He took a plastic sample bottle and filled it with the contents of the natural basin.

He placed the small bottle back into a little pocket on his pack and took a deep breath. The fresh air in the mountains never disappointed him, even if it was a little chilly. A few more minutes and he had climbed to the top of the ravine and was looking down towards the Soap Valley below. Named for the product mined from the area in the late 1800's, the valley was nearly fifteen miles long and ten miles wide at the base of the mountains and foothills that surrounded the town of Fallcast.

Larger than the most of the valleys in California that held cities of millions, Soap Valley was hardly populated more than the 2,500 advertised on the sign as you drove into town. WELCOME TO FALLCAST! Pop. 2,531. Underneath that sign was nearly a dozen others each representing a church or organization such as the Presbyterians, St. Ignatius of the Valley, Rotary Club, Moose Club, Elks, etc.

The valley had a whitish hue at the long drawn out base from end to end, the result of the rich minerals that made up the floor. The foothills were colored with reds and gold, some turquoise and varying shades of browns. Some purple from germanite, the reds were from realgar, the gold from chondrodite and serpentines, copper and limonite, hematite and pyrite.

Granite and basalt comprised the mass of the mountains themselves with small fissures of broken bedrock from volcanic activity centuries past. Cheat grass and other fire fuels clinging to lush hillsides of manzanita in the upper elevations, bitterbrush and sage in the lower and scrub and tall juniper everywhere completed the desert scene.

There were no pines this far south, the mills, fire and drought had taken their toll on them in the early days after man had walked on the virgin soils for the first time. Erosion and runoff from heavy snows created ravines and gullies, thousands of them along the side of the mountain and each had a quarry of its own unique minerals pushed up from under the crust.

Since the Eastern Sierras were the result of two tectonic plates colliding, the mountains were pushed upwards to the heavens with the force of more energy than any one could imagine, the farther south along the range the newer the ridges and mountain tops were, so they looked ragged and sharp as compared to the rounder and smoother looking hills and mountains to the west of where Jason was standing.

Finding a flat slab of basalt balanced over a smaller round one at the peak of the hill he was on, Jason sat again for another shot of water and a look around. Even though this was work, there was still beauty in his surroundings.

He pushed pause on the Shuffle and took an energy bar out of his pack and chewed while looking around. He had taken a bite of the granola and raisin conglomerate when he saw a juniper that looked out of place in the next gully over his right shoulder. Often scrub juniper grew on the sheer sides of a ravine, and this was a tall juniper, about six or seven foot tall. It was all alone. But something about it made Jason think it was out of place.

Jason fished around in his pack for his Bushnell binos and popped the caps off. He balanced his elbows on his knees and focused the lenses on his prey. He was right, the tree was out of place, and it looked like from his position that it was planted in some sort of large container made out either a large tractor tire or cut-off fifty gallon drum or barrel. There was a small black tube protruding out of the ground at the root line of the juniper, and it snaked its way towards the top of the cliff wall-almost as if it had been hidden on purpose-then it was hooked over the top of the ridge with an elbow and settled in a little circle of hand stacked rocks, arranged into a circle to trap water from rain.

He brought the glasses back down again to the tree and noticed the rock wall behind the evergreen was darker than the rock on the visible sides of the bush. He pulled the glasses away and rubbed his eyes then refocused them on the wall. It wasn't darker, it was an opening. A mine or a cave in the wall of the gully about two hundred feet below him. Jason did love these things.

A mine? It wasn't on any of the survey maps from the area, nor was it on any claim map or assay report. He drug his map from a slot on the back of his pack to check and make sure, and after a few minutes using his handheld GPS, he confirmed there was no claim or any mine on the regional map.

Curiosity burned in his brain now. Jason loved exploring caves and abandoned mines as a kid; the latter was so dangerous that when his father found out he was grounded for a month. From that point on he never mentioned what he and his friends did on the weekends. They still took their flashlights and handpicks on camping trips; most trips were planned near the open shafts of former claims.

A thought turned his internal excite off for a moment. There was no dump. No tailings at the mouth of the opening; tailings were rarely carried farther than the mouth of the hole in a wheelbarrow and dumped down the ravine. Dumps were always a tell-tale of a mine, the fresh picked and crushed rock was sometimes used for a bed for a small ore car track. No signs of anything like that. And the juniper. There was something fishy about a small tree used to hide the mouth of a mine, perfectly plumbed to keep it green as it grew in a small hole picked out of solid rock. Someone didn't want this place discovered.

Jason took a few more minutes deciding whether he would traverse the dirt and rock wall that sat at a twenty-five degree angle to the streambed and then climb the rocky wall on the other side back up to the mysterious hole. It would take some time to get back to town and it was-Jason looked at his watch and the dial read 11:03-too late to try and make his lunch date if he went exploring today. Besides, he had a few more days here and the hole wasn't going anywhere. From the look of the ledge where the opening sat and the juniper, no one had come up here in quite a while. Several clumps of tumbleweed had collected around the hole.

Jason marked the spot on his map and placed everything back into the pack and set out down the other side towards the Jeep. It took him an hour and ten minutes to get to the point he walked from the Wagoneer; it would take him that at least to get back. He was going to be late for his first date with Carrie.

Carrie meanwhile was washing her hair for the second time. Dusty had gone off to Meg's house and she had some time alone to be in fear. She had never been on a date before she was on her own-and only a couple of quick bad ones since; she had never tried to make herself look presentable-she just never worried about it until today. Why today? She liked the stranger with the airplane; he was sort of mysterious and well educated at the same time. He was always smiling, even when Heather told him that he would have to talk to her husband about getting his fuel.

He smiled when he saw the restaurant was packed solid and he didn't even pout when he found out his table was taken the night before. He just seemed always happy. Carrie hoped so. She also hoped he wasn't taking all the gossip about her. Everyone in town talked about her and her family, small towns were like that, especially when the people who owned the mines were involved.

Carrie had tried to comb her hair out straight and then it started to curl as it dried. She got frustrated and went back into the bathroom and dunked her head into the sink again. She decided it would be fine if she just braided it.

"C'mon Marie." She whispered to herself. She always referred to her own middle name, a habit she picked up from her mother. "Get it together; you're going to be late."

After drying her hair for the third time and coming to the conclusion that a light feathering with outward curled bangs on one side and evenly pulled up on the other would have to do it; mainly because she had less than fifteen minutes before Jason was to show up at the diner, and Carrie had a ten minute walk from her place.

It was half way down the rut riddled road when the right front tire blew. Jason kind of liked the old Jeep Wagoneer up until this point. After nearly sliding off the embankment into a sixty foot drop into a rocky canyon and managing to get the giant box of a vehicle to stop just short of slamming into a sheer rock wall on the other side of the road, he stood outside of it and kicked at the flat tire.

"Is this fate?" He asked, looking upward to the sky.

He pursed his lips together and shook his head as he walked to the back of the ancient SUV and opened the hatchback to get the spare. He did say an apology to whomever he was speaking to earlier under his breath and small prayer that the extra tire had air in it.

It did and it took ten minutes to remove the failed rubber and install the rounded, bald, and somewhat misshapen spare on. It thumped the rest of the way to town. Jason looked at his watch as he passed the county sign that told him that the road was not maintained at this point- someone had turned it around years ago and the sign was never moved back facing the dirt road. The time was now twelve fifty-five. He was going to be late for sure.

Carrie walked in the front door to the Salt Lick at exactly five after one. Gloria was sitting near the back window looking out over the valley below and was smoking. When she saw Carrie she stubbed out the butt and stood with a smile.

"Hey honey." Gloria seemed to have been sleeping or in a heavy daydream and hadn't gotten her full cheerful voice back.

"Hi Glo." Carrie pointed to the window nearest the front of the diner. The view was of the mountains behind the valley.

Gloria nodded and went to the drink vending station and poured a cup of coffee. She walked slowly back to the table where Carrie had sat herself and set the cup down in front of her. She pulled her ticket book from her apron and a pencil, and in true TV waitress fashion, licked the end of the pencil before putting it to the pad.

"Same?" The waitress asked.

"Uh, no. Jason was supposed to be here at one. I'll wait for him."

At the sound of Jason's name, Gloria's eyes drooped to the floor and she turned slowly and picked a menu up off of the table behind her and sat in front of the empty spot. She sighed so heavily that the big blond curl above her eyes wriggled.

Carrie heard this and looked up to meet her eyes. "Not spoiling something, am I?"

Gloria smiled a very sad grin and shook her head. This time the curl was hanging on for dear life. "Cass; you know better than that. It's just that I'd figured you two would hook up in the end that's all." Gloria turned and headed for the drink serving station, she mumbled over her shoulder, "Guess I was right."

"Glo, we're not *hooked* up. He asked me out to lunch and I said yes. Simple as that."

Gloria looked above the wooden divider that separated the service area from the diner. She was going to ask Carrie if her dad knew about the lunch, but decided against it. Even though she was the most eligible bachelorette in town, Carrie was also a good friend. Gloria had to cry on her shoulder more than once and didn't want any bad blood between her and Carrie.

Carrie looked out the window and sighed heavily this time. "But he's late."

"If he's driving that old junker that Marcus loaned him from the mine, he's probably broken down somewhere." Gloria said with a slight hint of satisfaction.

Gloria came out from behind the service counter and sat down in front of Carrie. She had brought with her another cup of coffee and sat it in front of herself. She gave a once around the diner-which was empty- and leaned in towards Carrie.

"Just so you know; I like him. But I would never leave Joe for anyone. He's been a good husband and I should be thankful for somebody like him, not even Mr. Pilot from Colorado."

Carrie just smiled and leaned back towards her hostess. "I like him too. He seems…"

She drifted off; most girls in town knew the last few words Carrie didn't have to say.

"Unlike the local boys." Gloria finished for her. "And he's rich and can fly you right out of this dump and into a life of luxury."

Carrie blushed. She looked up quickly and then back to Gloria's eyes. Gloria turned red as a Chinese flag and lowered her eyes to the table. "He's standing behind me. Isn't he?"

"No. But close enough to hear you." Came a jovial reply from the front door. Jason had slipped in while they were taking. "Is there a wait?" He asked in even a happier voice.

Gloria took a deep breath and put on her sarcastic waitress face then stood. "No sir. Your table is ready. The rush won't be here until around two, that's *his* lunch time."

She stepped out from the table and placed her hands on the chair then winked at him. Jason walked over and thanked her, and then he sat down with a slight groan. Carrie sat back a little, she was confused as to why he would show up for a date wearing his work clothes, and they were a little dusty and dirty, just like the other day in the mercantile. *Maybe this guy's a slob!* She though almost out loud.

"Nice, uh, shirt?" She whispered.

Jason took the cup of coffee and sipped for a second. "Had a little trouble getting down the hill."

"Oh."

Jason closed his eyes and let the coffee sooth his system, he was a little frustrated and way nervous. He opened his eyes and rubbed them after setting his cup down. In just seconds, his stomach and heart rumbled. She was a raving beauty! He had never seen her made up like this, she had made her hair into something elegant, and this was no simple lunch. She was treating this like a date. Now he felt like a cad for not at least changing his clothes.

"I'm so sorry. You look beautiful by the way." He lowered his head in mock shame, hoping she had a forgiving side.

Carrie smiled with glittering gold in her eyes and said, "Thank you."

"I didn't have time to change. I was lucky enough to get here at this time."

"It's okay. Gloria and I were having a chat about you."

"Me?" Jason looked over his shoulder and saw Gloria standing next to the cash register nodding her head. "I hope it was all good."

Carrie just smiled. "I see they got most of that train wreck cleaned up."

Jason looked lost for a second and remembered that a boxcar had flipped over onto the highway. He had totally forgotten about it, his mind was focused on Carrie all day. He shook his head in disbelief and said, "Did they? Obviously they did if you went home to change."

"We went home early this morning. The secondary road was cleared earlier, about five am, and then 201 opened around eleven. There was a rail crane just an hour away and the railroad brought it in last night."

"Obviously the spill wasn't very toxic…" Jason added.

"No, I guess not."

Jason took a sip of the coffee that Gloria had sat at his place earlier. His eyes darted around the empty diner. "Where's Dusty?"

Carrie took a glance at Gloria and then her eyes settled on the condiment tray at the side of their table. She played with the sugar holder, trying to find the right words.

After a sigh she brought her voice to barely above a whisper, even though the place was empty and Gloria already knew. "He had a bad morning. I sent him to the sitter's."

"Sitter's?" Jason set his cup back down slowly. "Is he okay?"

This was going to be hard, Carrie thought, but she also decided this morning she was going to tell the stranger about her little brother. The truth never hurt as bad as it does right at first. But, she also decided that some things were going to be left out. Some things were just no-one's business.

"He likes you, you know." She started. Jason nodded. "You've noticed that he's different?"

"A little. I mean he looks normal and acts like a kid, but he seems…"

"Slow."

Jason didn't want to hurt anyone's feelings so he kept his full observations from last night to himself. "Yes. Is it autism?"

"Three years ago he was… in an accident. He's had brain trauma, a bad kind. He has a memory disorder, one doctor in Vegas calls it *mixed retrograde and anterograde amnesia.*"

Jason didn't change his expression. "Wow. Is he going to be alright?"

Carrie's eyes were welling up behind with burning tears. "I… I don't know. But there is hope, I mean everyday he seems a little less… lost." She wiped her moist eyes with her paper napkin. "Sometimes he can't remember me or other people, other times he can't remember who he is. That's one thing I want to point out to you; sometimes he likes to be called Dusty, other times he wishes to be called Dustin. We don't know how that came about, though."

Carrie paused to sip her coffee and Gloria came over to the table. "Hey guys. Cook's back from the store. Would you like something to eat?"

The Cook, aka *Cookie* or Jim Blantz, was a large man in his sixties. Of course he earned his nickname

82

Cookie in the Army during Vietnam, where he was a mess sergeant. He had the traditional half white half sweat-stained chef's hat that he wore while cooking; it covered his mostly bald head of white hair. All that was missing to make him look like the cooks in all the war movies was the stogie hanging out of his mouth, but that was given the kybosh by the health department years ago.

Cookie was always late or having to run down to the mercantile to get something he had forgotten to order from Sysco Food Service. He worked the diner from six am to three then he returned at six and cooked till nine, when the diner closed. Sole proprietor or not, he had very little life outside of the place, so this was his life. He was as much a part of the diner as was the collection of memorabilia hanging from the walls.

Jim's father opened the diner in 1952, the original being the triple-wide trailer portion. In 1973 when his son returned from Asia, Jim's father took out a loan to build the newer extension and when the work was completed, left the diner to Jim. His father died in 1983, the life insurance policy paid for the refurbishing loan and now Jim made mostly profit, after paying the expenses.

"The usual for me please Gloria." Jason said with a forced smile. He saw the revelation that lay before him was painful for his friend. New friend.

"Laws almighty. I might as well have a pig tied out back for you."

"Just a fruit bowl and milk please Glo."

Gloria saw the pain in Carrie's eyes and knew she was telling Jason about Dusty. *She must like this guy a lot to give him the burden early on…* It took weeks for Gloria to understand it herself. "Okay sugar. Back in a flash."

Gloria left the table and the padding of her shoes could be heard as she walked back behind the counter. She didn't envy poor Carrie for having to tell the tale over and over to new folks, and she especially didn't want to be in

Jason's shoes either. It was hard enough telling someone the sad story-even though it sounded as Carrie left out the nature of the accident-but how were you expected to respond? Most folks just said they were sorry and changed the subject. She glanced back at the table and noticed the couple was avoiding eye contact. Uh-oh.

Jason said his apologies for Carrie's troubles and then looked down at his clothes. He didn't have time for a shower or even change and now he regretted it wholeheartedly. He took a deep breath and heard a little sniffle coming from Carrie. He raised eyes from his open jacket to meet hers and they were fixed on the varnished tabletop. He cleared his throat.

"Hi." This got her attention. "My name's Jason David Parmenter. I'm thirty-three years old and I come from Denver, Colorado. What's your name?"

Carrie smiled, it was hard not to. "Carrie Marie Dodson. My birthday is May 10th, 1991 and I was born here in Fallcast, Nevada."

Jason slowly reached out from in front of him with his right hand and offered it to her. She took it and softly took his grip, but she was sure to give it a startling firm squeeze. She watched as his eyes enlarged a little and then a smile of respect crossed his lips.

"Nice to meet you Miss Dodson. I'm glad we had the time to share together today."

"Me too Jason... uh, Mr. Parmenter." She giggled.

Their hands stayed in place, Carrie turned hers a little to the right and Jason followed with his. They were now holding hands. Gloria heard a laugh and she came around from the kitchen area and saw the youngsters were looking at each other in the eyes and joking. *My God he's a catch*! She thought to herself.

"Sorry about my attire, but I had a rotten morning. The Jeep blew a tire on the way back and I almost ran off the road." Jason reciprocated.

"Oh too bad. I'm glad you're alright though. Did you have fun?"

"Just the usual rock and dirt and sand and stuff." Jason was about to lower his eyes for a second out of mock pity for himself when he realized he had an insider, "Hey! I did find a cave or a mine out there on Dinosaur Back. Do you know it?"

Carrie shook her head, "No. How far up?"

"Bout three miles. It's just a few clicks from a USGS Marker and I have the coordinates written down for research. There's no such mention of it on the geodetic maps or the assays. I thought maybe it was a private mine or an old Indian cave."

Carrie shook her head. "I think it's the place the high school kids hang out, or used to."

"Hmm. When I was a kid I loved to hiking into those things. Still do, I might go out this weekend, since I don't have any fuel."

Carrie smiled one of those I know something you don't know smiles and squeezed Jason's hand a little tighter. He saw this and crooked his head a little to the left.

"What?"

"You said you need a special gas right?"

"Avgas. Yes."

"John Dickson, a farmer at the far end of the valley, he has an old airplane. I bet he would have a few extra gallons of Avgas lying around. For a price of course."

The hair rose on the back of Jason's neck. This girl was listening to everything he said!

"Can I ask you a question?"

"Sure, as long as it isn't about geology. I have a friend who's good at that."

Jason guffawed and leaned in towards her, looking both ways as if to convey it was a secret, "You are very well educated. Did you go to school around here?"

Now it was Carrie's neck hairs turn to come to attention. He just flattered her. He knew she was a local with no college education, and now he asked like she was a scholar or something. She didn't know how to respond. The truth again. It would be less painful later.

"I was home schooled." She pulled her hand away from his. "My father and mother taught me."

"They did a very good job. Is your mom a teacher here in town?"

Carrie's face went red then nearly purple. She pulled her hands completely under the table and folded them together in her lap. This truth hurt. "She... left us years ago. When I was twenty-three."

Jason's heart sank. He had blown it again. First with the question about her brother and now her mother. He raised his hand to his eyes and rubbed them.

"I'm sorry. I'm not very good at this dating thing am I?"

Carrie let go a tiny crack of smile, it was her fault for bringing it up and he was taking the blame. She liked this guy, a lot. She wanted to know more about him.

"Okay. It's alright. Things weren't so good back then and you couldn't have known. She wasn't a teacher, but she was very smart."

Gloria brought the plates to the table during another silent moment and she excused herself after setting them down and backed off towards her stool at the counter where her newspaper was.

Carrie took a bite of watermelon and looked at Jason; he was cutting his immense ham steak into pieces. "Now you. Your folks were killed?"

Jason had just plopped a piece of meat into his mouth and was trying to chew it fast enough to answer in a manner able way. He forgot to swallow. He coughed a little and took a sip of water, then said, "Car accident a few years ago."

"I'm sorry."

"Don't be, it happened a while ago, I'm okay with it… now."

Carrie just sighed maudlin at best, she turned the conversation, "Is it fun being a geologist?"

"Well, one time it was. Now days everything is so much about paperwork or permits for this and permission for that. It's hard to get any good science in. It's kinda like when I first got out of college; I hated it."

"Hated it?" Carrie's eyes went wide, "Why still do it?"

"It's not so bad now; but when I first got out of school I went to work for this company in Lovelock…"

"Nevada?"

"Yes. They made me do claim surveys, which meant climbing mountains and hillsides looking for registered claim stakes, then recording the info. This was way before GPS, so everything had to be done by hand, and foot."

Carrie smiled, "Not even an ATV?"

"No." Jason frowned to emphasize his displeasure. "I walked eight to ten miles a day, and all uphill it seemed. Frying summer heat, freezing winter cold, didn't matter. I thought being a geologist was going to be fun, finding new rock formations and studying strata."

"Strata?"

"The layers of rock and sediment that form along the ground as time passes, then as the tectonic plates shift-those are these little islands the continents float on-when they shift and run into one another it causes earthquakes and even drives the mountains higher, sometimes millions of years of layers or strata is exposed. Geologists examine these layers to determine things like weather, moisture, air content, volcanic eruptions and even how the dinosaurs disappeared."

Carrie was now resting her chin in her palm as Jason explained geology 101 to her. Most of which she knew from her studies, but this was the best course a conversation could take. She didn't really want to talk about herself, even though she would eventually have to.

Jason took a breath and asked her if she was hungry. Carrie realized she was just staring at him and her face went crimson as she picked up her fork and nodded. He finished off his ham and began to work on the eggs with the corner of his toast.

There were little bursts of talk between each other, but the business at hand was to eat. Jason hadn't eaten since last night, and Carrie hadn't eaten but a handful of chips in the spare bedroom of the hotel office before she went to sleep, dreaming of Jason. The door squeaked wide at exactly two o'clock.

"Afternoon Ron." Then she turned to Jason, "Our lunch rush…"

Gloria was addressing the bartender from the Horseshoe Club from last night, Jason noted. He was dressed pretty much the same; light blue shirt with a turned up collar, blue jeans and he wore a small windbreaker that he took off and sat over the back of the first stool at the counter. He was probably Jason's age, maybe a few years younger, and built like a man that spent most of his time indoors standing behind a bar and not getting out for a little exercise. He was a little overweight and would probably have a heart attack if he had to run for any reason.

"Mornin' Glo."

Ron nodded at Gloria and then scanned the rest of the diner and his eyes rested on Carrie for a few seconds, then in a flash of movement and surprise his gaze fell upon Jason. There was no nod or acknowledgement, more of a moment of jealousy and then a twinge of fear. He looked forward after a few seconds and held out his coffee cup for Gloria to fill.

Carrie leaned forward to Jason and whispered, "That's Ron Benjamin. He's the bartender at the Horseshoe. He's here every day at two."

"Lunch rush huh? I know him." Jason whispered back and added, "I don't think he likes me too much."

"He's just jealous." She confirmed one look. "He's asked me out about three times a month. Until my brother trashed his bar one night when he found out. Ron and my brother never got along too well."

Jason felt the urge to get up and leave right then and there. He had seen her brother the other night and knew there was nothing but trouble on the other end of this date. He managed a creaky, "Well, I hope I get along with him."

Carrie laughed out loud, which made Ron look their way and then turn his eyes back towards the kitchen shaking his head.

She said, "You won't have to worry about my brother. He's not allowed close to me. We had a fight some years ago and a judge ordered him to stay away or face jail. I haven't seen my brother closer than fifty feet at church in three years."

More complications Jason thought. He had finished his meal and pushed his plate to the center of the table to indicate so. Gloria saw this and walked over with the check and laid it out on the table in front of him, then patted his shoulder, which seemed to enrage Ron at the counter even more. His face was red as a sugar beet now.

The bill came to $11.63 so Jason laid out fifteen dollars and told Gloria to keep the change and Carrie stood in unison with her new friend. Jason helped her out with her jacket under the watchful eye of the only other diner in the place and then slid into his own coat.

Carrie walked out in front and smiled at Ron as she passed him at the counter and said, "Hi Ron."

He just nodded back and pretended that he was busy reading the menu.

Jason passed him next and nodded when the large man's eyes came up to meet his. Jason knew it was a bad idea to even speak to the man, but he couldn't resist and whispered, "Ron." As he passed.

The bartender pursed his lips and lifted the menu back into place. When Carrie and Jason closed the door to the diner behind him he looked to Gloria and spoke loudly, "Does Tom and his dad know about them?"

Gloria just shrugged her shoulders and smiled back.

"Probably not!" He finished as he set the menu down hard onto the counter. "Probably not."

"Not another happy town folk type." Jason said as they turned right, heading towards the area that was closed last night due to the railcar accident.

"Like I said, he's just jealous." Carrie snugged her jacket closer to her as they hit Sluicebox Avenue, the wind had picked up a little and the breeze was chilly.

They walked in silence for a few minutes; Jason didn't know what to say. He wanted to see the train wreck or at least what was left of it, since there was no real entertainment in town after the last movie theater closed two years ago. Carrie had made the turn towards this side of town after leaving the diner as if she read Jason's mind.

As they approached the crossing, just after the shoofly where the railroad tracks crossed Highway 201 and headed for the lower half of town and then into the mine area spurs, Jason caught a whiff of a familiar smell. Diesel fuel.

When they reached the accident site, the marks of the railcar were evident on the asphalt where it had scraped after falling over onto it; Jason saw the barrels marked with the fuel's labels. That was the toxic spill.

They stopped at the crossing and saw the ground was littered with super-absorbent material to soak up the fuel, and the ground from the track line to the lower access street was also covered in the white powdery substance.

Jason looked to his left back towards town and sitting on the shoofly set of rails was a flat car with a squashed box car on it. In front of that was a huge rail crane, used primarily for lifting freight, rail maintenance and resetting derailed rolling stock.

There were people everywhere, a group of about six men were standing next to the flatcar, all dressed in railroad overalls, they were the crew from the crane; another group of three were corralled by the forward of two engines, most likely the crew of the locomotive that pulled the fateful freight car into town.

On the other side of the highway were several official cars that consisted of two county Sheriff vehicles, two Nevada Highway Patrol cruisers, two more cars that had state seals on the doors and one car that had GSA motor pool license plates; most likely the National Transportation Safety Board here to look into the accident.

Carrie and Jason stopped just on the north side of the tracks at the crossing and took in the scene. On the other side of the tracks near the collection of law enforcement cars stood Deputy Darrin Parker. Parks saw the couple and smiled over the heads of the other cops standing around drinking coffee and shooting war stories at each other, and then waved. He nodded and said something to the other officers and they looked towards Jason and Carrie and then waved also. Parks started jogging towards them.

He seemed chipper today, not as grim as last night when he made the announcement of the derailment, and was nearly out of breath as he reached the onlookers at the crossing guard stanchion.

"Hey Carrie. Hi, uh Jacob is it?" He panted as he slowed his pace a few feet away.

"Jason. You know me?"

"Sorry. Got to know everyone in my line of work, Jason. Everything okay Carrie?"

"Fine Parks. Did you stay out here all night?"

"Ah no. I went home about two a.m. and then came back about ten this morning. Quite a mess huh?"

"Anyone hurt?" Jason asked.

"No. But the tracks are screwed up. The Feds," Parks nodded towards the two casually dressed men in jeans and windbreakers, "say that these rails are going to be messed up for a week or so."

"At least the toxic spill wasn't too bad." Jason added.

"Yeah. Just diesel fuel. The car had some ten or fifteen barrels of the stuff for the Cooper Mine. Made a hell of a mess and it's going to stink around here for a while too."

Parks took off his drill sergeant hat and wiped his brow with a hankie he retrieved from his back pocket. He was dressed in a lighter Ike jacket today not the bulky Tuffy, and seemed in better spirits than last night.

"Where you all headed?" He asked like a kid looking for a ride.

"Nowhere. Just wanted to see the wreck and stretch our legs." Carrie answered. "Already been by the lower street on my home and back to the Lick this morning."

A familiar *I don't trust this newcomer* look crossed Parks face as he glared at Jason and addressed Carrie, "You two stayed *together* last night?"

Carrie shook her head and placed her hands on her hips, fists balled. "Darrin Parker!" His attention swung back to her, "Why would you suggest a thing like that?"

"I'm not suggesting anything. I just don't want any trouble brewing because of rumors that you and Jared here are dating or something. Your brother is a handful as it is."

"Jason." Jason corrected.

"Jason." Parks apologized. "We just don't know you too well and it takes folks a while to get used to someone."

Jason was about to tell Parks something but Carrie cut him off, "He's going to be here through the holidays, so you better '*get used to him*' now."

"I'm sorry. I didn't mean anything by it. I just don't want any trouble that's all."

"There won't be. If Tommy starts anything up, he's going to jail and this time no one can bail him out."

With that Carrie spun on her heels and started walking away leaving Jason looking sheepishly at the deputy. He just shrugged and walked back to his compatriots at the police cars. Jason took a few seconds to take all of what just happened in before turning and following Carrie.

When he caught up to her, she had her head down and was walking a little unsteady, like she had too much to drink, but Jason knew it was because she was crying. She had one hand over her face and the other arm was crossed over her chest. Tears slipped between her fingers.

"I'm sorry about that." Jason said as he slowed his pace with hers. His heart was pounding in frustration.

She sniffed back a tear and wiped her eyes, "It's not you. It's everyone in this stupid town. I can't even have a friend without causing some kind of suspicion that I'm sleeping around."

Jason didn't know what to say.

Carrie continued, "Don't let these idiots scare you Jason. They're all just jealous that I like you and they think you're going to break my heart and leave town."

Now things were moving a little fast, Jason thought. "I didn't think we were like, you know…"

Carries stopped, her eyes had an almost blue hue to the usual golden hazel. She smiled and that did something weird to his chest all of a sudden. "Jason, were friends right? I know everything is crazy about me right now; my little brother, my big brother. Does that make us less than friends?"

"No of course not."

She began walking again in the direction towards the Salt Lick. "Good. Because I need a friend now more than ever."

Jason walked a few steps behind her for the rest of the way to the diner. He didn't know why he felt attracted to her, other than looks and maybe her smile, but there was something deep about her that made his heart feel funny when she talked, she did seem to need a friend-if all the talk about her was right.

He had heard the old timers at the mercantile a time or two talk about her situation, being that her brother and father was very strict in raising her. They didn't allow many if any friends over to the house, they kept her out of school-now he knew why, she was being home schooled by her mother-and many were afraid to even say hi to her.

She passed the diner and walked towards the Sage and Juniper office, up the tailing hill and into the glass cubicle that surrounded Mary for most every day. Jason quietly followed along behind and smiled at his landlord as he closed the door.

"Hello Mr. Parmenter. Sleep well?"

"Fine Mary, thanks."

"Darn power outages. I wish the county would get their act together and get us some reliable power lines from Vegas."

Jason just nodded and smiled. Carrie had walked over to the guest accommodations table where a small old Compaq computer and HP inkjet was for overnighter's use, and a telephone. Carrie picked up the receiver of the phone and quickly dialed in seven digits. She was breathing like she had been jogging.

Her voice took on a soothing tone, "Hi Helen, its Carrie. Fine. He's fine too. Sure, I'll bring him by soon. Listen, is John around? I need to ask a favor. Thanks."

Carrie turned from looking out of the west window and faced Jason. Her face went to a smile that hid any feelings she was having earlier, like she had just turned her pain off. A second or two more ticked off, and then someone came to the phone on the other end.

"Hi John! Yes we're fine. I need to ask you something. Do you use Avgas in your plane? Do you have any extra that I could buy, like say a barrel?" She raised her head to Jason who understood her silent inquiry. He nodded. "Yeah. I can pay you for it at the end of the month. I don't care John, this is important. Okay, see you in a few hours alright?" She smiled at the receiver and switched back to looking out the window, "Great, thank you John. No, I mean it."

She hung up the phone and turned back to Jason with a triumphant look on her face and sighed. "He says you can give him one of your barrels when it gets here."

"He knows me?"

Carrie crossed her arms over her chest, "I'd have thought by now you would've realized the whole county knows you're here."

Jason lowered his head, "Oh."

She kept her tone enthusiastic, "And if they don't, they will after they see us together for a few days."

"Marvelous." Jason replied without exuberance. "I need to get something from my room, I'll be back."

Carrie nodded and waited for him at the front door of the office.

CHAPTER SIX
December 10th

The mine's Jeep wouldn't have been very good for hauling a fifty gallon drum of aviation fuel, so in less than five minutes after hanging up with a man she bartered the fuel from, Carrie had talked Jack Taylor out of his blue diesel F-250 Super Duty for the trip. Jason left the mine's Jeep in the parking space in front of the office and they walked around back to get the F-250. Carrie and Jason had been on a dusty road for the last half hour, heading southeast off of Highway 201 a few miles from town. Carrie was driving.

"So your mother and father passed a while ago? I kinda wish my father had, in a way."

Carrie and Jason had been in full conversation mode since they left town. She was learning more about him than he was of her, but for the moment Jason thought this was some kind of response thing. She wanted to feel comfortable about knowing his innermost details before she would reveal herself to him. Tit for tat. Quid pro quo.

Jason sighed and looked out the window at the passing sage clumps. "It's okay."

"Did they travel a lot?" Carrie hoped to back out of this situation.

"Basically, yes. They traveled so much my father would have saved thousands if he'd had his own jet."

"Your father flew?"

"Yes. He taught me when I was ten."

"Ten?"

Jason smiled, "How old were you when you learned to drive?"

"About the same age." Carrie smiled over her shoulder at him. "But that's not the same." A wave of relief chilled her shoulders, she handled that well.

"Sure it is. Flying is easier than driving, there aren't too many folks getting into your way up there and if you have a reliable plane, it's much safer."

"Really?"

"Yes, you're going to find out, since you got me the fuel you have to go up with me."

An evil laugh rumbled from Carrie's diaphragm, "There is no way in-I'm not getting on a plane that looks like one of Dusty's toys."

"Sure you are. And Dusty too. I think he'd love it. And you need to see what your efforts have brought. If you won't go, then turn around right now…"

Carrie glanced over to her rider again and this time she was not smiling, but her eyes were. She was pretending to be mad at him, or scared, but Jason saw right through her ruse. He wanted to spend more time with her too.

The Super Duty rambled on the road for another ten miles, the winds had turned the last five miles of dirt into washboard, and the corduroy was annoying to say the least to Jason. He hadn't heard a word from Carrie in the last three or four miles, since he told her she was going flying, but he had nothing to add. There were many questions though, about her, and as she rounded what seemed to be the last big turn towards the mountains on the far east side of the valley he cleared his throat.

"What about you? Now you know almost everything about me, what will you tell me about yourself?"

"One thing I don't know about." Carrie redirected.

Jason sighed surrender for the moment, "Okay."

"What happened to your girlfriend? Did you and she just fall out of love or did something tear you apart?"

The question was personal. Deeply rooted sadness would be the best to explain the situation, but Jason knew if he confided this last bit of truth about himself, then Carrie would have to open up about some dark things in her past.

"Both yes and no. Lindsay was a complicated woman; we met while she was doing her undergraduate work at the University of Denver. She was studying to become a biologist. She was studying ecosystem dynamics, sort of a person who loved the outdoors, and wanted to see nature in its purest form.

"We dated for several months, and then moved in together. She had a knack of knowing me well inside and out and knew how to keep me happy and at the same time get what she wanted. It was a great relationship."

"I can tell." Carrie said with a smile of compassion.

"Well, we had been together for five years; she was finishing off her senior year and was getting ready to graduate, and she-changed. Almost like overnight, although it had been a long time coming and I should have seen it.

"You see, many of the courses she took were in direct opposition to mining and the way I planned to make my living when we were, if we were to get married. She became more and more argumentative about what I did and wanted me to become a field geologist in earth sciences. Then she had this professor, he thought he was God's gift to man-if he would have believed in God-he took Lindsay to the side and began a special session with several other *concerned* interests."

"Environmentalists?"

"Damn you're smart. Yes. She and her new friends began to do the opposite of what I was doing; impact studies that I knew were flawed. The science wasn't there, just tons of speculation and theoretical results that were made to look like fact. There was this mine in North Dakota, it would have created thousands of jobs and brought a small city back from the brink of extinction and her professor and his group was hired by an anti-mining outfit to do the environmental impact statement.

"Well, let's just say the town disappeared and the mine was never started." Jason looked out the window at the miles of flat white alkali bed surrounding them. He felt sick to his stomach reliving this part of the last year.

"So that broke you up?" Carrie slowed the truck a little; she was caught up in the story.

"The company I work for was the one hired by the mine to do the geology of the area."

"Uh oh."

"I was the one appointed to the work assessments, to do the surveys. The woman I loved and I butted heads on every turn. In the end, she moved in with her professor and now they go around the world fighting mining claims for the preservation of the earth."

"That was it?"

"No. Not exactly. I found out she was pregnant a week before we separated." Jason's voice cracked, "I don't know what happened, but when I saw her a few months later at an alumni dinner, she wasn't, you know, anymore."

"Oh god, I'm so sorry."

"You couldn't have known. Besides, it feels good to tell someone the truth for a change."

"I'm the first?"

"To hear all of it. The end I mean. No one else but she and I know."

The diesel truck made a small climb on an S curve and then dropped down a mile long coarse road and the outside views of white dust and parched earth began to turn dark with green and brown. The farm was near the base of the western slope of the Specter Range; east beyond that was the Nevada Test Site; 883,000 acres of land that is run by the Department of Energy, the most famous know area is the proposed nuclear waste depository at Yucca Mountain.

Over 900 atomic tests were done in this area; and about 100 were done above ground since the 1950's until the ban in 1992. Much of the land is public and can be used, but large areas are still closed for testing and military training.

This side-the eastern side-was owned primarily by the Dickson family ranch, affectionately called The Glow Worm Ranch, the name coined by one of John Dickson's friends in the early fifties when the atomic bomb testing was going on behind the mountain.

Carrie worked the steering wheel back and forth as the dirt-slick road wound down a hill to an open area of plowed and disked dirt rows, fenced off from another area that held about one hundred head of cattle. In the early spring and all through the growing season this area would be green with alfalfa and corn.

Three buildings sat at a diagonal angle away from each other. The first was the main house; a large two story white and blue home with huge dormer windows on the second floor and a wrap-around porch on the first. There were seven rooms in all for sleeping, five bathrooms and two large rooms, one for dining and the other was a study.

The main dining room was more of a dining hall, where the workers and owners would gather each morning before sunrise to consume steak and eggs, bacon and potatoes along a forty foot table. Talk at the table was limited to what had to be done throughout that day, and maybe some patter about sports or hunting.

The next building back about one hundred feet from the main house was the bunkhouse, where the help slept. In the winter months the cattle were kept close to the ranch, about ten men stayed here and in the spring feeding run, about twenty more all lived in the largest building on the compound. Bunk beds set next to each other like in an army barracks three high were the best accommodations in miles, a huge common area the workers called "The Pit" where they had a ping pong table, billiards, television and dozens of board games that could be played on the five card tables set up in there.

Behind that building was the barn. Horse tack and stalls were located here with six stalls on one side for the Dickson family and ten on the other for the winter help. A tack room about twenty by twenty held all the leather and buckles needed for saddling horses, even team equipment when the chuck-wagon was taken out during the spring and summer on drives.

The barn currently held nine horses, three goats that roamed on their own but preferred the barn this time of year, five feral cats that kept the mouse population to a minimum and a dog named Skunk. An abrasive encounter with the smelly namesake earned him this handle.

On the south end of the big curtilage was a lean-to of sorts, large enough to cover the three tractors, two squeezers, one bailer and several ATV's used for transport around the ranch's perimeter. Chickens roamed the ground everywhere in this area because the roost was located at the back end of the sheds, a fifteen bird coop and one rooster inhabited it most of the time during the night. Encircled with chicken and barbed wire, the birds were usually kept safe from coyotes by two semi-friendly security patrolmen.

One was Skunk the dog and the other was a brown and white llama that had free roam of the entire ranch within the fenced areas. The llama named Hawkeye from the book *Last of the Mohicans* was just that. He kept watch over the ranch and coyotes never ventured very close to where Hawkeye patrolled.

Carrie pulled the F-250 to the perimeter gate that crossed just in front of a rusty old cattle guard. She stopped and looked at Jason with her eyebrows raised; he knew what she was demanding with her dazzling eyes. He hopped out of his side of the vehicle and opened the gate, waited till she was all the way through and then secured it behind the truck.

"Thanks." She said as he climbed back in.

She floored the accelerator and the diesel spun the tires towards the main house.

Helen Dickson was your typically average fifty-five year old woman. She wore a blue and white flower print dress that had flour all over the front of it, even the apron she wore in front was covered in it. White hair that was pulled up into a bun and kept in place with a butterfly clasp surrounded a slightly tan and weathered face.

Her clothes looked like something out of the Walton's, but she wore them with practicality and grace. She greeted Jason and Carrie at the door with a smile and a hug for Carrie.

"Hi honey! How's that brother of yours?"

"He's doing alright Helen. He's still in and out of it once in a while."

"That's too bad." Helen looked at Jason and smiled even bigger, "And this is the pilot from Colorado huh?"

Jason nodded and offered his hand. She took it with her flour covered right hand and gave it a firm handshake; she built a good grip kneading dough over the last thirty years as the wife of a rancher.

"Jason Parmenter."

"Great to meet you Jason. I've heard a little about you."

This made Jason a little suspicious of whom.

"C'mon in and have a seat. John's out back oiling his tractor and he'll be just a few minutes, I'm sure he saw you two coming."

Carrie stepped in first followed by Jason; the room was warm-heated by a fire in the immense fireplace in the corner. The smell of breakfast still hung in the air and was being joined by the new smell of freshly baked bread.

Helen stepped lively back to the kitchen and spoke over her shoulder as she went, "Got to get the last couple of loaves in for dinner honey. Have a seat and I'll bring some coffee out."

"Thanks." Carrie said as she looked for a soft couch.

The furniture in the main house was right of an old western. Antique oil lamps on small tables in every corner, lace and doilies everywhere. The doorframes were huge, with huge open rooms behind them, long flowing heavy draperies were pulled to the side to allow the meager sunshine in.

The traditional book shelves and curio cabinets filled in the walls with dozens upon dozens of photographs dating back over a hundred years to current. A tongue-in-groove wood panel rose halfway up the walls then wallpaper took off from there to the ceiling; the wallpaper was old and curling in some places near the crown molding at the top, the hand carved woodwork molding including the crown, the doors, windows and halfway up the wall had been painted over and over again, leaving thick brush marks in some places.

Trinkets and whatnots decorated the table tops and cabinets, Hummel figurines, china, fancy crystal glassware, and more photos graced the shelves and curios. Jason liked this kind of decoration; it showed the progress of the family throughout the last hundred years here in Fallcast and not in a blingy tacky way like the Salt Lick's memorabilia.

"Would you too like some cookies or maybe a sandwich? I could whip up a couple of briskets on bread in about five minutes..." Helen called as she headed back to the immense kitchen to finish her bread.

Jason shook his head no at Carrie and she answered for the both of them, "No thank you Helen. We've got to get back to town, Dusty's at the sitter's."

"Pity. Mr. Parmenter should get a chance to have a little of home grown, home cut, home smoked and homemade beef sandwiches." She called back from just inside the door, where the kneading table was.

Jason's stomach was now rumbling. He gave Carrie a pity me look. She returned it with a mock pouty face and held up a finger to indicate to hold on a little while. There was a thunderous stomping sound at the front door and in walked John Dickson, heavy wool jacket covering overalls, and giant work boots.

"Hidey Ho!" He called as he removed his hat and set it on a peg that protruded from the clothes tree at the door. "How are you honey? And how's that big boy?" His voice was ragged from dozens of years of smoking. He fished one out of his pocket as he acknowledged Jason. "Mr. Parmenter."

"Fine John. He's getting bigger."

Jason nodded back with a smile. "Good afternoon sir."

"Sir? Now don't go putting that old man elderly respect crap on me. We're just old fashioned country folk here and you're welcome at our place." He struck a match on the end of his yellow thumbnail and lit the cig that dangled precariously from his lips as he talked. He smiled as he exhaled blue smoke above his head.

"Are you smoking in my receiving room John Dickson?" Helen scolded from the kitchen.

"Yes. But I'm headed out with the couple here." He winked at Jason and gave him and Carrie a wave towards the door.

They walked for about five minutes towards the storage barn, John talking all the way as the ashes flitted here and there from the end of the smoke. When they rounded the corner to the man door Jason saw an old white with red striped Cessna 172 sitting on a plump of grass, the windows were covered by a tarp and the wings were anchored to the ground with small chains.

"She ain't been in the air in several weeks. I thought I lost her after the wind last night. Geez what a blow!" John

104

took the hardly smoked cigarette butt from his mouth and tossed it to the ground in front of his feet, grinding it into the pasty white dirt with his old boot. "Fuel's this way…"

He led them to the man door and opened the hasp.

Inside the barn was as dark as possible, John reached in and flipped on a switch and the room was bathed in fluorescent light. Heavy canvass tarps covered everything except an old wooden wagon, the chuck wagon, and some old wooden barrels. John walked over to one of the several piles of tarps and pulled it down to the ground. Underneath were four bright blue barrels marked with the flammable triangle and the words AVGAS.

"Got a barrel sling and winch over there…" He pointed to another lump of tarp. "Cass, why don't you go get the truck and drive her up to the big door there huh? Me and Mr. Parmenter are gonna heft them onto the bed."

Carrie nodded her head and shot Jason an apologetic look and disappeared out the man door. John and Jason pulled the tarp off the cherry picker with the barrel sling on it and maneuvered it into place at the first barrel. John fished another smoke from his pocket and lit up, not really caring too much for the fact the barn was filled with flammable gas and dusty remnants of hay. The cig flapped in his lips as he spoke again. "Probably should take two."

"If it's no problem Mr. Dickson."

"You got a fancy for our young Carrie here?" Even though the voice wasn't accusatory, there was a sense of needing to know.

"We're friends." Jason tried to hide his ambushed feeling.

John paused while blinking his left eye in the trail of smoke that drifted into it. "Uh huh."

"Honest. We just really met and I have no other expectations."

John curled his lips around the smoke stick and pulled it out of his mouth while blowing smoke in Jason's direction. "She's a good kid. Had a rough few years but she handles herself well. She must see something in you if she's with you."

"She just drove…"

"Listen young fella; Carrie is smart as anyone in town and few treat her like it, say like her old man and big brother. She's been good to us out here and we want her to stay happy as she is now. If she even lets you hang around her at all its cause she sees something that you don't even know about yet. Be careful, you might fall in love with her." He smiled and put the cigarette back in his teeth.

"I will sir."

They heard the diesel F-250 rumble up to the barn door and John went over and pulled out the old four by four that held the two huge doors shut. He opened it wide and waved Carrie, who had already backed the truck to the door, into the barn.

It took a few minutes and one cigarette for them to load the two barrels onto the bed and secure it in place with ratchet straps. Jason sat on the bedrail to catch his breath from having to do the lion's share of the work. John was picking around in his pocket for what Carrie thought was another cig, but in turn he pulled out a pencil and walked over to the barn wall.

He found a bare spot in between several markings already on the wood and motioned Jason over. He began to scratch something on the wall with the pencil and stood back when Jason arrived at his side. He had written a makeshift contract, it read:

TWO BARRELS PLANE GAS FOR TWO BARRELS WHEN MINE GET TO THE MERCANTILE JASON PARMENTER.

"Just put your mark here…" John pointed with the pencil. Carrie covered her mouth and turned to hide her smile and Jason complied.

"Thank you John for your help." Jason nodded.

"I'm always willing to help this young lady and her friends"

John shook Carrie's hand first then Jason's and asked again if they wanted something to eat and again Carrie said no thank you. The couple from town boarded the Super Duty and Carrie fired the engine and bid goodbye to John as she maneuvered out of the barn and onto the gravel driveway. John waved and winked as he closed the doors.

Ten minutes later they were braving the washboard road again.

"Why didn't you want to stay for lunch?"

"Because lunch would turn to supper and supper might end up being a sleepover. John and Helen are probably the best hosts in all of the valley and they are a little lonely. Didn't he chat you up a little as you were waiting for me?"

"Yes."

"What'd he say?"

"Just what I already know. You're a good person and to respect you."

Carrie smiled and looked over her arm at him, "You knew that?"

"Yes. I think you are the best person in Fallcast, you treat me like a person instead of an outsider."

"Well, you're still an outsider, but I…like you."

CHAPTER SEVEN
Late Afternoon December 10th

The blue F-250 powered up the last hill of white dust and sand before the downhill plunge into the eastern part of the valley and the town. Jason had been questioning Carrie about her life in the desert.

She had been hesitant to reveal much, but she knew eventually if she were to stay friends with Jason, she would have to disclose a lot. She sighed and kept looking back and forth from the road she knew well, to her passenger, "My mother disappeared about eight years ago. My father and brother were distraught as I was at first, but in time they seemed to cope. It took me quite a while to adjust. She was rumored to have run off with a guy that came into town for a month; he ran a crew of survey guys up on the backside of Diamond Ridge behind the town."

Carrie pointed to the crown of the mountain ahead of them and continued, "My little brother turned to me, he was devastated as you can imagine. He was spoiled because he was the youngest."

"Been there." Jason added quickly.

"Well…" She took a breath and closed her eyes for a fraction of second longer than she should have and the truck slid sideways a little. Jason's eyes went wide as saucers, but he kept his tongue. She said, "Although my father never beat me or molested me, he did more damage than anyone could imagine. I was never allowed to have a boyfriend, never allowed outside of the yard until I was eighteen. I've never been with… a man."

Jason inhaled slowly and asked himself in microseconds how he would respond to this. She was a virgin at the age of twenty-nine; not only was that unheard of now days with someone of her looks, but it was also a cause of shame in many societal circles, and many would think she was just lying. He took a quick breath and hoped he didn't put his foot in his mouth, "So, basically you've never been on a date."

Carrie was looking forward at the road ahead; a smile crept up on her lips as she stared at the curve they were coming upon. Jason sensed she was amused by his response and he continued.

"Well, I guess you could say you're lucky. Sometimes I wish I had never had been so eager to become sexual. It happened so fast and I never had a chance to enjoy it. It also tells me one thing…"

Carrie bit, "What's that?"

"You have one hell of a lot of patience!" He let out a little laugh at her expense. Carrie laughed along.

"It's just that I've been so busy with Dusty and…"

She cut herself off and Jason looked from the passenger window on his side to her to see what was wrong and her face was white as a sheet. Her eyes were white wide as well and there was a look of fear plus anxiousness on her lips. Jason looked out the windshield to see what the scare was about.

The column of smoke rose high into the air and the duo didn't smell it until they were closer to town. Carrie sped up her already maniacal driving on the slick road to get to town faster, but both in the cab of the truck knew where the smoke was coming from. The smell was unmistakable; it was not from a farmer burning his field or trash in the dump on the east hillside, it was coming from the Sand and Juniper II.

There were three engines here from the fire department's main house this time. One was on 201 blocking incoming traffic from getting too close to the entrance, another pumper was at the hydrant at the corner of the old mine dump and hooked to it with hoses running from the pumper to the last engine which was set in the north lot in front of Jason's-or what was left of-room.

Carrie brought the Ford as close as she could when she was stopped by a deputy doing traffic control at the first turnoff towards Sluicebox and Mylar. He raised a hand to her as she approached.

"Hi Mike, we need to get up there." She said with a calm tone.

Mike Tenner grew up in Fallcast and went away to the academy in Washoe County when he turned twenty-one. He returned to Joshua County after two years there. Mike was a pleasant looking individual with small acne scars on his face; he had blond hair, a short crew-cut and a bright smile that few could argue with. He took a look in the back of the blue Ford and shook his head.

"Are you crazy? Two full barrels of gasoline and you want to get closer?" He said almost wide eyed.

Both Carrie and Jason had forgotten about their cargo. They looked at each other and Carrie just nodded at the deputy who was about to hail an oncoming car from the other direction. Carrie pulled to the shoulder and the occupants hopped out and ran up the hill made from tailings.

The scene was surreal. The north top part of the T was nearly gone. All that remained from the intersection of the top to the leg of the T shaped building was where the two met, and then the wall gradually declined to the ground level where Jason's room once stood. The fire was out, but smoke still curled up in small columns into the breezeless afternoon air.

Jason took several steps towards the spot that was his room and was stopped by Deputy Parker.

"Hold on there cowboy. No one gets close till this thing is out." Parks spoke with the toothpick bobbing up and down in his teeth.

"Just trying to see if anything is left. I had everything in there…" Jason replied, trying not to sound as upset as he felt. Carrie joined his side.

110

"What happened?" Carrie asked.

"Looks like an accident. An old light socket or something…" Parks began.

"Or a match in a trash can." A voice prompted from behind the trio.

Fire Chief and town businessman Marshal Tedford was standing off to the side and behind Carrie, Jason and Darrin. "Looks like the fire started in a trash barrel behind your room; that is your room I heard you say?"

Jason looked as the others did to the Chief. "Yes, it was."

"Fire started in the trash bin, went up and took to the eaves, then made its way into the attic. By the time enough smoke was seen at the office the roof was on fire and then by the time we got here the roof had collapsed and spread to the rest of the rooms over to there." He pointed to the wall that rose from where Jason's room was to the intersection where the building runs west to the office. "That's why your room got the worst of it."

"It'd have to be a big fire in the bin." Parks said.

"Don't know what was in the barrel yet, pretty burned up, but the investigator will figure it out." The local arson investigator was also the town's coroner coincidentally, and the brother in-law of Tedford. "I'll let you know when I find out. By the way Mr. Parmenter, you don't smoke do you?"

"No."

The Chief ran his filthy soot covered hand across his chin, "Hmm."

"Is it safe to get closer?" Jason asked him.

"Yeah, just stay out of the rubble till the investigator gets here from the bank." The Chief's brother in-law runs the bank.

Jason wandered a few feet ahead, Carrie at his side, and stood where the door to his room once was. He ran his eyes over what was once the mattress, now a heaping lump of melted sponge-foam and springs in the center of the room. The mirror that sat on the table next to the TV was broken and darkened by smoke, the TV was still in its position, only it was a glob of plastic and glass. Jason could see where his laptop had sat next to the television, now there were two flaps resembling two burned beyond recognition pancakes.

The wall that separated the bathroom from the bed area was gone, some pipes and wires stuck out of the ground where it once stood; the tub looked perfectly intact and still had a pink color in the charred porcelain.

The cinder block walls had collapsed under the intense heat near the corner of the room, and the rest was pushed down by the firefighter's water from the hoses after the fifty year old mortar crumbled. Few pieces of wood remained, the framing was gone; the only thing that stood out was the wooden table where the TV and mirror was still sitting. Everything else was covered in alligatoring marks on the beams and cross members of the roof that now lay over the floor.

Carrie took Jason by the hand. If he wasn't so shaken up by the fact everything he had was in the room, he would have felt it. She squeezed it a couple of times before it registered. He turned to her with a smile of desperation.

"What do I do now?"

She smiled her best reassuring grin and squeezed his hand again. "Let's go talk to Mary."

As they walked to the office, Jason kept looking back over his shoulder at the carnage, hoping that is was some kind of dream. He turned at the last second when they approached the glass cubicle-shaped room, which was full of people when he spied the mine's Jeep Wagoneer. A flash of relief hit him as he ran to the driver's door and fished the keys out of his pants pocket.

"Thank God." He whispered as he reached for his backpack on the passenger seat where he left it before heading out to the Dickson ranch.

"Your stuff?" Carrie asked as she leaned over his shoulder.

"Yeah! I've got my personal stuff here, well most of it anyway, my cell phone…" Jason read the inventory aloud to Carrie as he pull items from the bag, "Maps, the movie I rented from the store and was going to return today; good Lord thanks, I didn't want to have to replace that. Let's see; ah… keys to the plane. I just lost my laptop, paperwork and clothes."

"Good."

Jason closed the door to the Jeep and followed Carrie inside.

"I'm sorry Jason, but there's nowhere to put you." Mary began explaining, "The fire department has closed off two rooms on the south wing and two rooms on the south side of the main building. Then all those folks that had to be moved are taking up the last rooms we have."

Mary Taylor sighed and looked at him apologetically. "We have tried the Miner's Inn, but they're full."

Carrie was standing behind Jason and spoke over his shoulder. "What about your spare room?"

"Oh honey, we've given that one to the Parson family. They've two young kids and lost everything in the fire…" When Mary said fire she shot her eyes to Jason as if he had something to do with it. "We won't have any rooms until the Chief say we can reopen the rooms closest to the fire damaged ones."

"Guess I'm going to have to fuel up my plane and get to Vegas and then I'll get a room there. Can I use your phone to get my boss to wire me some money?" Jason said, with resign and a touch of annoyance.

Carrie curled her upper lip to her nose in both contempt and thought. "Okay." She took Jason by the arm and led him to the back of the cacophonic filled room. She talked barely above the din, "Okay, you'll stay with me."

A two-fold feeling hit the young geologist at once. One was that of relief and anticipation, the other was of dread and fear. "What of your dad and brother?"

"I told you that they are not a part of my life. They have nothing to do with me and what I choose. It's my house, I own it and that's that." Her tone was grave.

"But the people around here will…"

"Talk?" She cut him off, "They always talk. Let them, we know it's strictly legitimate and you're only staying until you can find another place."

"That's not at all what I meant. Your father's related to the owner at the mine that hired my company, if he thinks for a moment that we're… you know…"

Carrie had no response to this. She would love to have her father think she was having premarital sex with a stranger, it would infuriate him so… But it would be bad for Jason both with his job and his-if any-encounter with her brother. "Leave the Jeep here and get in the truck."

Carrie turned towards the hotel manager who was joined now by her sullen looking husband at the counter and spoke in a firm tone that had bearings of disappointment, "We're going to drop the fuel off at the airport and bring your truck back and then *find* Mr. Parmenter a place to stay, for his duration here." She turned on a heel and grabbed Jason by the hand like a mother would do with her child in the toy department at the store; then led him outside.

"Sorry…" Mary said as the door to the office closed.

Getting the fuel off the truck was no easy task. There was no convenient sling winch or cherry-picker at

114

the airport hangar Jason's Cessna was in. Carrie backed into the Quonset hut as far as she could go with the truck and then they sat on the lowered tailgate as Jason thought about lowering each of the three hundred and thirty-five pound drums to the ground.

Carrie turned out to be a strong woman as they finally decided to try and lower them down without any MacGyver-like gadgets. Besides, there was nothing to build anything with in the hut. Jason tipped the barrel over one at a time and rolled it to the end of the bed, then hopped to the ground and with the help of the young woman, lowered the barrel down slowly by its end. Although there was a thump as the heavy things fell about a foot, there was no damage and better, no leaking. Jason then rolled the barrels under each wing and with the help of Carrie again, sat them upright. There they would stay until this weekend when he would return and pump their contents into his wing tanks.

As promised, Carrie returned the truck and personally thanked Jack for its use, she also avoided Mary, for some reason she didn't like the way Mary insinuated that Jason had something to do with the fire. Jason and Carrie boarded the Jeep by this time it was nearly sundown, and then headed off towards Mylar Street and Carrie's house on Crucible Way.

The approach to the house at 1675 Crucible was down a dark street, the few lights that were on at the neighboring homes cast little in the name of the gloom that surrounded the occupants of the Jeep.

Carrie knew that Dusty would be home in twenty minutes, enough time to get Jason situated with his new living conditions, even if they were temporary at best. She knew that losing everything in a fire was hard on a person, at least he didn't have his entire life in the room like photos of family or friends, things he had collected since childhood, knickknacks that took his mother years to collect, memories of a childhood stolen by a deep religion.

Carrie realized she was transferring her pain onto his. She had an inkling how he felt.

Jason stepped up the finely made wood staircase up to the wraparound porch that was covered by opaque fiberglass corrugated panels. The four by four support posts had plant pots hanging off each one of the five in the front of the house and Jason could see them full of springtime flowers in his mind. A large swing sat near the corner.

A large bay window was curtained so he couldn't see inside while he waited for Carrie to unlock the door. He felt alone in a way, and also nervous inside. Here he was on the stoop of a beautiful woman's house after he was forcibly evicted from his room by fire, she was understanding and even tried to keep his spirits up.

He knew he liked her, she was fascinating in an enigmatic sort of way, her dark skin and features told of Native American Indian decent, maybe even South American. Her eyes were spectacles of innocence and an alluring color that made you feel almost intimidated looking into them. There was a deep intensity that could penetrate into a soul it seemed.

It had to be fate, or maybe Karma, but prior three days ago it seemed the world was out to get him and now there was a sense of life pushing him one direction, towards Carrie Dodson. She was his beacon of hope, everything that went wrong, the power failure, the train wreck forcing her to stay at the hotel office and Mary sending her to tell him about the wake-up call thing put her into his proximity again, the fire that now has her opening her home to him, things were looking up.

"Can't see the stars through that..." She said as the door squeaked open on its hinges.

Jason looked back down at her and smiled, "Just breathing in the fresh air."

Carrie smiled back and said nothing as she walked into the darkened house. It was just after six but then sun was down and the cold was creeping into their skins. She flipped on the light switch and the room was bathed in a warm yellow glow from antique lamps made to look like oil lamps hanging on the wall.

Jason noticed there was little glamor to the inside of the house. A small living room about fifteen feet by ten in front of him; the room had two old couches one on the far side of the area and the other in the center in front of an oak bookcase that held an old 36" TV. He looked to his left and saw a long hallway begin with three doors along it; looking to his right he could see the kitchen off to the right, the dining room being part of the living room.

Carrie took his backpack from him as he looked around; she sensed he needed to get his bearings a little so she left him to look around while she took his pack to the room he'll be staying in. As she opened the door to the room the chill washed over her, she hadn't opened this room in weeks or maybe even months and the chill had been sealed in behind the door.

Flipping on the light she noticed the bed was out of place with its fancy frilly sham and spread. A barrage of pillows covered it from headboard to near mid-way and there were several stuffed animals taking the rest of the room to the foot. It was an old double, but it should do for him she hoped, he might have to sleep diagonally in it to keep his feet from hanging over the edge.

There were sparse furnishings in the room; a chest of drawers made from cheap particle board and bought in Vegas at Wal-Mart was the only thing that seemed practical in the small eight by eight room. She sat his pack on the bed after shoving a few of the stuffed residents out of the way. The curtains were closed, the floor was clean, the room smelled a little of the mothballs that were in the pockets of the old jackets in the closet, but all in all it was in good order.

Carrie had lit a fire in the fireplace near the kitchen area of the house. It was an old brick and steel stove used mainly for heating but a rod on a hook and sway-arm was installed for cooking in a handled pot, maybe just for decoration, but it still gave the place a look of warmth and security along with the nicely done hand sewn curtains and odds and ends from the antique shop.

It had been silent since the door had been opened and Carrie let them in. She went to the kitchen, she was nervous as well. She had first seen Jason Parmenter the day he flew in. In many places an airplane landing at the airport was no big deal, just an everyday event, but here in Fallcast with the airfield just a half mile from her house it was.

Carrie and Dusty were in the yard playing on the swing-set on a nice November afternoon when the buzzing of the Cessna broken the welcomed silence. It made several large turns and then three passes about a thousand feet over the airstrip, before landing.

Dusty was beside himself, he loved anything new and while not out of the ordinary, it certainly was new to him. Everyday something was new to him that was old news the day before. Carrie sighed at this thought. During some summers when the fire season was at its peak, helicopters would stage at the little field once and a while and Dusty kept Carrie busy running back and forth to watch them circle, hover and land up close. Every now and then when a fire would be burning nearby, Carrie would pack a lunch and they would make a day of it.

She and her little brother watched as the Cessna landed then she had to deal with Dusty begging for an hour to take him to the airfield and show him the plane. So she helped him put on his walking boots and she donned hers and up the dirt road they went. When Dusty reached the perimeter fence, he was nearly lathering at the mouth over the new thing, while the pilot idled the blue and white craft to the hangar made of steel.

By the time Carrie managed to get Dusty to the gate by following the fence line, the tall handsome looking man had already pushed his ride into the Quonset hut, and was now struggling to get the second door slid shut. With the Cessna out of site and the noise gone, Dusty's mind began to drift away from the reason they walked down here.

A man that worked at the mill pulled up in an old Jeep and the newcomer was a little animated in his conversation, something about being promised something and the preparations were not made. Although he was upset, the pilot seemed more resigned than angry, more or less like he felt he had lost the battle before it had begun. Carrie knew right then and there that the man had other issues, more than whatever he was waving his arms about was actually bothering him.

"Hungry?"

"Oh, yes I am a little. Do you want to drive up the street and get a burger when your brother comes home?"

Carrie smiled, he thought of Dusty and not just himself. "Nah. I have a half a chicken defrosted from the other night in the fridge. I'll whip us up something in a jiffy."

She could hear Jason moving around looking at things. That was okay, she had nothing to hide. He called from the far side of the living room near the hall, "Okay."

Just as Carrie took the white butcher papered fowl out of the refrigerator, Megan's Bronco pulled into the gravel driveway behind the mine Jeep. There was a look of confusion on the boy's face as he exited Meg's car and walked slowly to the little gate on the four foot cyclone fence that surrounded the house. Meg's face was contorted into a strange look also, she was curious too.

Carrie set the chicken on the counter and stepped fast to the back door, she didn't want Dusty to barge in and discover a strange man in his house. Even though Jason and Dusty had met once, she wasn't sure if the boy would remember him and go into a panic over seeing a man in the house, there had never been one in here before alone with his sister.

The back screen door screeched open and Megan turned the handle to open the back door at the same time Carrie did, so they met nearly face to face as the door swung open, startling them both a little.

"Oh!" Meg leaned back a little, "I saw the truck and I didn't know if you had company."

"It's Jason's on loan from the mine. He lost his hotel room in the fire…" Carrie began to explain as fast as possible but was stopped by Meg with a wave of her hand.

"No need… I heard all about it."

Dusty shot in past the two of them as they were talking and headed for the living room as if he were on a mission. Carrie tried to catch up to him, but it was too late, the boy reached the open area past the dining room and was stopped, open mouthed as he stared at Jason. The pilot and geologist had seated himself on the couch alongside the wall just as Meg had pulled up.

"Hi Dusty!" Jason said before Carrie could remind him about what she had said earlier.

The boy just stood there, staring open mouthed. Carrie had grit her teeth together and inhaled making a little hissing sound, expecting her little brother to scream and run to his room to hide where it would take hours of coaxing to get him to calm down and come out for something to eat. She would probably have to send Jason outside and tell him to ring the front doorbell when Dusty was in the living room. He adjusted to people coming over much easier that way. Carrie took a step towards her brother.

"*AIRPLANE MAN!*" Dusty screamed with joy.

The room froze. Well, Carrie and Megan froze, now they were opened mouth in astonishment as Dusty slowly walked towards Jason, smiling like a child his first time at Disneyland. *He didn't correct Jason about his name like he does me nearly every day! He knew this man on sight and seems happy to see him, what gives?*

Meg tapped Carrie on the shoulder and shrugged her shoulders with a look on her face that silently said: *Are you seeing this?*

Although he didn't exactly jump into Jason's arms, Dusty made his way slowly in front of him and Jason offered the boy his hand. "How ya doin' Dusty?"

Dusty was at a loss for speech and just moved his mouth to the words, "Airplane man!"

Carrie had a tear form in her eye. She wiped it quickly with a finger, but her insides were melting. No one ever connected to her brother, something is going on…

She was going to say something like '*Dinner's on its way*' but her voice was muddled in the dust filled open mouth. Instead, Jason played his part right on cue, "Your sister and I got some gas for my plane today, what say we go for a ride tomorrow if the weather's good?"

You might as well have asked the boy if he wanted a ride on a rocket ship to the moon. His mouth popped all the way open and he slowly turned towards his sister who was trying not to cry at this latest development. He cocked his head to the right and didn't even have to say anything; the look in his eyes was enough. To add to the silent conversation, Carrie just nodded with a half crying, half bewildered look on her face.

"Cool!" The boy bounced off towards his room. Jason watched as he went, smiling and shaking his head.

Meg grabbed Carrie by the arm and led her back into the kitchen and whispered, "That's new…"

Jason heard the voices behind him and turned, "Oh hi."

Carrie introduced Meg to him, "Megan Cooke, this is Jason Parmenter."

Jason stood like a gentleman and walked to the five foot six woman. He regarded her short hair for a second and then made full eye contact. She was a small town beauty, maybe head cheerleader or at least the quarterback's main squeeze at one time. There was still an edge on Carrie's looks to Meg though. Meg seemed so… so… typical. Carrie was anything but.

Meg took his hand and gave it a firm grip, like everyone he had met so far in this town, and she curtsied a tiny bit, her eyes never leaving Jason's.

"Pleased to meet you Jason." She let go of his hand but not his eyes and said over her shoulder, "Seems Mr. Parmenter has a way with Dusty."

"I know. It's like there's some kind of connection between them." She wiped her eyes with a dish towel and said, "Wow. Would you like to stay for dinner?"

"No thanks Cass. Steve is taking us into town for dinner and a movie tomorrow night, I've gotta get home and pack."

Jason turned and made his way back to the couch when he saw Dusty heading into the living room pushing a toy fire engine. The boy was making siren sounds as he pushed the ladder truck toy around in circles and was making talking sounds-as if the firemen were talking to one another. Jason sat down as Dusty drove his engine back down the hall towards his room.

Megan gave Carrie a smile of confidence and a peck on the cheek and headed for the back door. "I won't say anything to anyone, if that's what you want."

Carrie thought about this for a minute and nodded, "At least till we figure out if it's going to last…" She sighed heavily and looked out towards the living room. "I hope it does."

Meg let herself out and Carrie began to un-wrap the chicken for cooking, listening very carefully into the living room, in case any new revelations took place. She turned to find the iron skillet she kept in the stove and bumped into Jason.

"Oh!" She chirped.

"Sorry."

"I thought you were on the couch!" Carrie was on the verge of panting from the start Jason gave her.

"I wanted to see if I could help you." He walked to the window just in time to see Meg driving away. "Baby sitter?"

"Life saver." Carrie added as she pulled the pan out from the oven and set it on the stove. "If it weren't for her, I'd never get anything done."

Carrie began wiping the remnants of the last frying episode from the pan with paper towels as Jason continued looking outside. Something bothered him about the way Meg looked at him as she paused at the end of the driveway. She stared right at him through the window; her eyes were accusatory, narrow.

"She the jealous type?" He asked over his shoulder as Meg left the driveway and headed up the street towards town.

Carrie laughed at what she thought was a joke, "No. But she is very protective. Why?"

Jason turned towards the beauty at the stove; he crossed his arms and smiled at her.

"No reason." He sighed like a child who was told to go to bed and said, "I want to thank you for everything so far."

Carrie smiled as she tossed the greasy paper towels into the trash can and passed him on her way to the counter. "You're very welcome."

Dusty drove his fire engine through the kitchen and was promptly scolded by his sister, "Dusty, I told you not to run your toys through here, please."

"Dustin." The boy defied.

Carried sighed. Her heart sank a notch as the realization came to her that the signs of recall had faded from when the boy met Jason. "Dustin." She retreated.

123

"Megan took me to see the fire today!" The boy exclaimed with delight.

"*Reaaaaaaerrrreaaaaarreeaaaaaar!*" The siren sounded as he maneuvered the red ladder truck back into the living room, "Stay in the car. I'll get this okay?" He mumbled to himself as he went.

"Comes and goes huh?" Jason asked quietly.

Carrie took the chicken parts out of the paper wrapping and found a large Tupperware bowl under the cabinet. "Sometimes. It was a shocker though, tonight when he saw you. He never remembers people after meeting them once or twice."

Jason huffed out a laugh. "He just wants me for my plane."

Carried stood up and placed the bowl on the counter and nodded in agreement. She found the flour decanter and measured two handfuls into the bowl. "He does lock onto what he wants."

Jason shifted from the counter by the sink to the kitchen table, which was about the size of a card table with three metal chairs. He cocked his head to the right as he leaned on the back of one chair, "It is alright to take him flying? I mean I'm not jumping the gun here, I just thought that…"

"It's fine." She opened the cupboard and pulled out a few select spices for the breading. "It's just…"

"You're afraid of what might happen when I leave."

Carrie finished mixing the spices with the flour and walked to the fridge where she retrieved three brown eggs from a carton. She nodded again, this time slowly and didn't make eye contact, or say '…*for me too*…' like she wanted to.

"Brown? Are those eggs any good?" He protested.

"They're fresh as yesterday. They're farm eggs, not the processed stuff you buy at a store silly." She responded by smacking one egg at a time on the edge of the bowl and with one hand opening the shell to the let the whites and yolk run out into the flour and spice mixture.

"You're pretty good." He added with a note of impression.

"My mother was a good cook. She taught me everything kitchen."

Jason sighed. He had used the egg thing as a distraction while he thought of something to say about her fear; he took the time to carefully word his next thoughts out loud, "Don't think about me leaving right now okay? We should be good friends, after all, I'm here in your house right now and you know I'll be in town at least for the holidays."

She looked at him and grinned. Then Carrie sighed too and let a little of her feelings slip, "I'm glad you're here. It's like fate in a way you know? First the Avgas and now the fire."

Jason's smile frowned south. He had almost forgotten the fire, the loss of his camera equipment, his clothes, some important papers and the sheer knowledge of visible violation or vulnerability. He hated to have to rely on someone else. His was usually the bigger shoulder.

"I'd almost forgot about that. Can I use your phone?"

"Sure." Carrie nodded and pointed her eyes at the old Princess phone mounted on the wall near the back door. "Just leave your credit card number on the counter there."

"I'll have to dig for it tomorrow in the rubble…" Jason said flatly as he headed for the phone.

Carrie finished mixing the eggs together, scooped a couple of serving spoons of bacon fat from a container under the sink, plopped them into the frying pan and then washed the chicken parts off in the sink as Jason dialed the number to his company in Denver. He leaned back against the counter as the ringing began and took a deep breath to think about what he was going to say. Carrie pat-dried the chicken and pushed the pieces into the whipped eggs, turned the burner on and made sure the chicken was soaking properly before heading into the living room to check on Dusty.

"Hello?"

"Sorry to bother you at home boss." Jason began.

"Jason." Dave Selnick began, sounding a little irritated.

"Bad news Dave. The hotel I was staying at burned to the ground."

"Holy…" Selnick censored himself, "Are you alright?"

"Yeah, I wasn't there at the time, but I lost nearly everything that wasn't in my pack."

"Samples? Reports?" Business as usual after Dave found out Jason was okay.

"Samples I got, the reports and assayers evaluations are gone. Plus my laptop, camera and clothes."

Jason listened to his boss issue his apologies again for the losses and a promise to send a new laptop filled with the software needed to complete the job, and a small check for purchasing clothes. He kept to business more than anything and seemed irritated that things would be delayed another few weeks while Jason waited for the FedEx truck to show with the new things.

"Fuel is coming Tuesday right?" Dave asked.

"Doesn't matter now, I have obtained a hundred gallons from a… friend here. I'll be airborne tomorrow."

"But you don't have a camera."

"Very observant boss. But I know someone who could lend me one." Jason hadn't asked Ed Baylee Sr. if he could borrow the Cannon SLR he saw on the shelf behind the hardware counter yet, but at least he would try.

"Okay. Stay safe will ya?" Dave seemed pressed for time and wanted to end the conversation, "Call me if you can think of anything else, I gotta go."

"Alright Dave. See ya."

Jason hung up the phone and found during the conversation he had turned his body to look out the window in the door and was staring at the mountains miles away as the sun on the other side of the valley cast a ruby-blue glow on the eastern range's top as it sank. He sighed heavily and inhaled. A smell of overheated oil caught his attention, he turned to see Carrie hadn't returned to the kitchen from checking on Dusty and the oil was near a flashpoint.

Jason craned his neck to see if he could catch a glimpse of Carrie around the corner but he couldn't, so he turned the burner off and headed into the living room, there he stopped dead in the near center of the floor as he saw Carrie. She was sitting on the couch, crying into her hands.

When she had entered the living room, Dusty had earlier gone to his room and exchanged his fire truck for the little blue airplane that his grandfather had bought for him six years ago. It was an old F-4U Corsair and the propeller had long broken off. What caught her attention was the fashion Dusty began to play with the plane in the living room like he was landing the toy, the same way they saw Jason land his plane weeks earlier; the boy circled the plane around a couple of times then made a make believe final approach and then landed. The similarity was uncanny and it made Carrie feel uncomfortable as excited. Dusty had never revealed his memory to be so strong before.

What brought her to tears was what her little brother said just before Jason walked in. He had a plastic man figure that he had stuffed into the cockpit of the plane; he pulled the little man out and stood him next to the plane. He looked at his sister and in the manliest voice he could muster;

"Howdy ma'am. I'm Jason the airplane man. Would you like a ride?"

CHAPTER EIGHT
Evening December 10th

Carrie was sitting on the couch facing the TV, though it was off. She had changed after dinner into flannel sweatpants and a thin sweater in light blue. Her stocking feet and legs were pulled under her and she was turned towards Jason, who was sitting on the other couch facing her. She had supplied him with another pair of red flannels and a T shirt, fortunately she was a tall woman and her clothing fit him snug, but enough to keep him warm in the cool house.

Carrie had cried for several minutes after her brother acted out some scene he saw in his mind, she was able to return to the kitchen and without a word finished the fried chicken dinner. Jason helped, but kept quiet also, not knowing what to say or offer to her. She added three large ears of corn to boiling water and hand tossed a salad in the time it took the frying to complete and Jason was more than complimentary at the dinner table, it was his first real home cooked meal in weeks. Dusty ate silently, as much as a distracted twelve year old would and went to his room to play.

Jason helped wash and dry the dishes since Carrie didn't have an automatic dishwasher, Carrie opened a bottle of chardonnay and after he returned from his temporary room where he changed into his night clothes, they sat staring at the cozy fire Carrie maintained after she was able to get Dusty to sleep.

"Was that good?" Jason finally asked, nodding down the hall.

Carrie considered him for a moment and then turned her eyes back to the fire. She knew what he was referring to, the white elephant in the room that had been there since just before dinner was made. "He's never had a moment like that." She sighed and wiped her eyes. "I don't know what made him say that."

Jason nodded. By her reaction he knew it was a good thing, but unexpected and maybe a little frightening. It scared him a little.

Carrie continued without looking at him, "His memory usually only lasts for a few hours at a time. Almost every day I have to remind him who I am." Her eyes glistened now in the light of the fire. "This is... new."

The fire crackled as the smell of burning oak wafted around the room. Jason inhaled and looked steadily at his new roommate. He had a million questions, but one was all he could think of, "What happened?"

Carrie took a deep breath as she closed her eyes. A tear dropped from her right eyelid as she did, she quickly lifted it away with a swipe of her hand. She kept them closed as she drew the crystal wineglass to her mouth and took a sip; the alcohol warmed her throat and chest, all the way to her feet. When she opened her eyes again, they were focused on the fireplace and its glowing embers at the bottom of the log. The yellows, blues, greens and whites blurred and the past came alive. In a quiet and determined voice she went back in time just a few years, back to when life made little sense to her.

"It's amazing how all these homes were built to look alike. Actually they were built alike because most of the homes in this town were built at the same time. The house my father lives in is nearly identical to this one, the house I grew up in and spent twenty-six years of my life is nearly the same as this house.

"The fireplace, the wood floors, the draperies, all the same. My mother kept the place the way I do now, I don't know why; maybe it's in my blood." Carrie glanced at Jason with a flat look, "You would have liked my mother. She was full blooded Shoshone; her features were dark like mine, except her eyes. Her eyes like mine are what set her apart from many of the tribe, one elder said she was the embodiment of a goddess, others accused her of sorcery. My father met her on a business trip to Idaho for a mining conference when he was a young man."

Carrie looked back to the fire, "They married and had my brother Tommy ten months later. I was born three years later, Tommy looked like my father, and I looked like my mother. Then seventeen years after that, by accident my father would say, Dusty was born."

"Accident?" Jason kept his voice quiet also.

Carrie didn't look away from the hearth, "Whispers around town said that my mother had cheated on my father because he was gone for two months when Dusty was conceived, supposedly, but that wasn't true. My mother was faithful up until the day he drove her from the home."

Another sip of wine for the both of them and Carrie continued, "My grandfather died the year before my mother disappeared. My paternal grandfather, my mother's family would have nothing to do with her after she married my father. Grandpa was an active member of the American Society for the Defense of Tradition, Family and Property; or TFP for short. I didn't know much about them until I looked it up a few years ago on the internet at the library.

"The TFP is a dogmatic version of the Roman Catholic Church, the very strict version you read about in history books before the liberal revolution in the Vatican in the nineteen sixties. You know," She turned to Jason again; "women were not allowed to wear pants or use makeup at all. Children were homeschooled and friends were not allowed over-especially sleepovers-we never went out to the public pool, we didn't have mirrors in the house because my grandfather believed that looking at yourself was vain and vanity was a sin. Hell, everything was a sin to them."

"I've noticed there's no Catholic church in town…" Jason added.

"Burned down in nineteen seventy-three, suspiciously." She added a note of sarcasm and a sip of wine. "Some say it was my grandfather and his cult-that's what the townsfolk called us and his friends-a cult. They strived for the day of the old church, the church that beat heretics into submission and the wife's place is in the home cooking and cleaning and attending to her husband's every need sort of thing."

"Seems a lot of things burn suspiciously around here." Jason interjected humor. But Carrie's eyes remained focused and her expression was flat.

"Fire is the purge of the mining towns. I've read about it happening everywhere; the old wood used in the buildings, poor fire plans, fireplaces for the main heat source, few hydrants and lots of mining chemicals. Bodie, Virginia City, towns that grew up in the mining industry all burned nearly away at one time or another. Fire cleanses, my grandfather said once. "

She took one more sip and returned her gaze to the fireplace, "Fire purifies. Anyways, after grandpa died my father changed. He became like his father in some ways, demanding my mother be more of a housewife and a slave than a human being. Some say she was carried off by a wayward stranger to live a better life, my father said she was cast to hell for her sins. I was left to raise Dusty at age twenty-three. I'd never been on a date, never been to more than three or four movies till a few years ago when Meg and I would go. I've never had a real romantic kiss or a moment that made me feel alive inside like you're supposed to."

Jason tried to ease the conversation again, "So you were telling me the truth in the truck then."

She nodded, not breaking eye contact with the flames. "Yes. I've never been with a boy fully, in that way. I had this date one night three years ago. My first date, a guy that made me feel so free inside, tickly and tingly. Paul

Davis was his name. I announced that I was going out and was headed for the door," Carrie rose to her feet, this startled Jason a little. "Dusty was playing with his toys over there…" She pointed to an area of the floor near the fireplace.

Jason swallowed a small sip of wine, he was becoming a little scared; she was acting like it was happening right here…

"My father and brother had made sure that I was observant of their rules, I was not allowed to date nor be seen or see boys my age. They were trying to keep alive my grandfather's legacy of the TFP, even after it drove my mother out of this house, her house. My father grabbed me by the hair and called me a whore and threw me to the ground. Tommy, not wanting to look weak in my father's eyes, picked me up from the floor and pushed me hard against the fireplace bricks."

Carrie looked up, above the hearth and mantle and stared at the blank area above the fireplace. "My father kept a hunting rifle in a set of elk antlers here." She pointed to the empty space, "At our house I mean, the house we lived in before." In her mind, Carrie was there.

"I hit the rocks so hard that the wall rumbled and the rifle fell to the floor. Dusty picked the rifle up, or tried to, it was too heavy for him and Tommy ran over and grabbed the gun. He pointed it at me and yelled he was going to shoot me in the leg so I couldn't run like my mother did. My father jumped over to him and grabbed the rifle, shouting '*that was enough*' and he and Tommy struggled with the gun for what seemed like hours.

"In reality it was just seconds, but in the struggle the gun went off. I was sitting on my butt near the hearth crying and the bullet hit me."

Carrie pulled her hair back to reveal a pink and white swollen tuft of flesh about the size of a nickel on the right side of her neck just in front and below her ear. Then she slowly turned her body to the right allowing the back of her neck to be seen, and directly behind her ear and across from the entry wound was the exit wound scar. Her eyes were misty at this point; she was on the verge of tears.

She took a breath and did not engage Jason's eyes. Instead she looked back into the fireplace and stepped close to the brick hearth. "The bullet went through and it ricocheted off the brick," She ran her finger along the grey stones as if she was in her old home tracing the mark the projectile left, "the bullet then hit Dusty in the head next to his temple and went in."

The tears came. Jason was uncomfortable up to this point, now he was anxious and sick to his stomach. Carrie took a few minutes to compose herself, Jason started to push himself up so he could go over and comfort her but just as he got to his feet; Carrie put a finger up in the air in front of him. She shook her head with her eyes closed and head down, still facing the fireplace. Jason sat back down.

"The… fire truck was the first there," Carrie spoke again, this time referencing the incident as it happened at the other house, for some reason she no longer insinuated that it occurred in front of her, "and then Parks came. He was only a young rookie then; he saw my wounds and Dusty's and nearly passed out."

Carrie looked over to Jason and her eyes were red but clear, she shot him a smile as she headed for her place on the opposite sofa. Her story went on, "He…" She laughed, "Parks threw up on the kitchen floor." Her face went somber again, "The other people started coming in, there were so many that I lost count as I went in and out of consciousness. Chief Tedford put a cloth to my neck and Parks helped a couple of the other guys stop the bleeding on my little brother.

"Then while the firemen were loading Dusty and I on the gurneys, I saw Parks handcuff my father and another deputy was wrestling with Tommy on the ground, trying to get him cuffed. They both were arrested and taken out of the house before the helicopter arrived."

Carrie sat up straight and took the last sip of her wine and looked at Jason through the empty glass. "You wonder why I'm afraid to fly? On a windy stormy night three years ago, me and Dusty were in a helicopter on our way to Las Vegas University Hospital with gunshot wounds."

Jason saw she wanted him to say something so he added, "Understandable. Is Dusty afraid?"

Carrie shook her head, "I don't know. He doesn't seem so, in fact he seems drawn to them."

"So that's why you care for him? His dad and brother were arrested?"

"Sort of. It had a lot to do with it; you see when I was released after only four days I was visited by Social Services. They had already been to the house and interviewed neighbors and folks around town about us. They wanted to know if I thought I could take care of Dusty if and when he was released, he was in dire trouble. The bullet lodged in his brain and that's what caused his memory problems. It also made him slower than the rest of the kids his age, so school was out for a while.

"The doctors said he would get some of his memory back, but not all of it. It took him six months to learn to walk again and another six months to be able to speak. He gradually became closer to who he was before the shooting, but nine years old..." Carrie began to cry again.

Jason got up forcefully and fast. He moved this time without delay and was sitting next to Carrie in an instant. This time she didn't protest. Jason could smell her tears, a shampoo he had smelled on her before as she passed him in the mercantile and the laundry detergent. The same detergent he could smell on the clothes she lent him for the night. He placed his arm around her and squeezed for comfort and she leaned in towards him. A few minutes later she had regained herself and pushed back at him a little. The closeness made her nervous and anxious inside.

She took a deep breath and started her tale again, "After the trial and hearing Dusty was awarded to me as his guardian, my father got six months in the county jail and Tommy got a year in Carson City for the shooting and aggravated assault on a police officer.

"The court, some great friends in town and Megan helped me move into this place; the state pays me eight hundred a month they take from my father for care of a special needs person. My father and brother are ordered by the court to stay away and they do. When my father wants to see Dusty he has to call them and they set a meeting place and have an advocate there the whole time."

She touched Jason's hand with hers. It was warm and it trembled a little, out of fear and the new sensations she had been feeling since she met the young pilot from Colorado. "Would you get us some wine? The bottle's on the counter by the window."

Jason did as she asked and when he walked back into the room he saw Carrie was stoking the flames to the fire. She stood and accepted the glass from him and stood back by the fireplace. She was forcing herself to keep her distance.

"Tommy has become a problem here in town and many rumors were started when things settled down; bad things were said about him and dad. Then rumors were started that I was a sex slave. Things like that."

Jason sat back down in his seat on the couch by the window and poured the last of the chardonnay into his glass. A question came to him and he didn't know why he asked it, but it seemed important, "What happened to Peter?"

"*Paul?* He left town after my brother beat the hell out of him the week he was to go on trial. That didn't help my brother's case at all, another reason the judge added time to his sentence. I've never seen him since."

"Was he your first love?"

Carrie smiled indicating she knew where this was going. "We kissed once, the first and last time I kissed someone… like that. There's been a few dates since recently, nothing serious."

Jason lowered his head; he felt he had crossed some kind of line.

"We never had sex either. Yes, I'm still a virgin if that's your next question."

Jason went bright crimson. "No! Not at all, I mean you already told me and I…"

"Forget about it. I'm probably the oldest virgin in all of Nevada, and some parts of California." She pinched her lips together, "When you're busy as I've been with Dusty, nothing else seems to matter. Every now and then, I feel so…"

Jason stared at her blankly. Carrie's face went south again, she had more to add. The end of the story which involved Dusty's current state of health and that hurt her. She sat down; this time taking up most of the sofa, indicating Jason wasn't invited.

"Five days a week we do home schooling for three and a half hours. It's all he can take before he gets restless." She looked to her left at the fire and let out a quick breath, "I never know how much he learns, or how much he retains. I spend the afternoons at the library learning myself. So I can be a good teacher.

"Dusty spends one or two hours a day while I study with Meg and I pay her fifty dollars a week. She doesn't want it, but takes it because I insist; I know how hard it is to take care of him sometimes. When he comes home…" Her eyes narrowed and a tear formed in each corner of them.

"It's called anterograde amnesia. There's list about five pages long that describes his symptoms and another that is ten pages long that describes in a thousand different ways why doctors don't know how to help him with anterograde because *the precise mechanism of storing memories is not understood.*" She finished with a roll of her eyes as she quoted the last sentence of the pamphlet word for word. After three years, she had come to memorize it.

"My little brother," She nodded down the hall to indicate Dusty, "paid the biggest price of us all. He might never know what happened to him, he might never be normal or ever know he was once normal." She took a long sip of her wine while keeping her eyes closed, "He wakes up some nights with terrors. The doctor here says it's nightmares about what happened, but Dusty says it's the darkness."

"I was afraid of the dark; maybe it's harder on him because of his injury." Jason added.

"I don't know. He says it's the darkness, the *'darkness in the shadow'* that scares him."

"Darkness in the shadow?"

"That's what he calls it. I wanted you to know that part because he might wake up screaming and I didn't want you to be upset. It happens and I'm used to it."

"I'll be alright. Are you sure you are?"

"If you're asking if I need company to keep me safe tonight, the answer is no."

"I... I..." He was struggling for air.

Carrie laughed out and very loud. Then she sighed with a smile and a look that made Jason a little scared of her. He took a big sip of wine.

"I like you *Airplane Man*. I've never told anyone but a few souls about the story you just heard. Only my very closest friends."

Jason took the hint, "Thank you." His smiled nervously, "Cassie."

Carrie's face turned sour, her voice became gravelly, and "You don't get to call me that."

One full minute passed after she scolded him and they never broke eye contact. Finally a smile crept across her lips. "Dusty calls me Cassie. Only because he couldn't pronounce Carrie when he was four. Meg calls me Cassie because Dusty does. One or two others do, but they know why."

"Sorry?"

"Don't you like my name?" She asked.

"I was just kidding."

"Me too." Carrie moved over to the end of the sofa, "You can all me Cassie."

Jason's cell phone rang as he moved an inch closer to her. She had taken a slight breath in anticipation, but the ring shattered the moment. He looked at the caller ID and frowned.

Holding it up he smiled at Carrie and whispered, "I've got to take this. Sorry."

He winked and walked down the hall to the bedroom. Carrie crossed her arms in front of her and pouted a little.

CHAPTER NINE
Friday December 11th, 2009

Jason woke at six a.m. His room was unfamiliar but cozy enough for a full night's sleep, after retiring around ten the night before.

Carrie and he sat up watching the flames in the fire die to a flicker of occasional white and red and then the coals glowed ominous orange. They tried watching TV, but the lack of a good show and sound seemed out of place. So he and Carrie sat in quiet, listening to the crackle and hiss of the oak logs surrendering themselves to ash.

The bed was firm, much stiffer than the one he had at the Sand and Juniper, so his slumber was undisturbed. When he was younger, he slept outdoors on the ground on rocky slopes and crevices all the time, the comfort of a slab of concrete would have been more than a hint better than the worn out mattress at the hotel.

The sun was peeking in just lightly through the cracks in the heavy drapes, and Jason was a sun-up boy. He laid there for a several minutes, getting his bearings and thinking about last night, the tale that Carrie told him, opening her heart to him, the pain she suffered and suffers on a daily basis. By comparison his troubles of late seemed minute.

He rose quietly so not to disturb anyone. He found some slippers in the closet and made his way into the living room. Frowning at the frigidness of the place he searched for a wood pile out the back window until he saw one in the corner of the yard, covered in a blue tarp. He shuffled outside without a jacket.

Once outside, his tummy told him it was hungry.

Carrie on the other hand had trouble sleeping all night. It wasn't just the fact a man was sleeping in her house, a kind and handsome man, a guy she liked; he was good with her brother, he was patient with the things that would drive her near insanity on occasion and he was still seemingly calm about it.

Three times before midnight she rose from her bed to go to him. The first time she made it to the foot of her bed and stopped there. The second she made it to the door and a girlish tickle on her sides made her stop and cover her mouth before she woke anyone-namely Dusty. The third time she made it down the hall three steps from his door, after taking painstakingly slow steps and opening her room door without a sound. Again a sensation in her insides made her stop and think about what she was doing. They had sat next to each other on the sofa till the fire died, her legs pulled underneath her, his straight out in front of him and crossed over one another.

They finished the bottle of chardonnay, and lounged in silence for nearly an hour. She was thinking about what she had told him and how much she left out plus how much she shouldn't have said. He must have been quietly digesting, *what a crazy bunch of people that live in this forsaken town.*

She finally dozed off around three a.m. and went into a deep dreamless sleep till five-thirty, when the dreams of a normal life played out before her closed eyes. She was walking along a streambed in the mountains looking for Jason; he was walking ahead of her but he was stepping fast, climbing a rock wall to a cave somewhere. She was in love; she knew it and it felt good.

Suddenly a sound like rocks falling woke her from her dream. There were voices in the living room, no-the kitchen-someone was in the kitchen talking. She glanced at her alarm clock and it read 8:15. Startled by the fact Dusty hadn't been in to wake her and the noises made her nearly jump out of bed and dress quickly into last night's clothes.

"Good morning…"

Carrie looked around the kitchen. It was a mess; a bowl full of pancake batter with drippings sat on the counter next to the stove, the frying pan had been wiped out and set on the burner with a dab of butter melting. The smell of fresh bacon still wafted about, strong caffeine gurgling in the Mr. Coffee on the other counter. The scene wasn't as startling to Carrie as much as the fact that Dusty was sitting at the kitchen table eating pancakes and bacon.

"I'm sure Baxter would have understood Terry." Marcus Doward said calmly in the front seat of the Excursion.

"I know." Terrence Dodson sat on the opposite side of the vehicle, sipping from a Styrofoam cup of Salt Lick coffee.

Marcus was the epitome of the old time miner, even though he relegated the hard work to his two hundred person workforce now, he dressed the part. His grey hair and bald spot gave an indication of a man in his sixties, but Marcus was only fifty-five. He had mutton-chopped sideburns and a little dip under his nose with a giant hand waxed and tooled moustache springing out on both sides and curled to a near perfect circle at the thin ends. His eyes were sad, but hardened with nearsightedness, so he kept cheater glasses at the end of his nose most of the time. Marcus was dressed up today; it would be a day of celebration-if everything went right.

The elders of the last remaining mining families, they had come to discuss business; one with anticipation, the other with a heavy heart. A heavy and exhausted heart. Marcus had been trying to talk Terry into shutting down the Dodson Mine for years since very little profit was pulled from the ground anymore. He wanted the business to himself of course, but the real reason behind the closure was his retirement and Terry running the Doward Mill and Pit.

Terry was a hard man; he had years of experience running mines and the people needed to keep them open, his six month jail stint a few years ago seemed to harden the man even more. Marcus was a man's man. He was not harsh or mean and he needed someone to take over the reins of his family owned business and not worry about the competition buying him out when he did.

The open feuding but quiet partnership of the only two operating mines in the area was a symbiotic one. They fought for every ton of borate in the dry ground around the town at one time or another until Doward opened the Pit. But when dirt worshippers came around to see the mines closed for environmental reasons, the at-odds businessmen joined together to fight the tree huggers in court and in the halls of legislation in Carson City. And they fought hard together as any ally would. A quote from Aristotle says: "A common danger unites even the bitterest enemies." and that was the case here.

The Hatfields and McCoys of southern Nevada were at each other's throats since the respective founders of the two biggest mines who were a branch of the same family that broke the dusty soil over a hundred years ago. There were even rumors of murder or at least tendered homicide on more than one occasion between one family member or another. But it all ended today with a swipe of a pen.

"Listen Terry," The slightly older and portlier man said to his new open partner, "we've been at this for longer than most countries exist. When things get burned out on our side of the ground, you can reopen this side and start another pit here. It'd be your retirement package."

Terry just stared out the window to the soon to be abandoned building. The mill had been worn down over the last forty years and was looking more like a shack that sat in the middle of ghost town somewhere; hundreds of them were within miles of here. The corrugated steel sides and roof had been damaged by wind storms over the years, some gales twice the strength of the one on the ninth; the wood that was once whitewashed yearly now had been neglected for the past three, the paint peeling and flaking off, leaving little piles of white on the ground near the footings.

One hundred and thirty townsfolk worked here still. They would have to be laid off, then possibly be rehired a mile and a half away at the Doward Pit and even though many of the rumors around town about Terry being a hard man, he had mellowed in the last few years to a point and in these hard economic times, the last thing he wanted was more unemployed in Fallcast-for any length of time.

"You can start next Monday, in my office. You have the run of the place and I just sit back and write your checks. In a few months, we'll be sittin' pretty."

"Yeah."

"Besides, from what I hear from Monolith, this Jason fellow has come across something that might put you in the millionaire's seat and me in the Governor's Mansion."

The mention of the outsider's name curdled the coffee creamer in Terry's stomach.

"In a month we'll have what we need and then the Doward-Dodson Mining Company will be the biggest combine ever in the west."

"If I don't kill the messenger first." Terry growled through his teeth.

"Will you stop crying please?" Jason asked through the door.

Carrie had felt the blood run out of her body and face as she saw the two closest men in her life acting as if the world had never dealt her the bad hand, and as if Dusty had never been shot. She had locked herself in the bathroom and tried to hide her tears and whimpers, but

Jason heard her through the door. When he quietly knocked she refused to answer at first. Then she opened the door a crack and sat back down on the commode with the lid down. Jason took a seat on the edge of the iron clawed-foot tub.

"How?" She sniffed through her hands.

"I don't know. He walked out and saw me carrying in the firewood, he stopped like he was going to scream and then he went back to his room. After I started cooking the bacon, he came back out and acted as if I was here all the time. He started playing with his toys in the living room while I cooked."

"I'm sorry Jason. It's just that I'm scared." She straightened up a little.

"Of what?"

"Of everything. You, his reaction to you. How he acts when you're around."

"He doesn't seem that bad…"

"He's not. Don't you see the point?"

Jason sighed heavily. "I guess not."

"Okay, he's had stretches of days without a fit and bad days that last weeks. But in the last few he's been off and on, and what happens when you're gone?" She wiped her tears on a hand towel.

"I don't know. I'm sorry."

"It's not your fault."

"I guess I'll go get dressed. I'm gonna meet the fire chief at the hotel."

She looked over to him. He pulled his cell phone from the pocket of the flannel pants and showed it to her, "I called him this morning. He says I can come by and see if there is anything recoverable." He stood.

"I'm sorry. Breakfast smells good. Shall we eat first?"

Jason didn't know what to say. At first it sounded as if she was mad at him, then he feared she was so upset that

144

Dusty had appeared to have taken a liking to him that she was confused; now, she was open and ready to go for a ride with him today.

"Are you sure you want to go?" It was all he could muster.

Carrie saw the consternation in his eyes. She knew immediately that she had given him a jolt by being so upset this morning and it really wasn't his fault. She was upset that things were going well, *too* well so far and it scared her that the other shoe would drop soon and there would be pain. Of course she was shocked about Dusty's behavior, she had always thought that if she had found someone she really cared about, there would be a confrontation or at least she figured Dusty would be so upset about the new person that he would hide or throw temper tantrums. He had done it a few times in the past, but Carrie had never brought a man home before.

Maybe that was it. Maybe it was having a different man in the house that made the difference for Dusty. Maybe it was the fact that Jason was a nice man, who was patient with the boy and even played along with him. Maybe Dusty could see things in people that she couldn't. She would have to try it out today.

"Yes, if Dusty can come; Meg won't be available today, so I have him the whole day. Fridays we usually go on field trips." She wiped the drying tears from her eyes and patted her cheeks, trying to get the puffiness out of them.

"Sure. We'll have fun, well as much fun as you can expect scrounging through what used to be my possessions." He started to walk out the door and turned back in, looking at Carrie. A huge smile crossed his lips, "Field trip huh? Okay." He spun on his bare heel and walked out, down the hall and to the spare room, his room.

Carrie lifted her brows in surprise and then scrunched them back down to her eye level when she thought, *what the heck does he have planned*?

"Look at it this way Terry, you won't have to lay anyone off…"

"It's not the point." Terence Dodson grumbled with his hoarse voice, "This mine has been in my family almost as long as the Doward has been in yours."

"But if this deal works out the way we hope and that idiot from Colorado isn't full of road apples, you'll get your half of the new mining operations plus enough to retire fully."

Marcus and Terrence were still sitting in front of the soon to be chained-up, boarded façade of the Dodson Mill. Terry was sipping out of a polished steel hip-flask now; Marcus was slurping out of a cardboard covered cup filled with hot coffee and Bailey's.

"That's the whole thing Marcus; I had plans for that rock-sniffer. I want him out of here as soon as possible."

Marcus made a sour face as the liquor burned his throat, "Yeah, well that fire at his hotel room set him and us back nearly three weeks, according to his boss. Everything he had written down was lost."

"Too bad he wasn't sleeping in it." A deep throated growl emanated from Terry.

"Careful now. We don't want folks talking bad things until this little twerp acknowledges what we think. We could be millionaires by next August."

"When the cash is in my hand, I'll believe it."

"Just go easy on that kid. I've heard the rumors too and I don't want you ending up in the big house over that kid."

Terry glanced over the top of his flask as he sipped, "I have special plans in mind for him when he finishes." There was no evil smile, or a happy one, just the same flat powerful and mean expression when he lowered the flask and he didn't break eye contact with Marcus.

The acrid smell of a burned out building still hung in the air almost like a fog. Even as Jason pulled up the dirt mound of spent ore to the parking lot he closed the vent on the Jeep's circulation system. He and Carrie were sitting in the front of the Wagoneer; Dusty had elected to stay in the back-far back. The Wagoneer had two rows of seats and the large open area accessed by a tailgate with a window, enough space for a full month's of supplies from Sam's Club in Vegas or half a dozen backpacks for the surveyors or miners crammed into the passenger seats on work related outings.

Dusty had climbed in back before Jason or Carrie even got in, and they both elected to let him. Carrie knew her little brother could be a pain in the rear-rumpus sometimes about seat-belting up and she was in no mood for that this morning in particular.

Jason grew up in a small town and was riding in the backs of pickups and cars without the aid of safety devices since he could remember. Small towns afforded certain freedoms that have disappeared in the big cities, the same freedoms that mining and farming towns still offered from the vast politically correct movements. Besides, if the kid was happy, so was his sister and if his sister was happy, then the day would be perfect.

The weather had perked up a little and was nearing a typical southern desert winter temperature of sixty degrees by the time they had reached Sluice Box or Highway 201. As they entered the lot, Parks the deputy was standing by the front entrance talking to Mary and Jack. His patrol car was parked off to the side by a white and red 1985 Ford Crown Victoria. The words FALLCAST FIRE DEPT decaled on the side. Jason smiled about the new prowler the cops had and the antique equipment the firemen had. The difference in many small towns between the city and county finances.

Jason pulled the Jeep in as far as the police tape would allow and parked near the mid portion of the lot near his former temporary residence. He saw Chief Marshall Tedford digging through the rubble in the back of the former half of the building, picking up pieces of charred whatever and then tossing it back into a pile.

"Why don't you guys hang here for a moment?" He asked Carrie and Dusty as he opened his door.

Carrie smiled and nodded, not taking her eyes off of Marshall.

Jason ducked under the yellow tape marked CAUTION - STAY BACK - JOSHUA COUNTY SHERIFF and walked to where the fire chief was standing. The air was still muggy near where the fire was; the heat from the flames and the spray from the fire hoses that evaporated created a small weather pattern against the hilled wall at this ends of the valley.

A man walked from behind the cinder block wall that was once three rooms from Jason's. He was a short man in his mid-thirties had enough hair on his head to be mistaken for a Beatle in the 60's. He was dressed in overalls and a white T shirt underneath. He wore leather gloves and had tall work boots with the cuffs of the denim overalls in the top of each boot.

"Can I help you?" The man asked with a touch of authority.

"Mr. Parmenter? Over here!" Marshall Tedford called just as Jason opened his mouth to answer the short man's question. The short man frowned and shook his head then returned to his spot behind the burned out wall.

Jason shook the fire chief's hand as he as soon as he got close enough and turned, surveying the damage around him. He had to skip over a piece of melted something or another on his way to the fireman. Marshall was dressed in

148

a white shirt with a black tie-official fire uniform-with black pants and rubber firemen boots up to his knees. He seemed to be sweating in the sixty degree heat.

"Anything new about the cause?" Jason asked.

"Might have been a simple electrical failure or an errant cigarette butt…" A voice from behind Jason called.

Darrin Parker was standing at the edge of the debris field, his hands on his hips. He looked annoyed for some reason and that reason became evident when he began casting irritated glances from the Jeep which contained Carrie and Dusty back to Jason. Parks was a bit jealous, Jason had seen it before.

"Or," The fire chief began, "We *may* have found the real cause." He shot a look of contempt at the deputy then stepped back from Jason and called for the short man.

"Mike! Come on over here."

The man did, first looking over to Parks then to the chief and finally at Jason. His glare wasn't so demeaning this time.

The chief said, "Mike Baker, meet Jason Parmenter, the former occupant of this room." Marshall waved his hand over the area in front of them.

Jason took the man's gloved hand and nodded with a smile. A small grin appeared back and he looked to the rubble.

"Do you smoke Mr. Parmenter?" Mike asked with a hint of accusation.

"Nope."

"Were you with anyone who does yesterday? I mean around here in your room or in the back of the hotel?"

"Nope."

Mike made a sweeping motion with his eyes towards the Jeep and Jason knew what he was looking for, even if Carrie was a smoker he wouldn't dare accuse her without proof.

"It seems Mr. Parmenter," Marshall started again, "that a smoldering cigarette may have started the fire in this glob of metal that was once a trash barrel. It could have smoldered for hours, but…"

Marshall looked to Mike and Mike nodded back to him.

"Someone wanted this thing burning hot and bright eventually."

Jason's eyes opened big, "Pardon me?"

Mike finished the chief's thoughts, "Mr. Parmenter, I'm a schooled arson investigator from the fire academy in Las Vegas, true I own half the bank in town but by inheritance only and there's seldom work for what I love to do here, investigate fires. Trained right up there near Elko and everything and was going to be a big city CSI guy, but my mother fell ill a few years ago and I watch over her here now.

"This fire was smoldering for hours, not by accident I've determined, and there was a substantial amount of accelerant here in the area," He indicated where the barrel once sat with his right hand, "and along the wall, through the window to the bathroom and onto the floor of your room."

Jason knew what this meant. He glanced towards the Jeep. Carrie looked back with a quizzical look.

Marshal ended Mike's accusation, "What we have here Mr. Parmenter is pure and simple arson. Someone intentionally burned this part of the building down with little or no regard for the others staying here."

Jason looked back at the chief and Mike and they both had their arms crossed in the same manner in front of them. He shook his head and gave his best look of disbelief.

"Are you saying I did this?"

Marshall took a second and looked into Jason's eyes. He slowly shook his head, "No, not really. But you're

150

alive because the device was set up for such a long delay. Rarely do folks tend to hang out all afternoon in their rooms."

"Device?"

Mike pulled a paper lunch bag out of his side pocket and opened it. He took a sniff and held it out for Jason to do the same. "Kerosene."

Jason took a nostril full and nodded.

Mike began his theory, "I found remnants of a hemp rope in both what was once the bathroom and the outside here where the hotel keeps its trash barrels. Look…"

Mike pointed to the four barrels; three were still easily made out as fifty gallon drums but burned red, black and white. The fourth was nothing more than the lump of melted metal.

"This barrel had something in it to cause it to melt more than the others. Kerosene. There seems to be some evidence of cotton matting lightly soaked in kerosene and placed in this…" He removed a plastic box that had melted beyond recognition from the bag, "The box was probably some type of fishing lure holder with four sections. The cotton was in two of the sections as can be seen by the residue here and here." He pointed with a pencil he drew from his bib pocket.

"The missing sections probably contained lighter fluid or gasoline, more likely lighter fluid."

Jason was becoming uneasy. "So?"

"So, based on what I've found so far, a rope was soaked in kerosene and dangled into your bathroom window here…" He made an imaginary wall with his arm motions and then Mike pointed to a glob of white and black plastic that at one time could have been the sink. Jason assumed Mike knew what one looked like after a fire, because he sure couldn't.

"A thin rope wouldn't be necessarily noticed. And each window in the rooms that have them in the back I opened easily from the outside, something that Parks is discussing with the managers now; in each window sill is a plastic plant to give the room a homely look, but in yours someone filled the pot with gasoline and magnesium."

"Magnesium?" Jason stepped back.

"Burns very hot, probably from a road flare. Notice the white crystalline substance on the ground there next to the tub? Magnesium. Seen it before. Now the flame follows the rope up to the window and into the flower pot dish and lights the magnesium and then the gas in the planter ignites, falls into the room and whoosh!, big fire."

"And this was lit and someone ran?" Jason asked.

"Didn't have to run. Light a cigarette, place it in a matchbook a few inches from the matches and fold it over. Instant timing device. Place that under the little plastic box which is above a gallon milk jug cut in half and filled with a little more magnesium; the matches light when the cigarette ember hits the sulfur, the matches burn through the case slowly via the cotton, the flame hits the lighter fluid eventually causing a hot flame to ignite the magnesium in the milk jug which starts the rope and you have your device."

"Sounds like a lot of trouble." Jason pointed out.

"This was a well thought out plan. Probably trying to get you to leave?" Chief Marshall Tedford added.

"If someone wanted me outta here, they would have been better off leaving me to finish. I want out as soon as possible too."

Carrie caught this; she lowered her head and began to fidget with the seam on her jeans. This was not what she wanted to hear.

"Wouldn't this make you go sooner?"

"No. Let's put this thing to an end here. I did not start the fire; if I did I would have taken all the material needed to finish up here at least. If anything, this makes my job harder and now I have to stay longer."

Carrie raised her head at the revelation.

"All my belongings are gone. Destroyed. If I wanted to get out of here I would need some of that stuff anyways."

Marshall raised a hand. "We're not saying…"

"Yes you are," Jason interrupted, "It really irks me that you told me everything about the fire so far as if I planned it."

"We just wanted you to know what we know so far."

Jason mulled this over for a moment and said, "Is there anything salvageable here?" He looked around where his room once sat.

Both Mike and Marshall shook their heads. Marshall said, "We'd be looking for anything to help us, but up until this point… it's all burned beyond or melted." He sighed and looked Jason in the eyes, "I'm sorry."

Jason turned and carefully waded through the smelly, wet and squishy muck trying to keep his boots as clean as possible and back towards the Jeep.

"We'll keep you informed…Where can we reach you?" The Chief yelled.

Jason stopped and found a business card with his cell phone number. He had these in his backpack-the one that was spared from the fire-and so he loaded a few into his pocket this morning in anticipation of just something like this. He pulled the card out and instead of walking back to the two men, shuffled to the fire department car and slipped it under the windshield wiper. He nodded at the card and went to the Jeep, got in and drove off without looking back.

Parks walked to the perimeter line of the burned out structure, he didn't want to get any muck on his clean uniform so he stood at the edge about forty feet from the fire investigators and hollered across the still steaming black and crusty remains of the room.

"Why did you tell him about the cause?"

Chief Tedford was examining a piece of charred plastic that was probably once someone's cell phone. He raised his head only slightly and spoke just loud enough for Parks to have to strain to hear, "Because I think he's right. If someone wanted him out of here they wouldn't have burned his stuff. This smacks as a warning of some kind."

"Warning?"

Mike Baker was standing a few yards further than Marshall Tedford and offered in a loud voice, "Wait till the fire blooms over him staying with Carrie Dodson."

Parks looked down and the resonance of this and spoke quietly, "I'm not telling him."

"Neither am I..." Tedford said as he bent down to examine another piece of plastic stuck to the blackened carpet.

"Don't look at me..." Mike said.

CHAPTER TEN
Friday Afternoon

The Cessna 182 swept low over the empty white crusted valley about twenty miles from Fallcast, sixty feet above the ground, close enough to make Carrie nearly sick and Dusty hopped up like a junkie on Ritalin. He was nearly bouncing in his seat as he stared wide-eyed out the windows in the back of the plane. With a view out the back and up towards the sky via the plane's rear window and keeping his seat belt loose enough to slide from one side of the aircraft to the other to glance out the viewing Plexiglas windows.

It wasn't easy getting the boy into the airplane. Jason thought he might have trouble with Carrie with her revelation about her helicopter flight to Vegas after being accidentally shot by her older brother and father. Jason thought the boy, who seemed excited as Jason turned the Jeep down Airfield Road off of 201 towards the steel Quonset hut and graveled runway.

But excitement turned to quiet, then to incoherent mumbling the closer they got to the only building which housed Jason's 182. Dusty remained in the Jeep as Carrie reluctantly helped slide open the steel building's two fifteen foot by fifteen and a half foot hangar doors.

Carrie was hiding her nervousness as best she could, "So this is your idea for a field trip huh? Taking us out in a rickety old bucket like that?"

Jason smiled. He took a small breath and stared right into Carrie golden eyes, "Scared?"

She just shook her head as Jason walked inside the hut and uncovered the gas powered Dragger aircraft tug. Basically a six horse lawn mower engine mounted on a rubber wheeled plate with two steel wheels that temporarily surrounded the nose gear of the Cessna; it would provide the power to pull the small plane out of the building and onto the tarmac without much effort at all. Jason had a 24 volt electric one at his home airport.

He gave the pull-starter a series of quick yanks and the engine coughed to life with a puff of blue smoke on the third pull. Then as the little tug warmed up he maneuvered it in front of his plane and set it into place. He flashed a smile at Carrie who looked green as a bell pepper.

Dusty kept his distance still in the Jeep, his head just above the tailgate and his eyes peering over the edge, watching the goings on. Jason lifted the nose gear a few inches off the ground with a push downward on the handlebar of the Dragger and slowly let the clutch out and the plane jerked slightly as the tug pulled on the front wheel. With the hangar's doors fully open there was slightly more than a few inches of clearance on each wingtip of the Cessna's 36' wingspan, so he had to be extra cautious.

Once out, Jason pulled the Dragger back into the hut and went into the corner where the fuel barrel dolly sat. He gobbled up a drum of Avgas he and Carrie delivered yesterday with the handcart and pulled it outside the building under the right wing of the plane. Back into the hut once more for the hand-pump and hammer shaped wrench that unscrewed the opening on the drum along with a step ladder. He inserted the pump and set the ladder up just to the front of the wing and opened the tank filler access and placed the handle in the opening and climbed down the ladder to pump the fuel.

Carrie was still trying to hide her jitters, "Aren't you afraid of spilling it?"

Jason grinned wide at her again and shook his head. "Nope. The filler has a shut off when the fuel touches it."

"Oh."

She looked over her shoulder at Dusty in the Jeep and he appeared to have the same apprehension she did; only he was smart enough to stay in the truck. Just as Jason predicted, the fuel lever clicked off after hundreds of revolutions on the hand pump. He climbed the stepladder and performed the same ritual on the left side of the aircraft. As he pumped he smiled at Carrie, who was getting some color back, if green was a good color.

Dusty finally made his way out of the Jeep and over to where his sister was standing. He took her hand and looked up at her. Carrie's eyes were fastened on the pilot and his fueling efforts, Dusty tugged at her hand.

"Yes honey?"

"Are we flying?" He said. More of a statement but it came out as a question.

"I don't know. The airplane man says so. But I say no."

Dusty pulled closer to her and wrapped his other arm around her waist. "Oh."

Jason finished off the barrel and went to the hangar for another. After he drained about two-thirds of the second barrel he opened the door to the plane and looked at the wing-tank fuel indicators. They were mechanical, meaning they didn't rely on any sensor or probes, the two dials were set directly into the fuel bladders. Each one read FULL. Jason stuck his head out above the door and said, "Full as she'll get."

That didn't impress Carrie much at all. She watched nervously as Jason moved the barrel back into the hut, then the ladder. She knew the more he worked at it what he was doing, the sooner they would be in the air. She could refuse, maybe even Dusty would, but somehow she knew this man would be able to persuade both of them inside the plane; then it was just a matter of getting it into the air.

Jason came out of the hut a final time carrying a glass vial with what looked to be a huge syringe inside. He took out the syringe and went to a spot under each wing and pushed the metal needle into the spot. A small amount of fuel came out and filled the glass tube and he examined it in the sunlight like it was gold. He caught Carrie's quizzical gaze.

"Water. Looking for water and impurities in the fuel." He said without emotion.

"Is there any?" Carrie wouldn't know what to say to either answer.

"Nope. We're shiny."

"Great." Her voice echoed doubt. *I hated that TV show*, she thought to herself.

"Water and other gunk in the fuel means we stay, but this is clean and I just need to make a few more checks and we're off."

Again her voice was cracking hesitation, "Great."

Dusty just watched Jason's every move like he was a magician exposing his secrets to the crowd. He was fascinated.

Jason started on the left side of the plane's engine and checked the oil and some other things under the cowl, or the engine cover. Then he made his way back towards the tail, inspecting each little thing, the wings from tip to fuselage; then he pushed and thumped on every little door as he passed to the tail. He checked the rudder and the little rods that stuck out when he turned it hard right or left, then basically the same thing when he checked the flaps on the back wing.

"Elevator." He said with a reassuring smile as he moved to little wing up and down, checking the connectors to it too.

"What does that do?" Carrie said, squeezing Dusty a little. He would be watching and he might as well learn something.

"Makes us go up and down." Jason said as he moved the little wing again to show them. "This is called the rudder." He moved the dorsal wing again for show, "It makes up move left and right. Little flaps on the wings make us turn by moving the plane in conjunction with the rudder."

"Nice." Fear was building.

After he was satisfied the airframe was airworthy, he opened the passenger door and moved some things around inside. Stepping back out Jason realized his passengers were now both shaking like a reed in the wind. He put on his best smile and asked, "Do you just want to sit inside and see if you want to go up?"

His tone inflected they had a choice, Carrie moved slowly towards the Cessna, Dusty was at her heal and just a hair behind, hiding. At the passenger door she paused.

"Can I sit in the back?" She asked. Mostly out of fear she might throw up and that was the last thing she wanted him to see.

"Maybe next time." He started as he put his hand out for Dusty, who still was shuffling his feet behind his sister, not looking at Jason or Carrie, just staring at the ground. Jason leaned in closer to Carrie, "I need you up front in case he gets excited and starts bumping the controls. If he handles this well, he can fly up front anytime."

Carrie took a deep breath and looked to her little brother. He had a look of anticipation on his face, and a twinge of fear. "C'mon Dusty."

She held her hand out and nodded towards the back seat, which on the Cessna had to be accessed by tilting the right seat forward. Dusty took a look left then right, not really picking his gaze up from the asphalt tarmac, but in hesitation. He moved a foot closer, lifted his foot and found the step. Carrie stood behind him and gave him a boost into the seats. He sat down slowly.

Carrie inhaled again and slid the seat back into place. She glanced around the cockpit; the dials, the levers and things that looked ominous sticking out of everywhere on the dash and the floor between the front seats. It was all she could do from not getting sick right now. She willed herself to be strong, she had to be strong. After all she held her brother in the hospital with a wound to both sides of her neck; she raised him for the last three years on her own, and really long before that.

She found the pull strap above her head by the door and pulled herself in. She half expected Jason to give her a boost, but then again only one part of her anatomy that was sticking out as she climbed into the confined space and it wasn't yet time for him to put his hand there.

Sitting down Carrie noticed the space was extremely limited to movement. The passenger seat had a lot more room around it, so it seemed, but she pulled herself back into the seat as far as she could go, she didn't want to interfere with the controls either, and there were so many of them. Even her feet couldn't be stretched out because a set of pedals were directly in front of them.

Jason walked around the engine and the three bladed propeller slowly, again examining details of each, looking for cracks and eventual problems. Satisfied he gave Carrie a wink and crawled into the pilot seat.

Carrie let out a breath that stuttered and even she knew it would be interpreted as fearful and shaky. If he knew how sacred she was, he didn't show it. Pulled his seatbelt on and looked to the back of the plane.

"Dusty? Could you put your seatbelt on for me?"

"Why?"

Jason looked at Carrie and seemed lost for a millisecond. Then he winked at her and turned to the back again and said, "'Cause this is a magic plane and I don't want you to be scared you're going to fall on the floor." He emphasized this by looking to the cramped floor in front of the boy.

Dusty looked to the floor also and pulled his feet up to him. Half a second later he found the mated ends of the center seat belt and locked them into place-like he had done it a thousand times. Aircraft seatbelts were less complicated than cars, only one clasp held the opposite strand of nylon in the buckle and there was no button to push, just lift the clasp. Jason smiled when the boy finished and gushed.

"Wow? Have you been in a plane before? You knew exactly what to do!"

The nervous look began to fade on the boy and even Carrie smiled at the fact her friend was now patronizing her little brother. She took a moment to build nerve and then asked with her eyes closed, "Are we going to do this?"

Jason nodded to her and looked at Dusty, "Partner, I'm going to give you something okay?"

Dusty crooked his head to the side like a dog trying to understand a familiar command. Jason reached above the boy and retrieved a passenger headset. Dusty began to squirm so Jason set them to the side of the boy and pulled his own set off the hook by the door and placed them on his head. With his hand hidden low, Jason nudged Carrie and she looked at him with surprise then smiled. She reached in front of her and pulled another set and put them on her head.

Dusty watched and carefully picked the headset up and tried twice to get the cups on his ears right, but the boom mic kept getting in the way. Instead of reaching over and helping the boy, Jason waited till Dusty's eyes were focused on him and he bent the boom mic on his own set. Dusty mimicked him. The ears were covered. Jason used his left hand to find the battery switch on the console and flipped it up. Gauges came to life, the radio panel displayed numbers, and Carrie tensed her hands along her legs.

But Jason kept his gaze on Dusty and spoke into the mic, "Can you hear me Co-Pilot?"

Dusty's eyes swelled larger than teacup saucers, his mouth dropped open and he couldn't speak. It was magic! Jason knew he hit a chord. He spoke again, "If you can hear me, say Roger."

"*Rrrog*…Roger!" Either it was the sound of his own voice in the intercom system or the fact he was included in something he only saw in movies, whatever it was Dusty began to laugh maniacally, in a deep chuckle-like sound.

"Okay! How about you Stewardess?" Jason turned his towards his other greener passenger.

"O… okay. Fine." She took a breath and looked at her brother who was beaming from ear to ear. "And I believe we are called flight attendants now." Her tone was meant to make Dusty laugh and he did, even longer than before.

"Okay. I'm going to turn the plane on. It's going to shake but that's okay, don't be scared, I'm right here with you."

Jason spun in his seat and found the proper switches to activate and he turned the key. The Lycoming engine sputtered a couple of turns and then caught. In seconds the vibrations were minimized by Jason adjusting the mixture till the engine ran smooth. He turned back to make sure he hadn't lost his co-pilot.

"Okay?"

Dusty turned and nodded, his big smile was gone and replaced by a look of concern. But he hadn't had that look of panic-like his sister did in the front seat. Jason throttled the power up a little and the Cessna Skylane 182 RG began to roll slightly. Dusty began humming quietly; Jason did this when he was nervous so he knew the kid was feeling a little tension. Jason thought for a moment and turned to the boy.

"Are you ready for the magic part?"

Dusty nodded very slowly.

Jason smiled at Carrie as he turned back and gave her a wink. He pushed the throttle handle in a little more and the noise increased along with Dusty's humming, but Jason put his hands behind his head, laced his fingers together and leaned back. He pretended he was taking it easy. Carrie started to bounce her leg up and down. Jason didn't seem to notice *she* was nervous.

When the young boy saw that the pilot had hands behind him and not on the wheel he became curious. He leaned forward as far as he could into the middle to look out the windscreen. The plane was moving towards the runway at a ninety degree angle and a turn had to be made, even Dusty knew this it seemed, because the closer to the runway they got, the louder he hummed.

Carrie noticed the proximity to the turn and cleared her throat while turning her head towards the pilot, whom she now believed had lost his mind. "Shouldn't we turn? Soon?"

Jason pretended he was yawning and nodded slightly. Dusty's humming was getting more intense as he lost sight of the turn and Carrie began tapping her hand on her thigh along with the jumping of her leg.

"Jason!"

Jason turned and smiled at Carrie and then slowly crooked and winked at Dusty, who stopped his nervous sound for a second. Jason put his hands as far out as he could to the side inside the small cockpit and said in a goofy wizard voice, "Alacazam!" The Cessna turned right from the tarmac to the runway with his hands in the air.

Carrie saw what happened, but put her head down into her hands. She didn't know whether to strangle the guy or laugh out loud. Dusty sat straight up and stopped humming. Now, he gave full attention to everything.

Jason used the rudder pedals to keep the plane turning and then straighten out. He knew the boy would be amazed at a magic plane and magic usually made everyone feel comfortable for a few minutes. If anything else, magic always made kids feel safer.

Dusty kept looking out the front of the plane and then back to Jason, astonishment never draining from his eyes and cheeks. He had altogether stopped humming. The

Airplane Man had made the plane turn without turning the wheel like in a car and everyone knew you had to use the wheels to turn-at least as far as Dusty knew from watching everyone when they drove him around.

Jason was making his taxiing adjustments to mixture and he had to look to the painted elevation numbers on the side of the Quonset hut once again to confirm the height above sea level. It read in four foot letters and numbers: WELCOME TO FALLCAST ELE. 4,113. Most pilots listen to ATIS or Automatic Terminal Information Service just before takeoff and when approaching an airport. Since Fallcast Field has no tower or even an assigned radio frequency, no ATIS was available and pilots had to make adjustments to their barometric sensitive altimeter gauge based on aeronautical sectional charts for the area and little things like the large painted numbers on the Quonset hut there at the field.

A noise emanated from above them as they traveled, a hum not unlike the one the refrigerator made when it came on, but a whole lot louder.

"Just the flaps. It makes the wings longer at the back so we need less room to take off, it'll stop in a second." Jason pointed out to ease tensions as he watched the indicator move to the 20 degree mark.

Once they arrived at the end of the runway Jason again used his magic incantation to turn the plane then he shook his hands in the air again and waved them.

"Stop." Using the top of the rudder pedals to actuate the brakes Jason brought the plane to a smooth halt after turning the plane into takeoff position. Again Dusty was filled with wonder and amazement that the plane would do as the Airplane Man commanded. Carrie was doing her best to be brave.

Jason lined the nose of the plane to the center of the graveled runway. He leaned towards Carrie as she was making sure her belt was tight, "Ready?"

She cleared her throat and tried to speak, but her voice was locked. She nodded as her eyes moistened with tears of fear. Jason turned back towards Dusty, who seemed as anxious as his sister, but showed it less-the magic had worked.

"Dusty; I want you to tell the tower we're taking off. Okay?" Jason asked.

Dusty nodded and he crooked his head a little and asked back, "What do I say?"

Jason leaned over and pulled one of his earmuffs off and Carrie did the same. He whispered into her ear and then sat back and raised his eyebrows at her. She smiled, albeit shakily, and looked straight ahead. Dusty heard her voice over the intercom next.

"Tell them 'This is zero niner mike tango, ready for takeoff', got that?"

Dusty mouthed the words as she spoke them and he nodded. Clearing his throat opened the mic and he said in a loud clear voice, "Zero mikey's forty niners are ready for taking off!"

Carrie had to hide her mouth in her hands so Dusty wouldn't see her laughing. Suddenly a deep voice came over the headsets, "ROGER ZERO MIKE NINER, CLEAR FOR TAKEOFF RUNWAY 1-8 RIGHT. WINDS ARE CALM VISIBLITY IS UNLIMITED, SAFE FLIGHT!"

Carrie had to look out her window so Jason wouldn't see her face turn bright red from amusement. Dusty's once again enlarged. Jason turned towards the boy and almost asked his next question in the "tower voice", but he changed it as soon as he heard it coming out of his mouth, "Okay guys, you're going to feel a little funny, like your seat is falling. But it's okay, then there's going to be a few bumps as the plane lifts off, don't worry."

Dusty and Carrie both nodded with hesitation and a fake smile.

Jason pushed the throttle all the way in and the Lycoming O-540-J3C5D spun the propeller and pulled the 182 forward. At each little bump in the runway Carrie inhaled sharply like she had an exposed root canal. Dusty hummed along with the bouncing as the plane picked up speed. At 45 KIAS (knots in air speed) Jason knew his passengers were going to have collective fainting spells if he didn't intervene.

"Look forward, out the windshield. It won't make you sick…"

"I'm already sick." Carrie replied, but she looked forward anyway.

"If you look forward, you won't see how fast we're going."

Carrie looked to her right just as Jason told her not to and she saw the sagebrush rolling past furiously now. Then the grey gravel from the runway, the brown and yellow dirt and the sagebrush all became a blur. Carrie looked forward and felt her stomach beg for forgiveness.

Dusty kept humming.

"MmmmmmmmmmmmMMMMmmmmmmmmmmMmmmmmmMMmmMMmmm!"

At 60 KIAS Jason pulled back on the yoke and pushed himself back into his seat. The nose gradually lifted. At 65 KIAS, just as Jason had said, there was a whump! And the nose-wheel lifted; seconds later the main gear rose from the bumpy gravel and there was just the humming of the plane's engine, and Dusty. Carrie felt her weight increase as she was pushed into her seat. Bile rose to the top of her throat.

Suddenly Dusty stopped humming and after a second of shocked silence, he began laughing like he'd done earlier. Deep gurgling laughs followed by little movements as he tried to slide to one side or the other to see the ground slowly disappearing. Carrie took a chance and looked out her window, since the view out front was just sky as the plane climbed from the earth.

She saw the field that went near her home becoming smaller, distant. There was still a little push backwards into her seat, but it wasn't as bad as she remembered in the helicopter three years ago, strapped to a litter and a nurse hovering over her and her brother. A few more little dips as the wings grabbed at the air-looking to keep that vacuum called lift-and she referenced her position to the wingtips as Jason pitched the plane to the left towards the center of the valley below.

Dusty had stopped humming and now was viewing his world as never before. When he was on his last flight, just as Carrie was, he was in and out of consciousness and unable to look over his shoulder. Not that he would remember the flight anyway, the damage to his brain had wiped all existence of that day, it never happened; just a black hole in time for him. He saw his house below, at least he thought so, but all the houses looked the same. He saw the Pit, he thought, he wasn't sure if that was what is was, but he had so much information coming in at once and so little time to process it before another snippet of newness came.

Another humming noise from above him made him sink back into his seat, he recognized it; the sound was the *flappers*. Jason said that was what the noise was called as they were going down the road before they took off. Then another noise and a thump! On each side of the plane near and under the doors. Carrie knew this was the bottom of the plane falling off. She clinched her hands into tight balls and ran them back and forth across her jeans.

"This is a Cessna Skylane 182 RG. RG means retractable gear; the wheels pull up into the side." Jason offered as he glanced at the near panicked young woman.

"That's nice. Just keep watching ahead please..." She hissed through her teeth.

"Hey," He responded with a comforting smile at her, "it's okay. Really. There's no cars or traffic out here to run into."

"There's the ground..." She retorted sarcastically.

Jason glanced down at his altimeter and looked back at her, "We're one thousand feet above it."

"*Nice.*"

"No worries huh? You have to trust me; I've been doing this since I was eleven."

Carrie forgot about her current situation and looked over to Jason, who was fidgeting with some kind of buttons on a thing that had LED lights. "How long?"

"My dad owned this bird long before I did. He had a 172 when I was a kid. He took me flying all the time; by the time I was eleven I was doing touch and go's on at our ranch."

Conversation seemed to ease her mind a little so she kept it going, "What's a *touch and go*?"

"Instead of landing and coming to a stop, you touch the ground and pull back into the air. Fly around again and then do it over several times. It teaches patterns and approaches and landing procedures."

"Oh."

There was not a hint of fear in his voice. Not a tremble of doubt or uneasiness that flowed from his lips. He was enjoying this! He must have flown everyday almost, yet he still loves to fly his plane. Carrie was running the thoughts through her head as she watched Jason make little adjustments to the switches and levers. He turned a little wheel called TRIM and soon she felt the plane settle like a feather on a whiff of wind.

Jason fiddled with the black box with red numbers for a second again, he was pointing to some numbers on a little map or something on his knee, a clipboard that was held in place with a piece of elastic, touched a couple of buttons and then he put both hands on the wheel. *Yoke*, he called it.

"Traffic, this is zero niner mike tango, type Cessna. Fifty-two miles northwest of Vegas Vortac, touch and go's." He turned and smiled at Carrie.

"What was all that about?" She asked.

"Roger mikey's forty niners…" Dusty said from his seat in the back over the intercom.

Jason smiled widely at Carrie. "He pays attention."

"Of course. He's not an idiot, he just has trouble sometimes. What were you saying earlier?"

"I was just telling any planes in the vicinity about us being here. See…" He pointed to the box he had been fiddling with. "That's called a radio stack. I dial in the frequency and monitor radio traffic."

"What was that other stuff? Vegas Vortac?"

"It's what is called a VOR or Very high frequency Omnidirectional Range. It's like having to stop and ask directions, without stopping. A VOR is a building that looks like a taco stand without windows, it sends radio signals that these dials pick up and I can navigate up here without maps or following freeways."

Carrie looked stupefied. "Oh."

"It even has its own voice, you wanna hear it?"

Before Carrie could object to another new thing-something she had no clue about-a voice chimed in from the back, "Yes!"

Jason pushed a button on the radio stack and an eerie noise came over the headsets.

'*Beep-Beeeeep-Beep-Beep, Beep-Beeeeep, Beep-Beep-Beep.*' Then a pause and '*Beep-Beeeeep-Beep-Beep, Beep-Beeeeep, Beep-Beep-Beep*'

Dusty's eyes opened wide again; Carrie worried they were going to get dried out.

"Cool!"

"What the heck is that?" She inquired.

"That's Morse code. Every VOR in the country has a different code, so you know where you are at all times."

She didn't have a clue about what he was talking about. "Oh."

Jason scanned the gauges in front and made the announcement, "Okay, we're up about nine thousand feet or five thousand AGL, which mean above ground level. Let's take a look around."

With those words he turned the yoke to the left and added some rudder and the plane made a slow banking turn towards the west. He lowered the manifold pressure, or power, and let the 182 cruise.

Fallcast was a small town, and it looked even smaller from the air. The flyers could see the railroad tracks coming in from the north towards and through town, then off into the smaller valley to the south towards Vegas. A freighter of about a hundred and twenty cars rambled along the steel highway about three miles from town; it would be just a short time before it would bring traffic to a stop in town for five minutes as it passed through on the temporary tracks that were utilized after the derailment.

The Pit was the most recognizable object from the air, the deep and open hole looked the top of a major volcano somewhere; the dump trucks and loaders looked like Tonka toys moving around as the Cessna passed over.

Hundreds of dirt roads littered the valley, each one visible from the height they toured, some trails were just the occasional traveler on a quad, or a late night romantic encounter in the brush-a detailed map of the vehicle's path drawn out in the tall grass and sage. Other roads were the heavily traveled ones, trails to small family mines or to the ranches at the far west end of the valley; shortcuts to the main highway over the mountains and through tight gullies.

Jason found a familiar dusty lane cut into the desert floor and followed it for a little while. He lowered the nose of the Cessna and that brought a communal sucking of air from his passengers.

"Just want to show you something…" He said with a slightly mischievous grin.

The plane came closer to the ground and then Jason turned the yoke to the right, causing Carrie and Dusty to feel the slight G force of the bank.

"There…" He said, pointing across Carrie's chest.

Dusty slid over to the right side of the seat to look out the window.

"That's the cave I was telling you about."

Carrie looked at the small tree and the shadow of the ravine and scrunched her eyes at it. She thought she knew the area a little, but exactly where she was she wasn't sure. She had almost forgotten that she was looking nearly straight down at the ground as the plane was in the turn.

She looked forward and asked in a wobbly voice, "Can you make this thing go straight?"

Jason gave a little chortle and complied. "Sorry."

Dusty wasn't complaining. This was the most exhilaration he had felt in his life, as far as he could remember. The thrill of being above the earth and look right down upon it like a bird made him feel large, full of life, empowered.

"It's the moaning cavern."

"I thought that was outside of Sonora California."

"Well, that's what we called it as kids."

"Dark. Scary."

Carrie turned so hard in her seat to get a glimpse of Dusty, her lap belt dug into her hips.

"You remember going there Dusty?"

"Cold. Dark shadows." The boy pulled away from the window, there was fear in his eyes.

Carrie turned back towards Jason.

"We went there once when he was little, before-well you know. I used to go there once and a while when I could sneak out of the house. Dusty's right. It's a scary place to be."

Jason was quiet for a second then he made a southerly turn and climbed a little. He looked over to his beautiful rider and asked, "So it's not a mine. It's a natural cave."

"Yeah. We only went in so far, the other kids in town think it's haunted. And it smells bad, like people peed in it." She blushed at her words and looked back out the window. "Kids used to party there, but then there was an accident. A couple of teenagers a year or so ago were drinking or something and fell. They both died and it took like three days to find them. Now no one goes there. Besides, I think it's on my father's private property."

Jason pondered this for a moment and rubbed his chin. This made Carrie nervous; she didn't like it when he only had one hand on the yoke. He gave the plane a little yaw to his side and Dusty slid back over to the left to look out the window, the scary cave must have faded from his mind. Jason seemed like he was going to say something, Carrie finally asked.

"What?"

"Well, it's just that the map I have says the cave is on BLM land. Not private property."

"It's what the sheriff's office told us; or the town I mean. The two kids were really popular at the high school and the funeral was bad, it took over a week for everyone to get over it; so basically the deputies said if they caught anyone on the road up to there, they'd be arrested or cited or something I think my father bought it from the government to secure it or something."

Jason said nothing, but his mind was working. The tree, the tree was being kept alive by artificial means by someone. Jason decided he might just tempt fate-or an arrest-by checking out the cave on future ventures. He had to get some mining claim numbers of the posts up there again anyways, since his notes were tragically destroyed in a mysterious fire. Maybe he will have to blow up the town to escape.

On its southeasterly heading, the Cessna and her passengers glided over the vast green fields below. The Dickson Ranch splayed out under them and Dusty recognized something right away, he pointed out the nickname of the ranch before Carrie had said anything.

"Glowworm!"

Carrie glanced back over her shoulder at him. *He knows the ranch from the air!* She had learned from a website at the library about head trauma and amnesia that, with most affected kids, they can pick up on small or even unnoticed landmarks when they travel to places. Sometimes symmetry in buildings, the certain way irrigation canals run and curve around fields, roof colors, etc. Carrie knew deep inside her little brother was not fully damaged and he picked up on more than he let on to during his daily lessons at home.

It was boredom, casualness, maybe even frustration that kept his logic to a minimum, to himself. He locked things away and recalled them when he could outwardly, but importantly more and more-since Jason arrived in their lives-he was telling people what he knew. This was an improvement that Carrie would've hoped to have unassisted, on her own; but she was more than grateful inside that someone like Jason came along and inspired Dusty to reveal his thoughts openly to other people. It was not quite a miracle, but it was a sign.

"Very good Dusty." Jason registered his pleasure with the kid knowing things from the air-that would come in handy later-if his sister approved. "Do you know which way is back towards town from here?"

Dusty sat back and put his hand to his chin like he had seen adults do all the time when they were thinking. He lifted his right hand and made a pointer with his index

173

finger. First he pointed straight in front of the plane, then quickly changed his mind and pointed to the left, which was west of the little berg; then finally with a big smile and sigh he pointed behind them and to the right. Nearly exactly where Fallcast lies.

A rush of warm air made Carrie feel like she was going to faint. Dusty was doing better than well, he was learning at a rate she had never witnessed before and the air around her felt like a spa with bubbles rumbling around her body. She was dizzy and then felt like crying, her eyes burned to release. Jason saw this and tried to change the subject, he wasn't sure, but he thought he saw pride in her near watering eyes.

"Wanna fly?"

She turned her head so slowly from looking behind her to face the pilot that she could almost hear it creak in mind. Her face went from sheer happiness to confusion to shock in less than a few seconds, seconds it took for her to be able to form a clear word, or a word that didn't insult her host in the captive quarters of the small airplane.

"*Excuse me?*" Incredulous barely touched the sound that left her mouth.

Jason nodded at the yoke and at the exact copy sitting in front of her, "Fly. You know, turn the plane here and there."

"You're joking." Though her tone suggested she knew he wasn't.

"Nah. It's easy. Just put your hands on the yoke and hold it in place."

Carrie didn't move, she was barely breathing at best

"You're *serious*, aren't you?"

Jason smiled, "Of course. Try it."

"No."

"Please?"

"Absolutely not."

174

"C'mon, it practically flies itself."

"Uh huh." She crossed her arms in front of her chest.

Jason was about give up when he saw her look down at the control. There was a glimmer in her expression of near acceptance, of curiosity and maybe a twinkle of challenge. Slowly Carrie reached out to the black handled posts, one hand on each side. She grasped the cold plastic at first like you would hold a shovel or hammer, with determination and firmness.

"Easy. Just like holding a fine crystal flute glass. Don't make quick or sharp movements, she responds with just the lightest touch."

Carrie sucked in her lower lip and bit lightly down on it, her teeth showing slightly. Inhaling a small breath of fresh air she relaxed her grip a little on the yoke and ran her fists up and down a little to get the feel.

"Now, no need to push forward or pull back on it. If you do, you'll change our altitude. So just keep it where it is and now turn it slowly to the right." Jason gave a quick glance out the windows for any errant traffic. "Okay." To add emphasis, he crossed his arms in front of him.

The Cessna began a bank, to the right, but it felt like it was sliding sideways in the air.

"It's not right; I mean it doesn't feel right." She slowly whispered.

"I know; I'll adjust it myself with the rudder." And he did. "Great, hold it there."

Carrie let out a little laugh of pleasure, "It feels like we're going to slide out."

The Cessna circled for a few minutes, a wide circle that took several minutes to perform and covered miles. By the time the plane ended up where Carrie started the turn she felt calmer, confident. It was the control that made her nervous, before she had no control over her flight, now she was in control-well, a little of it anyways-she still didn't understand the rudder things on the floor or the wheel Jason turned once in a while and she knew for sure she didn't want to push the yoke in or pull it out, but she was doing just fine. There was a sense of power, of being able to defy the law of gravity and she was the one made the 182 RG turn!

Jason didn't seem nervous at all. He was a little, though, you had to be if you let a woman who drives the way she did to the Dickson Ranch handle the turns, but she was doing alright and enjoying herself. She was relaxing and things seemed closer between them. He knew if he showed her he trusted her, she might trust him a little more.

Dusty was locked outside the left window of the plane, staring out into the sky not towards the ground like everyone else does on a bank turn. He was *flying* in the sky, the blue, the air above his home and town. He knew where the ground was and what it looked like down there, he wanted to see if you got higher in the sky would you see the clouds and maybe even get a glimpse of Heaven-the place that the Reverend Foster talked about on Sundays at church. He had been close to the ground for as long as he could remember, but he'd never remembered this high up before-taller than the mountains that encircle the valley, higher than the smoke travels from the chimneys in town.

Carrie leveled the plane out into a north westerly course taking her on a path towards town. They were a few miles away still so Jason persuaded her to let him lower the altitude for a better look at the town as they passed over. She kept her hands on the yoke and he eased it forward from his side, not much but enough to get a little sense of lighter gravity. Minus G's.

Carrie giggled again at the sensation, Dusty let out a little chuckle himself when his tummy tingled. The plane settled on its new altitude of five thousand five hundred feet or fourteen hundred AGL. Streets became visible, homes were easily discernible, cars could be seen on the highway moving through town, other cars and trucks were using the side streets and even a bicycle or two could be spotted.

The pass over the town was simple, just a glide over the top and then a slightly sharp bank turn made by Jason and another pass going the opposite way. At the north end of town Jason directed Carrie to make a right turn out over the airfield and they coasted straight across the grey runway. Jason was making final preparations for landing when he spotted something flash below them near the Quonset hut hangar.

Jason swung his body to the left to glance out his window under the plane and saw what looked to be red and blue lights flashing in the fading daylight. He grimaced. Now what? He looked over to Carrie who was still softly biting her lip, which was sexy he noted, and smiled.

"You wanna land her?"

Carrie's face returned to the 'Hell no' look. "No thanks."

"Dusty? You want to land the plane?"

His eyes went wide. A nervous nod and then he shook it no. "Tomorrow."

Jason smiled at him and nodded, "You got a deal."

The flying geologist turned back to the front and pushed himself back into his seat. He set the trim for a longer glide and began his checklist. Checking their orientation he gave small turns to the Cessna's controls to bring the plane in a quick upwind and a fast turn for final. The passengers were holding on and Carrie forgot about being relaxed.

At five thousand feet Jason lowered the flaps to ten and made sure he was jetting along below 140 KIAS. Then he lowered the gear and pulled the throttle out. There was several seconds of near silence as the wind whisked past the wings and the plane settled, descending slowly to the earth. Making his final line up with the center of the gravel,

Jason followed the side of the road that ran along the airport; there was a sheriff's car parked a few hundred yards from the road and indeed had its rotating lights on.

The 182 lofted quietly up and then Jason let it drop to nearly the tip of the gravel pile at the end of the runway then he pulled back on the yoke and the nose lifted as the plane flared. The main gear touched down without the fanfare of screeching, but the uneven ground made a loud rumbling and the vibrations caused Dusty to start humming along with it.

The pilot expertly guided the idling aircraft to a stop just in front of the hangar and thirty feet from Parks and his patrol car. The cop didn't look happy; he switched his lights off as Jason shut the plane down.

Parks took a deep breath and made a grim face as he pushed his butt off the car and walked in a hesitated gait towards the Cessna. *This can't be good*, Jason thought. The deputy stopped on the passenger side and opened the door for Carrie.

"Hi Parks. Just getting my Amelia Earhart on…" She said with a little smile, "What brings you out here?"

Jason helped Dusty out of his side of the plane and pulled the keys from the ignition.

Parks addressed Carrie only. "There's been a fatal." He paused like he usually does for drama. "Meg and Steve were in a wreck near 95. Steve died."

Carrie's expression changed to instant pain. "Oh my god." She put her hands to her mouth.

Parks finally looked to Jason and gave him a discerning glance. "NHP says there was something unusual about the crash."

Jason heard the word crash and wasn't quite sure what was going on. He cocked his head to the left and asked, "What happened?"

"Don't know yet. I heard your plane flying around earlier today, when the call came in from the highway patrol I rushed out here to see if Dusty was with you, I know Meg watches him this time of day usually on Thursdays and Fridays." He stared at Jason the whole time.

"Poor Meg. Is she bad?" Carrie grabbed at Parks' arm.

"She's banged up pretty good, she was airlifted to University. Steve was thrown clear of the car as it rolled and died on impact."

Carrie just shook her head and leaned back against the plane with her back. Dusty came walking over and put his arms around her waist. "Megan hurt?"

"Yes honey." She cradled his shoulders and neck into her arms. "Yes she's hurt."

CHAPTER ELEVEN
Friday Evening

The ride to Vegas was quiet. Jason was driving the Jeep, Carrie was lying back as far as the seat would let her and Dusty was sound asleep in the back seat. The news had struck a chord with Jason, even though he didn't know Meg all that well and he had never met her husband Steve, the way Carrie had taken it. Her eyes watered, she looked whiter than the borax that comes out of the ground in Fallcast sixty eight miles by road northwest of the giant city of neon lights, huge water fountains and billion dollar casinos.

Carrie at first demanded to drive but Jason said he wouldn't go if she did. She was tired, scared, upset and her driving was horrible when she was the opposite of those conditions. Parks helped when he pointed out that Carrie didn't have a license. Jason was glad for that help, for when they had come to the part of 201 near Highway 95 where the accident occurred, Carrie might have driven them off the road as well.

An ominous warning ahead of them on 201. Bad accidents meant time spent on the scene, which meant the Nevada Department of Transportation had time to place construction site reader-boards miles ahead of the crash on both ends of the highway. The bright yellow-green letters spelled someone's fate:

CAUTION: ACCIDENT AHEAD
SLOW DOWN

Only the worst accidents meant reader-boards.

It was a horrific scene. Meg and Steve owned nearly identical 2006 Ford Broncos, Meg's was green with white and her husband's was white with green. They had been using Steve's and what was sitting on its roof a few dozen feet into the desert was unrecognizable as a vehicle at all. The Ford's body had been rolled into an oval shape; every window was gone and little blue shards twinkled in the moonlight, debris littered the sand and sage with clothing from the suitcases that had exploded on their impact.

There were four Nevada Highway Patrolmen on scene; one was still directing traffic, fortunately there was little on this road, many heard on the radio of the northbound closure and that only residents with proof of residence in Fallcast or the area was allowed to pass. Two more troopers were arming surveying equipment, a Leica Flexline TS02 Total Station, used for mapping out accident scenes; the NHP was one of the best in the nation for accident investigation and their tools of the trade were the best available. Fatal accidents were priority and sometimes several hours were spent on the scene mapping and measuring every inch and detail for insurance companies, evidence, future testimony, reconstruction in court and even research into safety procedures and highway speeds.

The final officer was the shift commander, usually a sergeant, and he was with the last of the witnesses who had found the crash, no one had actually seen the Bronco leave the road, but the skid marks showed no sign of control loss. Most accidents on Nevada's long stretches of highways involved the driver falling asleep behind the wheel, drifting off onto the shoulder, and then snapping the wheel hard to correct the drift, causing the vehicle to roll.

The lack of skid marks was the question on the NHP's mind. Even the slightest amount of pressure on the brakes should have caused sideways skidding, unless the brakes failed, or the driver was incapable of using them.

Carrie had her hand to her mouth as they were guided through the area towards the Highway 95 interchange. Parks had called ahead to the troopers to allow Jason and Carrie through; otherwise they would have been turned around and sent all the way back through the valley to the north interchange, a mere fifty-five miles out of the way. Dusty was asleep in the back.

"Oh God, Jason. Oh God…" Tears were streaming down Carrie's face and making little dark pools on her blue jeans.

Jason shook his head in dismay at the carnage. A frown appeared on his lips, he was careful not to allow Carrie to see it. "Sad."

It took a half hour longer to get to Vegas and the University Medical Center on West Charleston Boulevard near I-15. The place was slightly chaotic, even for a Friday night. UMC is Nevada's only Level I Trauma center, and keeps busy with medic helicopters landing frequently.

Dusty was still sleeping on Jason's shoulder as he carried him from the parking lot; Carrie was nearly running from the parking area. Dozens of cars were rambling around the lot as Jason and Carrie dodged the less attentive drivers to make the Emergency Entrance. Parked on the curb near the doors was two NHP cars, one was marked SUPERVISOR.

The cacophony in the ER area was normal for Vegas. Dozens of car crashes, stabbings, a couple of shootings, several gamblers who had collapsed while dropping coins in slot machines or were overcome by alcohol that was served free as long as you play in the mega-casinos lined the hallways and chairs. Everyone was shouting at once, everyone wanted to be helped now.

The three nurses on duty at the desk were overwhelmed; a triage nurse was trying to justify acceptance order by asking patients their condition. Those with breathing problems and chest pains were moved to the front of the line, save gunshot and knife wounds and severe bleeders. Others were given a number and told to wait, usually those who had children with the flu or folks who forgot to take insulin shots on time. People who had slipped or fallen and were holding various body parts in pain and makeshift bandages were put on hold also.

Carrie barged past the front of the line and right to the nurse who looked like she was about to climb to the top of a clock tower and start shooting.

"I'm sorry ma'am; you'll have to wait your turn…" The nurse with the name tag that read Betty began. She was wearing a simple Peaches Flutter Strokes round neck nursing top and blue scrub pants.

Interrupting, Carrie asked with no disguise of her haste, "I'm looking for a woman who was brought in here about an hour ago; she was in a car wreck on 201."

"We've had several car accident victims in the last three hours ma'am…"

"Her name is Megan Cooke. Look it up."

The nurse stared at her blankly for a second, it wasn't a request and finally Betty realized the only way to get rid of this new annoyance was to placate her. She stepped to an unused terminal and said, "Fine."

Carrie crossed her arms in front of her chest and Jason finally caught up to her at the counter. Juking and deking was best left for his college hockey days, and the throngs of aid-needy folks were not happy about the young woman that had pushed her way to the front. To stand beside her-even with a small boy-made faces go red and words of anger fluttered from injured to sick.

Jason pretended he didn't hear any of the unwell-wishers as he passed them and finally took a spot next to Carrie, who glanced over to him for a second then returned her fire-branded gaze at Nurse Betty who was typing. Finally a smile crossed the nurse's face and she lifted her head to the impatient line crasher.

"She's in Intensive Care on two…"

"Thank you." Carrie cast her gratitude over her shoulder as she bound for the elevator hall.

The elevator ride was quiet enough, Carrie was wiping tears from her eyes, Jason was rocking Dusty on his shoulder-best he could anyways, and the preteen was heavy. The doors slid open on the second floor and the three passengers hooked to their right off the car and walked to the nearest visible desk, the only desk it visible. Behind the desk was a set of double doors with one-way glass and no handles. A black triangle pad was located on the wall four feet up and just in front of the door. A pass-key was needed to open the doors, or you had to be buzzed in from the desk in front of Carrie and Jason.

The nurse at this desk seemed a little calmer since there wasn't the circus atmosphere here as there was downstairs. She smiled from her chair as Carrie stomped forward.

"Good evening. Can I help you?"

"We're here to see Megan Cooke. She was brought in an..."

"Are you family?" The question was not aimed at being condescending, but it sounded that way when the nurse interrupted Carrie.

Carrie took a deep breath and closed her eyes in near surrender, "No. But she watches my brother..."

"I'm sorry. Right now only family can see her, she's in bad shape."

"Her family is *dead*; I'm all she has left."

The nurse, who was dressed in pink scrubs with red piping and a scanning card with her picture on it attached to a small retractable ID holder above her right breast that read SALLY, looked for a moment like she wanted to say, '*Do you know how many times I've heard that?*'

"I'm sorry. I don't make policy. The doctor will be making his rounds in about thirty minutes, you can request visitation from him."

Carrie took a deep breath to fight back with whatever she had left when she caught movement in the corner of her eye. She turned and that's when the both of them first noticed the highway patrolman in his uniform sitting on a tall stool. The man was doing paperwork in a

184

nook. He stood and collected the papers he was working on and headed for the desk with a semi-smile while wedging his hat under his left arm.

Jason saw the man coming and nodded at the trooper.

Sally said nicely, "You can have a seat in the room to your left there."

"Thank you." Jason gave her an expression of relief and he retreated to the waiting area.

The trooper reached Carrie, who was still at the desk impatiently trying to use her angry looks to persuade Sally to let her in; he jammed his paperwork under his right arm and offered a hand.

"You say you're a friend of Megan and Steve Cooke?" His voice was quiet and deep.

Carrie felt intimidation wash over her body and she stepped back from the counter, cast a glance over her shoulder for Jason who had abandoned her to lay Dusty down on a comfortable chair in the waiting area.

"Yes?"

Her voice nearly squeaked like a scared mouse. Maybe it was the fact the trooper was over six three or four, or his uniform was bulging at the seams with his biceps, or probably it was just the badge and the fact he had been waiting for someone to question and Carrie was the first in line. He had somewhat hardened features, probably from military service, a soft smile and dark brown hair that had dashes of grey in it, the same with his eyes, brown with flecks of grey.

His uniform was immaculate, the light grey-blue suit with navy shoulder straps and pocket tops was pressed perfectly in all the right lines, it seemed too clean for someone who was hours earlier up to his neck in the crash that was frightful just looking at. He had numerous award pins on his chest on the right side above his silver nameplate and several hash stripes on his sleeve. His Sam

Brown was polished within an inch of its life and of course the butt of a gun making its presence known. He had a dark grey-blue campaign hat under his left arm, also known as a drill sergeant hat.

The trooper's nametag read F. SULLIVAN. As he drew nearer his smile widened but he added a brow lift which conveyed a hint of sadness. Carrie took his hand and he gave a quick single shake and withdrew it. This dropped his intimidation level about five points in Carrie's mind.

"I'm very sorry about Mr. Cooke." His voice conveyed true regret, not like the overly repeated standard *'I'm sorry for your loss'* tone you hear on *CSI*.

Carrie took her hand back. SULLIVAN's hand was warm, softer than she had expected.

"Thank you. Can you tell me what happened?"

The cautious smile disappeared. In its place was now a concerned look or maybe a carefully ordered question was forming in his mind. "I'm Corporal Fred Sullivan. I'm in charge of the investigation along with my sergeant, who is getting a statement from a DUI." Another fast smile.

"Okay?" Carrie felt the intimidation level rising again. Five being the highest, she was at level two.

Corporal Sullivan gestured with his hand towards the waiting area, "Would you like to have a seat?" Level three.

Carrie led the officer into the area. It was darker than the rest of the hospital, only a couple of small lamps were turned on in an intimate setting of sorts, the look trying to inspire a homey feeling. Even though there were fluorescents in the ceiling, they were off, the most light in the room was given off by the glow of a thirty-six inch flat screen TV tuned to Fox News with very little volume, in fact if someone was whispering you couldn't hear the TV at all.

Jason had placed Dusty on the couch, a very comfortable looking one, and had sat himself in a similarly comfortable looking chair facing the TV. He had his eyes closed; Carrie was hoping he was just resting them, not pretending to be asleep.

She sat down next to her brother on a soft loveseat and the trooper drug a smaller metal and cloth chair to just in front of her. Level four. He sat his big hat on another chair then pulled out a small notebook and placed the papers he had under his other arm on his lap. He retrieved a nice Pentel pen from his shirt pocket and opened the little book.

"I'm going to ask you some questions. But first I'd like to say a few things straight out, let you know where we are and what we are planning ahead for." Corporal Sullivan's voice was low and purposeful, loud enough to block out the sound from the TV, but not so loud as to wake the sleeping Dusty. Carrie nodded. Jason opened his eyes and leaned forward.

Sullivan gave Jason a glance and nodded, "Are you her husband?"

Carrie blushed red, even in the dimly lit room you could see her chameleon change in color. Jason smiled big with mirth in his eyes, Carrie looked over to him and though she saw a look of thoughtfulness, like he was planning to say 'yes'.

"No sir. We're friends, she was with me today. We were out flying when this all happened." His voice trembled a little; Carrie thought she heard a ring of alibi in his voice.

Sullivan looked down at his notebook and began writing. He smiled at the flying statement and the smile got wider when Jason added Carrie's alibi. He looked back to Jason.

"You're name?"

"Jason Parmenter."

Trooper Sullivan scribbled. He looked back at Carrie. "Your full name please and could you tell me about your relationship with the Cooke's."

"Carrie Marie Dodson…"

Sullivan interrupted, "Of the Dodson Mill Dodsons?"

Carrie's color only flashed a little this time, "Yes. He's my father."

Sullivan gave Jason a glance that made his blood cold, it said in a look: '*Wow! You're a brave one!*' Carrie saw the look and fire roiled.

"Megan was my friend since we were kids. She watched my little brother here when I was busy."

The trooper noted her words and looked over to Dusty. He flashed a sympathetic smile at the snoozing boy and looked back at Carrie. His face turned solemn. Level five.

"Are you aware of any problems between the Cookes?"

Carrie's heart stopped. "Pardon?"

"Has there been any arguing in front of you, or say maybe a harsh word by Meg to you about her husband or vice versa."

"No! I mean they never would have fought in front of me, they always seemed great together."

Sullivan nodded as he wrote. Carrie felt as if she needed to vindicate Meg more.

She said, "They did everything together, matter of fact they were going to have a fling in Vegas tonight-this weekend…" Her statement was cut short by tears. She covered her mouth and Jason placed his arm around her.

Trooper Sullivan gave her a reassuring smile and leaned back in his chair. "We've found some things that are out of the ordinary. Let me explain."

The Corporal leaned forward in the chair to get closer. He spoke in a whisper, barely loud enough to cover up Bill O'Reilly on the TV, "At the scene of the accident, there were no skid marks and usually with the new vehicles and anti-lock brakes there wouldn't be any from braking, but a sharp turn or overcorrection would leave a distinct mark on the road both of which indicate a number of things. It could mean there wasn't time to apply the brakes and drifted off the road, in some situations something the driver couldn't react to fast enough.

"Or, the driver fell asleep and drifted off the road, not having a chance to hit the brakes before leaving the pavement indicating there was no sudden turning of the vehicle. *Or* there could be a mechanical failure of the brakes."

He paused for dramatic effect and suddenly Carrie realized this must be a cop thing, Parks does it all the time.

"Now, tomorrow I or one of my fellow troopers is going to attend the autopsy for investigation purposes, and it will take weeks for a toxicology report. Blood tests will be back tonight for alcohol content, but I doubt there was any drinking involved. In fact I think there was something a bit more suspicious at work here…"

The trooper looked directly at Carrie for a reaction. He didn't get what he wanted so he tried another angle. "We did a field inspection of the Bronco; a more comprehensive one will be done at the station. We found that there was brake fluid leaking out of the reservoir, now that could mean just a failure of a seal-or, it could mean the nut that holds the brake line in place on the reservoir was loosened to allow the fluid to escape slowly." He took a breath and pursed his lips.

"Now, ordinarily that would be no real indication right off, there's a warning light on the dash to indicate low levels of fluid, but the curious thing is the wire to the sending unit was taken off also, so the warning light wouldn't work. Meaning; it looks like maybe tampering.

"Another thing," Sullivan continued as Josh and Carrie looked at each other sadly astonished, "a car that was passed by the Cookes minutes before the accident said the driver and the passenger were arguing. Mr. Cooke, who was driving, was doing well over eighty-not unusual for these roads as you know-but the couple appeared angry and completely engaged in yelling at one another as they went by the witness."

Jason sat up straight at this. He leaned forward to the trooper and asked quietly, "I didn't know you could release information like that. Is there something we should know?"

"No." Sullivan paused and took a small breath. He looked from Carrie to Jason, Dusty then back to Jason and said quietly back, "I know Fallcast. It's a very small town and the Sheriff's Office is going to be involved in the investigation. I want you to know the truth out front, since you're here. Rumors are going to fly as soon as someone sees me or another investigator in town. I'm not accusing anyone or even can say whether or not my theory is real, but I wanted you to know that we are looking into the possibility that the Cooke's brakes were tampered with or the possibility that your friends were engaged in an argument that caused Mr. Cooke to be distracted.

"Tell who you want, or tell no one and watch what happens, but I know that if I say nothing to you, then things you hear might make you edgy. Besides, I know your father and I'm sure he would want a full update."

Carrie sat back and her color went to her usual olive. "I don't speak with my father."

Sullivan just raised his brow and said, "Either way, now you know the truth."

The trooper pulled his right pocket open, the navy flap was Velcroed down instead of buttoned. He produced a card with a badge pictured on it and a series of phone numbers.

"This is my office number, my private cell-please be discreet, and the NHP's satellite station number where I begin my shift Wednesday through Saturday. You can reach me there between seven p.m. and five a.m., after that you can use my cell number if it is important."

"What is important?" Jason asked.

"Anything you hear or find out about in the next several days."

Carrie took the card with a shaky hand. The trooper stood up and slid the chair back into its previous spot and tucked away his notepad. He nodded at Jason and said *Ma'am* to Carrie before he went around the corner and down the hall to the elevator. Just as the door opened, he sat his trooper hat on his head and stepped inside, giving one last look in the direction of the visitors.

Moments later the attending doctor walked into the waiting room.

"The nurse says you'd like to visit Mrs. Cooke?" The doctor directed his question at Carrie and Carrie only.

He was dressed in the traditional smock coat, not the usual blue or purple scrubs everyone is so used to seeing now a days. The full length lab white coat went below his knees and was buttoned to just below the neck. He had a pocket protector in the only pouch on the chest, the name of a pharmaceutical on the outer flap, the pocket contained two or three pens, a pen-light, a small mirror and two or three tongue depressors. His hands were jammed into the side pockets at waist level.

He had a sad smile, comforting and serious at the same time-maybe even a bit grave looking-a small pencil thin moustache carefully trimmed to the corners of his mouth and neatly clipped at the ends. There was a trace of grey in the brown hair, it was combed over to the right side of his head, but in the low light of the waiting room it was hardly noticeable he was balding. Blue eyes completed the man's face, they were tired looking, a touch of severity also.

Carrie stood to take the man's hand, which he didn't offer. He just gave hers a glance and then stared back into her eyes. "Yes, I'm her friend…"

"Yes. The nurse told me. You can have ten minutes," He switched his eyes to Jason, "alone with her. That's all."

Jason nodded indicating he understood he was to stay put. Carrie looked to her brother sleeping on the comfortable couch and nodded back at the doctor also. "That'd be great."

"The trooper didn't want anyone to see her until they had a chance to question her." The doc added as he turned and began to walk towards the double doors. "They're done. She's very weak right now, so just give her your best and that's all. Don't try to pry anything out of her."

"I understand." Carrie did.

The doctor pulled his ID from the left pocket of his smock and paused several inches from the black panel on the wall. He inhaled carefully.

"She's in bad shape and on meds so sometimes she won't make sense. We gave her a sedative and that should knock her out in about ten minutes, that's all you have."

He slid the card over the reader. The doors clicked in the center top and the magnets released the double set as they automatically swung inwards towards the I C unit. The doc continued.

"She has a broken leg, a cracked sternum, several bruised ribs and minor spiral fractures in her right arm. Be prepared for that. She'll be in multiple restraints."

The doctor walked to the end of the L shaped Intensive Care Unit and paused at a sliding glass door. He placed his hand on the handle and again paused. He looked to Carrie with tired eyes. He spoke in a whisper, "Be

192

considerate of her condition." Then he slid the door open and parted the privacy curtain to the side to let Carrie enter. She stepped in and he backed back out into the hallway and disappeared into a coffee station.

A TV mounted high in the corner of the nine by nine cubicle was tuned to *SpongeBob Squarepants*, but the volume was barely audible over the beeping and clicking of machines and monitors. Just as the doc had tried to warn Carrie, the woman in the center of the bed looked like a marionette. Tension cables and splints were hanging everywhere, just like you'd see in those old TV shows like *Marcus Welby* or *Emergency!*

Meg was turned towards the small window that looked out onto the roof of another wing of the hospital. Carrie could see her chest rising and falling slowly, cautiously, as each breath brought pain and near tears. She was wearing an IV gown, or *johnny*, not very dignified for a young pretty girl like Megan, but the slits and openings allowed easier access to body parts that needed to be poked or prodded with the slightest discomfort for the person inside it.

Carrie thought about sliding the door closed but she was afraid she would bang into it if she felt sick; trying to run for the bathroom she'd spotted on her way down the hall past the other ICU rooms. She took a small quiet breath.

"Meg?" Her voice cracked and only whisper of sound came out.

She watched as the young girl's hands twitched at the sound. Her left hand, the one that wasn't in a cast, balled into a fist and then Carrie saw the small struggle it was for her friend to turn her head towards her.

There was no smile of recognition. Only wet tears rolling down her cheeks over several layers of dried tears with makeup in the streams. She took a long painful breath with her eyes closed; tears ran faster to the gown she was wearing.

"Carrie."

"Are you, I mean… I'm so sorry Megan." Carrie was now feeling the water burning behind her own eyes.

"Steve's dead." That was it as it left Meg's mouth. Sorrow, but finality.

"I know; I'm so sorry."

Meg cleared her throat, which also seemed to hurt a lot and then she raised her unbroken arm to eyes and wiped the tears from them.

"It was my fault. I did it." In a loud and clear voice.

"Don't be silly honey. It was an accident."

"We were fighting, we'd been fighting for days, but today was the big one."

"I don't think that matters now…"

"We were fighting over you."

Carrie didn't think she heard her friend right. She leaned in towards her and stepped to the edge of the bed. "What?"

"Steve was in love with you." Meg began with no tears. "He wanted to get a divorce."

"Oh no, Meg that can't be true you've been…"

"He was jealous. Angry at your relationship with Jason. He said… terrible things."

Carrie was on the verge of hyperventilating. She felt sick to her stomach and her knees trembled at the thoughts crossing her mind. She tried to keep her voice steady, "How can that be?"

Megan looked back out the window, but kept her voice loud. "He thought you would look at him at times, look at him with affection. He told me that things weren't going good enough for us and that he wanted a divorce."

"Megan, I think you're a little drugged up. I think you're hallucinating."

Megan kept staring out the window, "Not all at once. This has been going on since high school. He's always had a crush on you." The tears came.

Carrie felt the floodwaters release now. "Meg I'm so sorry I didn't know."

Meg took a deeper breath, this time the medication was doing its job, "We fought about you in the car on the way here. We had been doing so well, and then Jason moved in with you…"

"How could anyone know that? It only happened just a few days…"

"The whole town knows. Steve was enraged, I think he set the fire, I think he wanted to scare Jason out of town. I killed him today Carrie, I did it."

"Meg, look I…"

"And Jason, well I guess the Dodsons get it all again huh?" There was a sharp sarcasm in her voice, anger, hate, jealousy.

"Jason?" Carrie felt a steel knot form in her belly, dropping towards her feet.

"Yeah, Mr. Flyboy Geologist. What a catch huh? Got everything you want here, huh Cassie? 'Cept your poor brother though. Guess you could put him in a… a…what ya call them things? Sanitarium? Yeah. You and lover boy can go on with your life. Steve's dead and Jason and you are playing mommy and daddy…"

"Don't talk like that Meg; you're on medication that's all."

"I killed him. Please, just leave…"

Carrie opened her mouth to protest when Meg reached over and tapped the nurse call button on the TV remote.

There was a click behind the bed on a wall speaker. "Are you okay?"

"I want my guest to leave now." Meg put her hand to her face and bit her fist.

In seconds the nurse showed and pulled the privacy curtain aside. "I'm sorry ma'am, but you'll have to leave."

Carrie turned to argue, but she knew she was on a losing trend here. She walked out with a shuffled twist. As she walked, it was more of a slow roll on her feet-each one quietly moving in front of the other, she didn't see the NHP trooper sitting in the next cubicle. She didn't see the nurses staring at her. Her face was turned down, in an almost melted look.

Carrie had felt something for Jason, but they weren't playing '*mommy and daddy*'. They weren't even an item. But that was it wasn't it. *Was Meg jealous of Jason? Could she have cut the brakes on the Ford to kill her husband to have a shot at Jason? Was Steve really in love with her?*

Sure, she knew a lot of guys growing up in Fallcast had put her on their conquer list. She knew that men and boys stared at her behind as she walked by; she knew that on more than one occasion someone had catcalled to her back. She didn't think of herself as a model type or a beauty queen. But she wasn't blind. It hurt her now. It hurt that Steve had a crush on her and that endangered her relationship with Megan.

It hurt her that Meg had a crush on Jason and that the fire drove him to her place. That damn fire, did Steve set that?

Carrie stopped at the door to the waiting area. There was a click and the doors hissed open in her direction, she had to step back to let them clear her. She walked quietly towards the waiting area, Megan's words now echoing in her ears, the ambience of the hospital drowned out. Steve was in love with her, Meg was enchanted with Jason, what about Carrie?

When would it be her chance to love someone?

She moved from the small hallway that the doors were located in to the main hall and turned right towards the waiting room. Just outside the opening of the hall that dumped into the room, she paused and took a quiet deep breath. A tear ran from her eye as she steeled herself to tell Meg's story to Jason, but would she tell him the whole thing? She looked at Jason; his hand was rubbing Dusty's back and he had managed to talk the nurse into changing the channel from Fox News to *SpongeBob*. Dusty was wearily watching the show, opening and closing his eyes like he was about to fade off into dreamland again, Jason was watching it with him, smiling at the silly things the yellow sponge-man did, at the antics of his pink starfish friend Patrick and his cranky neighbor who lived in a steel Easter Island-like face at the bottom of the sea.

Carrie felt it then. It came as a rush, like an epiphany, it hit her. She *was* in love. If not totally yet, but falling at least, with Jason. She looked at the sharp outline of his hardened jaw, the soft streaks of tanned skin near his eyes from wearing his sunglasses nearly year-round, the brow that seemed always turned down into a puppy dog look. He was caring; he understood what her brother needed and was never short with the boy who had a learning problem. He was what she was wanting in her lonely miserable life.

His age was just perfect, he was gentlemanly about her, opening doors, insisting to pay for meals. He complimented her on her looks without sounding like the pigs that ogled her behind her back. When he spoke to her he treated her like a person, not condescending like many of the townsfolk did, like they figured she was dumb because she didn't attend the local high school.

He taught her how to fly. Trust. Even after everything that has happened to him in the last few days, he still trusted her and he was still kind without saying anything harsh about the people from Fallcast, like Parks who practically accused him of setting fire to his own hotel room. Like Marshall who was indirect about it, but still the insinuation was there and Mike from the bank, did the same. Carrie overheard what had been said at the S&J II, she didn't ask Jason about it when he got back into the Wagoneer, she knew he didn't want to talk about it otherwise he would have brought it up, but she knew he was troubled by the fire, who set it and why. Then accusations flew and he took it all like a good soul would. He was gentle in his heart, he didn't lash out.

Carrie took another small breath and smiled, wiping the tears from her eyes. She was falling for the man here, would he feel the same for her. A frown crept onto the corners of her mouth, what if he didn't feel the same? There was a moment between them the last night, was it lust or was he really interested in her, and he would have to be interested in her brother and his future as well as hers, if he wanted to be with her, that was it.

Jason felt he was being watched and slowly turned his head towards the hall. He saw Carrie standing in the doorway, leaning against the wall. Her eyes were moist and she had a smile on her face. He didn't dare say anything right now or move suddenly lest he wake up Dusty, who had dozed off again. The boy had woken in a panic in strange surroundings with no familiar faces. The nurse even came in to see what the crying was all about, and she agreed to turn the TV station to something he might like. After a few minutes, Dusty laid his head back down and Jason began rubbing his back to relax him, after all Jason's mother had done that for him when he was a child and anxious about something.

He saw the smile turn upwards when he looked in her eyes, those golden eyes. He felt a tingle in his side, moving from his belly to the top of his arms. He was falling for the young girl from Fallcast, and that could be bad. For the last few hours he was trying to put together a plan for his future, he was going to have to leave this area soon, but if he fell in love and she did the same, it would be so much harder to just pack up and go. Did he really have to leave?

Carrie walked over and sat down next to him.

"Is he alright?" She whispered into his ear about half a foot away.

"Yeah. He had a start, when you weren't here, but thank God for *Bikini Bottom*."

Carrie scrunched her eyes at him, "Who?"

Jason pointed at the TV, "*SpongeBob*. He lives at *Bikini Bottom*."

He took a breath and smiled. Carrie blushed, she was lost in his eyes and didn't realize she knew the name of her brother's TV show, she knew it well as a matter of fact, but her mind was elsewhere. Her mind was focusing on Jason. He was saying something that she didn't hear.

"Huh?" A deeper red.

He smiled and whispered again, "How's Meg?"

The name made the smile disappear. Carrie frowned and looked away, towards the TV up in the corner of the room. "She's... medicated."

"Oh."

Carrie wanted to say out loud the things Meg had said, '*She's in love with you and wants you to run off with her.*' And '*Steve had a crush on me and now he's dead.*' But instead she stoned her feelings and said, "She's had a hard week it seems. Steve's death is going to be hard on her."

"I think it would be hard on the whole town." Jason said without blinking.

Carrie half-smiled. *Yes, would say something caring wouldn't you. You're not going to make it easy on me huh? You are going to let me fall in love with you, head over heels as my mom would say...*

"Yes. I think we should be getting back to town."

"I was thinking..."

Carrie just looked into his eyes.

"How about a motel or something?"

"Pardon?"

"Well, the NHP isn't going to let me through; I don't have a Nevada driver's license that says I live in Fallcast. You don't have an ID at all, and I don't really think we should drive by that... *that* scene again. Plus, to drive around the other side of the mountain would take us two more hours and that would put us home around midnight."

Carrie lifted a brow, "You thought about this?"

"I've been lonely out here. Had to do something with my mind." He smiled sheepishly.

"I don't think it would be appropriate that you and I share a room together."

"I'll get two. One for you and Dusty and one for myself."

Yes, you would, Mr. Gentleman... "That won't be necessary."

Jason drove the Jeep under the awning of the Cactus Rose Motel on Highway 95, just fifteen miles from the junction of 201 and less than thirty miles from where the Cooke's Bronco rolled off the highway and into the desert flats.

Even though it was ten at night and a Thursday, the place was bubbling with action. Two people were in line ahead of Jason, who went in and left Carrie and Dusty in the Wagoneer. One couple was on their way through to Fallcast like the Jeep's passengers; the other couple had just been married in Vegas and now wanted a honeymoon suite that didn't have all the crazy flash of *The Strip*.

Jason waited patiently as each in line ahead of him was served and when he finally made it to the counter, the clerk looked troubled at his request. An East Indian, very short with a broad smile and a bad haircut seemed to be confused over the room count.

"One moment my friend." The man whose nametag said GURMINDER.

He began searching the computer for something and seemed distracted.

He smiled sheepishly at Jason and offered an apologetic voice, "I'm afraid there is only one room left. There has been a terrible accident up the road and many people are stranded here."

Jason looked out the window of the motel office and smiled back at the clerk.

"I'll take it."

Jason drove around to the back of the motel following the map that Gurminder had given him and to the spot the man had circled on it. Next to the pool, second floor, halfway down the balcony. Number 225. Jason pursed his lips as he stared above him at the room's door; he looked over to Carrie who was mimicking him, looking up at the door herself.

He sighed a cautious breath and spoke quietly, "There's only one room left. The wreck."

Carrie didn't take her eyes off of the door and whispered back, "Okay, you'll sleep in the bathtub then."

Fortunately for Jason there was no bathtub, just a shower pan and a curtain with colorful fish all over it. Matter of fact, the whole room was done in a seafaring theme, with a giant harbor painting over the bed-the only bed, and the blue carpeting with many dark stains. A single lamp lit the room from above the small round table in front of the window, a writing desk that doubled as a TV stand with a dressing mirror in front of the bed and a nightstand with an alarm clock that had plastic numbers that flipped down instead of a digital readout. Both the table and the desk had one chair each.

Jason had Dusty over his shoulder and carefully laid him on the bed, which creaked with resistance as he did.

The boy immediately rolled onto his side, his hands blindly searching for a pillow which Carrie brought to his head. She pulled the blankets over him, clothes and all.

Jason went about pulling the chairs together as a makeshift cot. He found the drawstring for the curtains and pulled them shut and turned with a start to find Carrie standing next him, nearly touching him. She was looking up with her soft eyes and that golden flash and fleck in them, her breath nervously shallow and intense. Before Jason could say anything she wrapped her arms around him and squeezed, pulling his body to hers and inhaling his light scent of after-shave and sweat. Her own eyes moistened.

Jason shuddered anxiously.

"Are you alright?" He asked.

Carrie let out a small breath and he could feel the warmth through his polo shirt. "Yes. I am now."

She stepped back and loosened her embrace then ran her hand along his jaw, which had begun to tremble a little too.

She said, "Thank you for today, aside from the terrible thing, it was wonderful."

Jason smiled. "You're welcome. I trust Dusty had a good day."

Carrie glanced over at her sleeping brother and whispered even quieter, "I haven't seen him sleep like this in months. He seems so relaxed around you." Her eye found his again, "I'm very relaxed around you."

A flash of heat roared up Jason's spine and sent spider webs of tingling tickles over his entire body. He shook for a second visibly.

Carrie felt his twitch and stepped back further. She asked, "Are you alright?"

"Yeah, just tired I guess." He shot his eyes towards the chairs he had set together. The pillows on each one looked comfortable, but the fact he had to basically sit up, worried him.

Carrie stepped into him again and another bear hug ensued. This time she nestled her head into his chest and she could feel his heart beating. She felt his pulse race through his arms, and took a deeper breath of his aroma.

She said, "The floor would be much more comfortable." Indicating with her eyes.

He sighed, resigned, and nodded.

"I've never had a problem on the floor myself." She said as she rubbed his back. It was coy and tantalizing. "Maybe I'll join you later…"

Carrie gave him a kiss on his cheek. Jason kissed the top of her head, gingerly, because he still felt he was violating some world order if he ran his hands along her body. He moved back out of her slackening embrace and grabbed the thick black and white comforter off the bed. He gave the look of it a frown, but threw it out over the empty space between the bed and the table. Next he untied the pillows from the chairs and again the thought of placing his head where who knows who had put their butt at one time gave him chills.

Carrie had gone to the closet and rescued him.

"There's two extra pillows here." She pulled them down and fired them one at a time at him with a giggle.

Jason tittered a little himself as he caught each pillow and placed it on the floor. Now came the big question, to undress or sleep in his clothes? He decided a gentleman would sleep in his clothing so he just took his shirt off, polo shirts wrinkle and he didn't want to look like he had slept in the same clothes he had worn yesterday, even though he had.

Carrie saw Jason remove his shirt, and his dilemma became hers. She hated sleeping in her daily attire, only having done it once or twice, a bra was very uncomfortable thing to sleep in and her jeans were rather tight, any movement during the night would wake her as the material would constrict certain changes in sleeping positions and Carrie was not really a sound sleeper as it was.

She waited till Jason lowered himself to the floor and she heard the ruffling of the comforter, then she flicked off the light on the nightstand and removed her bra through her shirtsleeve. She didn't sleep in the nude, especially when her little brother occupied the same bed, she still felt her shirt and pants tug at her every turn as she wriggled under the covers.

Dusty was snoring now. Carrie envied the boy, how easily it was to fall asleep when things were going badly for the older folks around.

"You alright?" Jason whispered from the floor.

"Are you going to keep asking me that every ten minutes?" She breathed back.

"Sorry. I'm just worried."

"I've been through worse." Carrie felt her eyes moisten. It had been a long time since she felt this bad. "We'll get through this."

"Okay."

Carrie tossed and turned as easily as she could so as not to disturb Dusty. She thought about joining Jason on the floor, but she hoped he realized she was using some gallows humor, to ease the day off. She heard him lightly clear his throat.

She whispered, "Tell me about your folks."

She could hear Jason ruffle the cover as he turned towards the bed in the darkness.

He paused, took a breath, "Didn't I mention, they're dead."

"Yes, I'm sorry."

"It's okay. They were great folks, but one night they got into this accident and..." his voice trailed off. There was no need to explain further, or warrant a maudlin conversation about them. "My grandparents are still alive though."

"Oh. They stay in touch?"

"When they're around. Barbados, Italy, Spain; they travel a lot."

"Wow. How old are they?" Carrie smiled at the thought of traveling the world.

"Both in their seventies. But they act like they're in their mid-forties."

Carrie wanted to steer the conversation towards something that was bothering her.

"Was Lindsay the only one, I mean, were you two in love?"

"As far as I could tell. We were close at first, I mean you know…"

"Like teenagers?"

"Yeah. But love is a hard word anymore."

"Why?"

"Because so many use it as a weapon. People use it as a wedge or even a hammer. They use it to get what they want out of life, out of people and girls out of their pants."

Jason seemed to want that last part back, but before he could say he wanted to retract his statement Carrie interjected.

She let a small smile cross her lips, "I know."

"Really? I'm not getting too personal about this, am I?"

Carrie took a moment to listen to Dusty breathe. She whispered, "No. I'm no angel I suppose. I've been close to having sex with a guy, but…" She took a deep breath. The sound was agonizingly erotic to Jason. "Petting mostly, if that's what you're going to ask next."

Now it was Jason who felt ambushed and the heat of blood pumping into his face made him have to wipe a bead of sweat away. Blood was rushing elsewhere too.

Carrie took Jason's silence as un-comfortableness, she dropped the subject. Guys didn't want to hear about how close you were with other guys. "I really like you Jason. I hope I didn't go too far when I teased you earlier about sleeping on the floor with you…"

"No." He tried not to sound disappointed. Tried. He cleared his throat above the passing truck on the road outside, "How about you? Is what I hear around town true about your mom leaving you dad?"

Jason could hear her sliding to the edge of the bed, the covers being pulled around her shoulders. He could imagine Carrie leaning on her arm, looking over the bed to where he was laying, staring at where his voice was coming from in the dark.

Carrie let out a sigh of resignation, it was time to let a little of herself out, "She did. She disappeared about the time things were going badly. She just couldn't handle things anymore."

"Did your dad beat her?"

An easier breath, this was a simple answer, "No. But abuse can go so much farther mentally."

"Yeah."

"It was in my family's blood to be controlling. It was in my mother's blood to be forgiving." Carrie rolled onto her back and raised her voice a little as the sounds of traffic outside picked up, "I miss her. Sometimes love means you have to say goodbye, without saying it to the person who has forced you away."

A car pulled into the parking below their room. The headlights though the curtains lit up Jason and Carrie's face for just a fraction of a second before the driver shut them off. Carrie could see Jason was staring up at the ceiling, his eyes were focused and fixed, he glanced over at her quickly; her eyes were looking at him, they were misty, but he could see the bright gold in them.

After darkness returned, they listened as the new arrival closed the door to his or her car, walked up to the sidewalk from the gravel parking lot, up the concrete steps, down the hall and then began stabbing a key into the handle of the door to the room next to them. After a few seconds, the lock turned, the door squeaked open and then closed. Jason and Carrie remained silent. Carrie had rolled onto her back and she herself was now looking straight up. The tears that came quietly rolled from the corners of her eyes to her cheeks and then down to the rough sheets below.

"Sometimes I think it would have been better for us, Dusty and I, if my folks were killed in a car wreck."

"Don't say that. It was horrible. It's something I would never want to go through again. Identifying the bodies. Receiving their jewelry from the coroner's office. Thousands of documents to sign. Court proceedings, judgments. What a pile of crap." Jason voice rose as he spoke, but after a few seconds he realized that Dusty was trying to sleep, he lowered it to a whisper again. "Believe me. It's much more traumatic. At least you know your mother's out there somewhere. She might come back someday or at least try to contact you."

"Maybe." Carrie sniffed. "I get so angry that she left, that she left *us* behind. Then after a while, I think about what she had to deal with, *who* she had to deal with."

"So some of the rumors are true?" Jason asked gingerly.

"About what?"

"You dad kept you prisoner."

Carrie let out a laugh. Not a blast of air from the lungs with a giggle, but a full on chuckle, "Well, I guess if that's how it was put to you."

"I don't understand."

"My grandfather was a member of the TFP, this super conservative religious sect started in nineteen seventy-three . It means; Tradition, Family and Property. I didn't know about it or its initials until I could go to the library and look it up. The TFP is a very strict order of the Catholic Church. We weren't allowed to go outside with any skin but our face and hands showing. Forget about swimming in the summer. We couldn't fraternize with other kids whose parents weren't with the group."

"So it's like a cult?" Jason was up on one elbow now, looking in Carrie's direction.

"I guess. Not like Manson or Jones, but pretty damn close." Carrie replied, with a hint of displeasure in her voice, "We weren't allowed mirrors in the house because vanity was a sin. We weren't allowed to talk to other young men or girls…"

"*We*? You mean your brother and you?" Jason interrupted.

"Yeah," Carrie answered, not seeming to care about the interlude, "Tommy and I. Dusty wasn't born yet. Mom was six months pregnant though when things really got out of control, or I guess you could say in control. In my grandfather's control. I suppose if he hadn't died back then, we'd have never met. Or you'd be ridden out of town on rail, as he used to say."

"Sounds like your home was a prison."

"Only in feeling. The house was beautifully decorated with statues of the Virgin Mary, other saints and church deities. Always fresh flowers in vases on nearly every table, it smelled so good…" Carrie smiled at the thought of the sweet smell of her father's home back then, "Roses, carnations, tulips. Whatever the season, whatever the florist in town had. He loved our family, I suppose we kept him in business."

The room suddenly seemed to fall about ten degrees. Carrie lowered her voice to a deep sharp pained whisper.

"*But the rules*. I could be educated by only family members or other TFP people. Outsiders were forbidden, in our home, in our church, in our lives. For young girls, boys were illicit. Boys were allowed to see girls, but only in family settings controlled by my father or her father. It didn't happen very often though. There were only three other girls my brother's age in the TFP family, they weren't very pretty and Tommy liked this one girl at school-boys were allowed to attend public school-but dad and grandpa refused his requests to let them meet her."

Jason could only think of one thing to say, "Wow."

"When my grandfather died, my father and brother tried to keep the faith. But temptation wedged itself in. Dad was always a drinker, secretly of course-my grandfather would never allow it openly-but after his dad passed, my father began drinking every day. He wouldn't hit mom, but he tried to enforce the TFP doctrine on her still. Drunks have little or no regard for rules after a while and he started making things up. When Dusty was born he accused her of having an affair. She just couldn't take it any longer."

"Where're all the members now?"

Carrie took a small breath and let it out slowly as if she were relieved, "The church burned, remember I told you that?"

Jason nodded. He had forgotten she couldn't see him. "Yes."

"After a while, the patrons began to lose battles with the city council for a place to meet. They wanted to use the school, but were refused. They wanted to use town hall, but were turned down. State officers came in to investigate that the TFP kids weren't getting the legal education the state required, so many fled into California. You'll see a lot of Mexican families that still follow the TFP guidelines.

"Others just packed and left, but only after charging the town with religious persecution and suing. It's been like fifteen years and it still hasn't gone to court. It's seems no one wants to pursue it, for fear that dirty laundry will be aired on both sides."

Jason was quiet after her last words. Carrie expected another question and when it didn't come, she rolled to her side again to face Jason. Finally he managed a statement more than a query, but it sounded as if he were curious.

"You got all this from the library?"

"The last six years. If I had to pay by the hour, I'd have to have three jobs."

Jason was digesting what the young woman with the dark Indian features had just told him. It sounded like Islam more than America. He wondered what kind of hurt would drive an obsession to the point Carrie had spent time-wise researching everything. Then he realized his own little obsessions. He knew how she felt. He knew what she felt.

Carrie finally broke the silence. "I... I'm not really as bad as people say."

Jason sat up. "What does that mean?"

"Don't they talk about me? Haven't you heard about how dumb I am?"

"No. Not at all. In fact, I've heard quite the opposite."

"Oh."

Jason took a deep breath. "I meant what I said the other day. You're one of the smartest people I know. And definitely the prettiest."

Carrie inhaled quickly. "Thank you."

"Why don't you come lie next to me? I promise to keep my hands to themselves."

Five or six seconds passed. Jason smiled. He knew that was a difficult request, he just wanted to be close to her for a while, like she deserved it. Her story was sad, but metaphorically, Jason felt the same way about parts of his life. He laid back down and put an arm to his forehead. The thought of growing up having to cover your body wasn't bothering him as much as the thought of living with the pressure of being thought of as better than everyone else. No wonder some of the townsfolk talked so badly about the Dodsons. They were probably treated like second class citizens by the family, and in rebuff the town made up stories. Told lies about incestuous affairs, covering up murders, hoarding the town's wealth as a way of keeping the folk in line. The Dodsons didn't seem like the evil family the town portrayed, not the way Carrie made it sound and Jason knew Tommy. There was no way he would ever be close to that guy. He was mean as the day was light, but maybe there was a way to get to know the old man. His new plan needed that.

He could hear the covers ruffling on the bed. Then he felt a warm body lie next to him.

CHAPTER TWELVE
Early Sunday Morning

It was four a.m. when the nightmares started. Carrie was walking down the long hallway of the L shaped Critical Care Unit at the University Hospital. She could hear a woman crying, it wasn't Meg though it was coming from her little cubicle of a room. Carrie walked slowly down the hall, her hand brushing the rough surface of the wallpaper as she went making a scratching sound.

She could hear the crying getting louder and thought to herself that it was probably the TV in the room, so her pace quickened a little. Just as she reached the sliding glass door, Carrie noticed it was shut, but the crying wasn't muffled like it was behind a door, it was loud and clear as if it were coming from inside Carrie's head.

Crying and more crying, louder and louder. Carrie was shaking as she slid the door open slowly, the scraping noise of the metal track on rollers causing the hair on the back of her neck to stand up. When she pulled the privacy curtain aside, Meg wasn't in her bed, she was nowhere to be seen. A flash of light out of the corner of her eye, movement, and Carrie looked over in time to see Jason being tossed around the room like a rag doll, or like someone in an old sci-fi movie where a person tumbles around the room from floor to wall to ceiling to wall to the floor again, only it was happening very fast as if he were in the car. Yes! It was like Jason was in the Bronco, being thrown about by it rolling.

But where was Dusty? Why couldn't she see him? They had traveled together in the airplane at first and then in the Jeep to Vegas, but she couldn't see him. She looked, everywhere, in the closet in the bathroom, even in the little cupboards that keep your clothing while you're wearing a hospital johnny.

She rolled over hard and fell to the floor from her bed. Instantly she realized where she was, back in her bedroom, in her home. Carrie sat upright. Seconds passed before she realized she was panting, a sliver of cold sweat rolled down the crease of her spine on her warm skin and the sensation that her face and the rest of her body was covered in the salty coolant struck her.

It had taken her several minutes to realize that they had returned home in the afternoon Friday; Carrie was nearly inconsolable, it was that time of the month-God's little blessing came-and the image of Megan sitting up in her hospital bed confessing her sins to her made the day a waste. Dusty was full of energy and wound up like a Swiss clock, the springs ready to explode, so Jason took back him down to the airport for some more flying, Carrie hit the sack at two p.m.

She cried herself to sleep and the next thing she remembered was the dream. It was a horrible ending. Death had come.

Her mouth was dry as a desert lake, it felt as if she had shoved a spoonful of flour in there, she tried to swallow but was rewarded with a sting of pain as the back of her throat was cinched closed. Carrie pulled herself to the edge of the bed and slid onto her butt, she searched in the darkened room for her water bottle-she diligently kept one on her nightstand-and found the room temperature water soothing and cool to her parched mouth and lips.

She set the water down and lowered her head to her chest and took a deep breath to let the images of her dream escape her mind, to let real time pass. Once the faces and thoughts faded she rolled back onto her back and pulled the pillow to her face, hiding her head from the chance of another onslaught of ill-gotten reveries. Tactile thoughts filled her head as she considered Jason in the next room, sleeping like a baby probably; he seemed to have no reason to have nightmares, his life seemed to be perfect. Money, great education, maybe even a family that cared for him.

Well, it was more than that. Carrie knew her father cared for her and maybe even her brother had a pang of affection before alcohol and drugs took his heart away, but being cared for in a normal family is way different than the corporal world her grandfather instilled upon his son and he in turn cast upon his family. The iron fisted and willow whip tradition of expunging demons from children so they grew up to be God fearing faithful that filled the plate every Sunday at Mass.

It was more than a comfort to have Jason around, it was a small thrill and even a moment of tension filled the space between them. Sexual tension. Carrie knew the geologist had "surveyed" her over, she wasn't prude. She stole her chances at him also, checking out his muscled chest and arms when she could. Breathing in his scent of sweet after-shave and a tinge of musk from his day in the hills or nervousness around her. Yeah, she thought, she made him nervous. She made a lot of people around her nervous and she knew the signs.

The more she thought about the man sleeping in the next room, the more relaxed she became and eventually she began to doze back to sleep.

Jason was again awake, staring at the ceiling and the shadows that were pronounced by the dim light outside. He'd been wondering how long it had been since he felt like a teenager, like he did now. She was commanding, beautiful, caring and even a little naïve. He wasn't a conqueror; he had no ambition of taking her virginity for the sake of doing it like nearly every high school boy had dreamed of. No. He felt intimidated at her lack of sexual experience, he felt as if he were a molester of some kind if he parlayed for her charms, if he was the one who managed to sweet talk her into bed-sans clothing and inhibitions.

But something deeper ticked at him. It had been a while since he felt this way about a woman, Lindsay was the last, he was wondering how long it would be before he would force his lips into her prospective space, hoping that Carrie didn't smack him across his cheek, but instead close her eyes and press her full ruby kissers onto his.

A wave of confidence washed over his body. He was falling in love.

At five a.m., his cell phone rang.

Carrie woke to the sounds of the TV in the living room. Dusty was watching his shows on a considerately low volume, probably advised by Jason to do so. After pulling on a small white cotton robe over her sleeping attire-a T shirt and satin blue jogging shorts that were way too small and revealed a bit too much cheek-she rambled out into the front of the house. Jason was nowhere to be found, but a half-eaten slab of toast, a bowl full of milk and a couple of floating *Cheerios* indicated he had been up to feed Dusty.

"Mornin' Cassie." Dusty whispered with a smile of affection.

"Mornin' honey. Did you sleep well?"

Dusty just nodded and went back to *Animal Planet*. Carrie drifted to the back of the kitchen to fill the coffee machine and discovered it had already been done, the coffee was made and a note was tacked to the bottom of the maker.

Carrie:
Got up early, early start. Went to look at that cave and finish survey of markers in the hills behind the mill. How about lunch? I have something to tell you.
Jas

The hike across the ravine was a bit more rugged than Jason had anticipated. Everything in the grandness of nature made certain proportions seem out of context. After traversing the deepest part of the gully, his scramble to the top of the first ledge was frustrated when he paused to take a breather and noticed a walking path that emanated from the mouth of the cave to a set of makeshift stairs out of hand stacked flat flagstones. The stones ended just a foot above the dry creek that ran the bottom of the ravine, and a well-worn footpath worked its way to a small clear area where he could've parked his Jeep. He couldn't have seen it from his earlier vantage point.

"Figures." He muttered to himself.

Jason returned his water bottle to the pack and carefully wandered down to the opening of the cavern. At the mouth he paused to feel for a breeze brushing past his body. This would mean there was another opening and possibly another entrance. The cool wafting air across his sweat-soaked arms clued him in.

Jason set his pack on a large rock by the inside of the cave. He took out a pack of Cyalume sticks for emergency lighting. The small chemical lights were perfect for just about any nighttime outdoor hobby and were easy to use, even if your arm was broken from a fall in a cave that you were probably not supposed to be in in the first place. Next, he took out a fresh water bottle and shoved it into his back pocket, the cool water felt good against his butt. A packet of snack bars and of course his knife. A nice hunting job that he bought in a store in Lovelock, with a large eight inch blade, a serrated top for sawing and a glow-in-the-dark compass set in the knob. The hilt had a small curved portion that fit his thumb and forefinger perfectly, it was designed like an old fashioned Marine fighting knife, though the most danger it ever encountered was cutting fishing line when Jason was out on a lake or digging a hole to replace a fallen claim stake.

Jason stepped into the dark hole and the first thing that hit him was the smell. Decay. Rotting vegetation or probably some animal that had crawled in here to die. The odor was light, whatever was in here had been gone a long time. Jason flicked on his trusty exploring flashlight, a Streamlight rechargeable, and the hidden grotto was exposed.

Just ten feet into the opening, the floors shifted down at a sharp angle into a low over headed room. If someone was walking around in here without proper lighting, there would have been twisted or broken ankles, after smacking their head into the rock above. Jason shined the light beam around to get his bearings on the rock room then he snapped his first green light-stick on and dropped it. This would be his bread crumb trail. He carefully eased himself into the first chamber and walked close to the walls, illuminating them first to make sure there were no living organisms that would take a bite of him for bothering it. Ten yards in and the cave sloped even more downward till it ended in a large room about thirty by twenty and nine feet high.

At the bottom of the first decline there was a six foot fire-ring made out of rocks, a half-burned pallet sat in the center. Black soot covered the rock above the fire pit; three large cracks in the rock above were a natural flue to the world overhead, venting the poisonous gasses out of the cave and into the clean desert air in the open. Beer bottles and cans littered the ground in places and there were even a few half-empty bottles sitting on shelves that were formed naturally in the walls by falling stones or rushing water at one time. Party-zone. This is far as the kids usually went, Jason thought. Maybe a little further into the darker areas for some petting or what-have-you, but not much deeper in. Kids were dumb in most respects when it came to safety, but they knew enough to stay close to the entrance. Jason followed a tube into the far back of the large room, dropping another light stick as he went.

Several small tubes or underground paths led away from the main room, but a wave of the light revealed that they ended abruptly shortly thereafter either by cave-ins with millennial or centuries old shifts in the strata. The large one Jason was walking in seemed the best route.

A road block. What appeared to be a cave-in of shored up timber and rock sealed the tunnel off to adventurers from going any further. Appearances can be deceiving, Jason thought to himself. He knew this was a work of man's hand and not of a natural collapse. The wooden planks and posts were arranged just right, like they were stacked instead having fallen from the ceiling of the cave. This was no mineshaft; there was no need for support, so the wood was an embellishment, an adjunct. Jason thought for a moment, then decided he had come this far, he would go further. Tugging at the smaller boards, he managed a small landslide that revealed an opening. This is where the breeze was coming from, on it was carried a stronger mixed redolence of stale vegetation, mildewed dust and the natural soapy smell of borate. To the untrained teenager coming here to party, this is where the cave ended, but to a spelunker, this is where the adventure began.

An ante-chamber was obscured by just enough rubble to keep any fortuitous explorer from thinking about going any further. Jason pondered for a few moments, wondering why someone wanted this area sealed from the outside, why it was so important to keep this chamber a secret from the relentless barrage of thrill seeking and drinking teenagers from finding it.

After five minutes of carefully stacking the rock and lumber to the side, Jason managed to make a hole large enough for him to duck and step through. He washed the light over the new portion of the cave to make sure there were no creatures, real or imagined, then he slid inside the cavity. He stopped on the other side of the entrance and popped another Cyalume, dropping it behind him as he carefully stepped into the cavern. He stopped with his light held high.

He was wrong. This was a makeshift mineshaft, there were crude timbers that held small portions of rock in place, not sectioned every few feet like in the mines of Virginia City or any of the other ghost town mines, the timbers here were concentrated only on areas that seemed to have been test-dug by someone looking for color or samples to assay. Shining the light at his boots he found he was standing on a sharp precipice, just a few feet from a ledge that dropped several feet down to a huge natural bowl shaped room. Jason estimated it to be about forty to fifty feet around, created by the constant shifting and grinding of the earth; pockets of air in solid rock. This cave might have been used by Indians as they made their way around before the White Man came and ruined a lineage of old traditions and beliefs.

Jason coursed the light around the ledge and found it to be varying in length from the walls, from about six to fifteen feet on one side and just inches of footing at the far end. As he turned sharply to avoid a spider web, the light slipped from his fingers. This is when he found the other entrance. A sliver of white light shone through a collection of rubble and timbers that had fallen to the floor; there was another room ahead, probably an access shaft made by man before the natural entrance was found where Jason entered. The opening was obscured by years of debris and was at the widest part of the ledge, so he picked up his dropped flashlight then sauntered over and surveyed the amount of work it would take to clear an escape route to the surface.

Jason figured about twenty minutes of digging and removal of rock would be enough, just for the heck of it. It was here that his attention was drawn away from the newfound discovery. Something bothered him; when he was swishing the light around the massive vault something caught his subliminal mind. He turned and slowly shone the bright white light carefully this time, not to miss any details.

On the other side of the cavernous room, he made his discovery. Jason first frowned at the sight, the shock. Then a smile appeared on his face as he began to put the puzzle of the whole place together.

The warnings of this area being private property and off limits. The artificially watered juniper at the entrance trying to conceal the natural opening. The fake cave-in hiding the ante-chamber. The ease in which a person could dig in and out if need be. At this moment, Jason made up his mind; he knew exactly what he had to do, what had to be done. A process started in motion days earlier, would be fulfilled.

In the darkness of the mine/cave, with his light pointing at his discovery, Jason decided that his future was here in Fallcast, Nevada.

Carrie managed a cup of coffee before the first wave of sadness hit her. Megan was in trouble, no doubt about it. Steve was dead, and she was claiming responsibility. The trooper had mentioned the brakes had been tampered with. Did Meg have the ability to do such a thing? Would she try to kill herself and Steve because he had a crush on Carrie and she couldn't bear to feel his tension over it any longer. The nights lying in bed next to him knowing that he was thinking about someone else. Was Carrie's face plastered over hers when he lay on top of her making love?

She shook the images from her mind and was about to stand when the phone rang. The loud electronic bell startled her and a few seconds elapsed before she could bring herself to answer it. On the ninth ring she reached the receiver and pushed the talk button.

"Hello? Oh, hi Parks." She managed a smile at the sound of Deputy Parker's voice. Then the smile faded, her soft wavy lips turned down as a thunder-bolt of pain struck the pit of her stomach. "Oh my god. When? How could this happen Darrin?"

Jason pulled the Jeep up to the garage door out in front of the house. Darrin Parker's patrol car was blocking the gravel driveway that encircled the yard in front the house. Frowning and wondering what was going on, Jason took his pack off the passenger seat and slung it over his shoulder, double checking that the zipper was shut tight. He took a breath and entered Carrie's house.

"Jason." Parks acknowledged with a nod. He had his toothpick stuck in its normal place.

Jason was too occupied with the crying Carrie at the other end of the kitchen. She was leaning against the sink with her head in her hands, hands that were wet from tears. "What's going on?" There was a tone of impatience and accusation in his voice, it was directed at Parks.

Carrie raised her head and threw her arms out, "Oh! Jason. It's awful."

He cuddled her, "What happened Carrie?"

Parks seemed hesitant at first then he answered as Carrie became occupied with sobbing on Jason's shoulder, "Its Megan. She's being charged with murder."

A pit formed in Jason's middle. "What?"

"NHP says that the brakes on their Ford was tampered with. They got the results from the state garage an hour ago and a friend of mine called me. Service line nut was loosened, fluid drained out. The sending wire for the sensor was removed too, to prevent the driver from getting a warning light."

Jason patted Carrie's hair down softly to his chest, "That sounds a bit circumstantial, Parks."

Darrin looked at the floor, then he took the stupid toothpick from his mouth and looked Jason right in the eyes for the first time. There was resignation in them.

"She asked Sal Buford at the service station a month ago about the leak. He said if Steve didn't tighten it down, the brakes could fail. The report from the NHP garage said the leak had been dripping for a while, but the nut was loosened recently, causing the reservoir to drain."

"Still sounds like bull..." Jason started.

Parks interrupted, "A trooper was in the room next to Megan's at the hospital. He heard the whole conversation between Meg and Carrie."

Carrie pushed off of Jason and went to stand by the sink, looking out the window. The conversation. They heard her claim responsibility. "She was under medication..."

Parks just shook his head, like it didn't matter.

Carrie felt the world closing around her. She was suffocating and her heart was beating so hard it felt as if she was ready to collapse right on the spot in her kitchen. Jason wanted to step closer to her, to grab her, he saw the faint look in her eyes, the whiteness of her skin as the blood drained; he knew she was teetering on the edge. He inched closer, but Parks raised his head again, staring right at him. Jason felt like a third wheel on a *bicycle*. Parks, Carrie, Megan, Steve. They all go way back, back to high school. Before the outsider came.

An urge of instant bravery struck Jason. He finished his small shuffle towards Carrie with a purposeful stride; he almost marched to her side with nearly an air of defiance about him. Parks just stepped aside, lowered his head and leaned against the table. After a few moments of silence (except for Carrie virtually hyperventilating), Parks set the toothpick back into his teeth and pushed himself towards the center of the room. He touched Carrie on her shoulder, gave a nod of acceptance to Jason and walked out of the room without a word. He did manage to get a "Hey little man!" out as he passed Dusty in the living room.

Carrie took a few moments to collect herself. She was embarrassed at her meltdown in front of her houseguest, the man she was feeling strange inside about. "Oh god Jason. What do I do? She was out of it when she was talking to me. They had no right to listen in to what she was saying, they can't charge her with anything."

"I'm sorry." It was all he could think of, it was all he felt right now. Carrie brought her mouth up to his and in and instant he felt her warm moist kiss on his bottom lip.

"I'm so glad you're here with me, Jason."

The stone cold iron lump in his stomach grew several inches upward towards his mouth. He took a slow deep breath, tightened his grip around her and whispered, "I have some bad news."

CHAPTER THIRTEEN
Monday Morning December 14th

Jason folded his only clean pair of jeans and stuffed the rambled remains of his dirty clothes in the suitcase he borrowed from Carrie. He debated whether or not he should sit on it to zip it shut.

"This was really bad timing."

"I know. It's not your fault." Carrie was sitting on the edge of Jason's bed. Her hands were folded in the *church and steeple style*, finger laced and her index fingers meeting at the tips, pointing straight up.

Last night, Carrie had managed to calm herself with the help from a glass of red wine and lying back in Jason's lap. He caressed her shoulders as she sipped the warm relaxant, she felt like moaning a few times in comfort, but thought better of it lest her mood be mistaken for anything but sad. She wasn't ready for the next step. *Yet.* She felt the need for him tingle in her shoulders where his hand touched her bare skin, even as he carefully let his fingers pass over and not under the thin straps of her tank top. He seemed too cautious; he also seemed in control of his ambitions. She would not make him wait much longer, if he returned.

Jason had revealed that he had filed a flight plan from Fallcast, leaving Monday morning heading towards Denver, Colorado with a stop in Elko, Nevada for fuel. He had to return his findings, his samples and rebuild some of his lost possessions like clothing. He would be gone for three weeks. Three long weeks, but he promised his return. Carrie didn't care about the details, so she didn't press for any; Jason didn't offer any either.

"I want you to..." Carrie had begun.

Jason hushed her with a kiss to her cheek. "I will. You're my best friend. You were there for me when I needed you, you haven't asked for anything in return."

"Until now." Her face blushed lightly with the wine and blood. "I… want you to come back. Here. To me and Dusty."

His hands slowed their course on her shoulders. He let his index finger slip up to her ear on her right side and he tickled the lobe with it.

"I promise."

"I… I'll miss you and so will Dusty."

Jason let a smile draw itself across his face, "Of course."

"I…" Carrie continued, "don't have many friends. I just lost another one it seems." She took a deep breath, "Parks is an okay guy. But I feel closer to you than anyone here that I've known since I was little. I can feel it your touch," She leaned her head to his hand that was caressing her ear, "I can hear it in your voice. You're so gentle with Dusty, you treat me like an equal instead of someone to be feared or respected because my father owns half the town."

"*A friend is someone who knows everything about you, and still likes you*." Jason quoted.

Carrie smiled. She turned in his lap and stood, leaning back down to give him a replay of the kiss from earlier, this one lasted longer, they both engaged each other's lips like teenage kids in the back of a sedan at the drive-in. She allowed him to pull her closer and she sat in his lap, her body aching for what came natural to two consenting adults. But he stopped short.

With a relinquishing sigh in his kiss he pushed her hands from his chest. She broke off the lip-meld and looked at him curiously, cheated, spurned. She let a sigh of resign wash past her lips and whispered softly, "I want to."

Jason stiffened his back and pulled close to her, fast enough to keep her hands tied in front of her. "Me too. Boy ooh boy. But I want to come back, thinking about you like this, we can have the best reunion ever the night I return. I promise."

"Is there something wrong?"

Jason smiled sheepishly, "I wouldn't be able to fly straight in the morning, I'd probably slam into a mountain thinking about what we did tonight!"

"I'm afraid I might be falling in love with you."

"And I... feel so... afraid."

Carrie bristled at this. She pushed away from him.

"Don't take it the wrong way please. Lindsay and I were so close, I thought I'd never love anyone else the way I loved her. But..."

Carrie cocked her head, "But?"

"I think it's time to let the past go."

A slow smile crossed her face. She leaned in to kiss him again, this time her hands were on his shoulders and she took his chin with her right moments later. As she stroked the stubble she pulled back and whispered, "I'm not an angel. Don't pretend you're noble or anything, it'll be alright."

He hugged her tight and spoke softly back, "When I return, that will be the greatest night of our life together. One of many to come. I'm falling in love with you too. And with Fallcast."

Dusty was hugely dejected that he couldn't go flying this time. Even though Jason let him help fuel the plane by running the hand-pump, he still seemed sulky. Carrie told Jason that she would pick up his fuel drums on Tuesday when they arrived at the mercantile on the freight truck, and she would deliver them to John Dickson. At first Jason balked at the idea, but after a very promising plea with a mouth to mouth kiss and her confession that "...*doing something, anything for him, would make her feel needed...*" he acquiesced.

"Dusty? Would you help your sister load and unload those barrels? I'll teach you how to fly when I get back, okay?"

226

The boy's mouth opened like a cavern.

"You don't have to bribe him." Carried responded.

Jason whispered back, "I'm not. I was going to do it anyway, now he has a purpose."

The boy was already to get to the mercantile that instant, it would be a long two days now that he had a job with huge rewards. Carrie saw his reaction and leaned back towards her departing beau, "Thanks a lot."

Jason just smiled as he jammed his suitcase into the storage compartment. Carrie walked around to the side of him as he did his pre-flight ritual.

"You know, I really know very little about you." She offered.

Jason smiled. He began working the rudder back and forth looking at the connections and said, "I guess that gives me the edge. Everyone in town talks about you all the time. It's like I got a manual from the townsfolk about how to operate you."

Carrie's face turned down, her lips which looked to be semi-pouty when she smiled, now looked completely limp with displeasure. "Oh really?"

She crossed her arms in front of her chest and followed Jason under the right wing. Jason looked at her from his crouched position and smiled as a red blush flowed across his face, and he said, "I suppose that didn't sound so romantic."

"Maybe you should pick up a manual for operating alone, upon your return." Her face remained emotionless. "Or maybe one on how to find a place to stay on your own."

Jason stepped back from under the wing and stood up straight. He hugged her as tight as he could, her body rigid and cold, fighting his moment of compassion.

He said, "I'll have a nice Christmas present for you and Dusty when I return."

Carrie looked down at the ground. If she was putting on the pouting act before, now it was the real thing, "I'd forgotten about Christmas."

"Do you have enough? For you and Dusty I mean?"

"Yes. Things will be alright. But I didn't have time to pick you out anything."

Jason put his thumb under his chin, index finger to his nose as if he were contemplating something, finally he said, "You know this little cross," he reached out and carefully withdrew her gold cross from under her collar, "get me one just like it."

A smile snapped her face into her satisfaction mode; she reached behind her neck and undid the clasp, presenting her keepsake to him. "This'll have to do until you get back."

He took it, kissed it and placed it around his neck. Carrie stepped behind him to clip it together for him, a quick glance to see what Dusty was doing, and then she kissed the back of his neck, breathing in his scent.

"Careful, you're going to find out a whole lot more about me in a few seconds if you don't stop that."

"Yeah? Like what?" As she slipped around him to face him.

Jason rapidly adjusted his pants around his waist. Carrie blushed.

"Oh." She giggled quietly, "Sorry." Her face went solemn again, "You *are* going to come back?"

"I promised you. And more importantly, I promised Dusty."

"Please don't disappoint him. He seems to have become attached to you. Like a… friend." She almost said father, and that would have been bad. As much as she hated her father, she was in no position to appoint a surrogate.

Dusty seemed to sense that they were talking about him and he appeared under the wing. He took out his tiny toy plane he had in his room and discovered after spending days searching for it, and held it up for Jason.

"No thanks little man. You keep it for good luck. I wonder if you'd like a bigger one though?"

"Ask Santa for me?" His eyes widened.

"Sure. We'll both be in the air at the same time, I think."

"Don't hit Rudolph!"

"I promise. Now, do you want to help me program my GPS?"

Dusty didn't know GPS from PMS or even *UPS*, bur he knew whenever the airplane man asked him to help, it was something new and wonderful. He nodded emphatically and jumped into the cockpit.

Jason walked around with Carrie in tow to the left side of the Cessna and flipped the battery switch on. He showed Dusty where their airport was on the little screen of the *Garmin GTN 725*, then he entered Elko's airport info by typing in KEKO. After a few more instructions from Jason, Dusty was pushing prompt buttons to make a little line from between a small dot that read FLLCST and KEKO.

Jason tapped the boy on the shoulder and said, "Well done. Now I'll get there safe and sound."

Dusty just smiled over his shoulder and began turning the yoke back and forth making engine noises with his mouth and yelling out commands to a make believe co-pilot. Carrie turned around and stood up from peering inside and rubbed Jason's back.

She asked, "Why overnight in Elko?"

Jason stood back from the plane door and rubbed the wing above him. "To fuel up mostly. It's only a few hours from here to there, but it's six more or even seven if I have a headwind to Denver. And who knows what the weather is going to do. If it gets bad, I might have to lay over even longer. Flying those mountains are the scariest part of the trip and I don't want to do it at night."

Carrie nodded. "You'll call?"

Jason offered a reassuring smile, "Of course."

Carrie practically leapt into his arms. "Come back to me please. I want to get to know you better…" She winked and he blushed. "And even about who you are. I mean, even if it's for only a little time, you'll make my life easier for being there."

Jason frowned and kissed her forehead, "I'm sorry I won't be there for Meg."

Carrie nodded. He felt her embrace slacken, "There's nothing you could do anyway."

"I know. But I keep feeling like I could help somehow."

"Call me when you get settled. Maybe I'll know more about what's going to happen, then we'll see."

Jason's face twisted into a smirk. Carrie wondered if she had said something wrong.

"What?"

Jason kicked at a pile of gravel, "I don't know your phone number."

The wheels of Jason's Cessna touched the asphalt of runway 23 fifteen minutes after one p.m. He taxied to a parking spot on the tarmac, set the brakes and killed the engine. Nearly four hours in the air is enough to take a toll on the body, crammed and jammed into a space the size of a mini-compact car, unable to pull over and stretch your legs, or take a nap in the back seat. Auto pilot is a dream come true for being able to move a little bit and Jason was sure there were a few flyers out there that power napped or catnapped while behind the yoke, but he wasn't going to be one.

He had hit some rough air three times on his jaunt, and each one would have been easier had he not had his mind where the Garmin GPS said *ORIGINATION*; Fallcast. His mind was on the dark skinned, bright golden eyed, American Indian half-blood young girl that has walked in his dreams for the last week and a half. Carrie had grown on him like a third arm; you didn't want it at first, but it sure came in handy at times and eventually it became part of you and your life.

Not that he didn't need a relationship, there had been no one since Lindsay and there was little chance-okay, no chance-that she and Jason would ever be together again. Carrie was beautiful, smart, tough, and she seemed to like Jason. That always helps.

But half his mind was in that cave, or cavern the difference supposedly being one is manmade and the other is natural, depending on what teacher you had in school. Either way, there was revelation that would change Fallcast forever, and Jason's future if he played his cards right. He knew one thing for sure, Carrie's world would forever change. He wanted so badly to tell what he had found but until he got confirmation on some other things, things he brought with him here to Elko, she would have to wait. That made Jason feel bad.

After shutting down his aircraft systems and making sure he was properly secured to the parking spot, he grabbed his backpack from the back seat and his duffel from the locker behind the seats. He held the pack close to him, this was his future. He was going to have to look up some old friends and call in a couple of favors, but he could afford that. The borrowed suitcase containing the rest of his things that wasn't destroyed in the fire at the S&J II, he half –heartedly drug alongside him to the rental car office.

Downtown Elko was sight for the eastern traveler. Old west storefronts met modern architecture, a huge looming casino and hotel centrally located and near downtown, less than a mile from the west end of the airport was a brothel, just off of West Idaho Street. All the world has to offer in sin and vice in a little town set at the edge of a mountain range called the Rubies.

The Ruby Mountains with Ruby Dome sitting at eleven thousand three hundred feet high, and Lamoille Canyon, a gouge cut from granite by glaciers millennia before man. The beauty and sheer enormity of the Ruby areas thrill the lone backpacker or the family on an outing of America's great natural landscapes.

One of the few places in the world to hunt the Himalayan Snow Cock, plus the ranges are filled with deer, elk and other major game. Jason found his excitement in the geology of the land, not the animals as much, but the clash of earth and rock. A mylonitic shear zone can be traced along the fault on the western margin of the Ruby Mountains, marking the contact between the igneous and metamorphic rocks in the core complex and the un-deformed sedimentary rocks around it. The Rubies are the collision point of the North American plates. The rock surges high into the air as fault lines scatter around the outside edges of decomposing rocks, soft rock and rock formed by volcanic activity. It is a Mecca of geology all in an area eighty miles long and eleven miles wide.

Jason gazed out the window of the Toyota Celica, not his first choice for a car but he wasn't going into the mountains for work, he was staying in town for this trip. The Rubies were lit on one side by the reflecting afternoon sun, the tops of the highest ranges visible were covered in a slew of clouds, cotton candy pink colored and textured at the bottom, pure white and misty as the swirls disappeared into the sky of blue above. Ahead of him downtown Elko loomed ahead as he turned out of the rental car parking lot onto Mountain City Highway, heading northwest into the city's center.

Elko straddles the Humboldt River and is virtually cut in half by the country-crossing Interstate 80; the highway that stretches from San Francisco, California to Tea Neck, New Jersey in the New York Metro area. With the thickest part of Elko's residence and businesses on the north side of the transcontinental roadway, warehouse and industrial complexes to the south. A population of around eighteen thousand that fluctuates with the price of gold, as most mining towns do, set in the eastern half of *The Great Basin*, an area of the western United States that claims more than eighty percent of Nevada, half of Idaho to the east and less than a third of lower Oregon.

At an altitude of five thousand feet, the climate varies as the time of the year does. Thirty degree weather in January to ninety plus in summer averages keep the city buzzing with tourism, fertile farming and ranching. The town itself covers only fourteen and a half square miles filled with the traditional city parks enveloped by trees which also line residential areas and a fairly quiet small-town feeling. Downtown boasts a row of shops along Idaho Street, not much unlike any other Small-town U.S.A.; with small specialty shops, banks, bars, restaurants, clothing stores (primarily western and heavy duty mining wear), casinos and jewelry stores.

The name Elko was reportedly coined by Charles Crocker of the Central Pacific Railroad around 1868; an animal lover, he saw herds of elk roaming the nearby Ruby Mountains and added an "o". When the railroad crews were finished on the portion of the Transcontinental Railroad that ran through the area, the town remained as a service center for the mining and ranching.

Unlike Fallcast, Elko has a modern look and feel to it. The town with its transient population that ebb and rip with the price of gold and other precious minerals is always fluctuating with new and forgettable faces. Fallcast does have that one thing that Elko has lost, recognizability. When you pass someone on the street, they know you. If you're just passing through you still get a wave from sidewalk travelers, even a howdy or a hello. Elko has become a city of anonymity; not as easily hidden in amongst the throngs of people like in New York or San Francisco, but a person could fall off the map temporarily here if he wanted to.

Jason turned onto Spruce Drive, and began to feel a little at ease. He could've turned left and gotten a room at the *Shilo Inn*, one of the better hotels or even downtown at *Stockman's Hotel/Casino*, but he wasn't looking for the noisy clatter of slot machines and smoke filled hallways with drunken cowboys or late-night tourists. The *Shilo* was nice and quiet, but not what he wanted either. He'd called ahead and made reservations at a small ten room jobbie tucked away from the downtown core. He was here on business after all.

Carrie had waited till the small plane disappeared into the cloud line that hovered above the tall Sierras before gathering up Dusty and heading back home. A few tears had dried in the corners of her eyes and was now a little crusty. She picked them out with a finger as she tuned the stereo with the other hand, steering with her knee.

She knew she was going to feel a little lonely; everything happened so fast with Jason that she had little time to let it settle on her. If that'd happened, it may have been a worse goodbye than it already was. He didn't see her tear up, most of the salty springs were for Meg, the rest for the fact that she had developed such a strong bond with her boarder and as most things go, she couldn't help but feel that Jason was just making an excuse to return home forever. Sure, he left a phone number. He had written the address of his apartment in Denver, a place called *Premier Lofts* on Market Street. He'd taken her necklace and kissed her and *said* he would return, but what were the odds?

She knew inside something wasn't right. That he was hiding something from her. Maybe it was the fact he could go where he wanted, he had a plane after all.

Carrie pulled into her driveway with another added concern as Dusty shouted to his sister, "Parks is here!"

The house seemed emptier than ever. Just two weeks till Christmas, the time for family and friends, parties and celebration. Preparing for the New Year and light hearted conversations over what everyone was going to do different in it. But here, things were going to much different. A new role for Terry Dodson had emerged from the ashes. A Phoenix reborn, he'd hoped.

A new partner in a new venture over the next New Year. With the holiday looming the thought of having to send out one hundred and thirty pink-slips to his best workers at the mine did trouble him, even as much as some of the town believed he was a cold-hearted man with a will of iron and a stainless steel grudge against anyone who crossed his path.

Cold-hearted. He'd overheard that one while sitting in the back-booth of the diner one night after a rainstorm forced the closure of the plant. Rain was as scarce in the valley as was the most precious of minerals, and one weird day the clouds converged overhead, opened up and the water fell from the sky. Nevada is well known for its cloud bursts, inches of rain falling in just minutes over a small area of dried sandy dust. The water has little time to seep in to the sun beaten desert floor, so it collects fast and rushes downhill flooding highways, lowlands and creating pools of mucky alkali and mud thicker than pastry dough.

Every now and again (once every ten years or so), a rogue cloud wafts over Fallcast and the Soap Valley and dumps for a half hour or so. This one day in particular, flood waters were building up at a weir constructed for the purpose of stopping what was about to happen. Buildup to a collapse of the small wooden and rock dam above the mill was inevitable and Dodson ordered the plant closed for safety concerns. He sent workers home and stood on the roof of the mill and watched as the weir broke and water rushed down into the gully across from the mine area.

Instead of repairing the dam the next day, he sent the employees back into the pit and the offices. A freak thunderstorm built off of the rare moisture of the previous day's cloudburst and once again water poured from the sky. Since there was nothing to slow or stop the collecting rainwater, the mud-flood came and washed away three employees' cars and buried them in the silty white crust in the six foot trench across from the parking lot. Dodson refused to pay for the cars. He even reminded the owners that they shouldn't be late the next day.

Cold-hearted.

It was his father that cast his iron will upon his child. It was his imitation of his father that branded and confined Terry's children. And the old man hadn't helped. If he hadn't died, who knows how bad things would be. His father would've blamed him for Marie Ann's disappearance six years ago. He would have even mind-bashed him for letting Carrie become so independent from the Church's wishes. To let her strike out on her own, and take her young brother with her.

Dusty. His last hope of starting things for the better. And what happened? His eldest had taken his place in the quick-tempered department then Dusty had ended up hospitalized with a brain injury and he and Tommy ended up with a restraining order. He couldn't even pass them on the street of a town he and his ancestors helped build and say 'how's things?' He couldn't even see his own son for Christmas. All he had was his drunk and anger-laced son Tommy, who was on his way back to prison if he didn't stop the drinking and fighting.

The sun was waning, the light coming in the windows from outside was glowing an orange-pink hue, casting off of the yellowish wallpaper. Terry rose from his chair and shuffled towards the kitchen. At the center island counter he retrieved a rock glass, walked to the fridge and grabbed a handful of ice from the freezer. A nice glass of Glenlivet, a cigar maybe in front of the TV and then off to bed. Early.

He had a long day tomorrow. A few things had to be worked out at the old place, the Dodson Mill, and his new job at the helm of Dowards was set to begin the next day. The transition was to be handled by Tommy, who was to oversee the closing of Dodson Mill in three weeks. Tommy had a nice cushy new job at Dowards as operations supervisor. It was baloney job, all he had to do was show up for work every day and look out his office window out onto the floor of the processing center, nod once and a while at the foreman and sign daily production reports. Hell, he didn't even have to read them.

Then out of the blue this afternoon Marshall Tedford had called Terry at home and wanted to talk about something. He knew what. The fire at the S&J II. He probably wanted to know if Tommy had some kind of alibi. Terry was going to meet the Chief at the mill around noon. He'd have Tommy standing there with him, to both intimidate the fire boss and to put his son on the spot. He was trying to get that damn kid straight. He wanted to see firsthand Tommy's reaction to any accusation. He would know right then and there whether the kid had set the fire that caused a whole new mess of trouble for the Dodson clan.

Got that upstart geologist his business partner and he had hired from Denver to up and move. Right into his daughter's house. If he found out that Tommy did have anything to do with that fire, he'd throttle the dumb punk for it. Now his youngest son and daughter had a houseguest courtesy of the arsonist, and that wasn't setting well with the community. Talk was cheap and so were the revelations about the new roommates. Word gets around. Whoever started that fire needed a good beating.

The whiskey slowly dribbled into the glass, the ice snapping and cracking as the alcohol touched it. The aroma of single malt scotch was as refreshing and exhilarating as a cold shower to Terry. It gave him a chance to reflect and remember the first time he had sipped a good drink.

He brought the glass to his lips just as the front door opened. It startled Terry at first; he hadn't heard the old truck ramble up the gravel driveway. His head was out of it. Tommy stepped into the kitchen, his work overalls slightly dirty for some reason. Maybe the kid had put his hands to work today, or maybe he was tossed out of the Horseshoe onto his butt again. Terry let the glass pause just under his nose as he inhaled the relaxing fumes again with his eyes closed. His mouth was watering.

Tommy was looking wild-eyed. His hair was out of place and he was fidgeting with his fingers. Drunk, or halfway there.

His voice was quivery as he spoke, "That rat bastard Ron!"

Terry didn't even open his eyes. He heard the ice melting as it sputtered in the rock glass.

Tommy continued without being prompted, "He says Carrie's shacked up with that rock sniffer from Colorado. He says they're a real hot item!"

The glass lifted slightly, letting the booze slide from the rim to Terry's lips as he inhaled again, waiting for the liquor to touch his tongue. Tommy was becoming impatient, but he knew not to rile his dad. His hands were wrestling with each other.

"I'm going over there and straighten this whole thing out, and maybe that punk's neck too!"

The Glenlivet made contact and Terry sighed as the rush of satisfaction overcame him. He swallowed a little at first, then a little more, then nearly the whole glass. He left about a half inch of the drink settle in the bottom of the glass and he took it away from his lips and opened his eyes. He focused them on his eldest son.

"No."

"But dad!"

"No. Have you been drinking again at the Horseshoe?"

"I went by to see what the fuss Ron was making. He's starting rumors that sis is sleeping around with that…"

Terry interrupted him with a raised finger, "That wouldn't be true. Carrie is not like that and you know it, she's just being over-generous with that kid. What'd you expect her to do? His place was burned to the ground, lost everything I heard." So much for bringing it out in front of the fire chief, he'd try to judge his son's reaction now.

Tommy was indignant, "So?"

"They're not an item. Not yet."

"So, let's put an end to it right now! Let's go find him and pummel his head into the…"

Another interruption, "And then I'll warm up the car to drive you back to Carson City? Is that what you want?" Terry sat the glass down hard onto the granite countertop; Tommy jumped and looked at it as an ice cube leapt from the glass to the floor. Terry continued, "Pack your bags for thirty years right now if this is what you want. Carrie's not sleeping around, she's not bedding anyone."

"But Ron says…"

"I'll take care of Ron tomorrow. You keep your head in this." Terry sighed and headed for the living room and Tommy followed, his head sunken to his chest. Terry kept talking in a monotone voice, "I have plans for that

239

geologist. If he absconds here without giving that full report to Doward, then we're in big trouble. If he gets mad at us for anything, he could just pack up and go home, leaving us with no papers to attract investors."

Tommy just nodded; they sat simultaneously, Terry in his blue armchair, Tommy on the sofa facing the back sliding glass door.

"If this Jason writes what his boss thinks he's gonna write, then we'll get some hefty cash to back a full operation, Doward's has the people and equipment if need be until other things pan out the way I hope. Hell, I was even entertaining a thought about dumping that jerk into the trash heap myself. But not just yet. Let's get what we want first. Okay?"

Tommy nodded.

"What's up Parks?"

Carrie had stopped at the store to get some snacks and was hugging the plastic bag to her chest. Dusty was already rambling about the yard like he was an airplane. Parks had his typical toothpick in place; it was bouncing up and down as he thought about what he was going to say.

"Came looking for Jason."

"He just flew off to Denver."

The toothpick drooped down nearly flat against his bottom lip. "That's not good."

"It's just for a few weeks. Why? What's going on?" Carrie stepped to her front door and stabbed the key into the lock.

"Tedford wants to see him. He was supposed to call before he left anywhere."

Carrie stepped into the house and Parks followed. Dusty remained outside heading for the backyard and the swing set. Carrie was becoming annoyed as she walked to the kitchen with Parks in tow.

240

"No one told him that and you know it. I was there, remember?"

"I'm sorry Carrie. It's just that guy gives me the creeps and you let him stay with you here and all."

Carrie could've gotten a little angrier, but she heard the desperation of jealousy in her friend's voice. She took a breath, set the bag on the counter in the kitchen and spoke quietly, "I think Tedford can wait a few days. Huh? I'll tell Jason to get a hold of Marshall when he calls tonight."

Parks looked down at this point. He drew the toothpick from his mouth. "Okay."

Carrie smiled, "Anything else?"

"Tommy's been making threats over at the Horseshoe. Ron and he are going to come to blows."

Carrie shook her head. "I could care less Darrin."

Darrin Parker nodded and slipped the wooden pseudo thumb back into his mouth. He took a small breath and staggered over his next words, "Carrie, I think that that Jason guy is bad news."

"Why?"

"I don't know. It's a cop thing, a gut feeling."

"Gut… or heart…?"

Crimson rushed to the temples of the young deputy. He could feel his face boiling with shame as he struggled to find and answer without tipping his hand. "I… I like you. Never been afraid to admit that, but still…"

Carrie stepped towards Parks and gave him a hug. His gun belt squeaked as she did, his breath drew in.

"Darrin, you're a great guy. If it were up to me, I'd hope that you'd look after me and Dusty. Hell, I'd trust you to take care of Dusty if anything ever happened to me, but we're only friends and I know how hard it is seeing me and Jason together. You'll have to trust me."

Parks nodded. Carrie felt a wave of uneasiness pass. She changed the subject.

"How's Meg doing?"

The toothpick went up again, "She's doing alright medically. But they've remanded her to custody, or will as soon as she can be moved."

Carrie felt a knot twist in her abdomen, "Oh my…"

"She's under watch right now, for her own safety, but as soon as the doc says it's okay she goes to lockup."

"She didn't kill Steve, Darrin."

"It's not my call. Sheriff says she'll be arraigned next week, in the hospital bed or not."

Jason dialed the number Carrie gave him. It was eight o'clock already, the day went by so fast since he wasted two hours with a nap when he checked in.

The room was smaller than the one he had at the Sand and Juniper, by about three feet all the way around. It had the usual accoutrements; TV, writing desk, dressing mirror, small bathroom the size of a New York phone booth and bad paintings done in oil that you could buy in an airport hotel lobby with a sign over them that read "Artist Clearance Sale". The room reeked as all hotel rooms did of cleanser and fresheners, stale air from the air conditioner/heater unit under the window and stale cigarettes-even though this was a no smoking room-few ever observed it in small places like this.

Carrie picked up on the third ring. Jason felt his inside tingle at the sound of her voice, the sigh as she realized it was him.

"Hello?"

"Hi."

"Hi. Made it safe and sound then?" She had a tingle in her tummy too.

"Yeah. Long flight, lots of rough air coming up through back side of the mountains, but I got here safe and sound."

A short pause was filled with both of them thinking what they wanted to openly say to one another, but just couldn't find the nerve to talk about yet, the elephant in the room.

Jason broke the stillness, "How's Dusty?"

Carrie let out a small giggle, "He's fine. He wore himself out on the swing playing *Airplane Man* flying around the world."

Jason laughed at this.

Carrie continued, "I think he misses you."

"I miss him too."

Carrie's face turned down, "Parks was here, looking for you." She began to fiddle with the telephone cord.

Jason's face went solemn too. Even though she couldn't see it through the phone, Carrie saw it in her mind. His voice dropped to a whisper, "What'd he want?"

She told him he had to call Chief Tedford and explain his absence, and then Carrie filled Jason in on what Parks had said about Megan, about the arrest and the upcoming court appearance. As she talked on, her voice began to lower, there were a few crackles here and there and finally the tears began to flow. Jason heard the distress in her voice, the pain of watching her best friend being accused and probably locked up was more than she could take.

A feeling of dread and regret washed over the inner being of Jason. The power he felt over his emotions was waning; he had heard Lindsay cry like this only once, the last time he saw her when she had confessed that she was leaving him for her new boyfriend; the twenty year older instructor and fellow save-the-earther. But this side of Carrie he had yet to see, the desperate for help for her friend, and Dusty's watcher.

"I wish you were here."

Jason cleared his throat carefully, "I do too."

"When're you coming back?" Carrie knew the basic date, but wanted to hear it from him again; she needed reinforcement, coddling, surety.

Jason held his breath. The truth had to come out, "I'll be back there in three weeks." Most of it was the truth.

"I… need a friend." Her throat hurt from crying, it hurt even more to be open and honest right now. "I want you here with me."

Jason had done the best he could to calm Carrie. She had sniffed a little more throughout the conversation, and he'd avoided the rough spot of admitting that he had the same feelings for her, that the more he got to know her, the more he was falling for her. The conversation turned towards Christmas, Carrie was going out shopping for Dusty. She would distract him from her main purpose by taking him to the S&J II. Mary said she'd watch him for an hour or so, the TV in the office was always a big distraction to him, it was a difficult request that Carrie was forced to make, since Meg was in the hospital and there was no one else to watch the poor boy, plus the daytime TV at the hotel office was reserved for *One Life to Live* and *As the World Turns*, Mary was making a big sacrifice to tune it to *SpongeBob* or *Dora*.

She had already picked out some items for the boy, toys and some picture books, he had some clothes coming and his father and brother had bought him some things and left them at the Post Office to be picked up because of the restraining order. Then she had asked Jason what he wanted and the answer was simple, *"Don't spend money on me please… Save it for yourself and your brother."* He also told her he'd be heartbroken if she purchased anything for him and they went without. She agreed not to spend any moncy on him.

Right after he hung up, Jason dug through the drawers of the hotel looking for the phone book. He found the local Yellow Pages and ran his finger down the page to a place he was looking for. One that was close to the business he was going to be at in the morning, somewhere he could get what he needed.

Then he pulled his cell phone out of the satchel and plugged it in to charge. After he tuned the TV to a commercial for the upcoming football games on CBS for next weekend, he began scrolling unconsciously through his contacts. It was only when *Law & Order* came back on that he realized what he was doing. He stopped at a particular number and typed a text message.

Feeling that he'd be able to sleep a little better now that he'd taken care of a few things, Jason turned the TV off and lay there in the darkness, thinking ahead. Weeks, months-maybe even years.

Carrie was lying in bed doing nearly the same thing. She was running the last few days in her head as fast as it would pass through her mind. Seeing Jason in town at the mercantile, running into him actually, then fate took over and they had been seated at the same table when the power went out, then the train derailed causing them to be stranded on the same side of town, the fire and now here she was thinking about him before she went to sleep.

She wanted to think about Megan and what she could do to help her, but her mind drifted right back to Jason. She saw the look of happiness on Dusty's face when Jason took him to the airport or let him sit behind the wheel of the mine's Jeep. He'd promised to let the boy drive soon and that was another brick in the wall of promises that she knew Jason would keep. For the first time in her life she felt as if things were on the right track, as if Karma was rewarding her for-what did Jason call it?-patience…

CHAPTER FOURTEEN
Week of December 15th

Jason was nearly skipping as he walked down the street. He'd attended to his business at the Mineral Sciences Labs office at nine a.m. sharp. The whole thing took roughly thirty minutes and the prelims were quite promising. He hoped that the rest of the day went well.

He received a phone call from the person he'd texted last night after his conversation with Carrie; he was given some helpful information and made a couple of calls while he sat in the lobby of the assayer's office. Another thing or two was done and it made him feel exhilarated that so much good fortune was smiling upon him. He thought about Carrie and he'd take the cross out from under his shirt and let the aroma waft around him it once and a while, just the slight hint of her perfume was left, but it was enough to make him feel energized for where he was headed next.

He had popped into a floral shop and paid two hundred and ten dollars for a bouquet of twenty-four long stemmed roses to be delivered to Carrie at her home on Christmas Eve next Thursday. It cost more than he had planned, but Jason was feeling generous and if things went well, then he'd be out a couple more thousand in just twenty-four hours. He had no one else to spend it on anyway.

He walked for about three more blocks, nodding and smiling at everyone he passed and finally he was at the doorstep of his last stop of the morning, Great Basin Jewelers. With a ball of twirling feathers in his stomach, he pulled the door open and the chimes of the bells made his mood lift even higher.

Carrie woke with a start and sat straight up. She had a dream that she and Dusty were riding on a train and the car they were in ran off the track. She couldn't find her brother, she couldn't find Jason. Her father and older brother were standing by the derailed car and were laughing at her, she felt alone and abandoned. Tommy raised his hand up to the sky like the preachers did on TV and said loudly, "He has forsaken you!"

A small bead of sweat paraded down her back, along the outside of her spine and as it touched the top of the small of her back above her rear, she could feel chills shivering every muscle from her toes to her neck. She took a deep breath and slid her feet to the floor. Ready to start the day.

After she'd hung up with Jason she had realized that Dusty had a doctor's appointment in Vegas this afternoon. Meg had helped her with that usually, driving them to town and patiently waiting for the doctor to give his monthly assessment of the young boy's mental status. But Meg was not going to be there for her today, or, for a while it sounded like. After making two phone calls at nine o'clock last night, both met with someone or the other being '*tied up and unable to help, but they sure wished they could*', Carrie dialed someone she knew would drop everything and be there for her. Even though it felt she was using him.

It was ten fifteen when the man walked into the room. He was dressed in a suit, a very expensive one that looked nearly satin. Dark blue polished shoes and nice light blue tie. His face was pleasant, he looked to be about thirty or thirty-five, clean shaven with little round spectacles with a light blue tint. His hair was combed and sprayed within an inch of its life and sat on his head like Snoopy did on top of Lucy's in *Its Christmas Charlie Brown!* He reached into the lining of his suit jacket and produced a card. He placed it into Meg's unbroken hand.

"How'd you get in here?"

"The police are quite responsible when it comes to an attorney privileges." The man spoke softly.

Megan looked at the card. She had just given herself a boost of morphine before the man walked in. It read RICHARD L. FERRENCE ATTORNEY AT LAW.

"You're a lawyer?"

"Yes Miss, may I call you Megan?"

"I haven't even been arraigned yet. How can the court appoint me an attorney if I haven't even been in front of a judge?"

"I'm not a court appointed attorney Megan. I'm from a private practice for a firm here in Las Vegas and have been hired by another firm to represent you."

"I don't understand..."

"I have been given a briefing about your case from the local authorities, I have spoken to the state police and now I need to talk to you. First off, I have to ask, do you want my services?"

"I can't afford..."

"Retainer has been paid in advance. The other fees have been negotiated and are in the works with the firm that hired me."

"I didn't know what I was saying when I came in here, they had me on medication and..."

The lawyer raised his hand to stop her. He gave a quick glance towards the door and then winked back at Meg, "Do you require my services?" He asked again, this time his voice lower and firmer.

"I guess so. Who hired you?"

"A firm called Trent and Donovan out of Denver, Colorado."

Darrin Parks pulled up in front of Carrie's house just five minutes before the hour she asked him to. He was wearing a blue polo shirt and jeans with white trainers. Carrie had to take a second look, it had been longer than she could remember she'd seen him in street clothes and he was standing in front of his personal car, not a prowler. She had seen the 1969 Chevy Nova around town once in a while. Light green with the back-end lifted like a dragster and tinted windows gave the car a racy muscle-car look. He was leaning up against the fender on the right side when Carrie ushered Dusty outside to make their appointment in Vegas.

She felt a wave of relief wash over her he reached over and opened the passenger door, he was there for her in a heartbeat, and she knew why. He really liked her and that was never a secret. But all morning she worried that he would feel used by her, he knew she had feelings for Jason. He nodded at her like a chauffeur, ran his index finger to his forehead like a salute and his smile was warm and understanding. He was a true gentleman and she could tell from his grin that he was doing this for himself as well as her. He wanted to be close to her, even if it was for friendship and not anything else, he was happy.

"Megan, please listen carefully to what I have to say. Do not speak of any details of the accident to anyone but me." He nodded towards the door. "Don't talk on the phone about it to anyone, especially your friend Carrie Dodson."

"But…"

Richard nodded nicely at her with a soft smile, "There are ears everywhere, here, there." He pointed to the phone, "I don't need to know details today. We will have plenty of time to talk so don't feel obligated to chat with me about it. I want to let you know what I know, so all you have to do is nod or say '*yes*'." His smile and another nod indicated he was looking for a response like he'd just described.

"Yes." Meg smiled for the first time in days.

"Great. You are going to be charged with voluntary manslaughter."

Meg's face went white.

Ferrence continued, "I need to know right now though, take a few minutes to think about it, would you like to be out on bail?" His smirk indicated he was asking rhetorically.

Carrie was seated in the doctor's office. Parks had wanted to go with, but the nurse waved him off and into the waiting area with Dusty. Immediately the boy went for the toys set next to the TV stand in the corner of the room. The TV was turned to CNN and the volume was too low to hear, so Darrin picked up a *Highlights! Magazine* and thumbed through the pages looking for *Goofus and Gallant*. Dusty had just been in the back going through several tests to gauge his mental level of comprehension, alertness and attention span and now he was playing games he wanted.

The office was decorated plainly with just an expensive wooden desk, three nicely upholstered chairs and the big leather captain's chair behind the kneehole. Decorations were sparse; mainly children's drawings of unknown things or animals and of course the prerequisite fifteen or twenty diplomas, certificates of completion and other accreditations.

Doctor Thomas was a nice enough looking fellow, of about sixty years of age. His hair had gone grey and was missing a little around the crown of the head. His eyelashes were very bushy and seemed to have a life of their own on occasion when he spoke. His smile was always relaxed, he never frowned, but his brown eyes did find a little time for accusation if he wasn't getting the answers or treatment he required.

Thomas was reading from a manila folder he held in his left hand, the file was about three inches thick, and

250

scratching his ear unconsciously with the other. He cleared his throat loud enough to startle Carrie.

He said as he looked over the top of the folder, "He's gone up about three points in comprehension. He's level still in A S (attention span) but there is a marked improvement in his alertness. He's also seemed to develop a new motor skill."

"What kind of motor skill?" Carrie asked, her heart filling with delight.

The good doc laughed a little and said, "He makes motor sounds with his mouth."

Carrie blushed at the joke. "Oh."

Thomas pursed his lips and put the file on the desk. "Has there been anything changed in his lifestyle recently? A new dog or a cat? Maybe a new neighbor?"

"We've… taken on a boarder." Carrie said, blushing even redder. "He lost the place he was staying to fire, and well, I'm letting the spare room to him."

The doc smiled. Carrie wondered if the smile meant he knew she was in a little lather over Jason the boarder or he was just happy that things had improved so well for Dusty. He cleared his throat again and asked, "Is this man a veteran or maybe an airline pilot?"

"He's a pilot."

Doc Thomas nodded surely, "That explains the flying thing."

Carrie let a small smile cross her puffy lips, "Yes. He does do a lot of that."

"Does the pilot tell him stories of flying around the world or something?"

Carrie didn't know what to say, she felt the truth was the best. "He… lets Dusty fly his plane."

The look on the doc's face didn't change. He scratched and a bushy eyebrow for a second then said, "There's this thing in one of my medical journals I've been glancing over recently. It's called hippotherapy. It involves using horseback riding as a treatment for patients with multiple sclerosis. It supposed to help the mind and the body. Maybe there's something to the way Dusty's treated when he's around your roommate. It might be the added attention or even the understanding of the boy's condition from the standpoint of an outsider."

"*Outsider*?" The name the townsfolk had for Jason already. Carrie felt bad hearing it this time.

"Yeah. Someone who has no clue as to the condition of the boy, so he treats him like a normal child. This might help in the long run; maybe Dusty is getting better a little because your boarder treats him normal. Never the less, we'll see the both of you in three months. We'll do full x-rays, CATs and see how the scarring is."

Carrie left the office feeling exhilarated. It was one thing that Dusty's skills were improving, that in itself would have made her feel like she was on top of the world, but to have Doctor Thomas suggest that the reason for her brother's better prognosis was the new man in her life made her feel like a child again. The first recollection of Christmas. That first memory of something that stood with you forever, in your mind. That one thing that made you smile, no matter how bad things seemed around you.

Then another thought hit her. The *new man*? There had never been an old man. Why would the words come to her like that? Jason excited her in many ways at times, with her brother and the way he seemed to listen to what she had to say instead of just brushing her off like a hick-town dolt.

As she walked the hall towards the waiting area another thought hit. Christmas!

Dusty was engaged in playing with the toys the office had for children and Carrie walked quietly up to Darrin Parks, who was trying to watch the news. The volume was so low, she couldn't hear it, so she imagined him trying to read the news anchor's lips. She smiled as he looked up and saw her approach and like a gentleman, he stood to her presence and Carrie picked up her pace a step or two and wrapped her arms around him.

The sudden affection took Parks off guard and he nearly fell back into his chair. Carrie put her index finger to her lips and made the shush gesture. She leaned in close to his ear and asked, "I need another favor from you."

Parks nodded and Carrie whispered her request.

The rush of happiness quickly dissipated like the morphine in the auto-dispenser when she pushed the button again. The thought of Jason hiring a lawyer for her was a glimmer of great hope for a bit, then it settled to a dull ache in her stomach. Carrie. She got all of everything didn't she? Meg's face turned down.

"Megan, what I need from you now is a written statement to me and for my eyes only. Can you write?"

She nodded slowly, painfully. Richard the lawyer took a small pad out of his inner pocket and a pen. He helped Meg position the book and writing instrument so that she was comfortable and then she looked into the man's eyes for a question. He saw this and responded.

"A witness says he told you to fix the brake line. Did you?"

Meg scribbled.

"Did you intentionally try to hurt Steve?"

More scribbling, this time the pen quavered as she wrote.

"Okay. Great. Now I want you to write me a brief description of what happened that night, including any details of an argument you may have had. Remember, no one will see this but me."

Meg stopped writing for a moment and opened her mouth to ask a question, "Why did Jason hire you?"

Richard patted her hand and she began to scribble again. He said, "I have no idea who he is. An attorney called my firm to hire me. I have no other requirement here other than to see you get a fair trial and be set free."

"I…"

"Mrs. Cooke, please. Write it all down. We'll talk over this stuff later when you're out on your own. This is a horrible place to make conversation."

Meg nodded. *Yeah*, she thought.

Carrie was whipping her straw inside the ice tea she'd ordered while they waited for their food. She was trying to think about what to say. *Funny*, she thought, *words never escaped her before when she was around Parks.*

"Thank you for everything, Darrin."

"My pleasure. I don't seem to get enough free time anymore and this was the perfect way to spend a day-off. Away from the grind, away from the town."

Carrie knew what he meant. Even though Darrin Parks had disappeared after high school to go to college and then an academy somewhere to be a deputy, she knew nothing about where or why he went. She also knew that getting out of Fallcast, even if it was for just the day, was a relief in itself. The town had a way of dragging on you, hurting your psyche, tearing down your abilities.

They were sitting in the food court at The Boulevard Mall just a few blocks from the golf course. Parks had watched over Dusty in *Radio Shack* while Carrie had slipped off to buy some presents for the upcoming holiday. She found a few great airplane toys (she'd found a large plastic plane the same color and likeness of Jason's Cessna and the thing was about the size of a small bicycle)- she knew to cater to his latest mindset, some newer bathtub toys, and some clothes from *J.C. Penny's*. A couple of shows from Screen to Home Video Store, some *SpongeBob*, some *Dora* and a couple of *Disney* movies that Dusty loved to watch. Hiding them all in four large plastic bags that she nearly drug to where Parks and Dusty were waiting for her, the cop picked the largest two of the four bags and flung them over his shoulder like they were his.

Now, as Dusty played on the carousel and other rides meant for kids half his age in the center of the food court, Carrie was feeling about as uncomfortable as a tick on a hot steel plate. Parks was jawing away like they had been the best of friends over the last six years and that made her feel even more out of place. She was fighting off the buildup of guilt in her abdomen, the tingle of the sense she was using him, even though he seemed to know and acknowledge it.

"I was thinking," Darrin began after wiping the ketchup from his burger off the corner of his mouth, "we should pop by and see Meg while we're in town."

Carrie was mulling over the newly discovered fact that Parks didn't have that damn toothpick in his mouth when he ate. "Huh?" She lifted her eyes off of his lips.

The red tinge in his face signified he had caught her staring at him, and that she wasn't paying too much attention to what he was saying. In the nick of time though, her brain registered what Darrin had suggested and she answered before the situation became even tenser.

"Yeah! That sounds like a great idea!" She took a quick sip of tea.

"Okay. I'll watch Dusty and you can go in and see her."

Carrie frowned. "Darrin, I'm not going to saddle you with my brother…"

Parks found his toothpick next to the napkin on the table. He stuffed it into his mouth so fast Carrie had missed it. "Stop it Carrie. I know all about how you feel about me and that geologist, okay? I'm offering my services for as long as you'll take them, as a friend and nothing else. There is no debt to be repaid; there is nothing that you'll owe me.

I'm doing this because you need to get out once in a while, *and* you need to see your friend."

Now it was Carrie's turn to blush. "I'm sorry if I made it seem so obvious."

Parks laughed and the toothpick did its usual dance in the corner of his mouth. "We hardly knew each other growing up, but we see each other frequently now and I want a comfortable space between us. Jason may be your heart's desire; I just want you to call on me when you need to. No strings attached."

The attorney left Meg. He'd gotten what he had said he needed to pursue the case, and at least, he said, enough to go on to seek a reduced bail or even to get a judge to release her on her own recognizance. She lived in Fallcast all of her life, she didn't work there, but she had nowhere else to go. She had little money so fleeing the country or even the state would be a major operation and someone would talk, obviously. Perhaps, the lawyer said, she would have to wear a leg bracelet with a tracking device that operated from her home phone and be placed on house arrest, but again to Meg anything was better than the county jail in Vegas or Fallcast. Her lawyer assured her that since the accident was in Joshua County, that the trial would have to be held there and not in the metropolis of Vegas and that made control of things easier.

Meg pushed the button for her medication.

Carrie and Darrin were padding Dusty along the hallway just in front of the waiting room on the third floor. Megan had been moved from ICU Monday afternoon when it was determined her injuries were no longer life threatening, but the admitting nurse downstairs had advised both of them that there was a policeman watching her room and no one was allowed to enter except her attorney. The mention of a lawyer surprised both the visitors, and Carrie was even more determined to see her friend, to find out what was going on.

After promising that he'd be good sitting alone for a moment watching the TV in the waiting area, Dusty settled into a chair and then Carrie and Parks headed for the door halfway down the aisle. A small cubicle was located directly across from the room, which had an electric lock that kept the door held in place with a magnet, and was released with a push of a button from the desk in the cubicle. In case of a fire or other emergency, the lock automatically lets go.

In the little nook with a small TV monitor that looks directly at the door and the hallway in both directions is usually manned by a security guard from the hospital most days if the room is in use by a low key suspect or person of interest, but today a sworn officer of Joshua County is seated reading *Sports Illustrated*. He heard the ominous footsteps of visitors coming up the hall and looked from his magazine.

"Jimmy Tyler!" Parks called about ten feet from the opening in the wall where the cubicle sat.

"Darrin Parker. What are you doing here?" The policeman rose to his feet and put the magazine down on the desk. He lifted a clipboard off the side of the desk. "How's things in no man's land?" He began to make a notation of time and names on the paperwork.

"Day off, Christmas shopping with a friend," He nodded at Carrie. "…and look at you, scrub duty…" He shook the man's extended hand.

"Hey, if you see Mike, tell him I heard he's got the job if he wants it."

"I will. It might do him some good to get out of Palookaville." Parks' toothpick turned down for the dramatic effect, "What's up with Meg?"

"State police put the hold on her, but we're the ones who have to post."

257

The deputy pursed his lips and gave Carrie a grim look. He scanned back to Parks and shook his head saying, "Been ordered by the boss not to let anyone in. And her lawyer said no cops especially, unless he's here."

"Meg watches Carrie's brother for her. The boy is down the hall and they're both a little concerned, she'd just like to see how Meg's holding up."

The guard took a moment to consider this and nodded, holding the clipboard out. Family is allowed; just sign your name here and checkmark family."

Carrie took the clipboard and filled in the spot the deputy indicated then marked SISTER on the log. She handed the clipboard back to Jimmy, he nodded to the door and said, "Only you though, I'm not messing with any lawyers…" Parks nodded and gave Carrie a reassuring pat on the back as she proceeded in to the room.

The room was small, but obviously larger than the ICU glass cubicle that Meg was in when she first was admitted into the hospital by air-ambulance. A small window with "decorative" aluminum bars on the outside kept anyone from breaking the high strength glass and making an escape that way, the only other way out is through the door.

A bathroom door with no lock led to a small room with a shallow sink, no tub or shower, just a drain, no privacy curtain (no curtain rod to hold a hangman's noose) and a low volume toilet designed to keep anyone with suicidal thoughts from being able to stick their face into the bowl far enough to submerge their head and drown themselves. There were no safety bars on the wall, no handrails to hang anything on or tie a bed sheet to.

The room had no shelving, no coatrack and no hooks to hang anything on either. The IV tree was collapsible if any more than five pounds was hung on it, cables and wires had breakaway plugs. The morphine drip was located in a small compartment in the wall behind the bed with access by key only and the drip was monitored by alarm if tampered with, or if it ran dry. The room was basically suicide/break-out proof.

There was no need to tie Meg to the bed with soft cuffs, her injuries kept her confined to the adjustable mattress. The look on her face when Carrie entered went from surprise, to relief, to pain in seconds.

"Carrie." Barely a whisper.

"Hi Meg. How're you feeling?"

Meg curled her lips in discomfort and looked back to the flat-screen TV, mounted behind a glass panel in the wall. "Okay."

The room was silent for more than a few seconds while each searched for the right words.

"I hear they gave you a lawyer." Carrie said with a hint of optimism in her voice.

Meg just grunted. "Hrumph." She cleared her throat, "You didn't know?"

Carrie just shook her head and took a slow stroll to a chair that was bolted to the floor near the bedside.

Meg raised her voice, "Are telling me you didn't know that Jason hired a lawyer for me?"

The sound of Jason's name shocked Carrie. "No… I…"

"Why not? You too busy with pillow talk to chat about things like poor old me?"

"Megan!"

"Big old flashy attorney comes strutting in here this morning, telling me to keep my mouth shut as if the walls were bugged. He tells me not to talk to anyone about what happened or anything else that's going on in my life and yet you stroll in here playing dumb?"

Carrie steeled herself and her voice trembled, "Megan, Jason flew to Elko on his way home. I haven't seen him, we just talked on the phone last night, and I told him about you. He must've called someone early this morning."

Meg looked the other way.

"Meg? What's wrong with you?"

The woman turned her head so slowly to her friend that Carrie swore she could hear a creaking noise. "Steve's dead. I'm under *supervision*, because they think I did it and that I might try to off myself because of my failure to kill myself at the same time. They watch me eat, they watch me pee, they think I'm going to kill myself. *Oh yeah*. You're shacked up with a good looking rich college boy and what've I got to look forward to?"

"Megan." Carrie reached up to take her friends hand, but she moved it away. "Jason and I aren't..."

"Sure you are. You just haven't had a free moment to do it." Megan looked out the barred window. "I like him. Do you know how hard it is for me to say that? My husband's body isn't even cold yet and I think I'm going crazy over your boyfriend who sent me a lawyer to get me set free..."

Carrie had no words.

"Yes. I have the hots for your sheet creeper." Carrie's face turned bright red as Meg continued, "Steve wanted you, *I* want Jason."

Carrie swallowed hard, "Maybe you shouldn't say things like that, the lawyer might be right about the room..."

Meg turned and looked Carrie in the eyes. The coldness of her next words resonated for what seemed like hours afterward, "Carrie, I don't want anything to do with you or flyboy anymore. Please leave. I could really care less about anything right now. I want to be left alone."

Carrie stood and again tried to take Megan's hand, but the injured woman moved it farther away and grimaced in pain as she did it. Tears formed in Carrie's eyes and she walked to the door and rapped on it. A hum and a click and she was able to push it open, she paused and looked back to her friend of over twenty years and whispered in pain herself, "I'm sorry."

The door clicked shut and Meg turned to scan the room again for any persons. She pushed the morphine button again, waited for some relief and shuffled her butt on the bed towards the IV box in the wall with the plastic butter knife she absconded from lunch. The little plastic bag with the utensils had one too many. *One too many*, Meg laughed at the thought, *yeah honey, always one too many*…As long as she upped the dose a little at a time, no one would notice.

Carrie took a moment to regain her composure as she thanked the deputy in the cubicle as he noted the time she left the room on his blotter. She walked silently down the hall to the waiting area where Parks and Dusty were watching TV.

Terrence Dodson was beside himself with fury. Not only did Chief Tedford show up at Dowards with accusations of arson, but he showed up with a deputy as an escort. The fireman boss wanted to look into each of the mill's vehicles, including the ones he'd brought over from the Dodson Mill. He had no warrant, but as the chief explained, if there was nothing to hide then there would be no reason for one.

After an hour of examining each truck and SUV, Tedford nodded at the last one sitting in the parking lot. The paint was still fresh on the curb where the name THOMAS DODSON was stenciled. Terry thought for a second that maybe Tommy should be here for this, then realized the boy would deny anything if evidence was found.

"What exactly are you looking for?" He semi-demanded.

"Each vehicle has an emergency kit for accidents and breakdowns. Each kit contains a set of six road flares."

Terry surged with anger and frustration. "How'd you conclude that it was a mine vehicle?"

"Got a phone call from an anonymous source. Said they'd seen a mine vehicle leave the area of the S&J II just about an hour before the place burned to the ground."

Terry's face went white with anger. "No kidding! Are you serious? That geologist was driving a vehicle from this mill dumbass!"

Tedford turned, after two generations in this town he was used to being belittled by a Dodson; he calmly smiled and replied, "Yep. Searched it an hour ago at your daughter's place with the help of Deputy Tenner here. Six flares all accounted for." He turned towards Tommy's truck. "This is the last one. If I find all six flares, then everything is okeydokey. If I find more than one flare missing then I have a suspicion, that will lead to a report and then we'll let the sheriff and the D.A. decide what to do next, Terrence."

Jason had finished his errands and was eating at a little restaurant during the late afternoon hour. A large window gave him the view of Idaho Street just across from City Hall and a park with a couple of baseball fields. Winter had at least settled in here in Northern Nevada, snow covered most of the ground although the streets and sidewalks were clear and the temperature was hovering around forty-five degrees.

By Saturday Carrie would be getting her bouquet, and he'd be home in Denver. If the weather held; according to the weatherman and flight meteorologists, it would. His trek would be much better without the rumble and tumble of high winds and clouds heading over and along the mountains towards his home, but he had to stop here first.

He'd been a friend of an assayer here since the early days when he was sent out into the field as an apprentice. Several years later, he finally made good on a promise to visit, and he'd brought some work to him in the little canvass cloth bags he carried in his knapsack. It should only take two days for the fire assays and maybe a few days more for the atomic absorption finish. Jason would be able to fly out by Thursday, and be home in time to enjoy the rest of the holiday curled up by his fireplace drinking expensive wine and dreaming of a better life. If things work out.

Parks pulled the Nova onto the gravel driveway, making the small circle to the front porch. It was a quiet fifty minute ride from Vegas, there was a constant noise came from the backseat as Dusty played with one of his battered toys. The front seat was the quiet area.

Darrin slowly pulled the gearshift into neutral and shut the car off. Now even Dusty was quiet. For moments all that could be heard was sighs from the deputy, Carrie and her little brother, his were breaths of impatience as he waited for Carrie or Parks to open their door so he could get out, he felt the tension and just kept to himself, he knew that something was up-adult wise-and he'd have to do his best not to get things messed up any more than they already were.

"So," Parks began quietly, "she basically shoved you out the door?"

Carrie nodded; she was looking down at her hands that were folded neatly in her lap.

Parks pursed his lips, the toothpick shivered from side to side and he looked out the windscreen towards the house. The sun was going down and the reflection was caught in the front window, the purple-pinkish haze reflected back towards the car. He took a little air into his lungs and asked quietly, "Do you want me to go inside?"

The wait for her answer seemed like a lifetime although it was only a few seconds, "Sure."

Parks let out the rest of the air in his lungs and opened his door and was nearly cut in half as Dusty by now had learned to push the lever on the side of the driver's seat to disengage the lock that held it in the upright position. He managed to get the seat far enough forward for him to slide out and he made a beeline towards the front door. Parks let out a little laugh.

"Dusty! Be careful!" Carrie was exiting her side and scolded the boy as he raced for the inside of the house. She took two steps and stopped cold, staring at the mine Jeep that Jason had parked at the end of the drive, near the side entrance to the back yard.

Parks saw her eyes were locked on something and followed her gaze to the Jeep also. He saw it too.

"Someone's been in the Jeep." Carrie said quietly. Now it was Parks turn to nod in agreement.

"Seatbelt?" He asked barely above a whisper.

"Yeah. Jason complained the other day that it doesn't roll back up all the way and he has to toss it onto the seat before closing the door."

"Thought so." Parks took his toothpick out of the corner of his mouth and stuffed it into his front pocket. "I'll take a look. Stay out of the house for now, stay on the porch where I can see you."

"Okay. Dusty, come here." Carrie used her firm and demanding whisper, the one Dusty recognizes as the *I mean now!* tone. He trotted over to her on the wraparound porch as she made the last step up. She glanced in the window, but the shades were drawn.

Darrin pulled the right side of his jacket back, revealing a Glock in a paddle holster next to the shiny gold and blue deputy star on a clip-on holder. He clicked the thumb-snap loose and stepped forward, looking all directions, but one eye was glued to the Jeep for movement.

He got closer and he crouched just a little as he approached, glancing into the back of the Wagoneer, his left hand extending out and reaching for the handle, the right rested on the butt of the gun, fingers splayed out, ready for the quick-draw.

It was the first time in over an hour that Carrie smiled. She had to put her hand to her mouth to keep a chirp of a giggle from escaping. He looked so silly, like one of those TV detectives. Dusty's eyes were wide as dinner plates when he saw the deputy's hand on the Glock, he held his breath, not knowing what was coming.

At the passenger door, the first one back from the driver's door, his hand made contact with the handle and he used his thumb to push the button in. The door clicked open and squeaked like a tortured mouse as he pulled on it. He stood straight and closed his jacket.

"No one here." He turned to see the look of delight and mirth in the eyes of his back-up. "Great."

Carrie stepped off the porch, and went over to him. She gave him a friendly hug and thanked him for his bravery. Darrin puffed out his lips and shook his head in embarrassment, then he noticed the piece of yellow paper under the windshield wiper. He stepped forward and pulled it out.

"What is it?"

"Mike's card." Parks flipped the card over and read the scribble on the back, "Missed you two, here with Tedford, arson investigation. Everything is okay though. See you tonight. M T."

"Arson? Jason's hotel fire?" Carrie asked, her voice pooled with concern. She had forgotten the whole fire thing, with everything else going on.

Parks nodded and dug the toothpick from his pocket. He brushed off a piece of tan lint and slipped it into its place. "There was evidence of a road flare that was used to start the fire."

"Oh. I didn't know."

Parks exhaled. "Jason didn't tell you?"

"No. He never said anything about it when we left that day."

Darrin looked back at the rear of the Jeep, at the mine's lock box kept there. "Checking for flares would be my bet."

"But he said everything was okay…"

"Yeah."

Carrie looked at the lockbox then back to Parks. He had a look of sadness mixed with determination on his face. Jealousy.

"Let's go in, huh?" She offered.

The toothpick dove down then quickly perked up. "Okay."

"What the hell are you talking about?" Tommy Dodson was standing in the doorway to his dad's new office at the Dowards Mill.

"They found all six road flares missing from the box in your truck. Did you start that fire?" Their voices carried high and loud throughout the building, only the janitor was left and he kept out of sight, doing his job.

"I told you I didn't!" Tommy began to protest more, but Terry held up one index finger.

"Tedford and Tenner. They saw all they needed to see. Your pickup, six flares missing. Let me tell you how that made me feel, standing there defending you as they opened that damn box!"

"Dad…"

"Shut up!"

Tommy lowered his head in defeat; Terry took this for resignation and crossed his arms in front of his chest. He was sitting behind his desk, but now he rose to the center of the room to close the distance to his son. Tommy looked up and the look of fear in his eyes shook his father.

266

Tommy asked, "So now what? They lock me up again?"

Terry just looked at his shoes and shook his head, the anger had subsided. He said, "I don't know. They'll file a report; the report goes to the D.A. It's his from there. Right now all they have is a box missing some flares."

"Can they do a match? I mean, can they do some of that CSI stuff and tell if it was from those flares?"

"I suspect."

Tommy mulled over this for a moment. "It was that bastard geologist. I bet he switched boxes on me."

Terry felt two furies rising in his chest. One for his son's accusation, one for Jason Parmenter. "Why? So he could burn all of his stuff? To become homeless?"

"To get Carrie to ask him to stay with her..." Tommy added coldly. "I'm just sayin' this could get me off! We can tell the D.A. that the geologist..."

"You want me to tell the law that a nice quiet geologist set fire to a hotel so he could get a room with my daughter?"

Tommy shrugged his shoulders with a big sly smile, "It might work. Get them off of me for a while."

Terry looked away. In his mind, he knew that his eldest had done it now, how could his own be so clumsy and stupid as to think he could get away with it? All of his plans were falling apart now, if Tommy goes to jail then suspicion falls back to the Dodson clan, of just being a mob of tyrants, trying to stronghold the town. An image he wanted changed. He wanted to be seen as the savior of Fallcast, the man who had the foresight to join forces with a rival mill owner to pull money from the ground.

But he needed that geologist from Denver to say the right things, do the right things. He needed a report that favored what the kid had told his boss a week ago, he needed that Parmenter guy. If he or Tommy went to the sheriff with the cockamamie story about Jason setting the fire at his hotel to get a cozy room with Carrie, just to save his stupid son's skin, not only would they laugh at him, they might just put the fear of hell into the college kid and he'll fly right permanently out of this dustbowl and take his report with him. That hurts Fallcast. That hurts Terrence Dodson. He made the decision right then and there, he would have to act fast to enact his plan, the one he made while sitting outside of his mill drinking coffee with Marcus Doward, the future of this town and the Dodson fortune were depending on it. Tommy would have to pay for his crime. Maybe this time he'll wise up. Maybe.

CHAPTER FIFTEEN
Tuesday Evening and the Week Ahead

"Hello?"

"Hi! It's me. Miss me yet?"

"Oh! Jason. Sorry I was just seeing Parks out. He stayed with me and Dusty today after he drove us to Vegas."

There was a long pause, then Jason said, "Slow down, I think you're three sentences ahead of me."

Carrie smiled. She was so excited to hear his voice; she threw everything out there for him at once. She took a deep reverberating breath and started over. "Sorry. Been a long day. I forgot that today was Dusty's doctor's appointment…"

Carrie filled Jason in on her day, she started with the joy of what the doctor had to say about Dusty's progress, Jason laughed when he heard it and told her he was happy to hear that Dusty was doing better. He denied he had anything to do with it; it may be that Dusty was growing out of his injury and maturity will see him even better than he is now. Carrie *denied* that, she was insistent that it was the new interest in the Airplane Man that made Dusty more responsive. Then Carrie told her story about what had happened at the hospital, how excited she was to see Meg, how Meg treated her like a grocery bag of dog poop.

"Thank you for the lawyer by the way. I know Meg doesn't understand now, but she will. I can't ever repay you for what you did…" Carrie's voice trailed off as she fought back burning tears.

"I know she means a lot to you and Dusty. It's the least I could do for you after you took me in."

"But it must be so expensive…"

Jason almost blurted out that he might have a new found fortune coming his way, but instead he took the lesser route, "I had some money saved up. It was just going nowhere in the bank, at least it'll help someone who needs it."

"Thank you." Carrie paused to take a relaxing breath. It was so good to hear his voice. "So, yes. I do miss you. Dusty does too."

"Sounds like you've had company though." Jason said through a smile. He gave a little hint of fake jealousy to tease her a little.

Carrie had forgotten about Parks. "Oh! It's nothing okay? He was a friend indeed for this friend in need, he offered his services. We had a nice chat about Meg when we got home that's all."

"Oh really?" A double dose of mock jealousy.

"C'mon Jason. He's a friend of Meg too. I just needed someone to talk to and he was here, I wish I could've had your shoulder to cry on…"

Triple shot, "You cried on his shoulder?"

Carrie felt as if she was losing her defense for having another man in her house, but why was she so defensive in the first place? She knew why, she was falling in love with Jason and she had muddled things up by inviting Darrin Parker into her house, she…

Jason interrupted her thoughts, "Carrie. I'm just kidding. I like Parks; he seems like a good friend to have, I wish I was there for you, but if I couldn't be, I glad you had some help from him."

Carrie blushed. *Was he serious?* "Are you serious?" She asked.

"Of course. Parks is a good man. I trust the both of you."

"Trust?"

"Carrie…" Jason struggled to find the right words, "I really like you, a lot. This whole trip was bad timing, just when you and I were getting closer. If Darrin Parker wins your heart, then it just the way things must be. But I want to have a chance at winning it back."

Carrie smiled at the thought she was caught in the middle, then she realized, "Are you playing me with this jealousy act?"

Jason laughed. "A little." Another bout of laughter and then, "I know you feel something for me. No need to defend yourself."

"Thanks for the credit."

Jason took a slow breath, "I miss you. I'll see you after the holidays, I promise."

They talked for nearly an hour, both seriously as Carrie explained Meg's position, then half-heartedly about the upcoming holidays, and what she'd bought for Dusty."

"Anything for me?" She asked coyly.

"I bought you a necklace."

"You weren't supposed to tell me! It's supposed to be a surprise!"

"Oh. Well, in that case, I won't tell you what I really got you."

Carrie heard a beeping in the background.

"Dammit, it's my cell." Jason said. "I'll call you tomorrow okay?"

Carrie paused, and then smiled into the receiver, "Okay."

"I'm falling in love with you. And goodnight."

Carrie's mouth fell open, her heart squished rapidly and her chest felt light. A rush of adrenaline surged through her bloodstream to the point she felt a flash of heat, like the sensation on your arm when you drop a slab of bacon into a simmering pan. She heard the double click of the phone resetting on the other end and then the tell-tale sound of the three tones rising in pitch with a woman's voice saying, "*If you'd like to make a call, please hang up...*"

Jason smiled as he heard her catch her breath just before he pushed the plunger down on the phone. His mind wandered about her beauty, her smile, her kiss as he was getting ready to leave, and then his cell phone rang again, breaking his daydream. He frowned as he looked at the caller ID.

"Yeah Dave?"

Carrie finally cradled the receiver, as slow as she could, hoping to make the feeling she had in her body last as long as possible. The tingle started to subside a little in her chest, but it left a trail of shivers down her spine and a warm revolving sensation in her lower abdomen, her legs twitched sharply and she crossed them over one another.

Her face felt warm and cold at the same time, she could almost see the blotches of blush on her cheeks and the pale edges around her eyes as the tears of love and joy fought to break the barrier and seep to her cheeks. It is no secret now, at least to her. She's in love with Jason.

Years of wanting a relationship that didn't feel based on how her father or brother felt how she should run her life, she felt so alone at times, especially after the last few years taking care of Dusty day and night with just a few small breaks in between when Meg would take care of her little brother.

Meg. Oh boy, Carrie thought, *she's going to go through the roof with this one, Jason and me telling each other that they are falling in love.*

Jason hung up with his boss in Denver. Things had gone from happy thoughts to dread; from jubilation over talking with Carrie, to fear for what was coming next, and it was going to be big. The new foreman and plant manager at the Dowards Mill wants to see him as soon as possible. Terrence Dodson. Father of Tommy the drunk bar-fighter, father of Dusty the poor boy who was shot in the head, and father of Carrie Marie-the woman he just professed his growing love for.

272

He was dead. Dead as sure as anyone who had messed with her before at least. He was going to have to think of something fast, because his trip to Denver was cut short by two weeks, his boss ordered him to return to Fallcast the Monday after Christmas. *No ifs ands or buts about it*. Jason would barely have time to finish up what he had to do here in Elko, fly home (if the weather holds) and fly back to Fallcast (if the weather holds), and Dave told him weather was not an excuse.

'Get your butt on a commercial flight and rent a car if you have to.' Was Dave's response to Jason using the weather as an excuse. *'Dodson wants you in his office Monday the twenty-eighth, nine a.m. sharp, no excuses. Listen Jason, he's pretty pissed off about something that's for sure. He wants a complete update, he wants you to give it and he wants it yesterday.'*

A knot formed in Jason's stomach, he knew he could get out of any trouble with Dodson if he had to, there was a secret that few in town probably knew about-if any-but Jason also was falling in love with the man's daughter even though Terrence wasn't allowed around her by restraining order, Dodson would see that some harm or worse would come to Jason, if he had the chance and Jason wouldn't let that chance happen. He'd be there in two weeks, bright and early with bells on. His report would make sure that his boss didn't get any more angry phone calls.

Carrie had to go into Dusty's room three times to get the boy up and ready. She'd spent an hour after that with his lessons for the morning; with several more planned for the afternoon, but the boy's head just wasn't in the right place. He would stare out the window towards the airport. He would fidget with his hands in his lap. Carrie was exhausted.

She inhaled and looked at the boy sitting with face turned towards the window and asked quietly to see if he was listening, "I guess we should go get Jason's fuel from Baylee's, huh?"

Dusty's head turned so fast towards his sister she swore it was going to snap off or at least he'd need a cervical collar from whiplash. "Yeah!"

His feet barely touched the ground as they took Jason's lent Jeep up to the Sage and Juniper to borrow Jack's pickup, then they drove over to Baylee's Mercantile to see if the freight had been delivered this week, especially Jason's fuel. It had and after buying Dusty a rock-candy stick, he helped his sister and Eldred load the two barrels into the bed of the F-250. She was off to play delivery girl.

The cool air had come in to settle again, even though it had been in the fifties and sixties this week, the days were dropping into the lower fifties and forties and even down below freezing at nights. The Dodsons arrived around lunchtime at the Glow Worm Ranch.

John Dickson was strolling out of the barn when he saw the duo in the Ford coming up the last few miles of dirt and gravel washboard road and waved them around to the back of the barn when he saw the drums in the back. After ten minutes of wrangling the heavy fuel containers off the truck and onto the ground, then rolling them over to where the original drums were, John pulled a pack of Camels from his pocket and torched the end of one up.

He blew out a long thin line of blue smoke and smiled at Carrie, who was sweating a little and Dusty, who was playing with the drum-dolly. "So he'd figured you'd just bring them out here yourself and flew off ch?"

"He had to get back to Denver for some reason." Carrie said with an apology. "It's important. Besides, we needed the exercise." She nodded at her brother.

John just stared at her as he inhaled another lung full of smoke. He drew out his shortened pencil and licked the lead end, stepped to the wall where he had written the prior week:

TWO BARRELS PLANE GAS FOR TWO BARRELS WHEN MINE GET TO THE MERCANTILE JASON PARMENTER.

and added underneath,

PAID IN FULL

Carrie nodded her approval of the end of the debt and rubbed her dirty hands on a rag that was sitting on the old workbench. She felt as if she needed to add something to the conversation, to defend Jason for not being here himself.

"He had to fly to Elko Monday, so he could be back in Denver by yesterday afternoon."

The cigarette hanging out of John's mouth drooped. He'd had his back to her when she began explaining and slowly turned with a near flair of the dramatic to face her. "*Elko?*" There was accusation in his tone.

"Yeah."

John took the smoke from his mouth and looked for a spot on the dirt floor to drop it and stomp it out. The butt stuck to the bottom of his boot and he had to rub it on the ground a few times to get it off. His gaze went back to the young girl's eyes and he sighed heavily.

Carrie saw the reaction and felt a little puzzled, "What?"

John pursed his lips, then took a rag out of his back pocket and wiped his forehead. While stuffing the rag back in where it came from he began slowly, "Well… Been a long time since I flew up that ways, but I never went through Elko. I always flew through southern Utah and across." He rubbed his chin as if he were trying to think of a reason to fly north to Elko before flying west. "Don't know why he'd want to go so far out of his way…"

Carrie looked down. She knew Jason wouldn't intentionally deceive her, or at least she hoped he wouldn't, but she felt silly for thinking he had for a moment. "I guess he had other business there first, or something."

John saw the worried reaction in the girl's face and smiled when she brought her eyes up to his. "Yeah, that's what it was. Lots of mining goin' on in Elko." He stepped over to her and wrapped his arm around her shoulder. "C'mon. The missus has got lunch goin for us."

Carrie smiled at him and nodded. Dusty followed along. He liked eating here, it was always a feast.

After lunch, Carrie took the truck back to the S&J and thanked Mary for its use. She hesitated at the door for a moment and asked, "Mary, could you watch my brother for a little while? I have to go pick up something and he's a handful."

Mary looked up from the desk to protest, but she noticed Carrie was nodding at the fake Christmas tree in the corner and she got the hint. "Sure honey. Be back by four though, *Judge Judy* and all…" She gave a sharp twitch with her head towards the TV mounted on the wall.

Carrie smiled and changed the channel to SpongeBob for her brother and gave him a kiss on the forehead. "Don't be a problem for Mary and I'll bring you something back, okay?"

Most other kids would start making a verbal list of what they wanted brought back, but Dusty nodded, looked up to the TV and was lost in the world of *Bikini Bottom.*

Carrie dashed out the door before Mary or Dusty got the chance to change their minds. She headed on foot down Main towards the mercantile, her head in a clutter of why Jason would go to Elko, he hadn't said anything about business there, and John was trustworthy enough and a pilot himself to know the fastest route to Denver. She pulled her leather duster tighter around her collar and stepped across the side street towards the mercantile when she ran smack-dab, literally, into her father.

"I'm sorry." He started.

"You are not supposed to be anywhere this close to me!" Her voice was on the edge of a pant. She started to cross across Main to get out of his way when he put up a hand.

"*Carrie?*"

Maybe it was something in his voice, it was almost a plea. It touched her heart after being filtered through her mind. Over the years she'd learned to know her father's tones, from jealousy to condescending. This was an altogether new one out of the hundreds he had. It was sad, like a child who'd discovered his goldfish dead in its bowl or a young boy who'd learned of his favorite grandfather's death. She paused, but didn't look back.

Terrence cleared his throat. "I hear you have a boarder."

She spun, the anger filling her eyes and voice, she'd been tricked by this new approach. "*That* is none of your business."

His head dropped quickly. "No. It's not. I'm sorry." He took a deep breath and let it out slowly, buying time it seemed. He reached into his heavy jacket and pulled out a small package wrapped in Christmas paper. "It's for Dusty." He offered it forward.

"You've haven't bought anything for him since before we moved out."

Another sigh, "I know. It's just that I'm, well, things are…"

"Have you been drinking?"

"No. I've made a mess of things. Between us, my own children. I… I'm sorry."

Carrie took the package with a hesitation. "Why now?"

"I don't know. Things are so, so, complicated right now. I just want you to know…"

Carrie interrupted; her voice was flat, not imposing, "The restraining order stands."

"I know. Have a nice Christmas."

Terrence turned and his eyes cast a glance over to the other side of the street, Carrie was hiding her gaze from him, but was able to catch a tear in the corner of his eye before he wiped them with a sleeve, pretending to wipe his whole face. He stepped from the curb with one foot and Carrie took him by the arm.

She cocked her head to the side and asked quietly, "What is it dad?"

Without looking back at her he simply shrugged his shoulders. "I… I'm just missing your mother a bit. This time of year was the hardest for all of us when you were younger. My dad keeping to the tradition as much as possible, your mother wanting to have an old fashioned Christmas, you kids wanting to open presents like your friends."

A huge lump formed in Carrie's throat. This was a confession. Only a few reasons people utter confessions near the holidays, depression and loneliness or terminal illness top the list. For a moment, Carrie felt something for her father-it wasn't pity, it wasn't shame, she more or less felt sadness for him. He had carved his path out of solid rock; his prison had been created by only him and his attention to his father's ideals and his plan to raise his family like his father had. In a prison of shame and isolation from the rest of the non-believers in the world.

But still, Carrie couldn't help but to feel a pang of guilt for not wanting to hold him right now in a hug and tell him everything was going to be okay, because it wasn't. If she hugged him and someone saw, the court could terminate the restraining order and Terry Dodson would be back in his daughter and youngest son's life, and that was not an option. Carrie had to be cold.

She took a breath and looked away. "I'm sorry for you." She stepped back closer to the mercantile front doors and said, "But things have to be the way they are."

Terry nodded without looking at her. "I'm sorry too. For everything and I don't expect anything from you, but you're going to get a gift from me this holiday season anyway. A nice one." He took one last chilly breath and glanced at her for a moment, "I'm really, really sorry."

He turned rapidly and walked off towards the railroad tracks, his head down like he was hurting, he was tugging at his jacket as he walked. Carrie felt a moment of shame for saying what she did so coldly. She glanced at the gift and shook it a little then a small smile pulled the corner of her M shaped top lip up. *Had he begun to feel remorse? Or was he dying?*

Even though the sun was shining as bright as any spring day, winter was truly letting its cold settle over Fallcast. Carrie watched her breath billow above her head in little clouds of steam, all the while watching her father walk towards the other end of town. *What was he up to?*

The flight to Denver was a little bumpier than Jason liked, the weather patterns had shifted somewhat, bringing in a low that circulated some lesser atmospheric winds. The ten hour flight included one stop in Salt Lake City for fuel and then a medium elevation course that took him through beautiful scenery, but Jason was too busy looking at what he had to do ahead of him than the mountains or valleys, rivers or even the highway he was following below.

First order of business was to take care of the results he gotten in his reports from the assayer in Elko. Calls had to be made, favors had to be called in and with the holiday quickly approaching, deals would be a hard sell, especially if many of the people he knew were out of town with their respective families for the holidays.

Another worry, Carrie had sounded down and even a little suspicious of him when he called before he left Nevada. She didn't outright say it, but she cast a doubt about his real reason for flying to Elko first-to get fuel and a layover, an excuse he's concocted-and she mentioned that her father had stopped her in the street to give her a present for Dusty and he seemed out of sorts. When she couldn't explain what "out of sorts" meant, Jason took it to mean he was angry or plotting. After all, Jason was to be in the man's office first thing Monday after Christmas. *First thing* or he'd be out of a job.

Even Dave was a little short with him when he'd called. There was no room for debate over the scheduled meeting, the client was demanding a meeting and set the date and Dave was too weak to have it changed, or-*or something was truly up*. Like living with the client's daughter (cohabitating, not sleeping in the same bed). Like the discovery that Jason made in the hills outside of town in the abandoned cave. Like the fact Jason had hired a private assay firm to test some dirt he brought with him in his backpack. Maybe it was the fire? Maybe it was the fact Dusty was getting better since Jason had arrived? Too many maybes and not enough facts. That was a worry for Jason. Everything he did in his life had a plan of some sort, and this was not going exactly the way he'd planned.

When the Cessna's wheels touched down at Centennial Airport just southeast of Central Denver, relief didn't come for the pilot as it usually did. He taxied to the fuel stand and after topping his tanks off, pulled into the small hangar that he'd rented for eight years. Inside was his 2006 red Chevy Blazer, hooked up to a trickle charger that kept a constant charge on the battery and even de-sulfated it when he was gone on extended stays. Usually he would switch the two out-the plane on the charger after unhooking the Blazer-but his stay at home wasn't going to be extended.

Jason pulled the Chevy out of the hangar, and then drug his plane in using the gear-dolly and closed the huge doors. After sitting in the SUV for a few moments to let the fluids coat the engine and tuning in his favorite station,

Jason took off for the gates and eventually headed up north on I-25 towards the Denver Tech Center where his boss awaited him. Monolith Minerals was located in the back of the 850 acre business park, one of the offices in the 25 million square feet of office spaces in the metropolitan center.

Jason would fill him in on most of the details of his findings, fill out some forms and take others with him to fill out later. Get some expense money and head home to his quiet and nearly empty apartment.

Carrie was getting ready for bed. Dusty was a little off this evening, it seems the further in time that Jason was away, the more agitated Dusty became. Carrie was agitated too. Between her father's surprise visit and the foreboding of the holiday home alone with just her little brother, Carrie felt empty for the first time in years.

How could she be falling in love with a guy she knows little about? She can't remember more than a few moments of discussing her life with Jason, and he revealed little to her also. He was so quiet most of the time, but he seemed to be functioning in his head, like he was working things out on a regular basis. Some guys sit there and look like they are lost in the world of thoughts, vacant and bland. Jason looks occupied with a vivid picture in his mind and a look of thoughtfulness on his face. He seems so intense sometimes, Carrie would snatch glances at him while he was doing something and he seemed intent and content at the same time.

Ron, for instance, when he was sitting alone at the diner; he seemed like his thoughts hurt his head, he always had this pained look on his face like he was experiencing confusion over what he was thinking about. Glo would ask him what he was thinking about and usually he would answer, "*Just things…*" The waitress would walk away and moments later the same expression would wash over his face.

When Jason returned, Carrie would ask him about his life. Get to know him better. Share her thoughts with him and spend more time talking about herself, things she rarely did other than to talk about her little brother. That would make her feel better. She sighed over her resolution and crawled under the covers of her bed, looking over her shoulder to the window, the moon was casting a glow over the barren desert, the wind was cooing slightly as it passed over the sage outside. In moments, she was asleep.

Terry Dodson was on his last drink of the night. He thought about his brief conversation with his daughter. He thought about the plans he had and how he would rid this feeling inside that he'd destroyed most of the lives around him, taking a little comfort in the phone call he received earlier from Marshall Tedford; the D.A. didn't think the flares that were missing from the mine truck that Tommy drove was enough to press charges, but Tedford lowered his voice and whispered a warning, '*The Sheriff's Office was going to keep an eye on his son, a very close eye, so be careful and tell him to watch his ass…*'

As the ice clacked when it fell from the bottom of the rock glass and smacked into Terrence's lips, the tingle of cold made him shiver. He'd have to watch after his son's ass big time soon. Things were going to get dicey. Especially after he confronts that geologist in his office Monday after Christmas.

Meg had pushed the button for the last bit of measured morphine drip she was allowed. Her thoughts were of her dead husband, her future and Carrie. She was furious over the fact that the woman her husband was going to leave her for was now dating the very man she had her sights on from the moment she first saw him. Dating, well *seeing* is more like it. Living together. He's probably already sipped from the virginal fountain, and they've been sleeping in the same bed. Jason was a handsome man, strong, built well, smart. *He could talk a beaver out of its teeth.*

Meg giggled at her sick pun and thoughts. Her mind quickly drifted to her lawyer, the man Jason had hired for her, he came in today with a big smile and great news. There would be no court date set before the holidays, so she was going to be released on her own recognizance for the time being, as long as she didn't try to leave Fallcast. In three days, the doctor says she can be cleared to go home. Just in time for Christmas. Alone. But she didn't feel afraid of being home alone for the holidays; there were things to do-even if she was confined to a cheap wheelchair. For the first time since she awoke in the hospital, Meg was confident she was going to be set free from the charges.

Meg fell asleep in a drug induced haziness dreaming that her beau was with her; she was being held by the man she was going to get. He'd fly her off and out of this god-forsaken stink hole and Carrie Dodson would remain behind, her hopes dashed. Meg dreamed of Jason.

CHAPTER SIXTEEN
Christmas and the week following

Carrie awoke to the sounds of crying. She rose from her bed slowly, a late night of wrapping and tying bows along with a cheating husband movie on late night cable kept her up. She wanted to watch *A Christmas Story* for the hundredth time, but passing storm clouds kept the reception down on some of her channels, the problem of living in a valley with only one cable provider and the fact she didn't want to afford satellite. Carrie was tired. And the dreams didn't help.

She wasn't the only one having bad dreams on Christmas morning, Dusty was in his bed and he had just awakened from one of his darkness in the shadows dreams, the ones where he swears he sees movement in the darker parts of the room, the ones not lit by the streetlamp or moon, the darkest portions of the small bedroom that are darker than the others. Most kids see or hear monsters under their beds or in closets; but Dusty sees them in the shadows, more precisely, in the areas of shadow that are murkier than the rest of the eclipse of a doorway or object. Sometimes he says he's in a cave and the monster is in there, with Carrie and a man, more recently the man had become *Airplane Man*, or Jason in Dusty's incubuses.

"What's wrong honey?"

"I... I heard something and then the shadow moved..." He replied, tears caked his voice.

Carrie sat on the edge of his small bed and took him in her arms. She drew him as close as she could, feeling the trembling boy's pulse race. She stroked his hair softly and kissed the top of his chilled forehead, rubbing his shoulders, she spoke quietly as she looked at his *Donald Duck* alarm clock. 7:25a.m. Might as well start the holiday.

"I think Santa's been here."

The boys eyes lit up. For a five or six year old this is the treat a parent loves to see, the excitement build in the anticipation of a child, the anxiousness that comes with the Christmas morning, the keenness of opening surprises brought by the Jolly Elf. In a boy Dusty's age, the mere mention of Santa would bring a rolling eye parade, followed by some quick comeback of sarcasm like, '*Yeah, whatever...*' or '*I'm not a baby, I know Santa isn't real*'; but Dusty isn't a normal pre-teen.

"Is Jason here?"

Carrie stopped her caressing mid-stroke. Her hand trembled as a cold shiver of excitement shot from the bottom of her spine to the back of her neck; she had to brush the back of her head with a free hand to calm the hair that was standing up.

"What did you *say*?"

"Airplane Man. Is he here too?"

"You called him by his name."

"Uh huh." Dusty drew back a little, like he had done something wrong.

Carrie felt a tear drop from her right eye, it slowly tracked across the corner of her mouth and dropped to the T shirt she was wearing. She pulled her little brother closer to her chest as the warmth of excitement ravaged her mind now. "You said his name! For the first time!"

"He says to call him Jason." Dusty replied with a renewed enthusiasm for doing something right in his sister's eyes.

Then a wave of sadness splashed over her, washing her warm feeling of delight at Dusty's newfound word in his vocabulary-he'd only called Jason 'Airplane Man' since they had met-Carrie's happiness drained away as she remembered she was alone with just her brother this holiday. She took a small breath, afraid if she inhaled a larger one she would break down and cry. She was *so* falling in love with Jason.

"No honey." She thought fast, "Jason had to help Santa, his sleigh broke down and Jason gave him a ride in his plane."

The boy's eyes lit up. "Cool!"

"Where'd you hear that word?" Carrie had begun to feel like a new woman with Dusty's words this morning.

"Airplane Man says it all the time…"

So much for '*Jason*'. She sighed and gave her brother one last big hug. "C'mon. Let's see what Father Christmas has brought you and me, and then I'll cook us some eggs and bacon."

"Oink oink." Was Dusty's reply. Carrie sighed a deeper release this time. He goes in and out of it so fast…

As they rounded the corner of the hallway to the living room, the boy began a little dance as he saw the packages under the tree. Carrie went to the wall first and flipped the switch that lit up the mini-lights on the six foot artificial tree. Real trees were expensive and the lot in town the Boy Scouts ran usually ran out by the time Carrie had wanted one, so she had found this little thing at the thrift store a couple of years ago; it was used, but it served its purpose and Dusty didn't even notice the difference when she brought it home earlier in the week to decorate. He was as excited as he could be over the tree and had most of the ornaments on it before Carrie could get the lights wrapped around one time. Of course the decorations were all on one side.

Many people in town buy their trees two weeks before the holiday, some even earlier. Carrie chose to do it just a few days before the holiday, since it was her choice. With her father and her grandfather and their households, there was no Christmas tree. Christmas was the celebration of the birth of Jesus Christ and not a reason to give presents to the children. It was a day of family to sit around and reflect the Christ Child's life by reading scripture. There was no fire and a pauper's dinner was prepared to symbolize the days of poverty the Savior went through and they fasted that night to symbolize His forty days fasting in the Judean Desert (not at all connected to his birth or this time of the year, but tradition was tradition with the TFP). They were not allowed to speak to one another until after noon, then the women (Carrie and her mother and other female TFP guests) went to the kitchen to cook the meal that must be served before two p.m., the men (Terrence, Tommy, baby Dusty, her grandfather and the male TFP*ers*) would sit in the living room and talk about the state of the world, well, her grandfather would talk or *preach*. He would spout aloud how the Pope has ruined the Church with liberalism, with relaxed rules of Catholicism, allowing sinners to enter the Church without physical penance. His anger and the anger of others in the TFP Church was renowned for their hate and anger towards the modern Catholic Church, the Pope and the followers that celebrate Jesus in any way other than the scripture said they should.

The tree's lights sparkled off the TV screen, then Carrie walked to the stereo and found the local that station has twenty-four hours of Christmas music on, Bing Crosby was singing *Silver Bells*.

She then went to the fireplace and began stacking kindling, old newspapers and a log while her brother began arranging presents by name. He had a hard time reading, but knew a 'C' and a 'D'. He had made two little piles of presents. Carrie had purchased a few for herself and then there were the obligatory gifts from friends and neighbors for them both, she reciprocated of course, and then finally the last present Dusty handled was the one that his father had given Carrie in front of the mercantile a few days ago.

Carrie watched as she struck the wooden match and set her fire ablaze, she stepped back and could smell a hint of her present in the kitchen on the breakfast bar. Flowers. One dozen red roses, long stem no less and in a vase shaped like an hour glass. Jason's present to her. A smile crept to her lips as she walked over to where Dusty was kneeling and they began to open the booty.

Dusty reveled at his new airplane that Carrie had bought him, a model that closely resembled Jason's real one. He flew around the living room for fifteen minutes before opening his other presents: A book from Mrs. Taylor, *Bedknobs and Broomsticks*. Carrie just shook her head in wonder. A pocket knife from old Mr. Burke down the street, Carrie would have to find a way to make that scarce. Coloring books and puzzles from Miss Baker the librarian, DVD's like *The Muppet Movie* and *How the Grinch Stole Christmas* with Jim Carrey, and a few other older titles Carrie didn't even know.

She had opened her gifts and handled each one as she watched out of the corner of her eye what her brother was doing, but each time she thought of opening another present, she would glance at the flowers. Then she realized… she hadn't gotten Jason anything! Just the cross she gave him as he left a week ago. Her heart pattered in panic.

She was interrupted by Dusty who had come to her lap and sat in front of her. "What's this?"

Carrie took her eyes off the vase of roses and looked down at what he was holding. It was the present from her father-their father-a rusty old lock with a set of keys. Old fashioned. Antique. Carrie had seen the lock before but where? Then the chill hit her fingers as she reached for it. It was the ceremonial lock from the mill. The clasp that was locked to the main gate for over a century, her great grandfather had purchased it brand new from the mercantile that was only a tent covering a wooden frame when he came to mine Fallcast, before Fallcast was even really Fallcast…

Carrie stared at the lock. Why? She looked over the boy's shoulder and saw a note from her father amongst the wrapping paper. "Dusty, hand me the paper please." He complied.

The paper was folded neatly in half and was inside the box that the lock was in. It was a simple phrase:

It belongs to you now
Dad

What belongs to him? The mine and mill? What the hell as going on in his head? Has he lost it? The thought Carrie had as Terry walked away from her the other day crossed her mind again, was he dying? Her eyes glanced from the note to the telephone on the counter in the kitchen. If she called him, she could be accused of breaking the no contact rule and the door would be open for him and her brother Tommy to come and go as they pleased, to begin the torture of being in her face for everything; how she lived her life, who she saw, what she did day to day. But she had to know. Something was making Terry do strange things. She had to find out.

Just as she reached the receiver, the phone rang and Carrie let out a shout of surprise. Her trembling hand picked it up and pushed the answer button. "Hello?"

"Hi. Merry Christmas."

"Oh, Jason!" Everything she was worried about had been forgotten in an instant. "Merry Christmas!" She looked to where Dusty was sitting, playing with his toy Cessna. He was trying to jam the padlock their father gave him into the cockpit. "Thank you so much for the Christmas flowers!"

There was a pause, then "They weren't for Christmas, they were just because…"

"Oh."

"I have your present with me right now though."

"Jason, I didn't get you anything…"

"Don't worry about it. I just saw something I liked and thought of you."

"I wish you wouldn't have. But I guess I have a couple of weeks to find one for you."

"No."

"It's no big deal, really, I…"

"You won't have time. I'm coming back on Sunday afternoon."

Now it was Carrie's turn to pause for a moment of silence while she turned the thought over in her head. She had to clarify, just in case she misheard him, she didn't want to get all worked up, "You what?"

"I have to back by Monday for a meeting."

"Wow. I mean, that's good right?"

"Well I don't know. It seems the new boss at Dowards has my boss on a hotplate, he called Dave and demanded that I be there in the twenty-eighth first thing in the morning."

"Oh."

Jason waited for a few moments to see what her reaction would be, after Carrie offered none he decided to ask, "You know who the new foreman is right?"

"No. Not really, I don't keep up on the mine business, that's my father and brother's life."

"The new foreman is Terrence Dodson."

There was at least a full minute of dead silence. Carrie had quickly processed this information, but she couldn't speak. She couldn't move. Her body was frozen like someone in a night terror dream, where your life is threatened but you can't force yourself to move, you know you're dreaming but you can't wake up. Carrie didn't know what to say, she hadn't heard of course, it was none of her business and her father hadn't mentioned it when they met unceremoniously a few days prior. Now she knew something was up.

"My boss says he closed the Dodson Mill. Went to work for Marcus Dowards." Jason added, feeling inside that Carrie didn't know what was going on.

"I didn't know. I… I'm sorry. Do you know what he wants?"

"No. I'll find out in a couple of days I guess. Must be big though, my boss is nervous about the contract with Dodson, I couldn't make an excuse for getting out of it or delaying it until after the New Year."

More silence. Carrie was getting angry; her father had found a way to meddle into her life without making contact. He knows Jason is staying at her house, albeit they were not lovers, they've shared a kiss, Carrie wanted to kiss Jason at least once not knowing whether he'd return or not. But Terry had found a new way to torture her. But why not say anything the other day?

What did he say when she told him it was none of his business when he asked about Jason? *'No, it's not. Sorry.'* And he sounded as if he meant it. Then there was the lock. The lock! It was from the front gate of the Mill. It hadn't been used in decades, but it sat locked to the chain as a symbol, a tradition of the Dodson Mine and Mill for nearly a century.

"Jason, I think something is up with him. Things aren't right and it's not that I should care about these things, but Terry isn't himself." She went on to explain why she felt this way; she started with the meeting in front of the mercantile and then the lock for Dusty wrapping in Christmas paper.

Then a thought hit Jason as he was listening. The cave. Maybe Terrence found out that Jason had discovered the secret opening in the cave. Maybe Terrence Dodson knew Jason was aware of the contents of the hidden area; the secrets that could be used to control someone. Maybe Terrence thought Jason was going to use the contents of the cavern to take clout over him or maybe he thought Jason would use the discovery as a stepping stone into the family. Jason was silent for another few moments until Carrie broke the dead air.

"I'm sorry Jason."

He took a breath, "Not your fault. Don't worry about it," He had begun to relax when his thoughts focused on what he knew and what he could do if cornered, "I'll make sure my company keeps the contract. Unless it comes between you and I."

A tickling feeling of a thousand feathers crept up Carrie's spine and stomach, "Us?"

She almost could hear him smile at the other end, "Yeah, us. I won't let anyone come between us and our friendship. You were there for me when I needed help and I owe you so much for that, and…" He paused.

"And?" Carrie was tingling with excitement.

"And I think we're not done yet."

This could have meaning either way, but Carrie needed an optimistic look for a change for today anyway. "I think not." She was rewarded with a sigh of relief on the other end of the phone.

"Okay, I've got a few more calls to make and I'm going to visit my grandparent's and have dinner. I wish I would've stayed with you this holiday, I guess I have someone to spend the holidays with again…" There was almost a resignation to his voice. "And don't get me anything!" Almost resignation turned to demand.

"But the flowers Jason, they're so beautiful. I need to…"

Jason interrupted, "No you don't. I said I owed you. I'll see you in two days, I should be there around four or five Sunday evening. Could you have someone help drop the Jeep off at the airstrip for me?"

"I'll just bring it and wait."

"I don't know what time I'll be there for sure, it could be hours afterwards…"

"I don't mind. I can't wait to see you." Carrie felt a wave of relief as she said the words, she meant it. And his response was what she needed for her own self-assurance.

"I can't wait to see you either."

Meg was sitting in her wheelchair, a cheap run of the mill one, but it functioned as she needed. She was released Wednesday morning and had been in her home ever since. She was able to move out of wheeled throne by sliding forward and using the cast covering her broken leg as a pivot point, and then move her butt to where she needed it to go. From her bed to the kitchen, to the living room to watch TV (she saw no need to get out of the chair to sit on the loveseat or sofa) and use the toilet when necessary.

Her brother flew into Vegas and rented a car to drive to her home in Fallcast. He wanted to help with the arrangements for Steve's funeral, but she refused. Instead she postponed any memorial service till after she was out of the chair and back on her feet. And hopefully not in jail.

Richard Ferrence: Esquire, paid a visit to her at home on Thursday, the day before Christmas, he was grinning from ear to ear. It seems there had been some mistakes made by the D.A.'s office in collecting evidence. What he said was, "*Sal Buford who told you to get the leak fixed on the brake line changed a bit of his story, it seems that he thought he might have told you to turn it the wrong way...*" When Meg started to protest the attorney said sternly, "*I don't care if he told you to do anything at all, this is what he says now and the case has the first of its holes. Just keep your mouth shut about anything involving it and I'm pretty sure more will come up. There's no need to worry...*"

Staring out the back window now, alone because her brother had to fly home for Christmas with his wife and her nephew, Meg sipped from a cup of cooling coffee. The microwave was above the stove and she didn't feel like getting up again to warm it. She cried a few times for Steve and his death, she cried for a few times for her own sanity

293

and freedom and the possible loss of both, and she cried for her loneliness. Carrie gets everything. It goes way back to before Carrie or Megan were even born, before the town of Fallcast was little more than a stop off for prospectors heading through and needing supplies; when Carrie's ancestors owned the town in part and the Dowards family owned the other part. In a small town like this one, someone was always in control of your life.

Someone was always getting what they wanted and someone was always getting seconds. Meg didn't want seconds. Sure, Steve was her high school flame and hadn't even met Miss Dodson until after they graduated. If she'd known then that he carried a torch for that bitch, he'd be alive now somewhere else. She'd be the one who shacked up the young good looking geologist who flies around in his own airplane. She'd be in his bed now, and Miss Carrie Dodson would be sitting here feeling as if the whole world hated her. As if the whole world wanted her to be lonely. As if she was nothing more than the newest widow in Fallcast.

Megan Cooke turned her wheelchair to look at the saddest thing in her home, the unlit Christmas tree. Underneath were presents from Steve and her-to each other. Several from well-wishers who knocked on her door after she returned home from the hospital. Meg figured much of the stuff they brought in cheap wrapping paper was things she would need around the house; toiletries, canned food, etc. There were several gifts *With Deepest Sympathies* baskets with notes that said things like *"Sorry for your loss…"* and *"…"* one even read *"We'll miss Steve…"* with a list of names from the bank where he worked. Only a few of them said *"Get Well Soon!"* or *"I Hope You're Feeling Better!"* and nothing from Carrie. Meg guessed she closed the door hard on that relationship. She even got a nice visit from Parks, who brought her some fine wine, but she wasn't allowed to drink it along with the Lorcet tablets she was taking for pain and swelling.

More than once while she sat there sipping her now cold coffee, she thought about suicide. She had a bottle of ten 10mg tablets of the pain meds. That would do the trick. But she worried about Jason. What would he say if he found out she died from an overdose. She racked her brain to find a way to make it look like an accident; maybe if she lay on the floor and put the bottle next to her after swallowing the whole amount fingers in her mouth clutching a couple of pills, they'd think she tried popping one or two into her mouth straight from the prescription bottle but instead accidentally swallowed the lot.

Maybe she'd lay the bottle on the sink next her coffee cup as if they had fallen into her coffee while she wasn't looking, or maybe she'd just drink the wine and take three or four more than the recommended dosage, after peeling the warning label about the toxicity mixing the drug with alcohol off the bottle and hiding it in the trash. Maybe her brother could sue the pharmacy for giving her a bottle of prescription medication that didn't have the proper warning labels.

After a while she'd given up on the thoughts of killing herself, she wanted Jason too bad and she couldn't get him if she were dead.

Terry was dropping an ice cube into a glass of eggnog. He'd left the carton out when he went to bed around four this morning and the Booker's Bourbon he just poured in added to the warmth. He didn't feel like drinking a warm dairy product right now, but he needed the sweetness added to the high-end booze.

Tommy had drug himself in around the time Terry was going to bed. He was in a vile mood, having been tossed out of the Horseshoe again and ending up at a divorced friend's home, who would also be spending his

Christmas alone. Tommy was asleep on the couch in the living room, his feet dangling over one side and his arm on the floor.

Terry had actually bought a real Christmas tree when the fresh green conifers first arrived in town on the back of a flatbed, decorated a full one sparsely, and strung a row of lights around it once. It was pathetic to look at, but there was this inner hope that the world of his would heal and the family would be here with Tommy and him, but healing is a long process and he hadn't given enough yet to let the wounds start to coagulate. Soon enough. But then he also knew that the flying geologist would be a problem, living with Carrie and all, but he was out of town and that flickered a little more hope. In three days, he'd set the whole thing straight, if not on fire.

Fire.

Terry stared at the tree from the kitchen, it hadn't been watered in a few days and the thing was probably a fire hazard. He looked from the tree to Tommy, who was snoring loudly, and wondered what would become of him. Back to prison? Dead? He'd hoped to give the boy a better job at Dowards, but responsibility was not on of his son's greatest attributes. Dusty had more responsibility.

Dusty. The only one who knows absolutely nothing about what was going on. Terrence envied him. He slammed back the creamy drink and walked out of the room. He stepped into the living room and turned on the TV. Jimmy Stewart was rushing through the streets of Bedford Falls in the snow saying *"Hello!"* to everyone. Terry wanted another drink.

Christmas afternoon had come. Carrie and Dusty played with his new toy plane for at least three hours then she forced him to put it away to do some work. They spent another hour and a half reading, playing word games and coloring with the new books he'd gotten. While the young boy watched *Teenage Mutant Ninja Turtles* on DVD, Carrie cooked up a nice ham and mashed potatoes. She had peas and green beans (Dusty's favorite) and sweet potatoes. She even had a little time to make a pumpkin pie from scratch with a giant gourd that'd grown in her yard.

At five o'clock, she dressed Dusty up and got him into a jacket. She put a nice pair of tan slacks on and a light blue shirt then pulled on a turtleneck that was a darker blue and they headed out the door to Meg's house. Carrie wanted to surprise her, she knew that things were tense right now, Meg was hurt and sick over the death of Steve and she knew Meg even blamed her a little, but she wanted to make things right. She wanted to let Meg know that things were okay and if Meg wanted to lay blame on her for what happened to her husband, then she'd let her. Eventually Meg would come around and things would be back to normal.

Carrie scooped up the big bowl that had the rest of the ham, and the side dishes in little Tupperware containers. Dusty carried the three slices of pie that were left (Carrie put two out for her and Dusty tomorrow) and they headed out into the fading sunlight for Meg's.

Jason was eating a nice meal at his grandparent's house in Highland Ranch. The *Ranch* as Jason's grandfather liked to call it, was a huge community in itself with over eight thousand acres of lush open areas, twenty-two parks, golfing and hiking and quiet streets, the elderly flocked here, although the prominent age was just thirty-six years of age.

The talk was kept simple, *"How're you doing? What're you doing? Who's the new girl in his life?"* The answers were kept simple too, *"Not bad, working in Nevada near Vegas, and we're not really dating yet."*

Kathryn and Noel Harrigan were Jason's maternal grandparents. They helped him through the death of his mother and father both financially and mentally. Although they offered, Jason refused the two thousand dollar a month *allowance* because he always felt he needed to work and he loved doing his work. Besides, his mother and father died nearly paupers and it wouldn't be fair to their memory to reap the benefits after their untimely demise.

After dinner he sat and chatted with them for a while longer, catching up as much as possible, then he left for home. He'd get a good night's rest and then pack Saturday for the trip back to Fallcast. Jason didn't mention the fact he was falling in love with Carrie, nor did he want to. His grandmother really liked Lindsay and was nearly heartbroken when things went the way they did.

"You listen to me. You're going back to Carson City if things keep going the way they are."

"You've said that before."

Terry and Tommy Dodson were eating at the diner. Since most folks struggled to make ends meet this time of the year, the Salt Lick was no exception. It opened every day of the year, hoping to catch a few extra bucks. Sometimes folks would stop in and have a drink or a piece of pie, other times it sat empty except for Cookie, who would nap at the counter.

"One more. Once more and I'm done with you, you're finished at Dowards, our mine and cut out of the rehabilitation." Terry was not raising his voice at all; there was actually a sense of calmness to his lecture, sort of a "matter of fact" tone to it.

Tommy looked at his dad. He hadn't had anything to drink today, he was jonesing for a beer or vodka, anything with booze, but abstained because Terry had asked him to, for Christmas' sake. He was becoming impatient though with his father's tone.

"Look, I can take care of..."

Terry held his breath for a moment, this made his voice grow deeper and his face turn redder, "You're not hearing what I'm saying. Come home drunk once more and you're out. Come home with some BS story about how you were victimized at the Horseshoe and you're out. Mess with your sister or your brother and you're out. Do you understand me?"

Tommy just sat there with disbelief in his eyes and an open mouth.

~

Sunday afternoon was not as nice as the weatherman had promised. Jason had called ahead as usual to the National Weather Service and AWC or the Aviation Weather Center, and was given a report of cloudy around seven thousand and light to moderate winds with little chance of any significant shear or downdrafts also known as micro-bursts. Even though the latter was true, the winds buffeted the Cessna around like a balloon, the shears and bursts were not evident at all. A good thing really, considering several fatalities have occurred in the last decade or so from the winds that basically blow straight down to the ground then out and taking whatever is in the air with it. Jason had lost a friend when he was younger, just getting his pilot's license, a man who was at one time an instructor had been caught in a freak wind shear just a few miles from the airport and his plane was tossed to the ground like a toy.

He was only an hour and a half out from Fallcast according to his GPS; the sky was littered with clouds so flying by instruments was crucial. It had been a while since he'd flown blind, but instinct took over after a few minutes and the only thing that rattled him was the shifts in wind direction at different altitudes. He'd left Denver at six in the morning, really before the sun had begun to rise and was now looking at his watch which read (after adjusting for the zone changes) ten minutes to noon.

Carrie and Dusty would be waiting for him at one o'clock, he'd thought his original arrival time was four or five but he called ahead and let her know he was running ahead of schedule but the winds and some other obstacles had slowed him a bit, so he was running about a half hour behind the readjusted time. Jason smiled when he remembered Carrie had told him she'd wait there all night and even camp out till next Thursday for him. She had missed him that much.

A cold puff of dry dust rose from the pea gravel runway as the Cessna bounced twice and settle to the ground. There were some slight winds blowing across the east-west runway and the little extra lift gave Jason an extended ride. He taxied the 182 towards the solitary hangar, a mine Jeep and two anxious welcoming party members were obviously waiting for his trip to end.

Carrie ran over and was tapping her foot on the ground as Jason killed the engine and began shutdown of the plane's systems, he had a smile on his face as wide as one could get. He wished he'd had a reception like this everywhere he went, the feeling inside of being home (in a home away from home sense) trickled from the base of his neck, along his spine and into his feet. He opened the door and before he could slide out Dusty was in the other side of the plane and at the controls.

Carrie waited impatiently as Jason's feet touched the earth after more than six hours in the air. Before the grey-blue hue of dust could coat his sneakers, Carrie had her arms wrapped around his neck. He pulled her close and could smell fresh strawberries and cream shampoo, mild perfume of some sweet nature and excitement. He returned the hug with the same intensity and lifted her off the ground a few inches.

"Airplane Man look!" Dusty was racking the yoke back and forth making his engine noises.

Jason nodded and was trying to say, 'good job' but the choke hold from Carrie was blocking his airway partially. She planted a warm and sensational kiss on his cheek next to his ear, he supplanted with a kiss to her neck. The aroma flourished. He was in love, and he was sure she was too. Absence makes the heart grow fonder, return makes the heart full.

Carrie began to chatter after the five minute welcome, as Jason unlocked the hangar to retrieve the nose dragger from the empty shed and hook it to the wheels of his plane.

"So how was your flight?" She began.

"Long. My arms ache from the damn wind."

"Did you miss us?"

"Of course."

"Are you staying for a while this time?"

"Yes. Yes I am."

"Meg hates me."

This made Jason stop in his tracks and the plane too.

"What?" He looked up to her, the eyes that were minutes ago wet with joy now seemed to have changed from their golden color to a burnt umber tone. "I don't think she hates…"

Carrie interrupted him with a sniff and a wipe of her eyes after checking to see if her little brother could see from the cockpit. He was still madly turning the wheel back and forth, pretend flying. "I took her dinner Christmas. She ate two bites and said nothing to me. I offered to help her get around and she'd basically told me to go to hell."

"Well, I don't think that means that she hates you." Jason began tugging the plane again, completing the 180 degree turn to have the nose face out of the hangar. "She's been through a lot, she has a rough road ahead, maybe she just needs some space right now."

"She blamed me for Steve's death."

"I don't know how she could."

"She said he was in love with me and that he was driving crazy after they fought about me and that they lost control."

Jason was at a loss for words. He just shook his head and took the crying young girl into his arms.

It took ten minutes to coax Dusty out of the plane and they were on the road for the short drive to Carrie's house. It was a semi-quiet drive, Dusty was revealing what Santa had brought him for Christmas; Carrie would correct him once or twice about which gifts were from the jolly old elf and which were from friends in town and the ones that she'd bought for him. As they approached the half circle driveway, Jason turned to Dusty and asked him to hand the knapsack up front. Dusty complied and sat back quietly for a moment as Jason pulled out a small wrapped present for the boy.

Then he pulled out a larger one for Carrie, who balked at it.

"I don't think you should've gotten me anything…"

Before the Jeep came to a stop Dusty exclaimed out loud, "Wow!"

Carrie turned and saw her brother had already opened the package and was holding up what looked like a video game with a picture of a Concorde airliner on the front.

"What is it Dusty?" She asked, not quite sure herself.

"A game!"

"Microsoft's Flight Simulator." Jason said proudly. "My own copy. It has real time flight displays, air traffic control communications and more. He can fly any plane he wants to, and see scenery he'd never get to see here in Fallcast. Like Pearl Harbor or Mt. Fuji."

Carrie flushed. She could never thank him enough, but she felt a little sad that she couldn't be the one presenting her brother something like this. She looked down at her lap and said in a quiet voice, "Jason, you shouldn't have."

"Nonsense. Might as well open yours!" He said beaming.

Carrie fumbled with the book size package and tore a small corner first, then she looked to Jason with fear in her eyes and a touch of shame, "I made you dinner, for your present. A real home cooked meal, and a nice bottle of wine. I think the best part of my present is Gloria from the Salt Lick is watching Dusty tonight for me. We can spend time alone together."

Jason felt blood surging. He realized what she was suggesting, "I hope you're not planning what I think you're planning?"

Carrie's face turned crimson, "Oh! No! No, not that…I… I just wanted us to get to know each other better that's all! I mean, just us no interruption! Oh Gawd, did I sound like I was going to…?"

Now it was Jason's turn to blush. He laughed a very nervous laugh and patted her leg, "So sorry! My brain is tired, I was thinking from the gutter. Forgive me?"

"Okay. I'm sorry too. I guess I could have framed that better."

"Speaking of frames, open your gift!"

"The flowers were enough. I could never have expected those, they are so beautiful."

"Geologists don't give flowers. We study rocks."

She nodded and kissed him on the cheek and peeled away the rest of the paper. Her hands started to shake, slowly at first, then rapidly. Her face turned white as a sheet and a single tear fell from her face onto the small glass box that contained a diamond necklace. "Oh God Jason."

The diamonds were small, but added up the choker necklace had about three and a half carats including the oval Citrine center stone. The grey clouded sky flickered sparkles from the necklace to Carrie's face. More tears fell. "I can't accept this. This cost a fortune." She whispered.

"Then sell it."

Carrie's mouth flew open in shock. She turned to see if he was joking. He wasn't.

Jason said, "I bought it for you because I wanted to repay you for everything you've done for me so far. If you need the cash, sell it. You'll probably get about three or four hundred…"

"Shush! I will not. I just, no one has ever bought me something so, so, special."

"You deserve it."

Carrie gave Jason a tear moistened kiss on the lips and a bear hug. It took several minutes, but Dusty was impatiently waiting to get inside and play his new game. He began slowly kicking the seat until the couple in the front stopped, laughed and opened the doors.

"I don't have a computer." Carrie said quietly.

"Relax," Jason replied, "I bought a new laptop for me and a yoke and peddle kit for him to use."

Carrie rolled her eyes in mock disgust, "You aren't really frugal are you?"

"That's why I have to work for a living…"

They both laughed and went inside. Carrie cooked dinner and Jason helped Dusty with his new game.

At six o'clock Gloria came by with a pecan pie and picked up a very disgruntled and cranky Dusty. He liked Gloria, but his new video game was the big hit of the season. He was trying to learn to fly a Mooney Bravo through some creative hoops that hung in the sky and was not in any hurry to quit. Jason finally went over and told him he needed the laptop for a while to do some work. That did the trick and the boy left with his head down, but his heart pattering hard from his new found talent of flying simulated airplanes.

Carrie lit a small fire in the fireplace, put on a pot of scented flowers and potpourri that smelled of pine and cinnamon, turned the radio up low. Burl Ives was singing *Silver and Gold*, she opened the bottle of wine and they sat back on the couch together, silent for a few minutes as the wine breathed and they tried not to too heavily out of nervousness. Finally Carrie couldn't take it any longer and she broke the ice.

"Did you have a nice Christmas dinner?"

"Not bad."

She decided it was time to get more out of him. She scooted close enough to Jason so she could feel the heat radiating from his body, and she knew he would feel the same from hers, especially now that the wine was warming her up. "What're your grandparents like?"

Jason smiled at the thought of them, "They're nice mostly. As nice as Irish immigrants can be."

"Oh, so you're Irish?"

"Half. The other half is German. On my father's side."

"Did you tell them what's going on; you know being here and the job and all?"

Jason nodded. "And you." Carrie blushed.

She took a deep breath and thought about her next words carefully; then asked, "What happened with your parents?"

Jason didn't skip a beat, that made Carrie feel more confident, "They were killed one night a few years ago, in a car accident."

"I'm sorry."

"Wasn't your fault. Besides, the blame lies with someone else."

"Who?"

"The person who ruined their lives. They were flat broke the night they were killed, they were out celebrating that." His voice turned cold, uninviting. Carrie backed off a little.

"Are your grandparents rich?"

Jason laughed easily, "Yeah, a little. They would've taken care of mom and dad if they asked. They wanted to take care of me, pay me a huge allowance for just being there for them when they needed me. But I refused. I wanted to keep earning my own money."

Carrie sipped her wine and her voice was raspy from the light burn of alcohol, "Very noble of you."

"Don't get me wrong, they're great people, but I wanted to be able to come and go as I pleased, they did pay off my plane for me though." Jason took a sip of his wine and put his feet up on the ottoman. Leaning back with his head he let the cabernet swim around and his brain joined in as the day was finally wearing him down. He was exhausted, from flying and worrying about tomorrow. He found a question in his thoughts.

"So, tell me about your dad. What am I up against tomorrow?"

Her sip of wine lasted for several seconds, this was a tip off that things might not go to good, "He's rough. Strong, strict and demands respect." She looked over to Jason, "He's been through a lot I guess over the years," She paused remembering the man who stopped her outside the mercantile, he was fragile looking, he seemed hollow. Carrie eyes drifted off of Jason for a second and then flashed back with a new thought, "maybe he's changed a little over the last few years, but be on your best behavior and guard. He can strike a blow without notice."

Jason's eyes went wide, "He'll hit me?"

Carrie laughed this off, "No, probably not, but he will try his best to intimidate you."

Jason took a sip of wine and closed his eyes after leaning his head back, "Great."

Carrie whispered almost seductively, "Tell me about yourself, and why do you like flying around looking at rocks so much? Do you have siblings? Do you want children?"

The last question caught Jason's attention. He looked over with his head still on the back of the chair, "Kids? Someday. I'm an only child; I grew up well off in many ways. Private school that sort of thing, my neighborhood was always nice and upper scale. My folks traveled a lot so I was left in the care of my grandparents quite often. I guess I'm going to inherit the rest of their fortune someday. But I've got other ideas for securing my future." He took a small breath, "How bout you? Kids? Aspirations?"

"I definitely want a couple of kids; one boy, one girl. Cliché I know, but it would be so good for Dusty to have someone close to him so to speak. I've always wanted to be a teacher, with Dusty I get the effect, but not the satisfaction of teaching a classroom full of kids."

"Sounds like you enjoy cacophony…"

"*Cacophony*, a meaningless mixture of sounds." She replied with a little giggle.

"It was on my 'Word a Day' calendar last month." Jason giggled back. His voice dropped to serious tone, "Why do you say you're not as smart as you'd like to be?"

Carrie took this as a surprise, "Where did you hear that?"

"Once you were talking on the phone to someone, Meg I think, but you said that I was too smart for you, that you weren't smart enough for me…"

The wine wasn't strong enough for that one; Carrie blushed, even though her skin was naturally dark toned, it was almost as bright as the red bulbs on the Christmas tree. She couldn't think of anything to say, "I… I meant…"

"It's okay. I wasn't meaning to eavesdrop on you, but when you said that, it made me kind of sad. I think you're one of the smartest people I know. I think you're shorting yourself, you'd be a great teacher."

Bing Crosby began singing *White Christmas* that second. Carrie leaned over and kissed Jason on the cheek next to his ear, this time with more lip and a touch of her tongue. She could feel the goose bumps rising on his skin, his breathing adjusted from relaxed to a little almost panting and he put his arm around her. He brushed her brown hair off to one side of her face and stroked her cheek softly with his index and middle fingers. Her lungs began fluctuating faster also; the air in the room was filled with soft holiday music, the smell of cinnamon and light smacking of lips.

Carrie moved closer to Jason, pulling his hand to her side, hoping he'd use his imagination and make good utilization of it, massaging her sides and her front, her belly and her breasts, but it lingered where it was. She began to softly tickle the back of his neck with her fingertips, tracing the line along his spine to his middle back, reaching though his Polo shirt's collar to keep contact with his skin. His inhales and exhales increased and the intensity of his kisses were strengthening, both their bodies were warming up fast. He finally moved his hand forward and Carrie scrunched down at the waist to indicate that it was okay to caress her there. He did.

Several minutes had passed, they were on the verge of a full connection, Carrie undid the string that was holding her sweatpants up; she could feel Jason shivering in nervousness. She slowly moved his hand with hers to the top of her navel, and then moved it in a circular motion around her navel. His breathing became shallow and quick, small beads of sweat formed on his brow. Her kisses were deeper now, filled with passion. She flipped the top button of his 501s open.

The doorbell rang.

Then a knock. Not a slight rapping or curious one, two, three; but a furious banging, like a child. Dusty. And Gloria. Carrie looked at the clock; it read 9:45, still forty five minutes before they were due back. In a flash the couple that had somehow managed to go from seated to lying back on the soft sofa and they were now scrambling to get upright, refastening unlatched clothing parts and scampering to get things normal around them. The pillows from the couch off the floor. Carrie tried to adjust her hair, Jason was laughing to himself and Carrie was giggling out loud. They were like a couple of teenagers who'd been caught upstairs by her parents.

It took all of a minute or two and knocking became louder and almost enraged. After checking themselves for tell-tale signs of impropriety, Carrie went to the door and opened it.

Gloria stepped in first. A quick glance at the pasty bodies in front of her made her tingle a little inside. She let out a small giggle that quickly hushed by covering her mouth.

"I'm sorry." *Snicker*. "He couldn't wait any longer; he wanted to play his game…" *Titter*. "Are we… interrupting anything?" *Chortle*.

Jason cleared his throat from the cloud of passion and answered, "No, not at…"

Carrie forced her voice into a sharp interruption, "Yes. Yes you did." She sighed as Dusty came over and gave her a hug at her legs. "But it's okay. Jason has to get to bed; it's going to be a long day for him tomorrow."

Gloria looked from Carrie to Jason, then back. Her smile was sly and curled in a look of satisfaction and sorrow. "Well, again, I'm sorry." She winked at Jason and Carrie then bowed her head as she said, "Goodnight guys. Be, uh, safe."

Carrie closed the door behind her and muttered, "Well I guess there's no point in keeping it a secret any longer."

Dusty made his way to Jason's laptop that he'd set up for him, the yoke controller and rudder pedals still attached. Jason went over to help the boy boot up the simulator and winked at Carrie as she went into the kitchen to pour another glass of wine. An hour later, they were all in their own beds.

Carrie drifted off with the touch of her hand where Jason had caressed her tummy. Jason could smell the musk of Carrie's perfume mixed with the skin from her neck on his lips and dozed off in minutes without a thought of his meeting with her father in the morning. Dusty dreamed of airplanes and him behind the controls. All of them were satisfied that this was one of the best Christmases ever.

Jason was sitting in the mine and mill office at the south end of an old building that reeked of dust and sweat. Terry's office was one of the larger ones, about fifteen by fifteen, second only to Marcus Dowards by three feet on each side.

His foot was tapping softly on the thick carpeting that was a horrible blue-green and marked with scuffs of boots and spots of dirt and mud. The office was simple, three large filing cabinets, two were the normal letter size and the other one was long and flat, four feet high and six feet long. This one held assay maps and tunnel dimensions, pit mine information and future diggings. One solid oak desk was the center piece of the room, three soft chairs in front of that. A long couch against the back wall with a hat rack filled with raingear next to the door. Dozens of framed pictures of the mine in its beginning stages, several assay maps of the area, one huge picture of the pit and some with people in them. Marcus Dowards with family, miners and secretarial staff in others.

One window overlooked the parking lot and the mountains behind the mill; one could see the switchback roads leading to the other pits and tunneled mines scratching their way up the hillside. It was clear outside today, as usual, but cold nearing only the forty degree mark. Jason's stomach was rumbling.

Carrie had gotten up early in the morning to make breakfast for him and Dusty. Dusty was told his day was going to be filled with schoolwork, when he protested and asked Jason if he could play his airplane game, Carrie said no. She told Dusty that Jason had to take his laptop to work today, she glanced in the man's direction and he nodded and replied in kind. Dusty was heartbroken.

A kiss on the lips with a slight drag of the tongue from Carrie made Jason want to reconsider leaving, but she insisted. Then she patted him on the behind softly as he walked off the porch to the Jeep. Even though he'd had two eggs, three strips of bacon, one pancake and two cups of coffee, Jason was still feeling empty inside. Then he realized why. Carrie. She made him fell tingly and fresh. He wasn't with her right now and he was hungry for her company.

Jason licked his lips where Carrie had nudged them with her tongue this morning just as the door literally flew open and banged against the wooden hat rack behind it. Terrence Dodson walked in as though someone had invaded his private space and he was there to quell any further trespass.

He wasn't as big as Jason pictured him. He'd only seen him twice, both times sitting. Once at the Salt Lick eating, and once at the Horseshoe bar. In the way people talked about Terrence, Jason figured him to be six foot eight, thick as a redwood, with steel grey eyes that could pierce solid metal with a glance. Actuality made Terry Dodson about six foot three, half as thick as a tree and the eyes were burning a hole in Jason's head right now. Close enough for the intimidation factor. Even though he was in his early fifties, he was a remarkable specimen of hard work and a hard life.

The large man walked from the door, which was still vibrating from being thrown open, towards his desk, his eyes not leaving Jason for a moment. Jason didn't break eye contact, he also didn't let his gaze appear to be threatening, he just let it follow the man to his seat. But he didn't sit. He placed his hands one on each side of him, shoulder length apart on the desk and he leaned forward. The knuckles showed signs of wear and tear; this was a man who wasn't afraid to get involved in his work.

After several moments of just eye to eye evaluating of each other, Terrence Dodson offered a hand. In a gruff voice he spoke, "Mr. Parmenter."

Jason fought the urge in his voice to crack, "Mr. Dodson." He took the large man's hand.

"I hear you have some figures for me." There was no chance this man was going to waste any time with pleasantries.

"I have printouts of valuations, estimates of the best areas to test dig, some hand written notes on my physical finds and a few photographs taken from the air demonstrating strata changes that might lead to a…"

"Never mind that crap." The man's voice lowered even more, if that were possible.

Jason sat back as if surprised, he was a little, but he knew Dodson would try to establish the alpha dominance right away. He let out a confident, "Sir?" With his head cocked slightly as if to convey curiosity over fear.

Terrence sat down in his chair hard. The springs squeaked from the sudden weight, the wheels creaked from stress as he pushed himself to the front of the desk, jamming his big legs into the kneehole. He looked over Jason's shoulder. "Drink?"

"No thank you sir."

The man opened a drawer and pulled out several sheets of fax paper. He tapped them on edge then sat them directly in front of himself, aligning the edges again with his fingertips. He allowed a moment to clear his throat and then he looked directly into Jason's eyes again, this time with the most intensity Jason had ever seen a man do.

"As a geologist, I'm sure you are aware of mineral assessments that include assay markers?"

"Yes, I…"

"So let's say; if you took some dirt from a field in New York, then took it to be analyzed, it would have specific markers that would make that dirt specific by location."

Jason nodded as a knot formed in his stomach, he had a feeling he knew where this was going.

"Say an old man with a bucket went onto one of my claims and dug himself a bunch of sand filled with little nuggets of gold. Then he went to have it assayed for gold content and the assayer was a friend of mine and decided that after determining the bucket of dirt was taken from my land by use of specific mineral markers called me with the results, thinking that the old man had permission to dig on my property."

Jason's knot became a chunk of lead weighing a hundred pounds.

Terrence Dodson rose from his chair and walked to the window and gazed out of it, his shoulders slowly slumped to an almost resigned form. Several moments had passed since he'd last spoke now, Jason was intimidated as anyone could get, but he didn't let it show. Terrence lowered his head a little as he spoke over his shoulder.

"I understand you're living with my daughter and son."

Jason's nervousness increased a little. "I'm renting a room from her until I can find a better place to stay."

Terrence didn't even look back. "Nonsense." He turned slightly just so Jason could see his eyes and mouth, and his shoulders buffed again, "There's word around town that the two of you have hit it off, am I right?"

"I... I don't know..."

"I'm a man of few words Mr. Parmenter. I'm also a man of fewer tolerances than most."

"We've become pretty good friends." Jason said with a dry mouth.

A sad smile seemed to cross the man's face, but he turned back towards the window and Jason could see that his shoulders were tensing; there was an open defiance about Terrence right now. "Friends." It was a flat statement.

"I mean we're not... uh... sleeping..." Jason fumbled through the words. Terrence turned sharply and the look of anger in his eyes shot laser beams. Jason lowered his head in reflective defeat. "Sorry." In his mind he wanted to be the way folks in town saw them, lovers. He wanted Carrie to love him as much as he loved her now, being here in this office made it plain that he'd go through anything for her and the other things he was planning for them.

There was a moment of anger and the urge to step over to the small man on the other side of the desk and pummel him into leftovers, but Terry rescinded within himself. He took a deep breath and let out a long sigh of retreat himself. He had brought this boy here for a reason, to solve a decade of anger and hate, to resolve two decades of resentment from his daughter, to keep the helm of this company away from his drunken son Thomas "Tommy" Dodson.

Another breath of uneasiness, "Mister... uh Jason." Terry's voice dropped. "I hope you are being honest with me. I need honesty right now."

Jason nodded emphatically.

314

Terry took another small breath and let it out in a fast moving stream of words, so fast they barely had time to register with Jason, "I want you to take my daughter away from here. I want you to take my son Dusty and her to a safe place and let her run this company from afar."

She could hardly wait for him to leave. Jason was hesitant as could be this morning, for good reason. But, she needed him out of the house so she could get some things done, so she could get what she needed and the phone was her first stop. She dialed the number from memory, chatted with the person on the other side for several minutes then returned the receiver to its cradle with a huge smile on her face and a tickle in her tummy. She had been able to do what she wanted and get what she needed, now she had to get Dusty up and going, and away from that damn video game Jason had bought him. They had to get to town in two hours, keep out of sight from Jason, and anyone else who might tattle.

Dusty was in a mood this morning, the weather was chilly and he didn't want to dress warm, so it was a struggle to get him into his jacket and gloves. He wasn't used to this; Mondays were usually stay at home and study days, but not this week. Carrie had even mentioned this to Jason as he was getting ready to leave. Nervously tying his tie he'd asked what her plans were today and she suggested the home school thing. It was a fib, but a small one. She had to get out of the house for a few hours. Jason had indicated that he was heading straight up to the area in the hills that he'd been working for the last few weeks for some final samples after his meeting-if he still had a job-and maybe he'd be gone most of the day. That was all Carrie needed to get things done.

"Excuse me?" Jason nearly fell out of his chair.

"Are you in love with my daughter? Yes or no?" Terry had changed his tone only slightly.

"I... I..." Jason was going to say he hadn't thought about it, but he wondered if Terrence Dodson could spot a lie. He figured the man could. "I seem to be enjoying her company more and more, we've grown on each other I think."

Dodson turned towards the window again and spoke low and purposefully, "I love my daughter and sons, contrary to what people say or think. I've done some terrible things these last few years, trying to keep them safe from the outside world, the meanness, the anger and the hate that the world around us fills us with. He turned towards Jason; his face had dropped like a man who had just received bad news about his health. "And now, I have little time to resolve everything that I've done. Little time." He stopped talking and looked directly at Jason, his eyes filling with what some people called tears; Jason didn't know what Terry Dodson called them.

Jason knew immediately what his boss and father of his friend was going through. He'd seen the look in the eyes of his grandmother on his father's side. "You're dying." Without emotion, but maybe a tinge of apology.

Terry evaded the statement, "Carrie needs someone to look after her. Dusty, needs someone too. A father figure, since I've blown my chance. Rumor has it that his health has improved since you've come to town?"

Jason nodded but added, "I don't think it was all me, I..."

"Nonsense." There was that word again, Terry must like it. But this time it was full of compassion instead of negativity. "He... likes you a lot. He's talking more like a ten year old instead of a five year old. He's developing motor skills. I've heard he's flown with you."

"Yes sir."

316

Terry shook his head. "I would've never approved of that. But if it makes the boy happy, then it can't be of any harm. Your boss says you're a good pilot and that you're very trustworthy."

Jason could feel the blushing his face was doing.

"If, Carrie likes you as much as I've heard, then things will be better off for her and Dusty. I've willed the Dodson Mine and Mill to him."

Jason nodded. He knew that there was something more, something that troubled Terrence Dodson more than whether his daughter was safe and happy. There was an *if*, there were always *ifs*.

"No one, and I mean no one, not even Miss Carrie Marie Dodson will have any control over operations when the boy turns eighteen."

"Yes sir, but I don't see…"

Dodson turned towards the window again and this time his voice was angry, "Yes. Mr. Parmenter, I'm dying. I have less than six months. I want you to marry my daughter, and then Mr. and Mrs. Jason Parmenter will have control over the mine and mill as caretakers and guardian to Dusty Dodson."

Carrie had made it back to the house faster than she'd thought possible. Everyone in town was being so gracious, she didn't even have to lift a finger to get what she needed; Mary Taylor even offered to watch Dusty for a while so Carrie could finalize things. Carrie felt something was wrong, or at least something was going on. Her father could do that to people, make them fidget about doing things and not even let Carrie in on it, and those working errands for Mr. Terrence Dodson were sworn to silence.

Jason was wondering whether or not to reach up with his hand to check and see how far his jaw was open. He'd thought he sprained it seconds ago. *Marry* her? What the hell was going on? This is not the way things happen in Fallcast, at least not from what Jason had gleaned over the few months he'd been here.

"We go through life not thinking about the day we, we…" Terry reached for a glass on the desk; it had brown liquid in it. Jason didn't think it was tea. "I have been thinking a lot lately. About all the things I could've done, all the things I should've done. Then all the things I had done. The balance isn't quite in my favor for heaven." He laughed.

"I don't understand." Jason said cautiously, "Are you trying to make amends?"

"Amends. Reimbursement, reciprocation, maybe some retribution. We never think about what we're doing until it's done. Never consider the consequences until someone comes to collect for them, I lost the only thing that would've mattered to me this day, I lost the first thing I really fell in love with. Marie." He wiped a tear from the corner of his eye like he was only rubbing them.

"Carrie's mother…" Jason added flatly.

"All three of them. But I think Carrie misses her the most, outside of me. Dusty's too young and damaged, Tommy is too interested in his booze and power. Carrie's caught in the middle. They were two of a kind. They looked the same at the same age, they were nearly inseparable. Until the day she ran away from us. I drove her to run off; me and my father's *way*. A *way* I'm challenging myself to change, to fix if I can. To stop the flow of damage and start the healing."

Jason waited for the other shoe to drop.

"That's what this whole thing is about. The will, you and Carrie running things under Dusty's name." His voice wavered between anger and melancholy.

"Where did she go?" Jason asked, not a hint of sarcasm crossed his voice.

Dodson dodged the question. "Of course, there's going to be trouble." Terry began again, his voice calmer.

Jason nodded. "*Tommy*". He said the name out loud.

Now it was Terry's turn to nod. He sat down at his desk and drew out a sheet of paper from the top drawer. "This, is a rough copy of my will. Thomas Dodson will be given many of my properties around town. The bulk of my savings. Other things. But he wants the mine. He wants control of the mill when it re-opens next May."

Jason crooked his head, "May?"

"I haven't shut the mill down completely. I'm having it refit. For our new venture, involving what you found on my property. Marcus Dowards doesn't know about my plans, and he'd better not find out from anyone this room." Jason resisted the urge to glance over his shoulder at the open door, but he felt humor was not required right now.

Jason toyed with idea still of asking Carrie to marry him as Terry rose from his seat, walked over to the open door and closed it slowly, with only the sound of the latch catching. He returned to the leather chair and slowly sat back down, placing both hands on the oak centerpiece.

Terry said, "There's more. The reason I brought up the assay scenario is simple. You've gotten the results that I assume you wanted?"

Jason felt ill again. He'd been holding a trump card and now he was ready to play it. The cave. If Terrence alludes where Jason thinks he might, there'll be a price to pay. But why hasn't he gone there yet?

"I know about the samples you took, but not where. I know about the results because Ben Laudin is a friend of mine and as soon as he saw the trace markers of the samples, he called me to ask if you had permission. I know that you were supposed to be here looking for gold, Marcus is sentimental about the yellow stuff and he even thinks there might be enough of it in the hills around here to get this town rolling again. Nobody uses that much borax anymore."

Jason was twitching in his chair. Should he play his hand now? Or wait?

"I know about the lithium." Terry continued.

Jason let out a sigh of semi-relief. He wasn't home free yet.

Dodson continued, "What I don't know is *where*. I could hire another geologist, take months to find the run, but, I have you."

"I…" Jason began.

Terry raised a finger to hold Jason's response and said, "You see, this is more of a business deal than a marriage or whatever you feel is the best course of action. With you as my son-in-law, we can get this town rolling again in under a year. I'll be gone, but Carrie will be the town's matriarch. You'll be her confidant and partner. You'll be part of the reason Fallcast returns to the map, imagine, this town full of miners paying top dollar for rooms, food, clothing and supplies. The possibilities are endless."

Jason was speechless. Not only did the scariest man in town now want him to marry his daughter, he wanted Jason to become part of the rebuilding of Fallcast. He decided to keep the secret to himself for the moment and asked, "What if Carrie says no?"

Dodson lifted himself from the desk and turned to look out the window again. He drew a heavy breath and wiped his eyes. Jason felt a pang of sadness for the man. His head was swimming with possibilities, *with* the proposal *and* the proposal. It was true he was in love with this man's daughter, but marriage? He hadn't considered it to this point; Terry began speaking in a voice barely audible over the hum of the florescent lights.

"I had big dreams for this town. My father's dreams actually. We wanted to be like the big mining towns of the past, a father figure for the people to respect. But in the seventies my father got caught up in this stupid religious crap, he pulled me and my new bride into it, then our children. Suddenly his dreams faded, he became obsessed with this line of thinking.

"I've had big dreams myself. It takes a lot of hard work to achieve your goals, but goals and dreams are so far separate from each other that you can't see them both without sacrifice. And I sacrificed a lot. My beautiful wife, Carrie's mother, left me."

Jason stirred in his chair. *Why is he keeping this façade up?*

Terry continued, "I got most of my dreams, but now in the final days of my life, I realize that getting your dreams and realizing them are two different things. You came here at the request of my *partner*," Terry made quotation marks with his fingers in the air, "but now you'll be working for me here. I need you to show me where you got this sample that shows such promise, the promise of saving this dying town."

Carrie was setting up the dining room for a nice dinner. She had removed the expensive China that her mother received on her wedding day from the hutch, it was a little sooty, so she wiped every last dish down with a moist rag, when the doorbell rang. She checked on Dusty as she walked through the living room, he was busy flying some airplane on Jason's laptop, so she continued to the door.

"Darrin Parker. What brings you by?" Carrie could smell alcohol on his breath before he answered.

"Just in the area. I'm off today so I thought I'd pay you a visit. Is Jason here?" It was the last part of the question that made Carrie's ears perk up. Parks was not interested in Jason's presence, but in his absence.

Carrie shook her head, "No. He's at a meeting with, my father of all people."

Parks nodded. "Yeah."

Carrie turned her head to the side, "You know?"

"Everyone does. You know how this town is. Bets are he's going to kick your roommate out of town and add a boot print to his ass on the way."

Carrie frowned, "Come inside Darrin."

Parks shook his head and raised his hands in defeat, "No, that's alright. I just came by to say…" He clammed up and stepped back in retreat. "That…" He was off the porch now and walking backwards to his Nova, "I love you."

Carrie felt a rush of panic, and then as Parks jumped into his vehicle and started the engine, she felt a wave exasperation crush her, as did her feelings. She wasn't expecting that from him, but the booze made it easier for him to say. She felt sad for him and a little warm. He wasn't all that bad of a person, but what brought him to this? She was kindling a tinge of self-awareness; she was blushing at his statement and she even felt gracious towards the cop. She waved as Parks sped out of the driveway, spewing gravel as he went. Carrie shook her head and went inside.

Dodson returned to his original line of thinking, "Tommy is not evil, but he has a mean streak and a bad side. He'll fight with every last breath to get control of the mine, to get control over his sister's inheritance. He's a lot like his grandfather; he believes that women have no place in anything other than the home."

Jason felt like saying something positive about the guy, but he couldn't think of anything. He saw how Tommy intimidated people around town, from Ron the bartender to even poor old Eldred Baylee at the mercantile.

"You've gotten yourself a long battle ahead." Terry ended with a turn from the window as he sat back down for the final time of the meeting. He placed his hands in front of him and formed a steeple with his fingers. "You decide. Right now, go your own way and leave this town as fast as you can. Or, stay and help me and this town out, and win the hand of my daughter, who has been rumored to have fallen in love with you."

Jason spoke but his throat was muddled with phlegm. He cleared it out with a cough and swallowed. "Who told you that?"

"Everyone I know has seen it. You don't hold hands wherever you go, you don't kiss in public, you don't hug each other in public, but many have seen it in her eyes. Her mother's eyes. I saw it just before Christmas when I mentioned you to her. She defended you as fast as she could." Terry took a deep breath, that had an echo of some sort in his chest, "This is your last chance."

Jason felt shallow breaths coming on, his chest felt heavy. He had to throw out his ace in the hole, just a smidgen to see if he could get a bite, in case things turned south on him.

"I've been through the cave." He waited, almost recoiled as he expected to be either thrown out of punched in the face.

"The cave?" Terry's eyes crooked, he looked confused.

"The place on Forests Hill about ten miles up from your mill."

Terry shook his head, the look on his face and the question in his eyes either made him a very good liar, or he didn't even know about Jason's discovery. "Mr. Parmenter, are you talking about that place the kids hang out in? I wish there was a way we could just blow that thing up, before someone else gets hurt there." His eye rose to meet Jason's,

"What about it? If you want to excavate there, you don't have to get my permission…"

Jason didn't get the bite he was looking for. Something was wrong; could it be that Terrence knew nothing about the cave and its secrets? "It was in the original charter. I just thought maybe you knew something about it…"

"No. If you want I can have it thrown in as part of a business deal. Sort of a wedding present." Terry was at a lack of understanding what the significance was with the old hole in the ground. As far as he knew, it was simply an old digging that revealed nothing valuable and now the kids in town use it for under-age drinking. "I'll have the paperwork drawn up…"

"That won't be necessary, thank you Mr. Dodson. Can I have a few days to think about your proposal?"

"Two. That's all. I need to know by Wednesday, I have arrangements to make."

Terry Dodson stood and offered a hand. Jason shook it, the man's grip transmitted a message; Terrence Dodson would not like a "no" answer. Jason turned and headed for the door as Terrence offered one last thought, "No one finds out about this. Ever. I take this conversation to the grave, as well you do. Nothing about my eventual demise, nothing about the lithium mine or the refit at the mill. Nothing about how I asked you with a troubled heart to help make amends for my stranglehold on this town and my family. If Carrie comes to me with her eyes red from crying and a story that you were forced to ask for her hand in marriage, you'll never be found."

Terrence Dodson sat back down at his desk and turned his chair to the window as Jason worked the knob on the door and walked out.

"I'll bet." He said quietly to himself as he left the mill offices.

Jason didn't go to the mountains like he'd said he would. Instead he went to the cave. There was something he needed to find out. It had been four hours after he'd left Terry Dodson's office when he returned to Carrie's house. He headed for the kitchen, took out a long-neck bottle of beer and opened it.

Carrie walked in when she heard the front door open and close, she was expecting Jason, and had the dinner in the oven. When she reached the open archway that led into the room, she noticed something was very wrong; Jason sat at the dining table in his nice suit, which was filthy, and he nursed a beer like a ravenous newborn on a teat.

"That bad huh? What did my father do to you?"

Jason looked up to her, first there was this look of panic, then it relaxed into a smile, a sad and confused smile, but at least the threatening tone of it was gone. "Oh! Hi, how was your day?" There was a hint of sarcasm, but very little flowed through in his words. "Mine was exciting."

Carrie let a rumpled frown cross her face, her puffy lips turned down and the gold in her eyes darkened, "*What did my father do to you?*" There was no smirk in her tone this time, accusation flowed heavily.

Jason shook his head slowly and tugged at the golden liquid in the brown bottle. After a long swallow and the impending fizzle in his throat from the carbon dioxide, he gasped a breath and spoke softly, "Your father... was a gentleman."

Carrie pulled a chair across the floor loudly then sat down hard. "You're kidding?"

Jason took a smaller slug this time and looked at the woman in front of him. He couldn't let Carrie in on the full force of his lecture and eventual proposal he received today, he could however, pry.

"Carrie, do you like me?"

Her eyes furrowed, "Why? What did that *bastard* say?!"

Jason shook his head emphatically, "Nothing about that. I was just thinking, about us. I mean, there's a possibility that I might be here for a while, a long while. How would you feel about that?"

Carrie thought for a moment, she considered Jason's words carefully, absorbed the meaning and the innuendo of the resulting answer she would give, "I'd like that, a lot."

Jason smiled big and nodded at her. "Do you think, maybe, that you could love me?"

"Possibly…" There was a play in her tone; her words seemed to laugh on their own as they left her beautiful mouth, "Depends on what you have planned."

"Your father has offered me a full time job. Full benefits and an eventual bonus that would take care of me and you, and Dusty for the rest of our lives…"

Carrie face froze somewhere between disbelief and shock. "He *what?*"

"Do you think you could love me?"

Carrie let the fact that her father was now invading her life once again to answer Jason's question without hesitation, "Yes. *I do love you.*" The relief of letting the man in front of her know how she felt was exhilarating, her stomach rumbled and her blood chilled with excitement, but the opposite was happening below her navel, she was building in warmth and anxiety.

This is what Jason had been expecting, he knew she had feelings for him, he was developing strong feelings for her, he'd hoped that she wasn't just lonely and in need of some companionship.

"From the moment I got the results of Dusty's last exam. I knew that you were a caring and loving person, that you'd do anything for us if you had to. I just knew inside."

She scooted her chair closer to him. He wrapped his arms around her after setting his nearly empty beer down. He sighed into her ear, "I just needed to know. I wanted to be sure that if I decided to stay, that you and I had a chance."

She kissed his ear lobe and ran soft pecks along his neck as she whispered, "I'll be here for you, if you want me to be."

Jason pulled back far enough for her to be able to kiss his lips and he hers, he pulled her onto his lap and the first deep passionate kiss between them escaped, love was mutual now and they both knew it. He'd fallen in love with her also. Carrie broke free a few moments later, slightly panting.

"Why did the meeting with my father bring this all on?" Her concern had surfaced again. If it had anything to do with Terrence Dodson, it couldn't be good.

Jason shuttled her back a little on his leg. "Well, he does want to see you again."

"I knew it!" She stood from his leg. "He put you up to this, didn't he?"

Jason raised his hands in defense, "Not at all. He gave me the opportunity to think about what I needed to do."

"What was that? He'd force you to marry his daughter so you could bask in the riches of the Dodson family?"

"It's not like that…"

"Really? You spend five hours at his office and the next thing you know, you're moving here and asking if I'd need a live-in lover?"

"Carrie… I love you for you. Your father disapproves of the fact I'm here. But he wants my expertise on a new mine. I stayed; I wanted to stay, for you."

Carrie was mulling this over. She knew Terrence had something to do with this, but what?

"Besides, I was only there for an hour. I… walked for about two more around town, then I went up to the hills to clear my head. I've been up there this whole time. I had to think. I had to make sure what I was doing was the right thing, for you and for Dusty…"

Carrie sat back down slowly. She shook her head with anticipation, "You really want to stay?"

"If I have a room."

"You can have *mine*…" The coyness in her voice was hard to define, was she kidding or serious. Her hand brushed his face then dropped to his chest and flipped open the top button of his suit jacket. She was serious.

Jason reached up with both hands to stop hers from advancing. "In a few weeks, we'll talk about that. I want you for who you are right now, not what we can achieve together."

"Jason?"

"I have to make arrangements to get my life in Denver moved here and I have to be sure this is permanent. I have a ton of stuff, mostly junk, but I think I can get a storage shed at a reasonable…"

Carrie interrupted with a kiss to his cheek, "The garage will be fine." She perked up a little and sat up straight, "Oh! I forgot, I have a Christmas present for you!"

"There's no need for that…"

"Nonsense." Jason looked at her intensely, this is her father's favorite word, "If I can get that brother of mine torn away from the stupid computer of yours, I'll show you. Get your jacket!"

Jason saw she was too happy to refuse her. He complied and drew his coat off the bar stool at the breakfast nook where he left it when he came in. He could hear the howls of protest from Dusty as Carrie forced him to shut the game off. There was a moment of whispering and then the boy yelled, "Yay!"

"Keep your eyes closed! No cheating!"

Carrie led Jason from the mine vehicle. He didn't have the heart to tell her he knew where they were, he wanted her to remain excited; but the smell of the fumes, the tell-tale sound of wind blowing softly over a wide open field and the squeaky mechanical sound of the rotator light on the small twenty foot tower told him the location. The airport.

A smile crossed his lips as he felt himself being tugged towards the hangar, his feet making crunching sounds on the pea gravel, the echo of their movements against the giant steel doors. Finally they stopped. Dusty had him by the left hand, Carrie by the right, and then the sound of old metal tracks being drug against each other as the big hangar doors were slid to the sides of the Quonset hut.

"Surprise!"

Jason laughed as he walked around the three new barrels of Avgas.

"How can you afford this, I can't accept it!" Jason beamed.

"My father. Seems he gave us a little extra this month, for some reason."

The mill. He cleaned out the petty cash from the old mill… Jason thought to himself.

Terry was on his third scotch and soda, sans the soda. He'd tried to mend broken fences today, but had doubt as to the success; much of his effort had gone into investing in the new guy in town, the stranger who was living with his daughter. Rumors began to fly around the berg as soon as the fire had chased the geologist from his hotel room, a fire that points its ugly finger at his oldest son as a suspect, and the mill full of talk. Whispered things like; Jason and Carrie had begun a love affair, to; the flying outsider had moved in and decided to stay. But the phone call from Elko and the mineral assayer friend that Terry had confirmed that the boy from Denver was looking for something, *some reason* to stay.

"Hi Meg. How're you feeling?"

Megan had managed to get her wheelchair to the door in three or four minutes after the knocking started. When she was finally able to wrest the knob unlocked, she was staring face to gun belt of Darrin Parks.

"Okay, I guess. C'mon in."

He waited until she had turned the wheelchair around and he helped push her towards her small dining room table in the kitchen. There was several books, an ashtray, a bottle of rum, three opened cans of Coke, a deck of cards and a plate that looked to have a half-eaten sandwich on it in the center. Parks determined this is where Megan had been spending her day, if not days since her release from the hospital.

"Sorry 'bout the mess." She began as she pulled some of the clutter towards her and Parks stepped in to pick the trash up and toss it in the can by the sink. "Gloria was here a little while ago. She's been keeping me company before she goes to work." Meg tried a smile that might have failed, if the pain pills hadn't made her relaxed.

"No problem. I just came by to see how you're doing."

Tears slightly fell from Megan's eyes. "I'm okay I suppose. It… It's just so quiet and… lonely here."

Parks put his hand on Meg's uninjured shoulder. "I know. I'm so sorry."

Megan opened a bottle of prescription medicine and shook out an elongated pill onto the palm of her hand. She reached for a can of cola and slammed the pill to the back of her throat and washed it down. "Vicodin." She said flatly.

"Can I get you anything?"

Meg's face turned into a sour pale twist, "Heard that Jason's back in town."

Parks pulled out a chair. "Heard that too." He affirmed as he sat down, his leather belt squeaking in the nearly silent kitchen.

"Heard he had a meeting today with *her* dad. Heard it was cozy, not confrontational."

Parks just nodded. He hadn't received this much. This was new.

Meg just waved the accusation off with a hand. "Dowards' secretary told Gloria at the diner at lunch. Says they shook hands afterwards and all. '*It seemed real chummy…*'"

Parks exhaled sharply. "So?"

Meg felt anger rushing into her face at the same time the Vicodin was rushing into her bloodstream, "*He* isn't moving out. As a matter of fact, *they* were at the Salt Lick for lunch and Gloria says they were closer than ever. She says *they* were giggling and carrying on like a couple of teenagers."

Parks rumpled his brow and his toothpick dropped downward, "Look Meg. You can't go on blaming Carrie for what happened between you and Steve."

"He loved her, he told me right there in the car just before I…" She caught her words and put her hand to her mouth. "Nothing."

Parks tapped his hand softly on the arm that was in a plaster cast from the wrist to the elbow. "Everyone knows I had a thing for Carrie myself years ago, before I left for school. But we have to let things go as they will; we're just making it harder on ourselves."

Meg winced as she withdrew her set arm away. "She's going to pay…"

Parks nodded. He knew that the drug was taking effect and that Meg was probably the one drinking the rum, mixing the chemicals was a bad idea and it made her say things she didn't mean, but he was in her home and he didn't need to get her fighting with him. He stood and excused himself to her back door. He should've been on patrol a half hour ago.

"Things'll work out Meg. They always do."

Just as Parks was letting himself out the door he heard her say, "Yeah. I'll see to it."

The fire was crackling and the room was darkened by the setting sun. In the winter the sun was down by six here in the Soap Valley, the mountains subtracting time from the descent by their height. Carrie was sitting with her feet pulled up underneath her behind, a mug of hot chocolate between her hands and she was blowing the steam off the top. Jason was sitting opposite her on the loveseat; he was holding a cup of the same with a Kahlua enhancement on one finger through the handle. Dusty was asleep on the floor between them, his Cessna toy clutched in his arms and a peaceful smile of content on his face.

Jason was mulling over the words that had been presented to him today by Carrie's father, the somewhat indirect plea to take Carrie's hand and help with Dusty. Raise the young boy to run the family mill, if he can handle it. But that wasn't all that was rambling through his head. There was the cave, the secret of the cave that Terrence never mentioned, in fact, he seemed unfazed about it as if he didn't even know the importance or the existence of what the hole in the ground represented to the Dodson family. Maybe he didn't know, but that would be nearly impossible.

"Penny for your thoughts." Carrie said softly over the slow jazz playing on the radio.

Jason smiled over to her and took a sip of spiked hot chocolate.

He said, "Just thinking… Can we get a babysitter for Thursday night? It's New Year's Eve and I thought we'd go to Vegas, or something. Just you and I."

"Gloria is working, maybe Parks can do it."

Jason nodded with a slightly pained expression; he tried to picture Darrin Parker babysitting, which would be an entertaining spectacle to witness. "Parks?"

"He's done it before."

Jason weighed the price he'd have to pay for the deputy's time at the controls of Dusty for a night. "I have to make some phone calls, but if you can arrange the sitter, then we can have a date." The first phone call in the morning was to Terrence, he'd get his answer.

"A real date? Of course, this is something I have to see…" She said sarcastically.

It took a long time for Parks to give his answer fully. He was not exactly happy about watching Dusty so the girl he had a crush on could go out with the quarterback, or that is how the whole scenario seemed. Just like high school, he had this crush on Mary Lister, the dance squad leader. He built up enough courage to ask her out one day and she replied by asking him if he didn't mind driving her "friend" in his Nova along with them. Turned out Mary and the boy Nick sat in the back making all kinds of smacking noises while Darrin drove them to the old drive-in. Same feeling now, but with age comes heavier tug at the heartstrings.

"My place is a mess, not really a good time for me…" Parker responded.

"You can stay at my place." Carrie replied.

It took a few minutes more, but Parks agreed. It made him happy to hear Carrie happy.

At three in the afternoon December 31st, Carrie and Jason were on their way to Las Vegas in his Cessna. Two suitcases stuffed into the back seat and the tanks were full thanks to Carrie's last minute Christmas gift, they reached the general aviation portion of McCarran International by four and were riding the elevator to the fifth floor of the *Luxor Hotel and Casino* by four forty-five.

The Luxor was a grand spectacular; Carrie had never been in something so luxurious before, not even to visit. Her stomach trembled the whole time they were in line to check in. She was afraid to ask Jason what it cost to stay here especially on New Year's, so she averted her eyes when he produced a credit card to pay for the room.

The room. The Luxor was a giant pyramid in all respects, from the Sphinx guarding the front of the hotel, to the massive Egyptian architecture styled interior and even the way the inside of the casino rose in a twenty five degree angle to the top floor inward, just like it would look on the inside of a pyramid. Each hotel room door opened out to a railing so that a person could look directly down to the casino floor after stepping out of the luxurious accommodations. The room itself was richer than she had ever experienced before.

The space consisted of about fifteen by twenty feet, the huge queen adorned with four large pillows with satin sheets and roll cushions took most of the center. Across from the bed was an armoire that held a closet, a large desk that stood five foot high next to it and a fifty inch flat screen TV rested upon that. A smaller desk was attached to the larger one with a bowl of real fruit as its centerpiece.

Along the window wall was a small round table with two upholstered chairs, both appearing to cost more than the sofa and loveseat in her own living room, and the window was at the same angle as the wall to the doorway and the outer walkway. Just as the angle rose up to a point in the casino, the room gave the appearance of being inside the wall of a pyramid as well.

Carrie gasped when the door to the room was opened. She wandered for the next ten minutes looking here and there, out the window at the view of downtown

Vegas, then in the spacious bathroom, back out to fondle the fruit and then to the bed. A couple of bounces and she ran her hands on the soft spread.

"I could only get this room, one bed…" Jason began, "I promise to be on my best behavior."

"I don't think that'll be necessary." Carrie replied, with a twist of coyness and sultry apprehension.

Jason just cleared his throat. "I'm going to take a shower. The remote is on the nightstand." Carrie winked at him and he retreated to the bathroom, *probably not needing the hot water right now*, she joked to herself.

They ate at *Tender Steak and Seafood* inside the *Luxor*, both Carrie and Jason had to dress up, Jason in business casual with a smart soft dark blue suit and matching tie, Carrie wore a black fluffy and sheer cocktail dress she had bought years ago for a wedding and hadn't worn since.

After dinner the couple found themselves walking hand in hand around the casino, neither of them dropped any money on the machines or the tables, and eventually found themselves at a crowded bar. The *High Bar* it was called and the name did it great service. An intimate little niche by the casino, with soft music and generous drinks, the *High Bar* was the place Jason was hoping for, for what came next.

He'd gone absent when Carrie entered the shower, dropped down to the shopping area of the hotel and found a jewelry shop. He walked out in ten minutes, hoping Carrie was the type who loved a long hot shower; his suit jacket pocket was heavier with a small velvet blue box. His wallet was lighter by three thousand dollars.

Carrie was nursing her second drink, a Cosmopolitan; Jason was taking huge sips of a long neck Budweiser. A crowd at a nearby craps table began cheering and Jason slipped the box from his pocket to the table and discreetly covered the box with his hand, feeling the softness of the velvet against his rough fingers. Carrie returned her eyes from the cacophony in the casino to sip her drink when she caught Jason's eyes. They were a little moist.

"Smoke bothering you?" She asked.

He cleared his throat, careful not to let the cracking of the vocal chords affect him too much and whispered above the din of the bar and casino. "Do you love me?"

Carrie blushed slightly, "I think I do. I think it was easy for me, I am falling fast. Who couldn't with all that you've done for me."

Jason cleared his throat again, "What would you say if I told you I was planning to stay in Fallcast?"

"You said that already."

"I mean it. I want to be here, with you. And Dusty, forever…"

Carrie's eyes grew big with excitement, but then a small fog of discouragement drew into them, the gold flecks fading, "Why? You have a great life in Denver. I thought you were kidding about staying, really."

"You said I could use your garage…" Jason said.

"I know, but I mean, permanently?" Her voice began to crack now too.

"I had to ask you father something, and…"

"Jason, what did my father say? Is this about him or us?"

"It's only about us…" Jason moved his hand from the box and rapped the mahogany bar with his knuckle slightly to get her eyes drawn to the blue thing. "About you, and I and forever."

Carrie's eyes slowly tracked to where Jason's hand was. The closer they came to their destination, the wider they got, the brighter and shinier the gold in them became, then they flooded with tears.

336

"Oh… my… god…" Her voice disappeared into the music playing in the background.

"I have your father's permission, not that it matters, to marry you. Will you marry me Carrie?"

CHAPTER SEVENTEEN
Two Months Later

Carrie sat in a very uncomfortable chair, one of two that sat on either side of her father's office door at the Dowards Mine and Mill offices. It had been a very uncomfortable two months since New Year's Eve when Jason asked her to marry him, two long months filled with anger, sadness, hurt and forgiveness on both sides. Carrie twirled the one carat diamond ring on the fourth finger of her left hand, the gift from Jason, a center piece diamond the size of a large pea, with a sickle shaped moon around it, all mounted on a white platinum band with dozens of little diamonds around the crescent and along the band.

At first she had begged him to take it back, it was too much for him to afford, and then after hearing him with a return plea to keep it, she acquiesced. She didn't say yes right away, her eyes filled with tears, her heart with happiness and fulfillment; but then it occurred to her that Jason had mentioned he'd had Terry's permission, Carrie put two and two together. Jason had a meeting with her father on Monday, Jason asks Carrie to marry him on Thursday. She was angry, almost red hot but she calmed herself, she was in a public place after all.

Her heart began to beat hard against her chest, knowing that this was an arranged marriage of some sort, arranged by her father who couldn't help sticking his nose in where it didn't belong, and she would have none of it. After she had voiced her opinion in a not so subtle tone over the piano player at the bar, she saw Jason's heart break. His face fell, his eyes watered even more than they were-not from happiness or anticipation-but from rejection. Even though Carrie had spelled out the reason she believed he was asking her hand in marriage, even though he denied that he'd made a deal with Terrence Dodson for the bride like some East Indian dowry, even though he had said he'd been planning to live in Fallcast for a week or so prior to his meeting with the patriarch of the Dodson family and his love was the result of being with her for the few weeks leading up to his decision, Carrie refuted this. And she watched Jason melt down.

They returned to the expensive room he had rented for them, Jason had taken his clothes off and climbed into bed, his reddened and swollen eyes facing the window and the shining lights trickled in from below. Carrie had come out of the bathroom to find him like this, she tried to apologize for her reaction, but Jason remained silent. Carrie lay above the covers on her side, until she finally dozed off, lightly sobbing. Her father had come into her life again.

A lot had changed in the last few weeks, Jason had woken up early New Year's Day and packed quietly; he made coffee for them both and sat silently watching the TV news with the volume off and the closed captioning on. When Carrie woke, he smiled graciously and let her get ready to leave. They spoke little about the night before, Jason making small talk, Carrie nodding. The ring was in the little box it came in. Things had changed when they returned.

Jason seemed a little hesitant to talk about his proposal, Carrie felt cornered. One night, after a mysterious cell phone call at eleven o'clock p.m., Jason said he had to return to Denver for a few weeks to get things straightened out at *home*. Finally Carrie confronted him before he left.

"I'm sorry. I thought that my father put you up to this…"

"Why don't you talk to him? Just go and see him? What can he do in public to you? Nothing. Ask him for yourself what he wants; all I wanted was you and Dusty to be my family. Once again I find myself having to defend the way I feel. I thought you'd be happy. I thought you'd be glad someone was willing to be with you and help you raise Dusty. But now I feel like you're just using me as an excuse to get even with your father, he didn't put me up to any of this, he just suggested he'd help out with things if I stayed with you. Marrying you was *my* idea."

Jason threw his pack over his shoulder at midnight and headed for the door.

"Jason, please don't leave angry. Is that what you want? For me to say I'll marry you? Because I will, but I just want to make sure that this isn't some game for my father..."

"Then I guess you have a few weeks to discuss it with him. And as for agreeing to marry me, the moment is lost right now, I've lost the taste since I know our lives will be filled with doubt; that you only agreed because you think you've hurt my feelings..."

Jason didn't slam the door behind him, but he might as well have.

Carrie visited Meg three days later, after two nights of waiting for Jason to return her call. She just wanted to make sure he made it back to Denver safe, and maybe try to talk with him, understand what he feels and maybe try to explain herself to him. How the torture of her family brought her so much pain.

Meg was moving about now. Her wrist was in a brace, her leg in a smaller cast and a walking boot. Her mood had changed a little it seemed, she was no longer angry at Carrie outwardly.

Meg had gotten some great news, her lawyer Richard L. Ferrence (the lawyer that Jason hired for her) had managed to get her out of any more than one court appearance. He'd filed a writ of Habeas Corpus, demanding the evidence be laid out formally, that there'd be no more delays. He issued a statement to the judge that the testimony of the service station owner Sal Buford was tainted and that after interviewing the man himself, found his story had changed. This is what the D.A.'s office found too. Attorney Ferrence also pointed out that what the trooper had overheard in the hospital cannot be admitted as evidence simply because Megan was not given her Miranda Rights and anything she said was inadmissible.

The D.A. sputtered a quick plea bargain, two years probation and the deal was accepted. Meg was free, except she was not allowed to leave Fallcast without written permission and she had to visit her court appointed parole officer weekly or vice versa. Meg at first balked at the idea, but Ferrence convinced her it was better than a lengthy trial where she would still stand a slight chance of conviction. There was the testimony of the witness in another car that saw Meg and Steven physically fighting as they drove to Vegas, and she could get involuntary manslaughter if it was determined she had grabbed the steering wheel. The fact that no brakes were applied could indicate this, so she acquiesced. Two years was a lifetime, but better than jail time.

However, the news that Carrie and Jason had essentially broken up improved Megan's mood even more. She was sympathetic, caring and nurturing to Carrie. They sat and talked for a few hours, Carrie inviting Meg to come over and have dinner with her and Dusty when she got the chance and Meg agreed.

So, here Carrie was. In the last place on earth she'd thought she'd be. She didn't want to be here, she wanted to be in Jason's arms, begging his forgiveness. She heard a door close down the hallway of the offices, looked up and saw the scariest thing she'd ever known. Her father, walking towards her, with a smile. Sad but true.

His smile didn't faze her although it had a certain degree of evil in it, it was the man himself. Although he hadn't lost a lot of weight to make him thin as a rail, he'd lost enough to show; at least twenty pounds, maybe thirty. His eyes were hollower than usual, sunken back into his forehead in their sockets as far as it seemed possible. His face was pale white, not the burnish tan color he'd had just the week before Christmas, his movements were slow and determined, not effortless like before. Her father was indeed dying. *Why didn't Jason say anything?*

Terrence opened the door without offering a hello or any other salutation, Carrie rose from the chair and entered, catching a whiff of some bad smelling medicine flowing from his pores. She walked to one of the chairs in the office and sat down without looking up at him at first. Terry sat behind his desk and sighed, it was plain sigh like a relief had washed over him.

"You look like you've seen a ghost." He said flatly.

A tear crept into the corner of Carrie eye, "You're dying." Her eyes rose to meet his.

Terry stared at her effortlessly for a second and nodded with his lips pursed, "Pancreatic cancer. Found out about it in December."

Another tear grew in the other eye. Carrie felt bad for him at this moment and why? She couldn't answer that. He was a cruel man, he did horrible things, he deserved what he was getting; but, he was still her father. "*Why...*" She had to clear her throat, "Why didn't you tell me?"

He laughed a little, "You really didn't appear all that interested in even seeing me then, I didn't want to try and beg for sympathy. I wanted to give you Dusty's present."

Carrie composed herself. She came here for a reason and she was going to get right to it. She pinched the tears away and pursed her lips into a curl, the fluffy elongated M shape of them became a flat line as she spoke tersely, "What kind of deal did you make with Jason?"

Terry leaned back suddenly. His face went from bemused to hurt, "What did he say to you?"

Carrie raised her left hand demonstrating the ring for effect, "He asked me to marry him."

342

Her father shook his head and turned his chair towards the window and spoke softly back to his daughter, "I didn't tell him to do that. I only asked him to get you out of town and he refused, in a manner of speaking."

Carrie's eyebrows rose in surprise, "Oh?"

"He said he wasn't leaving town. I reaffirmed that I wanted him to watch out for you and Dusty, he said he would."

"How was that?"

Terrence Dodson began a speech that lasted ten minutes, Carrie never interrupted once. She could not believe her ears, what her father who she grew to hate was doing. Giving the power of the mine to his young son Dusty, granting Carrie the rights to make decisions based on the mine before he turned eighteen and after if Dusty is not capable of doing so. How Jason knew the exact location of a very precious run of minerals that would bring the town to life again.

"I figured you two for each other. I'm sorry if it went bad."

Carrie felt rage building, "It went bad because your name was brought up. He said he had your permission. It angered me that he'd even talk to you about something like this…"

"I told you, all I wanted was for him to take care of you. The proposal was his idea and he never made any mention of it. Maybe he had it in the back of his mind and the situation felt right, maybe he loves you. It had nothing to do with me." Terry turned from the window to face his estranged daughter, "You seem to have a lot of my blood in you. Anger, retribution, grudge, spite. It sounds like it's all there." His eyes forged a smile, his mouth was taught with disappointment.

Carrie was beside herself. She had come here to figure out what the hell was going on and now she was being insulted by the man who she didn't want to see ever

343

again, in his office on his terms. She was feeling fury brewing over rage now. "How dare you…"

Terry interrupted, "I have a present for you too. I wanted to give it to you when I last saw you, but you were in a hurry to get out of my way."

He reached in his desk while his daughter was still trying to find the words she wanted to pelt him with, his interruption angered her even more. He pulled out a gold locket in the shape of a heart and sat it on the blotter in front of him.

"This was a present from your mother to me." He sighed heavily like a hundred pounds of lead were sat on his chest suddenly and turned towards the window, his hand coming to his face, probably to brush away tears, Carrie thought. "She was a good young lady. She had a heart of a child when it came to love; she fell so easily for me. And I fell for her. Her beauty was more than any man could hope to have in his touch and eyes in all his life. She cared for me so, but…"

Carrie held her breath.

"But there was my father and his church. He swayed many of us back then, his ranting and raving over the Pope and the way the church was heading down a path to destruction. I didn't know any better. I just followed blindly." He turned to face Carrie, his eyes seemed even further back into his pale face, his brow wrinkled like a washboard, his mouth turned down into desperation, "And I took your mother with me into that hell. But even her strength couldn't stand the torture of confinement I guess. When she left…" He paused again, turning back towards the window, his voice cracked with pain, "I no longer believe in any god. Maybe because of who I am, but faith has no bearing on me any longer. Many people think I'm doing all of this to get in God's good graces for when I die in a few months. They're wrong, He is no longer a part of my life, nor will He ever be again. When your mother left

344

us, she took all that was good she could give with her. When you left with Dusty, you took all that good that was remaining."

Terry quickly spun in his chair and picked up the locket, he stretched his hand out with it in his fingers, offering it to Carrie. She hesitated.

"I've removed my photo, if that's what's concerning you. It's just a picture of your mother in there now. This was hers, she left it. I want you to have it; she'd want you to have it."

Carrie felt hurt, "If she cared for us so much, why hasn't she tried to contact us?"

Terry lowered his head and spoke quietly, "Perhaps she thinks we're all still together. She might think your still living with me or at least close to me. I don't think she could bear even looking at me, especially right now. Take it. I want nothing to remind me of who I was when she was here. I'm being punished enough for my sins, right now."

The anger inside of Carrie flushed. She felt a cold chill run down her spine and drop to the top of her legs, then each knee began to bounce nervously. She reached out slowly and took the locket, careful to avoid opening it in front of her father. She offered a coarse, "Thank you."

Terry wasn't finished. "I picked Jason not just because he knew where the profit was in those dusty hills up there, also because he was smart. He seemed to like you and I figured you two would eventually hit it off. He's educated, he is a great influence over Dusty, or so I've heard, and he has money. Which means he isn't marrying you for the mine or the claims, he simply loves you for who you are, just like your mother did for me. But I changed and she left. The shoe is on the other foot now, huh? You showed him my side; anger, hate, rejection. You've become me, instead of that caring blood that belongs to your mother."

Carrie took this all in. She wanted to get up and slap the disgusting face of her father, tell him to rot in hell when he dies, but something snapped. He was right. In his own horrible way he had hit the nail on the head, Carrie had rejected Jason's proposal simply out of spite. Just like her father would. She was trying to get the faintness cleared from her head, trying to get on her feet to leave, but she hesitated. Something was missing.

She cleared her throat and spoke in a soft, calm voice. "Where's Thomas in all of this?"

Terry nodded and looked her in the eye, "He gets the properties, the leases and some of the other things. You get to keep your house of course, but the rest go to him including our old home. That is, if he stays out of jail, which I doubt is an option. In case he ends up back in prison, his inheritance defers to you. All except the money. He gets to keep that, but I doubt he'll have much to spend it on in prison."

Carrie nodded her approval, not that Terry needed it, but seemed like she needed to show some respect, he was dying after all. She raised her head for one last sentence, "I guess I should call Jason."

"You haven't tried yet?"

"He won't return my calls. I'll try his work number today."

Terry scratched his pasty forehead, "I wouldn't."

"Why?"

"Because his boss called yesterday. Jason was fired two weeks ago for violating his contract. You see, while under the employ of Monolith Metals and Minerals, any agent cannot use his skills to gather information or collect samples for personal use. Jason was doing just that, and in even more he was going to use this information to help me re-open the mill."

"What?"

Terry explained that he'd never really closed the mill, that a refit was under way and should be done soon. No one was laid-off, the foreman was overseeing the refit and most of the other employees were brought here to Dowards. Those who didn't want to or couldn't come here was given a large holiday bonus to get them through the four months of the reconstruction, and would be offered their jobs back when the gates opened.

Carrie was beside herself. No one in town talked of this. This was benevolence from a man who offered nothing like this to his family; he was not known for his kindness at all. "Why hasn't anyone said anything about this?"

Terry smiled large, "Because they signed a disclosure statement. If they talked or if it got out, I'd find out who it was and tell them not to return to Dodson Mill. They know that I can play a hard game."

So much for benevolence, Carrie thought. "What about Marcus? Does he know of your plans?"

"Not really. At least at first, but now that I'm dying, he sees opportunity. He thinks he can take control of this town, even if Dodson reopens. He just doesn't know the magnitude of what lies out there in that dirt. I do. And that's why I picked Jason. I want Dodson to remain a name of power and control here in Fallcast, that's why I gave it to Dusty. Even if you run it for him; it will bear his name, our name. If you want to sell it you'll have to get dozens of documents claiming his inability to run the mine after he's eighteen and I know you better than that."

Carrie realized she was rubbing the gold locket in her fingers. She dropped the keepsake into her shirt pocket and stood. She had found the energy to leave, but offered no embrace of handshake for her father as he stood. He nodded at her as she turned for the door.

"One last request? Call it a dying man's last wish?" He asked in a quiet voice before she could turn the doorknob.

Without looking at him or turning, she nodded straight ahead.

"I would like to walk you down the aisle, if things work out with Jason."

Carrie stiffened at this request; she opened the door and walked out without giving him an answer. She closed the door behind her and tears were streaming down her face by the time she reached the parking lot.

"Jason? I'm so very sorry for what happened. Please call me. I love you, I miss you. Please? Give me a chance to say I'm sorry to your face."

Carrie hung up the phone. She knew he wasn't really completely gone; his laptop was still here along with his clothes and personal effects. He wouldn't leave those just to avoid her, would he? No, that's not the man she fell in love with.

Finally, after an excruciating period of silence, the phone rang. Two and a half months after Jason had left Fallcast, Carrie had almost given up on him. Almost. She was blaming herself now, for her short-sightedness. For her bloodlines that fed anger and spite into her veins and head. She was sitting on the front porch watching the sunrise as she rubbed the soft gold locket of her mother's between her thumb and forefinger when the bell on the old Princess phone tingled.

As if she was set afire, she jumped from the porch swing Jason had built and flew into the kitchen to answer it before Dusty woke up.

Her voice was gravelly, "Hello?"

"Hi."

"Jason! It's so good to hear your voice I was worried…"

348

"I'm fine. How's Dusty?"

"He's alright. He misses you and I swear he's going to wear out your laptop with that game of his."

Jason didn't say anything; he let out a sigh that sounded like a half-assed laugh.

"What've you been doing?"

A moment of silence, then his voice was barely above a whisper. "Packing. I'm still moving to Fallcast, no matter what. I've managed to rent a house on the far side of town near the railroad tracks, one with a large garage and a view of the dumps." Another feeble laugh.

Carrie felt excited. But her feelings soon waned as she realized he'd said he was moving into *another* house. She quickly tried to fix things.

"You're more than welcome here. Anytime, you know that right?"

"Okay."

"I mean you can move here, with me and Dusty."

"I don't think that's such a good idea right now. With all that's happened."

A sharp pain struck Carrie in the back near her spine, she asked in a quiet voice, mimicking his, "What's happened?"

"Between us. You being mad at me for asking you to marry me. Your being upset over the fact that I'd talked to your father."

"It wasn't right Jason. I'm sorry for that. I have no explanation for my behavior. We can work things out, alright?"

A long pause meant he was mulling this over, or avoiding the answer all together.

"Lindsay called me a few weeks ago."

The sharp pain turned to an ache in her chest.

"And?"

There was an even longer pause this time. "We talked for a few hours. Nothing between us has changed;

349

she ended the conversation by asking for a ride for her and her *boyfriend* to a Canadian border town. I gave it to them. Something about fighting a mining conglomerate about their claims or..."

"I know about everything. About your job, the mine and dad told me about your deal with him."

"So?"

"How have you been living?"

"I had some money put away. My grandparents have been very generous also."

Another long silence.

Carrie finally spoke, "When're you coming back?"

"The movers left here yesterday, it'll take them three days or so to get there. I'll leave tomorrow, to be there when they arrive."

Carrie asked where he was moving to and he told her the address. She knew the place well; an old run-down house with only a fireplace to heat it and a yard filled with waist high weeds. She said a silent prayer that she could convince him to move back in with her. She'd do everything she could to make things right between them.

Jason continued, "Your father and I made a deal, I'll be working for him full time, I suppose he's not doing too well?"

"No."

"Hmm. I'm sorry."

"Me too." Not only did she mean she was sorry about what had happened between her and Jason, she was sorry the way her father was dying. For his suffering.

"So... I'll see ya in a couple of days, maybe we'll have dinner."

"Sounds great."

"Goodbye."

"Goodbye, I love you."

The phone clicked dead. She'd hoped he'd heard her last words.

Jason indeed did arrive at the airport on the day he said he would. Instead of circling town like he'd done before and alerting anyone to his approach, he headed straight into the wind and lowered his Cessna to the runway. As he taxied to the Quonset hut hangar, he troubled over what he had to do next, the rules he'd set for himself when he arrive back in Fallcast. First, he wouldn't head to Carrie's. Next he would wait for the furniture to arrive before he made his presence known to the local townsfolk. Third, he'd start making appearances around town when he started his job at the Dowards Mill and Mine next week.

He wanted no complications. Jason wondered to himself if it was shame, or maybe embarrassment that he'd been turned down by the town's most eligible bachelorette, rebuked for getting a somewhat approval from her father and then told she'd be happy to let things go their way after a while. After he'd left town with no indication of return. After he made it plain he wasn't kidding.

In a month, maybe two, Carrie Marie Dodson would marry him. After she apologized and after it was well known that it was her that had put the brakes on the marriage to this point. It sounded a bit arrogant to Jason, but he knew by now the whole town was well informed as to the entire affair.

Jason retrieved the mine Jeep he'd left in the hangar, after several groans from the starter and the sputtering of the settled fuel in the carb; he was on his way to his new place on the other side of town. He'd wait for the movers, who were scheduled to be here in the next forty-eight hours, and then it was off to the hills for a reconnoiter of his "digs", or the land that was sure to be his soon. The land and his fortune.

Carrie, on the other side of town was struggling with her brother and her deep feelings. She loved Jason, she knew that now, after the way her heart pounded and ached for him to be with her, after he'd answered the phone and said he was returning. She had one last chance, when he got back, to make things up between them. Explain to him why her father's involvement had sent her reeling, why her balk at his proposal was not his fault, but solely hers. Why she needed him and how she had seen the light between her father and *his* proposal. She would be ready to accept his last will and testament. She would help raise Dusty as the future patriarch of Fallcast and she would even let her father walk her down the aisle-but only if it meant she was marrying Jason.

She was also struggling with Dusty right now. He'd heard Jason's plane coming straight in from the north. Like a Labrador listening for a small stitch of sound coming from a clump of sagebrush Dusty had jumped out of his chair in the kitchen and ran into the living room bouncing onto the couch; looked out the front window which faced west, then sat back on the sofa cushions. As if he'd been able to hear a gnat fart twelve miles away, he bolted for the front door, throwing it open and running out into the yard waving his arms. By the time Carrie had gotten off her behind in the kitchen to see what the ruckus was about, they both had seen the little puff of dust rise from the end of the runway where Jason's Cessna touched down.

"So, he's back." Carrie wasn't sure about the tone of her voice, whether it was full of excitement or remorse.

"Can we go meet him? Maybe he needs a ride?" There was no mistake about the excitement in Dusty's voice.

Carrie looked to the empty spot in the semi-circle driveway gravel where the mine Jeep was usually parked. Empty. "No honey. He'll be here when he gets a chance." It didn't even sound convincing to her. "Maybe we'll meet him in town later for dinner." She brought her voice up an octave in hopes she could persuade herself as well as her little brother.

Dusty lowered his head from the horizon and looked at his bare feet on the slightly greening grass. "Okay." It sounded as about dejected as a child could sound and it pulled on Carrie's heart.

"C'mon. Let's make lunch and finish your lessons."

"Kay."

The movers were an hour early, having drove nearly straight through. Jason hopped out of the Jeep and walked fast up to the garage door to the house. After unlocking it and telling the buff furniture guys to bring everything except the couch, bed and TV in, he stepped back and realized that Carrie was right after all. The place was a dump. It was much smaller that her place and very much smaller than his apartment in Denver. The car trailer holding his Blazer was unloaded first.

The living room was about ten by ten feet in size, enough for the couch and TV. It's a good thing he didn't want anything else in here. He walked back to the bedroom and found it was about the same size, but there was only one window and it looked straight into the mine dump behind the house. The kitchen had a stove and oven combo, with a four foot cubic fridge next to those and a microwave on a portable cart. As Jason made his way through the tiny home, he realized this was what the miners he had talked to in other towns complained about everywhere. The small one bedroom places that owners rented for high rent. Jason was paying seven hundred a month and he wondered if he was going to make a second month's payment or whether he was going to have to find a new space. The garage was roomy enough for his boxes and covered furnishings, with about an inch to spare on all four sides when the truckers were done off-loading the trailer.

Jason signed for his stuff, the movers had finished in less than three hours, and he gave each of them twenty dollars for beer and being careful with his things. They thanked him and left. Jason stood at the open garage door. Arrogant. Definitely. And now he was hungry.

Gloria nearly tripped over the counter stools when Jason walked in. She had been wanting to see him since she'd heard the rumors that he was packing up and leaving Fallcast for good. *Stupid Ron and his "grapevine" of reliable information.* Bartenders can't be trusted for anything.

"Hi Jason! How are you, I'm so glad you're back!" She shouted as she helped a man put his coat on the back of the stool she'd knocked off as she flashed by. "I have a booth for you!"

Jason smiled and nodded in the direction she came from, Gloria took the hint and stopped coming towards him. She waved her hand in front of her and into the direction of the back of the restaurant under the ancient dump truck toys on the rack above the windows.

"Hi Glo, how's things?" He offered back as she gave him a half hug, half kiss on the cheek.

"Okay, better. I know someone who will be thrilled to see you!"

Jason raised his brow at her, "Who?"

Gloria just pointed to the front door, where Carrie and Dusty stood. They were looking around the other side of the place for someone.

Jason felt his stomach grumble with excitement. Yes. He was happy to see her, her beauty and the way she kept her M shaped lip curled as she searched the diner for someone recognizable. Jason froze. Should he move to her? Yell out? He waited for what seemed an eternity as she scanned every seat in the place, and finally made eye contact with him. Her eyes seemed to tear up a little then she bent down to Dusty and whispered something into his ear as she kept her eyes on Jason. Dusty kept his gaze towards the hallway behind the counter, nodded and then walked off towards the restrooms in the hallway, unzipping his pants as he walked.

It was three, no four heartbeats before she moved again. Jason knew this because he could feel his heart pounding in his chest and feel the blood rushing in his ears making a squishing sound as it passed his drums. She was beautiful as life itself, he thought quietly, her steps were methodical. A simple dark grey T shirt that was tight around the chest and pink Wrangler jeans with the cuff of the pants tucked into her boots.

Carrie felt light headed, like she'd just stood up too fast or had a fourth glass of champagne. She took one slow step, then another. Jason seemed to be frozen in place, but his face had a look of surrender on them. He was wearing tight blue jeans, a T shirt and his pecks filled out the top, and his semi-washboard stomach rippled the cloth as it tugged to a scrunchy spot into his waistband. He was smiling a little more with every step she took.

They collided near the end of the counter, his arms wrapped tightly around her waist and hers around his neck. Their lips met furiously and after a few seconds of kissing they rested each other's heads respectively on each other's shoulders.

"I love you." Was whispered.

"I love *you*…" Was the reply.

The room had silenced, the chatter had slowed to a halt as they embraced and finally there were small bursts of applause, several *ooohs* and *aaahs*, and a big "Hey Jason!" from Dusty as he left the bathroom.

Not everyone was cheering. There was one man on the other end of the counter, Ron from the Horseshoe Club. The look on his face was jealousy and contempt, and another set of eyes that were watering up outside the plate glass window of the restaurant. Megan Cooke was out on her first trip to the Salt Lick since the accident. She watched as the two saw each other and her heart felt like someone was squeezing it. She heard a maniacal laugh in the back of her head, then the tears flowed when Jason and Carrie's bodies met inside, tears fell freely as she looked at her feet, enhanced by a third leg made of steel-a cane-and she shuffled the trio on their way back to her car. As she reached the door she looked through the window of the Bronco and her lips pulled tight, her voice was crackly and demonic, "Enjoy your time together. For now."

Meg pulled out of the lot slowly, her body ached for her to stamp on the accelerator and send a cloud of dust into the air, but she knew it was a better idea not to let onto her presence. Ron stood and shook off his windbreaker that Gloria had knocked off in her rush to greet Fallcast's favorite geologist, or at least someone's favorite. He made it up in his mind that he was going to let Tommy in on this one; he was going to see that jerk run out of town yet. If he could get on the Dodson's good side, he might have a shot at Carrie. Maybe. Jason had to go first.

CHAPTER EIGHTEEN
Sunday February 14th, 2010

Jason had moved back in as soon as his rent was due. The kindred spirit had brought them together; this time there was little talk of what separated them. Jason had his own reasons, Carrie hers, but the excuses seemed trivial on that day when they spotted each other in the Salt Lick Diner.

Carrie was preparing a nice Valentine's dinner for the three of them. As she danced around the kitchen to Finger Eleven's *One Thing* and swirled potatoes in a mixing bowl with a hand blender, she filled Jason in on the last few months of Fallcast News.

From Dusty's "even better than before Christmas" test results, to Meg's often bi-polar behavior. She hadn't mentioned Parks confession of love to her, nor his frequent visits, which was on the level of once or twice a week. Once Jason had returned, the visits stopped. But Parks always nodded and smiled at Jason when they passed. Carrie talked of her meeting with her father and his state just before Jason returned. Terry had been in the hospital in town twice, but had checked himself out days after admission although he was on heavy medication for pain. Carrie stopped stirring at the end of the song.

"He says he wants to walk me down the aisle." She said in a matter of fact tone.

Jason was silent in the living room. He was watching the Ag report on Direct-TV, but had muted the sound as Carrie made her last statement. His insides felt light as a feather and tingly.

Carrie waited. Nothing. She was worried that he hadn't heard her. She opened her mouth to find another way to repeat herself and Jason walked into the kitchen with a huge smile on his face. He kneeled, kissed her mashed potato crusted hand and as he looked up with tears in his eyes he asked, "Have you set a date yet?"

Dinner was exceptional, although Dusty looked confused as to why his big sister was constantly wiping her eyes and Jason's knee kept bouncing up and down rapidly under the table, causing the whole floor to shake a little. He also was wondering in his own way why he was the last one eating. It was usually the other way around, Dusty would polish off his meal fast so he could have dessert before his sister was done and not have to wait for her.

Jason rose to the sink with his plate and cleaned it off then put it in the dish rack, and then he did the same for Carrie's and he stood back for a second staring at Dusty's plate, which was half full.

"Well, you're a bit behind tonight aren't you?" He asked in a humorous tone.

Dusty just raised his brows and ate a little faster.

After dinner and Dusty had spent a half hour explaining to Jason how he'd reached the level on *Flight Simulator* so that he earned a simulated pilot's license, and then Carrie with tears in her eyes explained how Dr. Thomas was excited as she was that Dusty was excelling rapidly and was now learning at a ten year old level. Jason congratulated the boy and helped his sister tuck him in at nine thirty.

After Carrie put the clean plates away, she brought out two glasses of fine brandy with a slice of red velvet cake she'd made earlier today. She sat slowly next to Jason on the loveseat and held his snifter as he ate through his Valentine's Day cake.

"Good?" She asked.

Jason had a mouthful and nodded then winked. "Gooollfff." *Good!*

Carrie took in a breath of the brandy and sipped. "I found this stuff at the mercantile in the back room under an inch of dust. Ol Missus Baylee said it had been back there so long she didn't even know what to charge me." Another few swirls, an inhale and a sip, "Twelve dollars and twenty cents."

Jason was finishing up his last swallow and took the snifter from her as he sat his empty plate on the coffee table. He inhaled just as Carrie had done, having watched her and he even had noticed his grandfather doing the same thing for years. Not being a brandy drinker, he had no clue to why, but he figured it had to enhance the drink. He took a small sip.

"Wow! Are you sure this is alcohol?"

Carrie nearly spit out her sip and through a cough said, "Careful, this stuff is potent."

"I didn't know you were a connoisseur of booze."

She just smiled back at him and wiped her lips with the sleeve of her sweatshirt. A few moments of silence crept up on them.

Finally Carrie broke the awkward moment. "Lindsay, huh?"

Jason's eyes went wide. "No! Not like that. She and her tree hugging boyfriend needed a lift to the Canadian border and she paid *dearly*. And I do mean *dearly*...." Jason put a sinister emphasis on dearly; it reminded Carrie of that evil bad guy with the curly Q moustache on Saturday television.

"How much? If you don't mind me asking."

"Twelve hundred dollars plus fuel. About the cost of my move here, I tossed in an extra tank without her knowing it."

Carrie's mouth took a few seconds to close. "Are you *serious*?"

Jason laughed like satisfactorily, "It seems that Miss Lindsay Kavender and Dreadlock Dave, or whatever his hippie moniker is, have gotten themselves on the no-fly list for some kind of left-wing psychobabble on the internet. They were desperate and I was available. I guess they were going to hike over the border from where I dropped them.

Anyways, I guess it's a bad idea to bad mouth politicians on your website and threaten them."

Carrie looked forward and took another sip. This was the type of explanation she wanted and she uttered an emotionless, "Oh."

Jason turned to her and put his hand on her hip. "Jealous?"

Carrie shook her head and smiled back with a sly grin; she said, "How much would you charge me?"

"Free flying, as long as you join the Mile High Club." Jason snickered back.

Carrie shook her head. She had no clue what that was. "Pardon?"

Jason giggled a bit then said, "Well, let's just say we'd need a bigger airplane for you to join. Mine's too small."

About ten seconds passed before Carrie got the jest of his words.

"Ooooh!" She laughed and reached over and took Jason's hand.

Jason set his snifter down and used his free arm to wrap around Carrie's neck. In an instant they were engaged in a heavy, passionate kiss; their hands were exploring each other's shoulders, arms, and then the prizes under each other's shirts.

Carrie ran her hand over the washboard six-pack, it was a little softer than it looked but that didn't stop her excitement as her finger trickled over the tops of the ripples. She could feel a little tuft of hair at his waistband and tickled it with her fingernails for several seconds. She felt his breath grow hotter with each stroke of her hand across his abdomen; his pleas were expressed out loud in his throes.

Jason had found the treasure he was searching for; gently massaging the area around her breasts as she inhaled deeper and deeper. Each time she exhaled the air from her lungs vibrated like waves crashing on a shore. He felt the snaps of his 501s being undone slowly; he returned the favor to the string on her waistband. He had to free both his hands to work the bowtie she'd made in the cord, and her breathing became less shallow. He pulled back from her.

"Are you… sure?"

Carrie lowered her head into a provocative pose, then her lips dropped to a suggestive little pout, and she nodded her head ever so slightly. She quietly said, "Yes."

In just fractions of a second her sweatpants were at her ankles and Jason's were at his knees. They both paused for a moment to embrace and kiss each other deeply.

"*CASSIE!!!*"

Both jumped from the couch. Carrie grabbed the waistband of her sweatpants and pulled them up to her hips faster than Jason could fathom. He'd fallen to his knees and was rolling onto his back trying to get his jeans up and buttoned.

"Right there Dusty!"

Carrie had ushered a scared and pale Dusty to her bed. The shower was running in the guest bath and a small, sad, frustrated smile was locked on Carrie's face as she caressed Dusty's hair and held him to her side. She's pulled the sheets up over him and had one of her bare legs sticking out the side of her covers. Moments later Jason emerged cleanly and scoured, he quietly stepped into the bedroom and waited for Carrie to talk first.

"He's alright now. Another one of his nightmares."

Jason nodded. "What do you think this *darkness in the shadow* thing is anyway?" He sat down on the dressing chair near Dusty's side of Carrie's bed.

"Dr. Thomas feels it might be a repressed memory of some kind. Something that is fighting his damaged brain to get out. Dusty once told the doctor that he saw his mommy lying on the ground dead, and another time he said she's getting beaten up really bad." Carrie sighed softly, "I don't know how much he can remember of mom. The doc says it might be a dream of me or someone else that frightens him and he thinks it's his mom because he misses her so much."

Jason raised an eyebrow at this. "How much do you remember the day she disappeared?"

"Not much. She was wearing a flowery sundress that my father had bought her. I remember because she was in a good mood that morning, and I went out back to pick some flowers for her. Dad had forced me to go to Baylee's with him to get some things for dinner that night, I asked him if he could take Tommy too, but he said *'No. Just you.'*. Dad and Tommy were having one of their fights over something grandpa had said or something like that. I never got involved in their disputes."

Jason nodded slowly as he rose from the chair and bent softly over Dusty's head and gave him a kiss. He then turned towards the door when Carrie called out, "What about me?"

He smiled and turned back, softly grazing her exposed leg with his fingertips, Carrie sighed deeper at this. Jason bent over and kissed her passionately enough not to wake Dusty, but enough to stir Carrie's earlier drive. He relented as a tease and backed towards the door with a coy look on his face.

"May seventeenth." She whispered with a slight pant.

"Pardon?"

"I want to get married on May seventeenth. It's my mother's birthday."

"I thought we'd wait till June or July?"

"I can't *wait* much longer."

"Do you think we can stand it that long?" Jason asked with a smile.

Carrie let a seductive smile fly at Jason, "I think the odds are against us…" She nodded at Dusty. He was holding his body in a fetal position now, his right hand to his chin. He looked like an angel. "But we've waited this long. I think we can make it."

Jason smiled at Dusty, "It's going to be just as hard after we're married, you know."

Carrie winked and whispered, "But I won't feel as guilty putting him back into his own bed to be with you *and*, he'll know that we are sleeping in the same bed. I'll bet he respects that a little more."

Jason smirked his mouth to the right side and nodded, "Uh huh."

"Good night."

"Good night, I hope me running a cold shower doesn't keep you awake…"

Carrie rapidly moved her eyebrows up and down then flipped the light off on her nightstand by her bed and pulled the covers over her and her little brother. Jason sighed and closed the bedroom door.

Carrie had dreams too. Hers were more enigmatic than Dusty's, flashes of her life as a child or as her in the future at some event like a wedding or a funeral. She was dreaming this morning of a car crash, one not much unlike Meg and Steve's, and the smell of gasoline burning. As the odor became stronger, she woke with a start and found Dusty had left her room. She got out of bed and pulled on her sweatpants from the night before then slowly made her way down the hall.

First stop was Dusty's room. She opened the door ever so carefully and found him asleep, half in and half out of his bed covers, his feet dangling over the edge. Next, she tiptoed down the hall to Jason's room and again slowly opened the door. Jason was asleep on his stomach with his feet hanging out of the covers, one arm off to the side and his hand touching the floor, the other was around his back. She scrunched her lips at the thought of how uncomfortable this looked, when she smelled gasoline again. Burning fuel.

Then she heard the fire engines and the siren on the town's volunteer fire station. Her heart fluttered a little panic in and out and she shuffled to the front room to look out the window, she opened the curtains and peered out. As the sun was rising she could see no smoke, but the wafting redolence of burning gas became stronger as she walked to the north side of the house.

The fire trucks were four roads up heading north. Carrie found her flip-flops by the door and headed outside into the early morning chill, as she rounded the side of the house and entered the backyard her heart stopped. She knew where the fire was now. The whole town would know.

A huge fireball of red, white and orange flame shot up into the sky, black smoke surged from the ground around the airport. The hangar and power shack were on fire.

"Oh god!"

She ran inside and woke Jason up.

Not much was left. The Quonset hut was flattened to the ground, melted and molten in some spots, the wooden shack that ran the light system to the tower that had the rotating beacon was completely gone and in the middle of the smoldering remains was the skeleton of a Cessna airplane.

Carrie could see tears in Jason's eyes, but he didn't express his emotions out loud or anything by weeping openly, he just stood there holding Dusty's hand with his right, and Carrie's hand with his left. Carrie would squeeze every now and again, he'd squeeze back.

"Oh Jason, I'm so sorry…" Carrie whispered. He just shook his head in disgust.

"You can use my plane." Dusty offered loudly over the din of the idling fire trucks.

A smile crossed Jason's lips. He bent down and picked up the boy, hugging him tightly in his arms. "I just might at that little man. But you'll have to do all the flying."

Carrie put her head on his shoulder and wrapped her arm around his waist as a pickup truck with fire department markings came tearing up the road towards them. It was Fire Chief Marshall Tedford. Jason led Carrie back to the mine Jeep they had parked about two hundred yards from the airport, near the entrance, and he sat Dusty on the hood. Carrie opened her door and sat on the passenger seat with her feet hanging out. Jason just leaned up against the fender and waited for the chief.

Tedford jumped out of his ride and didn't even close the door. He was three steps into the twenty feet to where Jason was when he started talking, "Someone doesn't like you much…"

Jason pursed his lips and shook his head, "What?"

"This is the second case of arson in this town in a year. You know when the first one was too." Tedford offered a dirty hand.

Jason shook his hand and asked, "You mean this wasn't an accident?"

"Nope. Found remnants of road flares again. This time it was meant to look like an accident, but there's no reason for road flares to be there. Is there?" Tedford looked to Jason in an accusing way.

"I didn't have any in my plane if that's what you mean, don't see many accidents in midair to redirect traffic… Do you want to search the Jeep?" Jason waved a hand towards the back of the Wagoneer; his voice was sharp with criticism and pain.

"Yes."

Jason shook his head and walked to the back of the Jeep; he opened the back door and stepped back, allowing Marshall Tedford to do the rest. The fire chief leaned in, opened the supply locker and rolled his hand around in it.

"Six flares. All here, sorry Mr. Parmenter but if I went to the mine to search vehicles again and hadn't searched this one first, there'd be hell to pay."

Terrence Dodson would've been beside himself. If he were healthy, if he were not already resigned to the fact that his oldest son Tommy was going to prison. If his estranged daughter had not called him a day ago and announced her marriage to Jason Parmenter the geologist now on the payroll of Dodson-Doward Minerals Inc. If she had not asked him to walk her down the aisle that day. He glanced again at the desk blotter, May 17th. It was already on his calendar, it was Marie's birthday and he knew the significance of the day to both him and Carrie. It was an homage.

But now, today, here was his stupid son sitting in front of him again. Chief Tedford had been here yesterday again, another fire. This time it was Jason's plane and the hangar at the airport that was destroyed. The common factor? It was Jason's property. It was started by a rudimentary device using road flares. It happened while Tommy was unaccounted for.

Tommy lowered his head. He knew his father was on the way out, and he also knew that he was to get a large portion of the estate. Money to live off of for years plus all the rental and mortgaged properties they owned. This could net him six thousand a month easy, as long the places were occupied and he didn't go on any sprees with the cash, minus the eight-fifty a month for Dusty and four hundred fifty for his whore sister. But how long would that last? If Dusty got the mine and mill, then in a year or two he'd be bringing in six thousand a month for him and Carrie, and that jerk-hole, *Jason*. Tommy's expression was sour at the thought of that gold-digger. Literally.

"Do I make you ill?" Terrence asked. "Perhaps I should just have everything transferred to your little brother."

Tommy lifted his head. "Dad, I had nothing to do with it…"

"Tedford said all the flares were accounted for this time in your truck. But that doesn't take you off the hook. You've been bad-mouthing your future brother-in-law around town and good folks have heard it. Folks who like to tattle. Folks who could put you back in Carson City."

"I… I…" Tommy started.

"Where the hell have you been?"

Tommy took a deep breath. "I've been seeing someone."

Terrence waited. When Tommy didn't respond immediately he asked with anger on his breath, "*WHO?!*"

"Meg Cooke."

Terrence's eyes widened. "That girl that was nearly killed last year? The one who's on probation for killing her husband?"

"She didn't do it…"

"I don't care!" Terrence rose from his chair slowly, as fast as his failing body allowed, pain coursed his veins. "She's on probation, you're on parole. Neither of you two can see each other!"

"That's why we've been discreet." Tommy said quietly, as if the world would understand.

Terrence faced his window and looked outside. Rain had started about an hour ago and the mountains were runny with water and dust, but the smell had made its way into the office and it relaxed the dying man's soul for a little while. He kept staring out the window.

"You get just one more. That's what the sheriff said yesterday. He says he knows you had something do to with the fires and he wants you gone." Terrence turned towards his oldest son, "When I'm gone, there'll be no more power, no more favors owed to me. You can't rely on me to bail you out of situations like this. When I'm six feet deep, no one is going to keep the authorities at bay; they'll just march right into your house and turn everything over looking for any reason at all. It doesn't matter whether or not you had anything to do with it. They'll hang it on you. Period. End of story."

"Dad…"

"No Tommy. Listen to me. If anything happens to Parmenter, anything at all. I'll put you away. Get me? Your sister loves him and he takes good care of your brother…"

"He's a cheat and he wants our money. He gets to sleep with Carrie and Dusty will be my only blood left after you're gone, how can he carry on the family name if he gets adopted by that freak of the skies?"

Tommy was looking at his knees when he spoke, when Terry didn't respond he looked up. His father was bright red and staring into his eyes like a tiger that had just trapped a meal. If steam could escape from ears, there'd be little visibility in the room.

Terrence's voice lowered three octaves, "*If you even go near them. I'll see you off before I go. Do-you-understand?!*"

Tommy felt a surge of terror. Few people could put the fear of death into him like his father could, sick or not, and now was a moment that Tommy thought he was about to die. His old man could have a gun; he could just jam a pen into his eye. He knew he'd crossed the line his father just laid out.

"Yes, sir."

~

Another month and a half had passed since the fire at the airport. No one was arrested to this point and Jason was trying to get his insurance check sent to his new address. Preparations for the wedding of the century for Fallcast was underway, everyone thought it would be a huge blowout type with all the frills, since the daughter of one of the town's most influential was paying for it. But it was not to be. Even under his protest, Carrie told her father that she wanted simple to old fashioned. She wanted to get married at City Hall, just as her mother and he did, she wanted minimal guests. Since Megan was again not talking to her, Carrie asked Gloria to be her bridesmaid and Dusty was volunteered for best man.

Jason was working full time for Dodson-Dowards and he had plenty of time off to spend with his fiancée, since her father was his boss and the land that Jason turned on to the mine was rich with minerals. He was almost worth his weight in gold. He was fast becoming a person of interest in town, he was building a base of favors and some powerful folks even owed him a little here and there.

But not all were happy about this newcomer who flew into town, stole the heart of the town's most beautiful and available rich girl, befriended her brother who rarely talked to anyone, Jason even managed to pull a few friends in from Baylee's Mercantile namely Ed and Heather Baylee, John and Helen Dickson of the Glow Worm Ranch, Cookie and Gloria from the Salt Lick Diner. Among those who trusted him were Marshall Tedford the fire chief, and many other local business men who saw the opportunity in the land that Jason had found for the mines as a soon to be boost to the economy as miners and specialists arrive to unload the thousands of tons of minerals.

The list against Jason was almost as strong with Darrin Parker, Meg, Tommy Dodson, Ron Benjamin from the Horseshoe Club and several of the local miners who worked for Dodson for years who had an eye on his daughter, but were afraid to act on the impulse because they didn't want to end up fired or worse, dead. Rumors flew amongst the haters, *who was trying to scare Jason out of town*? Each eyed the other with suspicion as they passed by in town or in the mercantile, or were fueling up at Sal Buford's. Sal even had his doubts about the rich fly-boy, he was sure the guy was just here to make a quick buck and then he'd be off into the skies to find another town to rape of its treasures and women. He said so on many occasions and the accusations finally got back to Terry Dodson who sent a handwritten message to Sal that said basically '*The mine would find other means for equipment repair and fuel...*' Soon Sal was as quiet as a roach, and he kept the rumors to a minimum.

Three weeks before the wedding, an old light green Chevy Nova pulled into Carrie's driveway at midnight and the driver stumbled out and shuffled to the porch. Parks was disheveled as any drunk on his day off, but he was on an alcohol fueled mission. He'd heard at the Horseshoe that Jason had to drive to Vegas to drop off some new samples to Dodson-Dowards Inc.'s assayer and would be gone overnight. Carrie answered the door on the fortieth knock, as Parks just kept pounding.

"Darrin? What's going on? Is everything alright?" Carrie was wearing her sweatpants, a T shirt and was still wiping her eyes of sleep.

Parks hesitated, the alcohol had worn off a little, but his head still spun. Carrie sighed heavily when she smelled the booze on his breath; she crossed her arms in front of her. A prior moment she considered asking him in, now she knew that would be a bad idea.

"Parks," Her voice was lower and stern, "why are you here at this hour?"

Feeling on the verge of rejection he looked into her eyes his somewhat bloodshot ones and said, "I... m... sorry. Carrie. It's been a long hard week ya know. And...

and I was just sad tonight, today." He looked around to confirm the sun hadn't risen yet, "Tonight. Can… can I come in?"

"I don't think that's very appropriate right now. Why don't you come back in the late morning?"

"I'm sorry." Instead of backing all the way down the porch, he stepped to his left and fell into the swing. The chains protested his weight and then squeaked as he found humor in his misstep and landing spot. After five attempts to get back on his feet he simply smiled up at Carrie who had a look of tendered rage on her face and said, "I'll just sleep here okay?"

With that, before Carrie could object, he closed his eyes and his mouth fell open. He'd passed out. Carrie felt a surge of sadness for the deputy sheriff; she went back into the house and grabbed a blanket out of the linen closet and a pillow off the couch to place under his head. After covering Parks up and managing to wedge the cushion under his heavy head, she turned to go back inside when he spoke in a low, sad voice.

"It's not fair you know. I loved you first."

Carrie let out another breath of disapproval, but resigned to sit in the chaise lounge across from the swing. "I'm sorry Darrin."

He raised his head a little and looked over to her. "Did you know I killed someone?"

Carrie's breath caught, "*What?*"

"When I was gone, you know, at school. At deputy school." He giggled at his lack of definition on his words. "The academy. In Reno."

"I didn't know. Why hasn't anyone said anything…"

"Because it was all hush, hush." He moved his legs to get the blanket all the way over them. "I was in training and wasn't allowed to have a weapon on me. Me and this guy named Mark, uh-Mark Fye had a room together for the weekend. S'pposed to be on campus, but we got a pass. We weren't drunk or anything."

Carrie sat up and placed her warm hand to Parks' forehead. "Perhaps you better get some sleep Darrin. Tell me about it in the morning."

"No. Now. While Mark was at dinner downtown, this guy who was staying next door was so high that he tried to get in my room. He got frustrated when the key didn't work in the lock, so he kicked in the chintzy door. He saw me getting out of the bed and pulled this *HUGE* knife. Of course, being the cool cop in training you know, I had a revolver in my nightstand drawer; I pulled it out and shot him." He made a gun with his thumb and forefinger, then closed one eye like he was aiming. He let his thumb drop to his hand and made a "Boom!" sound.

"Oh Darrin. I'm so sorry…" Carrie felt truly sorry for him.

"Then the next bit of training takes over you know. I dropped the gun on the floor and ran over to the guy. He's kicking and screaming at me, calling me a killer and all that. I phoned 911 and looked over. The guy's eyes were looking right at me. Like these blocks of ice, only they're red and black. I moved slowly to see if he was alive, check his pulse ya know, and those eyes followed me. Right up to his head. They followed my fingers as I felt his neck for a pulse.

"They followed my eyes as I ripped open his shirt to start CPR. When my roommate got back, those eyes just stayed on me. The whole time. Even when the sheriff's came and covered him up, he was looking at me. Those things, those eyes just said, '*you killed me, murderer*'."

Carrie had her hand to her mouth, *her* eyes were watering.

Parks continued with a yawn and a smile after a burp, "Since I was in training and the furlough was approved, they simply told the news that it was a deputy

372

who shot the guy. They said I was going to be under review and I was. They found me as having committed 'justifiable homicide'. Wow. I committed homicide…" He used his shaking and misguided fingers to try and make quotation marks in the night air. "Weeks later, the whole thing got buried under because the story of that poor girl that was kidnapped from her friend's dorm and was raped and murdered. My story was all but wiped clean. Did you know that the guys at the academy gave me a fake medal? They said I should skip the rest of the course because I already earned my bonus points. They were all proud of me." He swallowed some saliva that was building at the back of his throat.

"Darrin…" Carrie began, but he interrupted.

"Mark said he wanted another roommate, he said he was afraid I'd shoot him if he came in late or something. They made me take three courses over, there was a write-up in my file and I was reprimanded."

"Darrin, please…"

Again Parks cut her off, "I lasted three months there ya know. Big ol deputy Parker who shot and killed a bad guy was afraid for his life. Scared like a chicken. That's why I came back here. To Fallcast. Less crime. Less chance of me shooting someone."

Carrie paused for a few seconds. She wanted to be sure that he was finished, there was no use fighting his will over this matter. When he sat there motionless with tears falling from his eyes, Carrie asked quietly, "Who do you think set those fires Darrin?" She hoped to change the subject.

He covered his eyes and shook his head. "Don't know Carrie. Probably your brother, more than likely. He's the most vocal about how much he hates your boyfriend." Parks sat up quickly. "Meg."

Carrie felt a blow to her chest, "What?"

"First fire was before Meg was hospitalized, then…"

"No. I will not accept that, she's my friend, she…"

"She and your brother are seeing each other."

Carrie felt the urge to throw up. She couldn't say anything. After a few moments of silence Parks saw his opportunity.

"I do love you, you know. This whole thing is a mistake. I'll prove it to you."

"Darrin, please don't do anything stupid. Please…"

"I will. I'll show you I'm a better man. I…" He laid his head back down and closed his eyes tight like he was fighting off the urge to puke too. "I will. I will…" And he was out again.

Carrie sat there for nearly twenty minutes before finding the courage to get up and go inside. *Should she call Jason and tell him what happened? No. Things are okay right now. Parks'll sober up in the morning and be on his way.* He'll keep what he said to himself. Then the thought occurred to her.

It was a simple thought that crossed her mind last night. Carrie waited another fifteen minutes to make sure Parks was fast asleep before going back to bed herself. When she woke from a fitful slumber at seven in the morning, he was gone. The blanket was neatly folded up and the pillow was resting on top of that, they both sat on the mildly rocking swing in the morning breeze. The day was going to be nice, the sun was already rising above the mountains to the east, a bright yellow and blue haze settled above the tops.

Carrie was unsure at first at what she had to do. Then it just hit her. It was time to talk to Meg, to find out what the whole hassle was about with her and her best friend. Carrie dropped Dusty off at the library for an hour; he was already excited about being in the wedding-especially excited about being able to stand up there with

Jason. Anything Carrie had suggested to him recently was readily accepted without argument or whining and that made life a lot easier, his schoolwork was increased a little so when Jason and Carrie left for the five day honeymoon Dusty could escape having Gloria or Mary at the Sand and Juniper try to tutor him.

That was another thing that bothered Carrie this morning. She just wasn't sure about letting someone else watch Dusty for so long. She'd never done that since she gained custody, been away for so long, and she hadn't burdened anyone but Meg with more than two days of babysitting before. But Gloria had actually called Carrie to volunteer, and then two hours later Mary called from the hotel and asked what the new couple's plans were for the week after the wedding. Carrie had told her about Jason taking her to Vegas (the original plan was to fly, but Jason had yet to secure a replacement plane) and they were to spend a week at the *Mirage*. Instantly Mary had offered her services and then Gloria and she had argued nicely over the job; finally both agreeing to split the time as much as possible. Carrie was also a little unnerved that so many people were so kind to her recently. Nearly everyone, her father included, had been nice in offering services or gifts.

Carrie pulled to the front of Meg's house and stayed in the car for moments, she parked far enough away to hide the fact she was sort of spying on Meg, but she was incognito anyway, Jason took the mine truck to Vegas because he had to get the oil changed anyway, so Carrie was left with his Blazer and few in town had seen it yet. After ten minutes Carrie realized no one was home, she could see into the garage and the remaining Bronco was gone, a quick walk to the kitchen window revealed that a night light was on, on the microwave above the oven. The house was a mess, clothes and food boxes scattered all over the kitchen, bottles of tequila and bourbon on the counter.

Carrie knocked on the front door. After four or five minutes she quit knocking and decided to walk around the property again. At least someone might see her and tell Meg that she'd been around and that it showed some concern for Megan's well-being. Carrie rounded the corner to the garage and peered into the window that faced the house. Nothing that she couldn't see from the front. Tools were scattered all over the workbench, mostly covered in dust so Carrie surmised that Steve was the last one to touch them, it kind of broke Carrie's heart to think of that. Then she saw the box of flares. *30 Minute Highway Fusees* the box read in bright orange on the outside.

Jason came home to a crying Carrie. After looking around to see if he was the reason for the latest outburst (things had been a little tense since the wedding date had been set and he found himself on the deeper end of the blame pool) he managed to coax the truth out of her.

"It might be just a coincidence." He explained as he sat next to her and massaged her feet with body lotion. "Maybe she wanted them for her Bronco in case she broke down."

Carrie swallowed back a huge lump of pain, "She's been seeing my brother."

Jason lowered his head, "Oh. Well, maybe he used some for…" And his mind went blank for several seconds. He sighed relenting, "Have you told anyone?"

"No."

"Maybe you should call Parks, I'll bet…"

"*NO!*" Carrie burst into another eye-flood and stood from the couch, walked to the kitchen and left Jason sitting there with lotion all over his hands.

One week to go and the whole town was on edge. The rumor about the Dodson Mill had finally escaped someone's lips and behind doors things were exciting.

People were really thinking that Fallcast might become a huge town, one that boasted the amenities that destination towns offered. Daily freight service, new rail crossings, a real airport, maybe even a bedroom town in a way appealed to the folks, a one hour commute to Vegas wouldn't be so bad if a another gas station opened up in town and gave Sal a run for his money competition-wise.

Carrie was on edge. She had been very reluctant to talk about what she'd seen at Megan's house. Jason was pressing her to tell someone, anyone and get the whole situation over with. Get it out of her head and get along with the pressing things ahead, like the wedding.

On May 10th, just one week before the wedding, Jason asked again. He seemed to fall short on his birthday present to her too; the flowers didn't seem to cheer her up any at all. The pain was obvious on Carrie's mind; it was hurting her inside and even though Jason could go to the authorities and tell them what Carrie had seen at Meg's house, but that would put the pressure right back on her to talk to them and add to the tension between Jason and her. If Carrie wanted him to tattle, then she would've asked him to.

The night of the rehearsal which consisted of Carrie, Jason, Gloria, Dusty, some of the other folks who were helping put the Hall in shape with decorations and flowers and of course, Terry Dodson. The wall of anger was breached a little between her father and Carrie, but little escaped as a snide remark or a test of her father's commitment to the wedding.

After the rehearsal Terry bought dinner at the Salt Lick; Gloria's replacement at the diner, Tanya was serving them. They ate in quiet; once in a while a comment was made about the design of the flowers, the smell of alcohol on the Justice of the Peace's/Pastor's breath or how Dusty skipped down the aisle as he marched towards the proscenium set up for the service. Terry barely touched his meal and excused himself, after stopping at Carrie's chair to kiss her on the forehead, he left.

"You must have a cast-iron will." Gloria said with a smile as the door closed behind him.

Carrie turned and looked at her with a stern flat smile. "Why?"

Gloria smiled back and shook her head, "No reason."

Carrie returned to the sad, pathetic look on her face as she nibbled at her pie. Jason felt sick over how she was holding this all in, he rubbed her hand and she offered a fake *'I'm alright'* smile, but he just squeezed her hand in a defiant *'no you're not'*.

When they returned to the house everything came to a head. Jason sat on the couch and tuned to the Vegas news and watched it with the volume off.

"Aren't you coming to bed?" She asked. "Dusty's in his room."

Jason shook his head slowly. He kept staring at the TV and said, "We need for you to either get over this thing with Meg, or just change our plans."

This stopped her in her tracks. Carrie replied, "What? You mean the wedding? What are you talking about?"

"We can't keep a secret like this and not have it take a toll on us in the meantime. It's tearing you up inside."

Carrie sighed loudly. "Jason, this is my brother we're talking about."

"He burned my hotel room to ashes, ruined my work and my stuff. He set fire to my airplane Carrie! He burned the hangar to the ground! Is that okay for you? Because it's not for me." Jason looked from the TV screen to his fiancée. "What if I'd been killed?"

"But you weren't…"

"What if someone else was killed? Mary of maybe Jack? What if a fireman was hurt putting the fire out?" His voice was bordering on losing sanity. It climbed with each question.

Carrie replied with a stern but quiet response, "Jason! Your voice please!"

Jason shook his head and looked back to the TV. A commercial for soda was on.

Carrie took a moment and with her eyes closed, but the tears dribbling out from the lids and she said, "I can't believe you'd be so selfish. This'll put my brother back in prison for life."

"Yeah, I've seen you've made up with daddy pretty good too. Glad I could be of service, fixing your screwed up relationship with your family and then find my life in danger with each step I take in this stupid town. Maybe I should just find another place to live?"

Carrie stood at once. She took one glaring, accusing glance over her shoulder at Jason then stormed into the kitchen. At once plates and silverware from the evening's dinner were being tossed into the sink without regard for their safety, cabinet doors slammed shut and the refrigerator door was slammed as Carrie put the evening's leftovers in.

Jason knew he'd crossed the line. A lump of self-pity forged in his throat, then he washed it back down with the sickness of regret, the fluidness of embarrassment and a helping of heavy remorse. He raised his voice above the clamor in the next room.

"Carrie. I'm sorry, I didn't mean that. Maybe we can talk this out?"

He was answered with the slam of the back door from the kitchen to the backyard. Jason waited for several seconds to get up and walk into the kitchen, he wanted to make sure she wasn't just throwing the trash out and coming back in. When she didn't return he stood and shuffled to the back door, looking outside the window in the door and saw Carrie sitting on the swing set's tire swing. Her head was in her hands, bobbing up and down with each tear that she was trying to hold back in, with each sob and with each feeling of helplessness.

Jason was right. She had to tell someone or they'd be at each other's throats for months, maybe even years. Maybe Tommy would do something so outrageous like Jason said he might, maybe he'd set *her* house on fire! Or maybe Tommy would go from arsonist to outright murderer; Meg had been accused of killing her husband and Carrie refused to believe it at first, but now Meg was refusing to even talk to Carrie and her big brother was seeing Meg. She had seen the flares in the garage.

"Carrie?"

Carrie lifted her head to see Jason on the stoop, looking as pitiful as any man could. She could see he was sorry for what he said, but the hard part-the actual truth of it-was what kept her anger flaring at the sight of him.

"Go away. I don't want to see you now." She turned the swing away from the house and faced it towards the cyclone fence surrounding the backyard.

"But…" His voice dropped with a gurgle as tears flooded his eyes and sinuses began to flow into his throat.

"*GO!*"

Twenty seconds of dead air enclosed between them; Jason turned and slowly walked back into the house, he took his windbreaker off the chair in the kitchen and glanced towards Dusty's room. The door was still closed and there was no light coming from under it. He was still asleep. Jason retrieved his keys for his Blazer and walked out the front door, not slamming it; he climbed into his Chevy and started the engine while holding his breath, hoping no one would hear him-like Carrie-before he was out of the driveway and his destination.

"Bud." Jason kept his voice to just above the confusion and the weirdest song he'd ever heard coming from the jukebox.

Ron saw his latest customer's expression and nodded towards the music machine, "Call it punk-country I guess. Song's named *Cotton-Eyed Joe*, but some fool put a disco beat to it and a bunch of stupid rap lyrics… I hate it."

Jason cracked a half smile and nodded in a sort of thanks to the information. At least the evil sound coming from the machine had a name. Ron walked to the reach-in and pulled out a longneck, twisted the top off and returned to Jason's part of the counter. It was slow tonight, but Jason didn't want a crowd anyway, he wanted to be alone with his thoughts. He would later tell the cops that he didn't see Tommy Dodson and Meg Cooke "sitting" in her Bronco at the dark corner of the parking lot with steamed windows.

Carrie considered calling the Horseshoe, but if Jason was there she'd have no idea what to say to him. Sorry, maybe. She did know that she'd say she loved him and that they would work this out somehow. She'd say they had to work together because they were going to be spending the rest of their lives together, and couples worked problems like this out every day. *And folks got divorced too*, her alter-thought whispered in the other ear from her shoulder..

It was now midnight. She rose to check on Dusty when there was a knock at the door, Carrie's heart jumped thinking that maybe he'd gotten a ride home after getting too drunk or maybe he'd locked his keys in the Blazer. She rushed to the door and looked out the small window next to it. Her heart sank, thoughts rushed to her brain; all filled with horror, all filled with dread, all her thoughts made her physically sick. She held back the urge to throw up as she slowly opened the door to see Deputies Mike Tenner and

Darrin Parker standing there with looks of men who just saw the end of the world.

"Evening Miss Dodson…" Tenner began.

Carrie could only nod, quick and jerky.

"Carrie," Parks began, he had no toothpick in his mouth which signaled something bad had happened. He had a bright red bruise on his cheek and then Carrie looked to Tenner, he was also a bit black and blue around his left eye, "there's been a serious incident…"

"Jason?" It was more of a plea, a request that they make up a lie and tell her that Jason was okay. Her voice sounded like a creaking door on a haunted house, the one that needed the most oil.

"He'll be alright," Tenner began, "he's at County. A few stitches and maybe an ice pack."

Carrie's heart picked up the pace, "What happened?"

Parks took over the conversation for the next three minutes, "Carrie, where's Terrence?"

"Why?"

"He's not answering his door; we have some bad news for him, and you."

Again the flutter to her chest, *"What is it, dammit Parks!"*

"Jason was drinking at the Horseshoe tonight; did you know he was there?"

Carrie nodded to the affirmative, even though she wasn't sure, but confirmation was now made.

"Tommy and Meg came in about an hour ago; they appeared to already have been drinking somewhere else. Now Ron Benjamin describes the following:" Parks took out his notebook from his breast pocket and read, "At approximately ten-fifteen p.m., after consuming several shots of whiskey, Thomas Dodson stood from the table he was seated at and threw his chair across the room, striking Jason Parmenter in the head. Mr. Parmenter then collapsed to the floor at which time Mr. Dodson ran over and began kicking him. Mr. Parmenter rose to his feet and deflected several blows directed at him by Mr. Dodson. Mr. Parmenter whispered something into Mr. Dodson's ear and then Mr. Dodson became even more enraged and threw Mr. Parmenter over the bar. At this point, Mr. Dodson was livid, he threw chairs; he swore out loud and even accused some of the five customers of..."

Parks' face went crimson as he read the next part, clearing his throat first, "Being...uh... related to whores and quote, 'I'll kill every mother-bleeping one of you, you conspiring whores and f-ing stooges! When my old man passes I'll control this dump and you all be dead', end quote."

Parks took a breath as Tenner finished, "When we got there he took us on too. Mike," Parks nodded at Tenner, "took a bottle to the face thrown by someone. One person said it was Megan Cooke, but when we looked for her she was gone, then so was the witness, so we can't press any charges against her. Your brother hit me in the face as I was trying to restrain him and I had to lock him up. Now Ron says he won't press any charges, but Tim Donnelly, the bar's owner is." There was a long pause, "And you know what that means."

Carrie knew. She knew that Tommy was going in front of a judge and that judge was going to send him back to prison. Everything she wanted to avoid doing herself by not telling anyone what she saw. Now it was fate. Tommy most certainly was headed back, not even her father could stop that. Her wedding seemed even less important at this point.

"Do you need a ride to County?" Mike asked quietly, breaking Carrie's thoughts. It took a few seconds for her to reason why.

"I... can't. Dusty's sleeping." She whispered to convey her point.

"Is everything alright Carrie?" Parks asked; there was a scent of hopefulness on his tone.

Carrie felt a tear leaving her eye; she tried to beat the answer out as the wet line dribbled from her cheek. "Jason and I… we had a… fight."

Parks seemed to revel in this for a moment, then he realized that he was in uniform and officially capacitated.

He asked, "Are you all right?"

She nodded emphatically, tears were flowing heavily.

He took a breath and looked to his partner, "Mike, I'm off in an hour, would you cover my shift?"

Mike nodded.

Parks turned his attention back to Carrie, "I'll watch the little man."

"Oh, I couldn't…"

"Please Carrie. He's busted up pretty good. He'll… need you." Parks dropped his head and his right hand went into his right breast pocket to search for a toothpick. "Mike'll drive you to County."

Mike seemed a little annoyed at the suggestion, but he turned to Carrie and nodded.

Joshua County General Hospital was a small old one story cinder block and brick building just north of the left turn in the railroad tracks as they headed towards the mills. Painted white twenty years or so ago, it resembled a school more than a hospital, and more often than not school bus drivers who weren't familiar with the area would stop there first as they came into town for football games.

Brenda Cashill was the receptionist/nurse on duty. Her sixty year old frame was weakened by rheumatoid arthritis, her back was curled into nearly a taco shape over forwards, her hands were curled like eagle claws, her feet caused her to slowly move about, but as for being a nurse of forty years, she was exceptional. Her hands could move instruments in and out of the hands of the doctor with speed and grace, with help from a little stool that made her able to sit up straight by leaning back gave her the appearance of a fit and lean woman.

Business at Joshua County General was usually slow, an accident victim maybe once in a while was brought here if it was close enough so the more serious injury could be prepped as the helicopter flew in from Vegas; the most common emergency was a child that had trouble breathing, high fever, an elderly person with a heart attack or someone who crossed her husband and he smacked her around. It seems most of the jail's traffic coincided with the hospital's. Like tonight.

Carrie walked in the main door; she had to be buzzed in by Brenda, and stopped at the counter. The old nurse was returning a manila envelope to the grey file box behind the counter and her movements were clocked by a snail's pace. She spun slowly when Carrie let out an exasperated sigh, her head lifted as she turned, giving her an almost robotic look.

"Hi honey. Lookin' fer that ol man of yours?" The nurse chided.

Carrie was not pleased with the term 'ol man' but nodded to speed things up a bit.

"He's back in four. Got that dick from the S.O.'s office with him. Askin' him lotsa questions they are. Doc's seen him and left. Says he's alright to go home if he wants, but someone should watch him close for concussion or somethin'."

Carrie nodded her thanks and sped off. As she approached ER room four, which was just like the other five, a thick white curtain that surrounded the bed and some machines in the back of the right side of the building, she paused. The voices were coming through and she wanted to hear what had happened, she hoped she wanted to hear what had happened.

"So, you're saying you didn't see him come in." A deep, sleep deprived voice asked. Carrie recognized the voice of Henry-Joe Deweese, the only real detective Fallcast had.

Jason answered, "No. I had my back to the door, I wasn't expecting any trouble."

A sigh; then, "You say that he grabbed you by the throat?"

"Yes."

"And threw you over the bar?"

"Yes."

Another pause.

"Don't get me wrong for asking this Mr. Parmenter, but you seem strong enough to carry your own weight. Why'd you let him pummel you like that?"

"Out of respect."

"*Respect?* Are you serious, how can you respect that crazy…"

"I'm marrying his sister. I love her and I'd never do anything hurt her. She cares for her brothers, Tommy included, and I had no right to hurt him."

The tears began to flow onto Carrie's face again. She felt like a cad, like she'd somehow betrayed Jason by being mad at him. All he wanted was to protect her and himself from her maniac brother and she blew him off. She swallowed and reached slowly for the curtain.

"But you know sir, that this will more than likely end him up back in the *joint*?"

No answer. Carrie suspected Jason nodded. She threw open the curtain and held her breath for the worst. The detective stepped back to let Carrie have a full view of Jason, after acknowledging who she was; first with a frown, then a smile.

Jason had his shirt off. His left arm was in a sling and there was purple bruising on his chest under it. She saw he'd had several stitches on his face above his left eye and

386

a deep red bruise on his right cheek. She could see some of his hair was gone from the back of his head when he turned it to look at her, more sutures there. His face looked ragged tired; his demeanor was that of a beaten school child in the principal's office, he smiled broadly as she walked towards him, until he winced from the pain in his face.

Carrie planted a big kiss on Jason's lips. "I'm so sorry for all of this, you were right." She turned to Henry-Joe and let out a deep breath before spilling the beans about her brother and Meg. "Henry, I need to tell you something. Something…" She began.

"Carrie, you don't have…" Jason began hoarsely.

Carrie interrupted Jason and began her story:

Her find at Meg's house in the garage, the strange way she'd been acting around Carrie and the threats she'd made. She backed it up by pointing to a few people in town who'd also heard the threats. When she finished, Carrie kissed Jason again. He lowered his head, he knew what this meant; this was Carrie turning her own flesh and blood in.

Detective Deweese stood there for a moment with his hand frozen in place on his notepad with a pen in it. He was digesting everything Carrie had just said, he took a deep breath and cleared his throat as he began writing fervently and saying, "This is going to be the final straw Miss Dodson, you're aware of that. The judge won't let him skate on this one, the flares are secondary, we'll have to investigate their presence and if they're the ones used in the recent arsons, but the fact your brother has been seeing a woman on probation is a violation. The fact he did this without provocation," Henry-Joe nodded at Jason's wounds, "is an arrest on battery charges, the fact he was in an establishment that serves alcohol is another violation. I… I'm afraid no one can stop this from happening."

Carrie nodded as she touched Jason's wounds here and there.

Deweese continued, "This could get Megan Cooke time in County Jail for violating her probation too. Are you aware of that?"

Carrie turned to the cop and fire sparkled her eyes, "I don't care. I want this to end. Now."

Deweese just nodded and returned to looking at the words he was scribbling on the paper.

The Friday before the wedding, a warrant was issued for Megan Cooke, who had disappeared from sight. Violation of parole and suspicion of arson was the two key elements of the warrant; the judge also signed a limited search warrant for Megan's house and Tommy's. When Henry-Joe and Mike Tenner visited Meg's house and searched the garage, the flare box was still where Carrie had seen it. Although the Bronco was gone, Tenner doubted she would've gone too far, someone was holing her up nearby.

The search later at Tommy's house revealed nothing more than the fact he was a slob, old food was left in the kitchen sink and bugs were crawling around the mess. Beer bottles and whiskey glasses littered the living room and someone had thrown an ashtray through the TV screen. The disrepair of the home revealed an angry man, who took out his temper on inanimate objects. The fact he took out the same frustration on people was already given, and he was going to head back to prison for that, a third strike, and in Nevada that meant very close to life in prison.

Terrence Dodson took it the hardest, even though everyone expected him to have seen this coming and in most respects they were right. He had seen Tommy ending up back in prison, he was just hoping inside-a dying man's last request from God-that Tommy would see the opportunity of having control of some of the town was a hand up and he could stop his angry ways of jealousy and drinking.

In just less than forty-eight hours he was to give his estranged daughter's hand away to a non-local boy, his fortune to his mentally challenged son, his life to whomever sees fit to take his soul. Terry knew his options there were limited. There was no delusion he was headed for the Pearly Gates-if there was such a thing-he knew in his mind he should be mentally packing for a very warm trip.

Terry had considered a few times changing his will since he took everything away from his eldest son if he was imprisoned once again, to restrict what Carrie and Jason got, he knew that Tommy was probably going to get out someday and might need something for another, if not ill-fated, start. He would meet with his lawyer soon after the wedding.

CHAPTER NINETEEN
The Wedding, May 17th 2010

Jason arrived at the Town Hall Building around ten thirty. He was supposed to be out helping Dusty find a decent pair of shoes, since the ones Carrie had bought him a week ago were ruined when the boy went out into the field behind the house and played in the irrigation ditch. Little did she know that Jason had already had a backup pair hidden, the ruse of the shopping trip was to help Gloria and Helen Dickson decorate the hall.

Inside the massive building made of granite and marble imported from California and Italy, on the pillars of white stone that shot from the floor to the ceiling twenty feet up, were blue and white ribbons done up for the day. Streamers lined the railings of the inner hall and stairs that wound up to the second floor where the official offices were, blue and white, which were Carrie's favorite colors.

The centerpiece of the hall this day was not a podium set up for a political event or a press conference, but a white woven willow arch. Two small steps led from the polished granite floor to the center of the cabana-like proscenium and stage, white with white rose petals already spread on the steps. Behind this area sat two white lattice panels, in front of each was a six foot fake ficus tree with white lights. An eight stick candelabra sat in the center behind the stage with a white upholstered kneeling bench in the middle and a small white musician's easel for the pastor to place his notes and ceremonial book on.

From the front of where Carrie and Jason are to say their vows, two runners of white carpet ran to the back of the first set of doors leading to the massive receiving foyer ending with two Corinthian columns and flower urns filled with fresh blue hydrangeas with anemones, and white peonies with amaryllis.

The hall's open space was decorated with white streamers hanging from the rafters; the central area under the dome shaped ceiling had a huge paper flower arrangement suspended from the center with white and blue crepe strips going from the granite handrails on the second floor to the center top.

One hundred and fifty folding metal chairs were set up in three rows fanning out from the center where the stage was to the rear of the hall; it made Jason a tad nervous thinking that this many people would be coming. Carrie wasn't aware of the size of the crowd, the decorations or what Jason had planned next. He was helping tie little blue and white ribbons with a small sack made of white mesh that contained four candy coated almonds when he heard someone walking up behind him.

"This is very nice." A throaty and phlegmy voice said, the hoarseness echoing off the walls of the nearly empty Town Hall.

Jason spun as the man spoke. It was Terrence Dodson, and he was looking the worse for wear. Jason slid a chair out from the aisle towards him and said with a draft of concern, "Here Mr. Dodson, take a load off."

The man who at one time looked twenty at forty but now looked seventy at fifty-plus nodded with a complimentary smile and groaned as he rested his behind in the seat. "Much obliged." He took a deep watery sounding breath and asked, "Everything looks great, but don't you think we'll need more chairs?"

Jason felt even tighter inside. "Are you expecting more? Carrie said just a few folks really, but I figured we wouldn't need more than one hundred or so…"

Terry nodded, "Never know. Mill's closed on the big day in honor of her ceremony, only a skeleton crew to keep the walls from falling down. I figure at least fifty more or so would wander in." He coughed and bent over. The cancer was now turning him into a cripple.

"Are you alright? Is there anything I can get you?"

Dodson just nodded and pulled a handkerchief from his pants pocket. "Yeah, time for my drugs, how about a cup of water." Jason walked to the water cooler and filled a cone shaped cup, Terry reached into his front pocket and took out a script bottle, shook three little white oval shaped tablets into his hand and threw them into the back of his throat, then swallowed.

"Three?" Jason asked as he handed the water to Dodson. He knew most pain killers for cancer were strong after one or two.

"Well," Terry said while chuckling to himself, "as long as I don't have anything to drink after taking them and I don't get stressed out. I see no harm."

Jason nodded with compassion.

Terry cleared his throat, which was a chore in itself and looked up to Jason. Jason felt bad about the proximity to the man and pulled a chair up for himself.

"I know that Miss Dodson won't be as happy as I am about this whole walking down the aisle thing."

"Oh, I don't know," Jason began, "I think she's coming around to it. She hasn't mentioned killing you once since…"

Terry smiled big and let go a laugh. It was the first time Jason had heard one this intense.

"I'm sorry about Tommy. I should've known that…" Terry started with regret in his eyes and tone.

"Nonsense, if it were my boy, I'd have never guessed it either. It's in the past, let's leave it there and get on with our future."

"Not much of a future for me." Terry began after a wheezing cough. "But yours? Very promising. Carrie and you will have run of the mill, the town and many other things once I'm gone. You're just a very lucky man."

"Yes." Jason agreed with a hearty nod, "For Carrie and Dusty. As for anything else, well, I can take it or leave it. As long as they're happy, I will be."

Terrence crooked his head a little and narrowed his eyes a little at Jason. He sensed something; there was a hidden place in this man's story. Something wasn't right. He let the feeling go and vowed he would pick up on it later at his office. "Well Mr. Parmenter, I'll see you in few hours then?"

"Yes sir." Terry rose and shook hands with Jason, Jason being careful not to squeeze too tightly and the dying man spun on a carefully balanced heel and walk back out the front doors.

~

A portable keyboard was brought in before the ceremony began and librarian Mrs. Baker had been playing little soft sonatas while the guests shuffled in. Terry was right, more than two hundred people had shown so far and even though there was only standing room at the back of the hall, there were at least fifty more outside talking to the wedding party and pastor.

At one fifteen she was told to play the wedding march and she did so, on time. It took only seconds for the crowd to hush and mere minutes for the rest of the folks to gather inside the hall.

Jason felt ill. He'd dreamed of this for years, to other women of course, but never to one so beautiful and soon to be powerful. His grandparents couldn't attend because of his grandfather's allergies to dust and pollen, something that was in the air full time around Fallcast. He sent an apology letter in the R.S.V.P. envelope with a check for five thousand dollars with best regards from Jason's grandmother and himself.

Jason heard the din from the crowd draw to a pin dropping silence and then he could hear his own stomach at work, trying to liquefy everything inside his body. *Here it goes…* Jason checked to make sure his rented tux cufflinks were tight and then checked his tie and cummerbund again for any chance of falling off and embarrassing himself. He walked to the little foyer and found Dusty impatiently waiting for him. The boy was tapping his foot on the marble floor and had his arms crossed. Jason shot him a look he rarely used on the boy, but it worked and the frustration melted away.

Jason and Dusty made their way up the center aisle to small oohs and aaahs and a few gasps from the younger women in the crowd. Men nodded at him as he passed- some as if to say '*good luck*' others as if to imply '*lucky bastard*'. He held his head proud at both and continued to the front where the pastor stood. There was a pause in the music and then it started over, the march was too long and somewhat boring to play all the way through, so the "organist" began it again as requested.

Carrie was already in the bathroom stall as the music began. Her stomach was ready to flip, the juice and toast she had for breakfast was making a plea for a re-debut. After months of planning, the trips to the dressmaker in town to have her mother's dress altered, the flower shop visits where Jason pretended he was interested, same for the bakery who constructed a beautiful three tiered white cake with white and blue frosting (cream not beef fat) and Jason's attempts to sneak a peek at the Bronco's football games on Sundays when they met with the pastor and the caterer. *Ugghhh*, food. She couldn't think about food!

After listening to the march almost all the way through, Carrie felt well enough to make her way towards the door, *THE* door that once she crossed over the threshold of, she was no longer the most eligible single bachelorette in Fallcast, or all of Nevada probably. Her financial future was set; her love for Jason Parmenter was exact, her life was seemingly at the part where everyone says "*And they lived happily ever after...*"

Just as she came to the door, a loud and impatient knock made her judder back a step and she felt her heart stop. Her father's sickly and phlegmy voice rose for a moment above the music, then he had to lower it as the second attempt was begun.

"Are you okay, honey... I mean Carrie?"

She opened the door and smiled at him. It was the first time ever, she could remember that she had, but he looked so cute in his tux. His face was sunken as never before, Terry's eyes were mostly sockets and small specks of coal inside, but with a visible tear under each one. A tear of pride and accomplishment, although he had nothing to do with raising her, she felt as if he understood that his life was ending and hers was beginning and she felt a little gracious that he had tried in his last months of life to make things better for her and her little brother.

She felt a pang of guilt as she stared into his eyes for a moment, her big brother was absent and that was sad for Terry. Thomas was Terrence's only best friend as well as son and would have been heir to so much if he hadn't gone and thrown it all away over booze and Megan Cooke. *Megan Cooke*, now that changed her mood.

"Something wrong Carrie?" Terry had seen his daughter's eyes fall.

"No... *dad*. I was just thinking about Tommy. I'm sorry he couldn't be here."

Terry dropped his eyes to the floor too and spoke softly, "Yes, well he had his chance. And now it's yours, I'm so proud of you, if I'm allowed to say that. I wish your mother..."

Tears fell. Hard and fast. Terrence the pit bull mine owner with fists of steel and a will of iron was now a muddled mess of soft tissues and tears. He shuddered and tried to regain his composure but it took nearly a minute and a half as he managed a sad smile for his soon to be wed only daughter. "I'm sorry Carrie."

Carrie bent forward and placed a kiss next to his one remaining tear, the one that was making a fast dash for his collar. "It's alright dad. I wish she were here too. I'm sorry…"

"No need to be, it was all my fault and now I'm paying for my terrible ways. I hope someday you'll see her again and tell her about today." He let a smile crawl across his face, "Just don't tell her about me crying, she'll never believe you…"

Carrie embraced her father and held as tight as she thought he could handle without breaking his fragile structure. She kissed his cheek again and presented her arm out in the air for him to take.

"I think it's the other way around…" Terry said.

Carrie smiled and waited for her father to imitate the move, which he did and with huge smiles on their faces (although a bit ragged), Terrence Dodson walked his daughter Carrie Marie down the aisle to astonished breaths and shock filled awes.

Jason was talking quietly to Dusty when the room fell silent. He felt the hair on the back of his neck stand straight up and he slowly turned towards the center aisle, his stomach and heart fell at the same time. He had never witnessed so much beauty in his life.

Among little gasps and whispers a glow of white lace and satin flowed from the back of the hall that housed meetings for determining whether or not dogs could run wild without a leash or how much the mines should pay in taxes to the city coffer, an image of an angel appeared in the first few feet of carpeted destiny.

The angel's choice of dress was exacted to fit her unusual frame of nearly six foot tall, of a robust chest that easily supported the strapless silk plunging neckline, it tightened around her small waist-a waist rarely seen out of a Pendleton wool shirt or oversized overalls that made her look flat and strong-now everyone could see that there was woman underneath that rough exterior, and incurved shapeliness from the bottom of her bosom to the tops of her hips. Her dress was closed in the back gently by a corset style lacework, a large white satin bow resting comfortably on her buttocks that ran to mid-back with its lengths of ribbon flowing easily into the train of the dress, the front of the bow was arranged in a floral design center of the visage's belly, her abdomen a harbinger of beauty and bliss, the future of her years as a wife and mother, the very essence of what lies beneath the satin and lace curls of the large petal flower.

The train flowed from behind her quietly like a soft waterfall of glassy linen, just a few feet behind her footsteps silently slipping along the thin white carpet not seeming to touch the ground but at times reacting to the smallest of ripples or bumps in the runner, like a wave crashing on a rippled beach. The dress was sprinkled with Swarovski crystals, glittering in the special lighting that was generally used to make a lying politician look like a deity, now graced the townsfolk with the glow of a goddess.

Even Mrs. Baker the librarian missed a couple of notes as she lost her thoughts in the spectacle of beauty that shuffled effortlessly across the floor; a woman moving towards her love, her new life, her only.

Now it was Jason's turn to feel sick. *How could such beauty find him?* Carrie's hair was pulled back to an almost ponytail at the top of her head, several newly highlighted strands flowed from the small bun tied at the crest of her crown and flowed to her back where it met with the top of the neckline below her silken brown shoulders. One filament of combined brown and blond mane loosely dropped from just below the top, over the side of her face and wisped around her delicately made up cheek. Jason could not believe that such a thing were possible that this woman the whole town now desired, men and women both, was sashaying his way, to the tips of his feet where she would pledge her life to him and he pledged his to her.

Till death do they part…

Even Dusty didn't recognize the Salt Lick. Cookie had gone out of his way to decorate the outside, and just as Carrie had become the flower from the seed for her wedding day, the man of many complaints and few compliments had changed the simple diner into a reception place that held way more than the legal limit the sign by the door said it could. Tables had been moved to the sides, some disappeared completely, only Cookie knew where they went. He had decorated the walls and fixtures in the white and blue motif, even dangling crepe streamers from the antique toy trucks and sleds, from dried leather ice skates to vintage mixing machines and soda fountain handles that sat on freshly dusted shelves.

Even the sign that spoke the name of the place in partially broken twinkling neon was adorned with large bows and flowers, the reader portion boasted "CLOSED FOR WEDDING RECEPTION TODAY". The first time the diner had closed for a shift since the great fire that cleared most of the older buildings in town out, the diner was a private place for friends and family to gather and enjoy the matrimony of the two most beautiful people Fallcast had at the moment. Carrie was dancing with Jason in her dress, the train flowing from her fingertips, Jason's face contorted into the shape of a man who had just been handed the keys to the country, not just a simple city. Music was provided by Wurlitzer, and each guest at the few remaining tables could request a song by simply dropping a quarter in to the little replica on the table and push a button.

As the room fell silent over the first few bars of Richard Marx's *Right Here Waiting for You*, Jason leaned into his new wife and he inhaled the scent of the gods, a jasmine and lavender mix with just a touch of sweetness like an orange slice that held a tinge of tart but was slightly overwhelmed with pleasantness. He so badly wanted out of here now; he wanted to show her the rest of his surprise, from the decorations where the reception was being held, to the honeymoon. She was in for a treat. He was feeling his body shiver each time he brushed a bare part of his skin against hers, anticipating the moment when he would have her soft supple skin against his in full length.

Carrie was not far from thinking along the same lines as her new husband. Her body ached under the warm satin and chilling open top; she wanted to be with Jason and his strong muscled body, the ripped tone that seemed to come naturally for him. She never saw him workout, but his sinew was as taught as piano strings, her insides tingled at the thought of the sensations she would be feeling as soon as they fed the town's desire to see her dance one more, then board the mine vehicle that had been cleaned and polished within an inch of its life, the magnetic sign that was attached to the door that read DOWARDS MINE AND MILL removed. He could have used his Blazer, but Terrence insisted on the mine vehicle, he even paid for the fuel and return trip refueling with a company credit card given to Jason just a few hours ago.

But, there was at least an hour of dancing and hobnobbing to go.

At the door of the diner as the crowd dispersed, Jason and Carrie had done the traditional flower and garter throws, Gloria caught the bouquet and the garter belt landed in front of Parks, who saw it but refused to pick it up. He crossed his arms and smiled as the celebrants egged him on to grab it before anyone else. A flash later one of the preteen sons of a mine employee scrambled and picked it up and held it above his head like a trophy then ran around as the older boys tried to grab it from him. It brought on a good laugh from the people of Fallcast, a laugh that was well needed, like the wedding ceremony and even the reception. The town needed a reason to go all out and cheer. Gloria took off early with Dusty so Carrie and Jason could get some crowd time and the boy was excited to be out of his monkey-suit and on his way to play *Flight Simulator.*

At the top of the first step just outside the door Jason approached Carrie, who had changed into jeans and a blue top with ruffled shoulders, she was being practically mauled by well-wishers, one in particular, Parks. Jason walked up with a smile on his face and cleared his throat.

"*Ahem.* Can you leave some for the honeymoon?"

Carrie whirled around and Jason saw a red faced Darrin Parker trying to hide the blush on his cheeks as he thrust a hand out in Jason's direction. "Congratulations."

Jason nodded and took his offer; the grip of both was equally firm, but not overzealous.

"Thank you. And thank you for all your help these last few months, it really means a lot to me."

Parks gulped back a thought and asked, "What did I do?"

"You kept Carrie company when I was gone. You looked out after us when Megan and Tommy went crazy. I owe you big time…"

Parks nodded in modesty.

"By the way, have you heard anything about Megan?" Carrie asked.

Parks shook his head no. "Nothing. She's got to be hiding somewhere in town but no one will give her up. Her leg shackle was found in her living room, cut off by a saw or something, probably by Tommy."

Carrie lowered her head at the sound of her brother's name. She tugged at Jason's shirt, he'd changed also into a pair of jeans and a light blue polo shirt; she wanted to go. She *wanted* him and no more talk of her family. She spun to make the last two steps down from the restaurant's front door when she ran, literally, into her father. They quickly pulled apart and then cautiously stepped toward one another. Terry offered his hand to Jason who was waving at Parks and following his new wife down the steps.

"Thank you." Terry said. His voice was trembling from pain and the meds he used to control the pain.

"No, thank you sir."

Terry glanced at his daughter and wiped a tear from his eye with a handkerchief, then smiled, "Thank you too. Thank you for letting me have the pleasure of walking you down the aisle."

Carrie smiled sadly and gave her father a hug. "Maybe things will be different from now on?"

"I'd hope so, but with what little time there is left I doubt I could make a difference. I'm sorry."

Carrie planted a kiss on his cheek. "Don't be. Things will be okay."

The couple spun and after a smattering of applause boarded the Jeep and drove off into the sunset towards Vegas.

Carrie watched as the sun lowered behind one of the huge mountains in the distance, she felt a warmth in her body she'd never felt before, it was calm. Peace and serenity settled over her for the first time she could remember in her life. It was a dream at best when she was younger, to feel this way. Now on the other end of her outstretched hand was a beautiful man who along with herself had the keys to the city and the hearts of the townspeople. They would be the best, generous family to hit town since the founders of Fallcast. Plans were already in the makings in her head for children, she wanted to get pregnant tonight if possible, she wasn't sure you could get knocked up on your first time, but she hoped so. She hoped that as she and her husband enveloped their bodies into one single entity; to feel the rush of their muscles contracting and nervous systems overflowing with sharp jolts of electricity generated from intimate contact, that a child-a boy for Jason-would be conceived.

The room in Vegas was nice, not as nice as the one they stayed in the night Jason proposed to Carrie. *The Mirage* was still a step beyond anything that Carrie had experienced in her life, the room was decorated and furnished more lavishly than any home she'd seen in Fallcast with expensive loveseats, dining room chairs (yes, there was a dining room in the suite) and bed the size of a small swimming pool with a chest of drawers in oak at the foot, tall curtains that rose from the floor to about fourteen feet high.

The windows overlooked The Strip, the panes were twelve feet long and once again all the way to the ceiling. Blue pastels were used for the upholstery and a huge throw rug was swirled in the same color, Carrie's favorite.

A meal arrived at the door twenty minutes after they checked in, surf and turf. Filet mignon and lobster tail, asparagus neatly arranged in a cylindrical pattern and tied in place with string made from carrot skin. Small potatoes with caramelized onions, two tall flutes filled with Philipponnat Clos des Goisses and a thin slice of cheesecake covered in a cherry sauce that was spiced with liqueur. Carrie ate with a vengeance, the feeling of the well prepared meal competed with the heated feeling she was having in her lower abdomen, each bite she watched as Jason took a morsel of his food and stared at her, into her golden eyes that shined like newly polished baubles.

They finished and took their glasses down to the casino for a walk around; Jason plunked a few twenties down on some 21 tables, without much luck. Carrie dumped ten dollars into a slot machine and reaped fifty back.

After an hour and a half in the lower levels; seeing the live dolphins in the pools at the aquarium, a quick walk outside to watch the volcano erupt twice and a saunter through the larger than life replicated lagoon pool complete with rock waterfalls and private lounging, each yawned and they decided it was time to head back to their room. The ride back up to their floor was just short of *R* rated, neither Carrie nor Jason cared much about the security cameras. As the doors closed, the moment was right for the first passionate kiss they'd shared in hours, not since arriving in their room.

Carrie wrapped her arms around Jason's neck and pulled herself up to meet his lips, he lowered his head to help. At that point she slid her hands down the front of his jeans and searched, he ran his hands in between her soft skin and the top of her dungarees. They caressed and kissed as the car floated to the floor which held their room, waiting for the newlyweds to taste the brilliant accommodations provided. It took four stabs at the card slot to get the door open when they arrived, Jason giggled as did Carrie when he made the lock snap open on the fifth try of the key.

Without turning on the room lights, Carrie guided Jason along, with her backpedaling towards the bedroom. At each step, a button was released on his jean's fly; an inch higher on her shirt. At the apex of the room, Carrie lifted her arms to help him clear the blue ruffled puffy shoulder blouse over and to the floor, she immediately drooped to her knees pulling the length of his jeans along with her. Standing, they embraced for another three or four minutes and caressed the tingling skins of the other.

Carrie removed her bra slowly as Jason suckled her lips, in a slight break in the action he slipped his shirt over his head, made an attempt to hit the dressing chair and missed terribly, the garment slapping against the window.

Moments later, Carrie was caressing Jason's chest; running her fingers slowly over his nearly wash-boarded stomach muscles, she teased at his neck and shoulders with biting kisses as he sighed deeply. Her moment was here. For the first time in her life.

A pinch of pain and the world exploded in passion and ecstasy, the fluid movements of their hungry bodies were bridled with the desire they had for each other and on many occasions denied by interruption. There would be no crying out in the night from her brother in another room, no one at the door telling them of another tragedy, no entity in the world to stop the lust that had built into a crescendo of trembling masses of epidermis and sweat, kisses of deep need and the *le petite de mort* that rumbled the walls. More than once.

CHAPTER TWENTY
The Following Week

Carrie sat quietly as the Jeep wrestled the mountain pass upwards towards home. Her body was weak from the last three days. Food brought to the room, exercise which burned calories but not a lot of getting around, sights that were unaffordable before, everything under the sun in five days. She was spent. And sore. A smile came to her face as her body relived the last few nights, the pure ecstasy that came from the honeymoon and the fact there was no longer a blockage between her and Jason, that the intimate knowledge of each other was complete. She no longer feared not being good enough for him, as a matter of fact she was confident that he was just as happy as she was.

Jason was humming along to a scratchy and static filled song: Chris Isaac's *Wicked Game*, as the radio station from Vegas faded in and out. At times when Jason would sing a part, he was left all alone and Carrie would glance over and roll her eyes as he hit the high notes a little-*not high*. He couldn't replay too much of his week in Vegas, he was driving after all and the sensations that the thought of him and his beautiful bride sharing the same bed and telling each other how much they loved one another would cause him to become erratic at driving. Same reason he would playfully slap Carrie's hand away as she tried to massage his leg gently, but higher than he liked when he was operating a one ton mine-owned vehicle.

The happy couple had left Las Vegas late, around four p.m., and the sun was threatening to set behind the purple mountains behind the town underneath the massive hills of rock and dirt. When approaching Fallcast from the south and on top of the pass, the little berg only seems a few miles away, but the real story is in the switchbacks and steep grades you must navigate to get to the valley below.

As they approached Carrie's house, the reality of being home hit them both; Darrin Parker's police cruiser was parked in the driveway, he'd been sitting there for about an hour. Both Jason and Carrie took deep breaths as they slowly turned onto the gravel driveway.

"Maybe he's just welcoming us home…" Jason said with a note of uncertainty.

Carrie was focused on dire circumstances, "God, I hope Dusty's alright."

Jason slowed the Jeep to a stop next to the deputy's car and used his control buttons to roll down the window; he'd pulled up on Carrie's side of the Jeep so she could talk to Parks while he sat in his car.

"What's happening Darrin?" She asked quietly and nervously.

He smiled and that was a slight relief for them both, you don't bare horrific news with a smile, at least the conversation would be lighter.

"Hi guys. Have a great time?" He beamed a little like he was privy to the week anyway, "Don't see any tan lines…"

Carrie was going to say 'not much sun in our bedroom', but restrained knowing the fact that the cop had a crush on her and she didn't want to toy with his emotions. "We gambled indoor mostly and saw some great floor shows. I've been to that town too many times to just lie around the pool."

Parks nodded and then cast an approving glance at Jason, then took a respective breath, "Well, there's been some trouble while you were gone…" He pointed across the dash of his prowler and indicated the front window of the Carrie's house. "Happened last night, maybe yesterday evening. I've been keeping an eye on the place, what with Meg missing and all."

Carrie and Jason both turned their heads at the same time to see the window was gone, broken glass covering the porch and the curtains outside blowing in the wind like torn sails on a lost ship.

"*Nice.*" Jason said sarcastically.

"Yeah. I'm sorry; I thought I was doing a good job, but…" Parks replied.

Jason turned back to Parks and smiled, "Not your fault. You really didn't even have to watch the place."

Parks returned the smile with a gratuitous wink and said, "I want to keep you guys safe until we find Megan. I'll be passing by here each night a few times and I'll drive by on my way to work."

"No need Darrin, we'll be okay. Did they take anything?" Carrie said from her window down to the deputy.

"No. I walked through, just in case and nothing looks disturbed. The brick was lying on the loveseat by the fireplace."

He held it up. There was a word written on the brick in chalk, the letters were damaged sailing through the tempered glass, but enough was left to recognize *WH ORE.*

Carrie felt tears welling up inside and behind her lids. "Dammit." It was all she could think to say.

Jason put his hand on her leg and rubbed it softly. "Don't worry babe, I'll go and get a sheet of plywood at the mercantile until we get the glass replaced."

She just nodded and let the tears fall onto her blouse.

Jason slowly opened the door and popped his head in first. Parks had a call and left, Carrie and he slowly made their way into the house after refusing the deputy's insistence that he go first. Carrie made him drive off and he did, shaking his head. Carrie had faith in her man, she knew no animal or other being was safe if it threatened her while Jason was around. She once wondered if he'd kill for her.

As they checked each room their pace quickened and mood improved until they reached the den where Jason's briefcase was and his laptop. Someone had rifled through his papers, and tried to open the *Windows* program. Only Carrie, Dusty and Jason knew the password so it locked up. Someone had been prying in here. But why not steal the damnable thing?

"Son of a bitch!" Jason exclaimed, which startled Carrie, she'd never seen him lose it so fast.

"What?"

"This pisses me off. I thought the cop was a good guy…"

"Jason! He is. Darrin didn't go through this stuff. Maybe you left it like this…"

"No, never. This paperwork is all out of order. The computer was not on when we left last week."

"Maybe Dusty and Mary came by and he played with the games…"

"No! Don't you see? The thing has locked out everyone but me. Dusty knows the password back and forth, whoever did this knew nothing about it and the thing shut down as a precaution. Dammit!"

Concern washed over her face as Carrie went to touch his arm; he jerked it away and went into a small rage as he stuffed the splayed papers back into the briefcase and slammed it shut. Jason then took the case and walked back to Carrie's bedroom, now to be theirs, and slid the case under the foot of the bed on his side.

"Is everything alright Jason? You're worrying me."

He just nodded with a look of hate on his face and went into the living room, got the broom out of the closet and began sweeping up the broken glass. Carrie joined in without saying a word and they cleaned the mess up in just under an hour.

Jason was pacing back and forth as he ate his toast Carrie had made for him and Dusty. It was Monday morning and her husband was off to work, a special meeting with her father, and Dusty (although he didn't know it yet) was eager to get to the schoolbooks and study after a lazy week and weekend.

"Do you want me to make you a lunch?" She asked as he paced.

He didn't respond with a word, he just looked at her and shook his head.

"Look honey, he's my dad. I know he can be a bear, but…"

"It's not that." Jason said with a hopeless tone.

"What is it then? Is it something I did?" She gave him a little pout.

"No." His face said no, he said no, but that didn't solve the problem of his anxious body language.

"Hi Anne."

"Oh hello Mr. Parmenter. Mr. Dodson will be just a few minutes; he's on a call right now."

Jason nodded at Dodson's assistant. A forty something with too much makeup and nice boobs, but a desperate look of sadness on her face and a wardrobe to match. Fair haired, but not a very tidy job of dressing it up, just a simple office bun. She'd been his secretary at the Dodson Mill and Mine and he brought her over to Dowards, he just couldn't let anyone else run his affairs.

After a few moments there was a slight buzz from Anne's desktop and she nodded at Jason, "Okay honey, he's ready to see you now."

Jason entered the office and saw immediately things were not going well for Terry today. His face was buried in his hands and there was an open bottle of prescription meds on the desk in front of him. Jason sat in his usual chair. He waited patiently for Terry to look up. He did after three minutes.

"Mr. Parmenter. Good vacation?" His voice was graven, hollow.

Jason didn't dare smile slyly or answer in a provocative tone; he let his emotionless face guide his voice as it came out of his drying throat. "Yes, sir. Thank you."

"Terry. Please call me Terry." The man rose from his desk and pulled a side drawer open, then yanked a bottle of expensive scotch up and two rock glasses. "I'm your father-in-law now, let's be a bit less formal, okay?"

Jason nodded.

"I've had a rotten day Jason. The judge gave Tommy twenty plus the revocation of his parole. He can't get out for at least that much time. My lawyer advised against leaving everything to Dusty, he says that Tommy should get something, that way if he does make parole in twenty he can't go after Dusty or Carrie for anything. The report you gave the assayer was short on some information and he's been on my ass to get it filled in. Best of all, I was sitting here early this morning and I realize that I'm not on top of my game right now, but you had said something to me earlier, a month or two ago about the cave on mine property."

Jason swallowed hard.

Terry continued, "I let it fly by me the first time you mentioned it, then the other day I was thinking; why would he say something about it unless it had some significance. I wondered, what was going on there, what you saw or what you found, what it could mean for our agreement."

Terry waited a full minute before he began his explanation of what was to come next, Jason sat and felt horrible, but eventually relieved at the same time.

410

"How was your meeting and day?" Carrie asked as Jason strode in the door at noon.

He stared at her for a moment, then grinned a little. "Okay." He seemed farther out from a certain line of thought than usual, something else was on his mind right now.

Carrie and Dusty were finishing up the day's lessons and she had made them all lunch which was waiting in the fridge, roast beef and cheese sandwiches. Carrie put her books away and made Dusty take his to his room. He complied slowly, but the prospect of eating drove his feet. Carrie took the lunch out of the cooler, a plate with four triangle sliced sandwiches and a pitcher of tea. Carrying it out to the back porch, she set the plate down and then waited for her two men to come along.

"What'd you two talk about today?" She asked as Jason sat down and slid a wedge off the plate as she poured his tea.

Jason hesitated then figured he would try honesty, a little anyways. "His will. My place in the company and…" He contemplated, then, "about that cave I found."

"The one on the property? Still on that huh?"

Jason smiled. "Sorry."

"I don't know what the big deal about that place is; I mean I don't even think the kids go there anymore. Too many bad things have happened there. Is there something of interest you found?"

Jason's face went pale. He shook his head and got up from the table, "I'm not feeling well honey, I'm gonna go lay down."

Carrie watched as her new husband shuffled off to the back of the house. She was saddened by his demeanor, he was under some kind of stress and she hoped it wouldn't affect their new marriage.

Six hours had elapsed, Carrie had crawled into bed with her husband and rubbed his shoulders, which brought a response that lasted for an hour and a half and left both of them sweaty and exhausted even more. Dusty was working on his commercial jet pilot's license on the computer game so he was not a threat. A few minutes after six thirty that evening, the phone rang.

Carrie pulled on a pair of sweats and a T shirt, stumbling down the hall to get the phone before it went to the new machine Jason had brought with him here from Denver; Dusty was still not allowed to answer the phone after an incident involving a telemarketer and 9-1-1. Jason could hear his wife curse (a very rare event) the stool in the kitchen that she'd just stubbed her toe on as she picked up the receiver.

"Hello?" A long pause. "Oh, hi Anne. What? Oh no, really? Oh *God*. No, that's alright. I'm sorry too. Thank you."

Jason couldn't hear any movement in the kitchen any longer, the phone was now beeping that it was off the hook. Worried, he climbed out of bed, dressed and went to see what was going on. He found Carrie standing in the dining room, she was leaning against the counter with her face in her hand; the other was holding the receiver and was dangling from her side.

"Babe?" He said quietly. Carrie raised her head and he saw tears flowing from her red eyes. "What's wrong? Are you okay?" He rushed over to hold her and she grabbed him, dropping the phone to the floor.

"Carrie?" Jason asked again, holding her chin up with his forefinger and thumb.

"Terrence is dead." She said flatly.

Megan Cooke sat in her Bronco three blocks from Carrie's house. She could see the front yard, the front door and the driveway from her vantage point, she could also see if there was any movement in the house once in a while. She wasn't really hiding anymore, she had no reason to. This was going to be all over soon.

"Oh God, I'm so sorry honey!" Jason exclaimed as he helped his wife to a chair.

She shook her head and wiped her face with her hand slowly, "I... I mean... Why should I care too much?"

"He was you father."

"He was a bastard."

"What happened?"

"Anne said that she found him slumped over his desk about an hour ago. They pronounced him right there in his office."

"I'm sorry."

Carrie turned her head to her husband, "Was he drinking? Anne said he'd drunk a whole bottle of scotch along with his pain pills."

Jason backed his up a bit, "We had a glass, but I don't know what happened after I left..."

"Was he taking his pills?"

Jason lowered his head and nodded. "He took three or four, I told him that that was a bad idea, but he said he was hurting so much inside that he needed a boost..."

Carrie hugged Jason as tight as she could, "What do I tell Dusty? I mean he was just beginning to understand that Terrence was his father, and now I have to tell him that the man's gone..."

Meg watched as she saw a Nova drive around the front of the Dodson/Parmenter household. It was Parks, she looked to her left and saw an open fence in an abandoned yard, as quickly and quietly as she could she pulled her truck in and shut the engine off.

"I have to go and give the M.E. a positive ID." Carrie said as she rose from Jason's lap and headed for the back of the house. "Will you watch Dusty?"

Jason rubbed his chin and took a deep breath, "I'll go."

Darrin Parks sat and watched for a few minutes, he hadn't heard about Terry Dodson yet, his cell phone was dead and he'd left his car charger in the prowler's glove box. He was about to head to the office when he spotted the roof of a vehicle in his rearview, it was behind a fence in a yard that was not occupied by anyone, the family had moved north months ago and the place was being fixed up. He put his car into drive and made a lap around the block; he was headed two blocks up and three blocks east, then he could drive back behind the house and get a better view of the strange vehicle. It wasn't that he was paranoid, but things weren't going according to the way it should be right now and he'd wanted to be sure everything was in its place.

"Probably a couple of kids getting high." He told himself aloud. He watched Jason get into his Blazer and drive off towards town, thinking to himself how the guy has managed to become a local now, marrying the woman Park's loved from afar for so long.

It took ten minutes to sneak up on the yard from behind, so the occupants wouldn't see him approach, nearly every kid in the town knew Parks' Nova and they also knew he'd do police work off duty. Parks was always carrying, he was considered always on duty. He'd drive up fast on the kids, jump out with his badge held high and then give them a scolding for a few minutes, promise to tell their parents the next time he caught them breaking the law and then let them go with a warning.

As he let his car crawl towards the open part of the gate he paused, his heart nearly leapt from his chest as he recognized the Bronco. He reached for his radio and remembered he was off duty today and in his personal car, he tried his cell again and found it had just enough power for an emergency call; he dialed 9-1-1.

He gave the dispatcher his name and where he was. Then, just behind him, he heard the tell-tale sound of crunching gravel on pavement being smashed by a shoe; he knew he'd made a critical error, he let his guard down-on duty or not-this is what kills cops every time.

He dropped the completely dead cell phone to his lap as the cold metal pierced his neck, the burn of a thousand candles focused where it entered, the sickly sticky soothing of warm blood cooling as it left his body and began pooling at his collar, followed.

Dusty was playing in the yard while Carrie was pacing around the kitchen after Airplane Man left. He sat in the swing shaking his head about the way things were inside for the last hour or so. His sister was tense and he could feel it, it was bad things. Bad things and probably the darkness in the shadow had something to do with it. He closed his eyes and pushed himself high into the air on the swing, he could feel the rush of the air over his cheeks, like he was flying without a plane, free and far away from the darkness. He heard a car approach. He drug his feet into the worn-out grass in a hole under the swing and stopped his flight, he turned and opened his eyes. He smiled.

"Hi big man, wanna go for a ride?" The familiar voice called to him.

"Hello?"

A long pause.

"Hello?" Carrie asked the scratchy open line into receiver.

"Carrie?"

"Megan?"

"Carrie? I have something to tell you, to show you. You have to meet me."

"Meg, the cops are looking for you…"

"I know, I just saw Parks spying on your house. I've managed to get passed him, but I can't go near your place again. Where's your husband?"

"Megan, please… Leave us alone, I can't…"

"Listen to me dammit! Is Jason there with you?"

"No, he went to the hospital, my father died and he…"

"Good. Meet me at the cave."

"The what? Didn't you hear me? My father died."

"The cave, you know, we used to hang out there when we were…"

"Megan, I never hung out with you guys remember? I wasn't allowed…"

"Whatever, meet me at the cave, you know where it is right?"

"I can't now…"

"If you meet me there, I'll turn myself in and tell everyone the whole truth, the whole story about what happened that night at the Horseshoe, and why I ran. And.. Carrie, Dusty will be with me…"

"My God! You have him?! Why, god Meg no!"

"Meet me at the cave; this has to do with your mother too."

"Megan, please… please!"

The line was killed at the other end and Carrie felt like throwing up, her blood was pumping so hard and so fast right now. Meg had Dusty, Carrie's whole world besides Jason, and that witch had him. She almost fainted, Carrie blocked out horrible visions by trying to see think about what else Meg had said; Megan was going to tell her the truth? About what and what about her mother? What would Meg know about her mother's disappearance? She fought off several moments of nausea and decided she would go. But she would call Jason and have him meet her there; she had to get her little brother back from that monster.

After trying to call everyone close and finding no luck, she decided that she would leave him in the truck. He'd mind or she'd take away his computer game. He'd be alright. Carrie called Parks cell and it went directly to voicemail, she nervously pushed Jason's number into her phone and cursed herself for not getting a cell phone after all these years. Jason's phone went directly to voicemail too. Panic started to settle in.

"Dammit! Where the hell is everyone?" Carrie took a deep breath and called for Dusty, hoping he'd hear the pain in her voice and appear.

Jason made the ID on Terrence Dodson, his father-in-law and signed the paperwork. There would be a huge memorial service for the man who kept Fallcast alive through all these years, for the man whose family basically founded the town and whose mine and mill employed and will employ even more soon. He left the hospital and was on his way home before Meg's call to Carrie. He'd turned his cell off in the morgue. He was glad he'd brought his jacket and had to put it on earlier, it was chilly in the place.

Carrie started the mine Jeep and fastened her seatbelt. It would take about fifteen minutes to reach the old streambed that led up to where the cave was. She'd been there twice only in her life, once after her mother ran away and another time with a boy who claimed he was looking for gold. Of course, she reminded him, the cave was on mine property and her father owned the claims in the area, but the prospect of finding gold on her father's land (a father she then hated will every ounce of her) made her excited. As it turned out, the only precious thing the boy was after was hidden in Carrie's barely worn jeans and under her blouse. After several minutes of wrestling and two very hard slaps to the boy's face, he reluctantly dropped her off back at home and they never spoke again. Carrie knew he would not bother her ever again, he was afraid of her father and what she might tell him, the boy spent the next several years afraid for his life. Until he became manager of the Horseshoe Club and Tommy's on again, off again best friend. Ron Benjamin. Time had faded the incident and he apologized fervently each time he saw her until she told him it was okay and that she might have leant to the passion a little. She knew Ron would say nothing to anyone about what happened that day, nor would Carrie; she didn't want the townsfolk to think she was a tease.

She turned the radio on to calm her nerves, finding a quiet pop station from Vegas and not knowing what was going on or why Meg had to abduct Dusty, but she knew one thing: her whole world was about to change.

The only thing that seemed to bother her right now was the tone of Megan's voice. It was hurried, impatient and driven. She seemed out of breath and nervous about something. Megan may have been capable trying to scare Jason out of town, but she really didn't think the woman she'd know since her youth would actually hurt anyone. But there was something about her demeanor on the phone; it was like-like she knew something that would change things forever. And Meg had her little brother; she would pay for preying on the innocent.

Jason pulled into the driveway and saw that the Jeep was gone. He pursed his lips and reached for his cell phone, realizing he'd turned it off at the morgue and forgot to turn it back on when he left. When it came to life it informed him he had two messages.

"Megan has Dusty at the cave, you know the cave? Hurry!" Carrie's panicked voice shouted over the sounds of the Jeep racing over a dirt road.

"Oh… God!" Jason yelled at the phone as he restarted the Blazer and spun out of the driveway, spewing gravel in every direction as his tires hit the pavement. He pushed the button for the next message.

"I'm on my way, hurry please, hurry, she's got him Jason, Meg's got Dusty…" The phone cut off. Out of range.

Jason felt tears coming to his eyes, they burned with release and the salty drops fell fast to his shirt. His insides were turning around like a tractor trailer in the middle of street, tight and awkward. He knew this was not going to end well. He had his foot pushing on the accelerator so hard it began to cramp on him. He hoped he could make it in time.

Neither the sheriff's deputies or Jason saw each other as they passed on the last turn-off before the road ended by the airport. The cops continued on towards the houses two blocks up from where Jason and Carrie lived, Jason stayed right off the forked road towards the mountains behind the airport. Towards the cave.

He cursed himself for allowing it to go this far, the secret. He should've told Carrie right away, but couldn't think of a way of doing it. He nearly cried as he thought about how things were falling apart, his beautiful wife alone with that maniac Meg, Dusty would probably be so confused right now it would take months to undo the damage that bitch has brought unto them. If Carrie walked out of there alive. What if he had to take care of the boy himself? Could he muster that? Given the circumstances, he knew he would. They would be inseparable. And Megan, that bitch. He should've known she was going to be trouble the first time they exchanged glances back at Carrie's house when he first moved in. She had that look in

419

her eye, that look that revealed all. His heart raced as he thought of the love he had for Carrie and Dusty, he struggled to keep the images of a dead Carrie and hurt Dusty from his mind.

As he pulled close, he could see only the Jeep, sitting by itself in the middle of the drainage gully, about one hundred feet down the hill from the well-known entrance. No sign of Megan's Bronco or any other vehicle, but Jason knew the area above the entrance was flat and could accommodate another vehicle-or two. He bet his willpower that Meg had parked up there; she would know the clandestine opening, the one cut there by someone trying to keep secrets. As he slowed to a stop at the Jeep, he kept his eyes peeled. Danger lurked from every rock or crevice. Jason pulled on a mine windbreaker and slipped alongside the Jeep and peered in the window. He opened the door and reached into the glove box finding another hunting knife and a Leatherman tool.

He stuffed the tool into his front pocket, the knife he wedged between his belt and waist, then he slowly climbed to the top of the gully and over past the opening to the cave, the one every kid in town knew about. But he didn't stop; he peered in the cavern as much he thought he should and then proceeded over the top towards the hidden entrance. He wasn't disappointed in his thoughts; Megan's Bronco was parked in the sagebrush just over the edge on the other side. Jason approached slowly and looked inside, no keys and locked. She was inside with Carrie and Dusty. He had to get in there now!

Inside Jason reached for his small penlight, which he didn't' have. All he had was two knives and a Leatherman. It was dark, but Jason knew the layout of this place. He would have to be careful not to step over the ledge below and fall ten feet to the bottom, but he also knew that if Megan and Carrie were in here, one of them would have a light. As he got further in, he could hear voices, one was angry and shouting; the other was frightened and crying. He shuffled towards the open archway that separated the two rooms by a small tunnel. As he made the last ten feet feeling along the wall, the voices stopped.

Then Jason heard another voice, it was Dusty, he was coming through the hidden opening! Jason spun to meet the boy before he got too deep into the abandoned mine, and when he did he heard the shuffle of shoes against a sandy and rocky floor. He turned too late. The shovel hit him square in the side of the head and Jason saw a bright flash and then darkness as his head hit the ground with a sickening thuck!

CHAPTER TWENTY-ONE
The Cave

Jason fumbled around in his pocket for the Leatherman. He could hear Dusty whimpering in the background while managing to get the tool out of his pocket and close enough to his second hand to open it up. In the middle of the plier-like device was a wire cutter, more than enough to slice through the rope, and he did it in record time. In just under two minutes since he came to, Jason had freed himself. He used the waning light in the cave from the entrance to find Dusty and walked carefully towards him. The smell hit him again, the odor of decay, rat droppings and musty air. He managed to get to the boy and put his hand on his shoulder. Dusty trembled at the touch.

"It's okay Dusty, it's me." Jason whispered.

"Airplane Man!"

"Sshh!" We have to keep quiet."

"Or we'll wake up the ghosts?"

"Yeah."

"I know them now."

"You do?"

"Yes. These are the darkness in the shadow. I saw them here before when I followed my Uncle Tommy here, hiding in the back of his truck. It was in my dreams. I know them now, they're the darkness. But they aren't so scary now Airplane Man, know why? Cause you're here with me. Tell the darkness in the shadow to go away; they can't hurt me when I'm not sleeping."

Jason took it all in. Even though he was excited, Dusty whispered his story. He'd been here in his dreams before. His Uncle Tommy, huh? Jason could see the figures against the far wall and just below them by about eight or nine feet. He could see a lantern swinging back and forth, casting a shadow on the walls of the cavern, the old mine. They both were like mummies, but there was no mistaking the dress, the shoes. The other person he didn't know, but Jason knew someone who did.

"Dusty, stay behind me." Jason said quietly as he moved to his feet and searched with his hands to find a weapon of any kind. His knife was out of his belt, the second one gone too. The Leatherman was a great tool, but did little in the defense department. Finally, his hand came to rest on a rusty old shovel he'd seen when he was here last time. He positioned Dusty behind him and moved slowly, the shovel at the ready to strike.

As he approached the opening, he could hear the voices again, it was Meg and Carrie. Same tone, same sound of worry and fright in his wife's voice. But Megan was pleading now; she was trying to Carrie to listen to her. Jason signaled Dusty to stop and the boy did. He moved silently ahead along the wall, careful not to shuffle his feet and give away his presence, Meg thinks he's still tied up and little did she know that Dusty had wandered away from her and was with him.

As he neared the sloping wall he had to duck down, he'd be hidden from sight as long as Megan or Carrie didn't look his way intentionally, he could hear Megan talking, angrily.

"It is true. So true in fact. I saw him do it!" She yelled.

Carrie was in a defensive pose, her arms out in front of her fists extended. Meg had a pick axe with the business end out in front of her, pointed at Carrie. They were in some sort of standoff.

"I don't believe you, Parks is not dead! Goddammit, where's my brother!" Carrie retorted.

"He is. I saw him kill Darrin just after I called you! He's a killer, you have to believe me!" Megan insisted.

"Jason didn't do it. He… Oh my god!"

Carrie had looked up and had seen Jason rising from behind his little rock pile. His face covered in blood, his clothing also. Dusty broke cover too and ran for his sister. Carrie reached down to scoop the boy up and she held him tight as she could, whispering into his ear and the boy was nodding. Crying and nodding. He looked at Jason and smiled, then he looked at Megan and dropped from his sister's arms. He had a look of anger and fright as he gazed at the ax wielding woman. Megan took one step towards him and held out her hand.

"Dusty, it's me…"

Carrie's voice was clear, frightened and pointed, "RUN! NOW!"

The boy broke for the other entrance; the one Carrie had come in. He ducked down as he cleared the mine shaft that led into the opposite room and they could hear him dive out of the cave itself, crying all the way.

Megan turned the pick-ax towards Jason. "Don't you move! I know it was you! I saw you!"

Jason had a look of confusion on his face; he cocked his head to the left a little and took a step forward saying calmly, "What. What did I do? You and Tommy set fire to my hotel room. You burned my plane to the ground. You tried killing me and Carrie! You kidnapped Dusty!"

"NO!"

Carrie was sick to her stomach. She watched as the duo circled each other. What Megan didn't know was Jason had the rusty old shovel in his hand at his side, the dark side, the blind side. Meg couldn't see it as she held the lamp out in front of her.

"You killed Darrin Parker! I saw you run away from his car."

"You're a liar! You're covered in blood! His blood!" Megan tried to convince Carrie as she looked to her.

"No Megan. I'm covered in my blood, the blood you drew when you hit me with the shovel. It's been you all along!"

424

Megan looked like she was going to lose it, she dropped the lantern lower for a moment and exclaimed, "You killed Terry Dodson!"

Jason took one step closer and she raised the lamp to head height. "Stop!" She called as she backed up a foot, one foot closer to the edge of the cavern.

"Megan, come on we'll get you some help…" He offered, slowly advancing.

Megan looked angry and frightened at the same time. Her eyes pled with Carrie to listen to her, they began to flood. She raised the lantern above her head and spoke in a calmer voice than before, like she was conveying a last testament.

"Jason started the fight that night in the bar. He told your brother that he was having sex with you in… in… you know, the bad place…"

Jason paused. He looked to Carrie. She'd turned her head towards him, he shook his head in rebut. "Megan…" She began.

Megan shuffled a few more inches back as Jason slowly approached her. She felt the edge at her heel and stopped. Her face turned from frightened to calm. She took a deep breath and slowly let it out. She raised the lantern as high as she could, taking her eyes from Jason to Carrie.

Her eyes looked back at Jason and she smiled at him, "I saw you kill Darrin, and I told the dispatcher that on the phone." She looked back to Carrie, "I'm sorry…"

Jason saw his opening as Megan was looking towards Carrie and swung the shovel at shoulder height, his arms stretched as far as they could go. The rusty spade caught Megan under the chin, two inches deep into her neck. Blood sprayed as her arms dropped the ax to one side and the lantern to the other where it rolled around on the ground. The swing completed and the business end of the shovel cleared the other side of Megan's throat, leaving a gash three inches deep in some places, nearly causing her head to fall off as her body fell backward to the edge of the cave and nearly to the long drop below.

Bright red blood sprayed for seconds from her neck, painting a macabre mosaic on the golden grey stone walls of the grotto in the flickering light. Carrie's mouth dropped open and she backed up to the wall then shuffled towards her right, towards the small cliff, her hands out in front of her, both wide open as if she were trying to hold back the sight before her.

CHAPTER TWENTY-TWO
Revelation

"What the Hell!?" Carrie screamed.

Jason took his knife from Megan's back pocket.

Carrie had nearly stumbled over the edge as she backed away from Jason. He hadn't advanced on her yet, but by his actions just now she wasn't sure whether he would stay where he was or step into her and finish her off like he had just done to poor Megan. She thought of a moment or two about letting herself fall down the rock wall into the pit below, but that wouldn't help her much if she broke a bone, especially an ambulatory one like a leg. She also knew that Dusty wouldn't get away if she became incapacitated.

"Where did you tell him to go?" Jason demanded as he looked towards the only way she knew out of the cavern. "Tell me and you'll live."

"What the Hell Jason! We're married, I thought you loved me!" She began to plead, it was almost an act, but she needed to buy her brother some time. "Why? Why?"

"Why do you think? What drives the world Carrie? Cash. Big bucks." He replied starting his right foot in her direction. He seemed like he was being cautious, maybe he didn't want her going over the edge. "Do you know what lithium will be worth in five or ten years?"

"Lithium? I thought you were interested in gold?" Stall, she told herself.

Carrie could believe what she was feeling inside. It was as if her mind was lying to her body and vice versa, telling her to flee but the man in front of her was the man she loved, married; there had to be an explanation, but he was telling her what she didn't want to hear.

"Gold will never get above twelve hundred dollars for long. The government will see to that. But lithium? It's the new platinum. The new benchmark of richness."

"I don't understand." Carrie was acting her best now; she was trying to be brave. In her heart she knew that if Jason was capable of killing Meg so swiftly, sufficiently, that he would probably kill her also, no matter what. She so badly wanted to rush her husband of less than a month. He had betrayed her, lied and hurt her friends, killed two of them and who knows how many more would suffer if she couldn't get away. Then a terrible thought struck her.

"You murdered my father." Her voice was cold, stabbing.

"Of course not. I just pushed him along on his destiny, I poured a few extra tablets into his scotch bottle before I left his office; I knew he'd have a few more belts. He shouldn't have so much booze with his pills. But that doesn't matter, didn't you know?"

Carrie felt tears burning at the back of her eyes, the pain was almost unbearable. She swallowed deeply, "Know what?" her voice cracked.

"He killed your mother. Tommy and your father killed your mother and she's about thirty feet from where you're standing…"

"NO!" Carrie couldn't believe the sound that came from her throat; it was like a hawk caught in a combine's reaper. "You're lying…"

"Not."

Jason picked up the lantern with his left hand and held high above his head while still holding the knife out in front of him with the other. Carrie couldn't take her eyes off the blade, shimmering silver and dried brown crimson, blood from Parks dried on the tip, nausea swept across her torso and she felt like she was going to vomit right then and there.

"Look behind you, to your left, against the far cavern wall." He made a motion to his right, her left with the Coleman. He smiled, "Don't you trust me?"

428

Her nausea was overcome by an instinct of fear, that lasted just a millisecond as rage and hate took over. 'Trust me...' that's what he said when he took her and her little brother flying. 'Trust me...' that's also what he said the night she lost her virginity. Her wedding night. The night they made love for four hours straight; straight through the pain of her first time, through the burning and then the pleasure, over and over, as much as he wanted. As much as they could stand, now he murdered her best friend and is holding a bloody knife out in front of him. Jason. She thought about the killer's name, and then she thought about how funny life imitates art, a phrase she saw online once. Jason. She smiled at her revelation.

"What the hell are you smiling about?" He demanded.

Carrie contained her rage, knowing that when she got her chance, she'd take it. She'd take that knife and shove up under his rib cage and find vital organs, that's how much she hated him right now. Her husband, till death do we part, she told herself. She almost giggled from the adrenaline rush and her thoughts.

Jason swerved the lamp again, "Look!"

She did.

The light was like the glow of twilight over the desert sand in the winter, just before the mountains behind the town snuffed it out. A figure lay crumpled against the far wall just as Jason had said; but this couldn't be her mother, the form was too thin. The clothing was a close match to something her-Carrie caught her breath. The dark waxy skin was wrinkled and covered by a blue flowered sundress...

"Mummified. Not bones but skin waxed over with soapy discoloration." He said matter of factly, "Six years is a long time, but it's not hot in here nor does it get cold this far back."

Jason swung the light over to the left even more and one more corpse frozen in time laid strewn out. Carrie gasped.

"Family and an enemy; we're cut from the same cloth I guess." He said it almost like it was depressing him, "Your family and I have a lot in common, maybe that's what your dad saw in me when he asked me to take you from this god forsaken place."

Tears were streaming down Carrie's face now. She still had her back to her assailant, her husband, her first real love. His words stung like ice on a wet hand, she tried to block out the images of what went on, she would have to find out who these corpses really were, but she pretty much figured she knew one. One figure lay prominent over the other; his shirt was the same one she had seen on him the night they were to go out. It was Paul Davis. He didn't leave town on his own accord, he was murdered and stuffed into a cave to rot-well, obviously not to rot by the looks of his waxy look of wrinkled skin. She couldn't see their faces and that was just as well, she needed her hate and anger to last, she didn't want to feel the sorrow right now, she had to…

"What are you doing?" It had finally occurred to Jason that she was stalling, "What the hell did you say to Dusty?" He took a step forward and lowered the light to see her eyes as she spun.

"I… I…" She began, she had to stall him some more. It took nearly five minutes to walk up here; it would take at least half of that to get back down the hill to the Jeep. "Why do you have to kill me?" She almost sounded as if she were pleading.

Jason stopped ten feet from her, it had blindsided him. She was stalling he knew that, but she also wanted to know in a calm voice why he was going to have to kill her. He was confused for a second, the last two people he'd killed begged for their lives like a child for a toy in the aisle most parents avoid in the grocery store. He had to think about what he was going to say.

"That was the whole plan, wasn't it?" Carrie began again when he stopped. "Marry me, kill my father, get my brother to be thrown in prison and kill me and Dusty in an accident so you would be the sole heir to the mine? To make millions off the dirt in this stupid place?"

"Something like that." Jason smiled a tad on one side of his face, "But not the boy. Dusty is a good kid, I wouldn't have the heart to hurt him. But he would be my charge and I could take care of him for the rest of his life. He trusts me." He paused for a beat and then said, "Why would think I'd kill him? I'm not a monster."

"You are. You are the worst kind of animal that feeds off the weak and…"

"You're stalling. You think the boy can drive that far alone? I bet he can, he's a smart kid, but he won't have a chance at getting out of here…" Jason put the knife between his belt and waistband of his jeans and reached into his pocket to fish out the keys to the Jeep with his right hand while his left held the lantern high. "But this is perfect, Meg's cell phone call to you. She'll be suspect number one, all I have to do is set it all up here, and then I kill her a little too late to save you, even Dusty can tell the cops that she hit me with the shovel and tied me up to kill you. Perfect..."

This was the moment Carrie was waiting for. She lunged at him. He dropped the lantern and it rolled to its side gasping and popping as it starved for fuel, but it kept glowing. Jason was surprised at her speed, her ingenuity to get him to holster the knife, and then her attack. His hand was already curled around the key ring so when he yanked his hand out in haste the keys came with it; as soon as he felt he cleared the pocket they were in he dropped them and reached for his blade.

This was her only chance. Carrie took a deep breath and in a flash she would be upon him with all her fury, but at the last moment he managed to get his hand free and the knife came out of the waist band. She saw the point being leveled at her abdomen just as her hand struck his jaw, he was stunned and stepped one pace back, but the thrust of the silver and already blood stained stainless steel was on its way. She braced for the puncture.

It hit just above the kidney on her left side. There was an initial pop sound as the knife went in, breaking the shirt she was wearing and the skin underneath. Then the icy-cold sensation of the skin being sliced by the blade as it went further in, the width enlarging the hole and nicking the top of the blood cleaning kidney as it passed inside. Then the burning. Hot as an ember from a campfire that snaps onto your bare leg at night, but it was deeper, all the way through. The pain was searing and Carrie became nauseous again, this time screaming at the top of her lungs. For two reasons:

Primarily because of the pain and the temporary relief it brought and secondly; she hoped her brother might hear her scream and hide. Jason had the keys to the Jeep, Dusty had to hide…

Jason was almost shocked by the experience of stabbing someone he had intimate relations with. It was the sense of depriving someone of their very essence. The knife made a sucking sound as he withdrew it. That was new too. When he killed Meg his heart was racing and it happened so fast, but as he was able to get the knife out of his waistband and in front of his body in time when his wife lunged at him, it was as if the world had slowed to a crawl. Like when you had a high fever or had the blood rushing from your brain, everything was clear as a digital picture; every sound, every movement. He could hear Carrie breathe as the blade went into her stomach; the draw was slow and then as if a door was opened to a cold room from a hot dry one-a rush of exasperated air.

The smell of Carrie's blood on the instrument of her death was exciting too. The metal and wet copper-iron combination made him feel exhilarated; it made him mad with pleasure. Carrie was bent over with her hands on her wound, now was his chance. He called to her and she stood as straight as she could. He drove forward for another insertion into her, this time he was aiming for her chest, just above her right breast, that beautiful breast he had kissed ever so gently, ever so softly to drive her to agony in ecstasy when they made love. He parried with the knife and made his move.

Carrie was not as incapacitated as she made out to be. She stepped to her left a half foot as her husband drove with his blade extended out in front of him like knight with a lance. His eyes changed from determination to surprise as he missed her body with the knife and as she moved her right leg out to trip him as he progressed. He had put all of his energy into his thrust and now she was using it against him, he was going to go over the edge and no one would stop him, not even his dear wife.

Her step forward and raising her leg to trip him hurt more than she could take. Carrie dropped to one knee and threw up in front of her legs. Her head was a swirling array of stars and blackness. The dark was calling her to come rest. Come in and relax honey, we're all friends here, it said. The light faded in her mind, in front of her eyes, the day was dying.

Carrie almost let the darkness have her, this was all too much all at once, her husband the killer that stalked Fallcast-not Meg like everyone had assumed including Carrie-her father killed her mother, her older brother was an accomplice as well to the murder and now she had been stabbed-probably fatally. She felt the warmth leave her body as the twinkle of the Coleman lantern faded in her eyes as the generator inside the lamp was starving for the white gas that vaporized in it and created the white bright light they were famous for. The she thought of how Dusty needed the light to get out of the cave, but now he had the flashlight and the thought of her little brother on his own for the rest of his life startled her. Her head spun. Adrenaline pumped and she fought off the nausea and pain, the pain that had been staved for the moment by the enzymes and endorphins coursing through her blood.

She leapt to her feet and started to run. Grabbing the lantern by the handle as she went, she managed to keep from bouncing off all the walls as she hurried out of the antechamber. As she rounded the first turn, the one where her brother or father had boarded the small hidden room from the outside world for years, she could hear Jason screaming at the top of his lungs in pain and in fury. The Coleman's fuel tank leveled and the flow started into the lamp again, brightening the path ahead of her.

"I'm going to kill you, you bitch!"

Carrie didn't turn or even lose a step. Every move her muscles made seemed to be tied to her abdomen and the sinew there, for every motion forward was a new experience in pain. She willed herself to go on, even with her dearly beloved calling from beyond.

"You can't run far! I'll find you and kill you!"

Carrie felt a tear raising to her eye as she saw the entrance to the cold dark cave ahead, the outside darkening light a contrast to the pitch black surrounding the globe of artificial light given off by the Coleman.

Jason felt his legs with his hands to find out where the pain was originating. As he tumbled over the ledge he had dropped the knife and his feet struck a small outcropping of rocks first. Then his knees hit and the rest of his muscled body rounded cozy over teakettle the way

434

down, ten feet below. When his body finally hit the bottom he was thankful almost that it was over-the downhill part that is.

He felt a warm and growing patch of wetness on his right knee and the patella or kneecap moved around like a fish being chased by a net in a small glass bowl. Upon inspection of his other knee the same problem occurred with the cap, but there was a huge swollen knot just below it and his left leg was underneath him. When he tried to pull it out, that's when he cried out in pain. His leg was broken, probably a spiral break, not incapacitating but very painful. The only thing to do was threaten his prey as loud as he could, and that seemed to ease the torture a little.

After he felt a rush of self-made pain medication try to relieve the hurt he felt, he rescanned his options. He had to get out of here, now. Next he had to get to Carrie and Dusty, not so much the boy but the woman. His wife. She had to be stopped. He knew he had gotten a good jab in on her, she was wounded and not as nimble and that made the odds even with him. He was no long-jumper or marathon runner himself, but he'd run her down. If she got to her brother, Jason would have to come up with a whole new plan…

He had to get her back into the cave and seal up the secret antechamber that was designed to fool the teenage kids from finding the crypt of the fallen townsfolk. Three bodies were easy to hide in a place that was rumored to be haunted by a ghost that actually killed someone, and that kept most of the teeny-boppers at bay, the rest who thought they were immune to such things and ventured in the cave with beer and building massive bonfires in the west end would see the way the timbers and rocks were set up to give the illusion of a cave-in and even the dumbest of all kids knew that cave-ins were bad and avoided them like the plague.

Jason pulled himself towards the bottom of the slope; each drag sent searing pain into his chest and head, but rage and fear of being caught down here by the cops before he had his chance to kill the woman who put him in this situation, kept him heaving.

As his fingers touched the rocks at the bottom of the wall, he felt around for something that would allow him to pull himself up with. Nothing. This was going to be painful and tedious.

Carrie had made it outside and was struggling to get down the path that had been littered with years of sagebrush growth and large rocks. Each rock was a stumbling block, each twig grabbed at her pants. She tried to call for Dusty, but knew if she did she would've sounded like a cougar warning off something with a low growl. Her voice was churning with phlegm at the top of her throat which came from the pain she was carrying with her.

At the crest of the rock face and the rest of the road downhill to the Jeep, she paused to see if she could spot Dusty and the flashlight beam somewhere. Nothing, just the twilight closing in with its common desert pink-orange hue that captivated travelers for centuries. She began what was sure to be a long and excruciating trip to the Wagoneer.

Jason had made it to the halfway point. When the cave was used by the Native American Indians centuries ago, they had carved small makeshift steps out of the rock face for the purpose of using the lower portion as a cool room. Jason hadn't seen these steps upon his initial discovery months ago, but his luck seemed to have improved. Hand over hand he nagged to drag his bulk up the face, and with each successful pull, his legs seemed to assist a little more also-even the broken one. Maybe it wasn't as bad as it felt?

As he reached the top he crawled onto the flat platform used by the Indians for sleeping on before the white man ever intruded on this land; he searched with his eyes to see if he was going to be ambushed from above. With no light he was still moving his arms around like antennae on an ant to forge his path. Minutes after pulling his body from the anteroom just to the entrance of the main cavern from the hidden room, he bumped into Meg's nearly headless body, it was still warm and as he drug himself across her legs they seemed flexible and mushy. An idea struck him and Jason smiled; a bigger smile than when he pushed the steel blade of the knife into his wife's stomach.

Carrie slowly pushed herself downhill. The sun was blazing its last hurrah as it lowered behind the range west of town, the pinkish glow was turning brown in the sky and the darkness had already spread its grasp around the areas the town lies in. Soon the darkness would creep slowly to the western side of the valley and night will close its cold grasp upon everyone, even those who were running for their lives in the desert mountains outside of town. Carrie wearily wondered as she stumbled over a small clump of cheat-grass if there would be a moon tonight. She chuckle to herself as her thoughts drifted, she regained focus by imagining her brother's face in front of her as she pulled herself to her feet again.

It was getting harder and harder to concentrate. The wound was still hot inside of her, she tried not to think about her attack or attacker, but his face kept shining through the cloud of pain that nearly strangled her with each step towards the Jeep. In situations like these, the knight in shining armor was needed, but hers was the one who just tried to kill her-and he may have succeeded anyways, by the amount of warm sticky stuff on her hands.

She dare not look down, not where she was wounded anyway. She would glance at the ground a few steps ahead, but that was rather futile as she was staggering, trying to keep her balance and avoid rocks and brush as the sky became murky around her. Just a few more steps, she told herself, have to find Dusty and get him to safety…

Ten arduous minutes later she was just those few steps and now gloom began to hit her; Dusty was nowhere to be seen. She hoped he was hiding on the floor of the backseat, maybe in the far back under a blanket or something, but her fears were realized when she was able to nearly throw herself onto the side of the vehicle. She was exhausted, bleeding and getting cold. She knew she was going to die out here in the middle of the desert, maybe even never found, just like the three mummies in the cavern.

The image of Jason dragging her lifeless body up the hill and stashing it back into the little enclosed room, placing her next to her mother-maybe even moving her arms around her for an eternal hug-made Carrie open her eyes and pound her bloody fist into the side of the Jeep.

A thought; she tried each door and found they were locked. What kind of fool would lock something out here in the middle of nowhere? A not so foolish fool who was going to trick you into the cave to kill you dummy! She giggled to herself, she couldn't remember if shock was wearing off or if she was going into it right now. As she used her hands to cover the sides of her face to peer in she had another thought.

The side window exploded, sending shards of blue square tempered glass everywhere. Carrie dropped the rock she used to open the window and reached in for the lock switch. She had a sense of urgency, she placed her head on the frame of the door after opening it and saying a prayer to God, thanking Him is some odd way for letting OSHA exist. OSHA and all of its overbearing rules, she remembered in her dizzy mind John Dickson once complained that OSHA had fined him $1,200.00 for having a bent rung on one of his ladders. She giggled again.

OSHA was good for one thing though, safety. Inside the mine-owned Jeep was a box required on every company vehicle that trod the grounds of any mine in the country. First Aid. She leaned in-in a great deal of pain-and felt what was left of wound that had coagulated tear open again. But no matter. Inside the little white box with a red cross on it was salvation, maybe.

She found the box under the seat, drug it out and placed it on the cushion. Just as she flipped the second latch, a hand grabbed her shoulder and she spun in fright. She screamed.

"Cassie, I wanna go home…"

Dusty was hiding close by. He was a smart young man, Carrie thought, he was waiting to see if I was alone. She reached out to hug him and he stepped back when he saw her left side.

"Cassie, you're bleeding! You're hurt!"

"I know baby. But I'll get all fixed up right here, if you'll help me, K?" She tried to sound brave, braver than she felt.

Carrie turned to the box and opened it. It was a gold mine in itself. Compresses, packs, a bottle of iodine, gauzes, tape, a box of bee-sting ampules, two boxes of Curads in various sizes, eyewash and eyewash cups, and the pièce de résistance: two envelopes of CELOX blood coagulant powder. That would be a lifesaver, she hoped. CELOX was designed for emergency room use, combat, paramedics and is not supposed to be available to the public, but in and around mines there isn't always a doctor around to prescribe it or apply it, so each first aid kit contained one or two packets; injuries that occurred around the mining industry were usually pretty severe.

Carrie leaned back against the seat, still standing halfway in and halfway out of the Jeep. She lifted her shirt which was stuck to the wound and her body from the blood. It crackled as she peeled, once the cloth got to the knife-hole, the pain surged. She tried not to scream, but instead she let out a crying yell. Dusty went pale and started to shiver as he watched. He was going into shock himself.

"Dust-Dusty...I need your help." She said in huffs and puffs. "I need you to hold my shirt up for me, okay? Can you do that?" She strained a smile.

He looked at her and nodded. A job, that was what he needed to do to keep his mind occupied. He gingerly grabbed the corner of the Pendleton just above where his sister's fingers were grasping it and held it tight in place just under her breasts. He looked at her tear streaked face and nodded.

"Okay Cass, got it."

She reached to the floorboards next her and pulled the iodine out of the box. She opened the bottle using her teeth and spit the cap onto the dusty desert floor. She inhaled a deep breath, knowing what was to come and poured the entire bottle over her abdomen and the bleeding wound.

A crow about three hundred yards away lifted into full flight as the scream ricocheted off the canyon walls. Carrie felt as if she was going to pass out for sure now. Her head began to shake uncontrollably and her eyes fluttered, her mind swam like a salmon headed upstream, her stomach was trying to show the world its contents, she felt warm inside-beside the pain-and tired.

"Cassie? Don't fall asleep okay? I'm scared..." Dusty pushed closer to her, she could feel his warmth gathering around her thighs.

The image of her little brother out here, alone with that crazed husband of hers made her wake up cold. She stiffened her lips into a curl and dropped the empty iodine bottle to her feet and rubbed Dusty's hair with her hand.

"I'm okay honey. Here, help me."

She tore open a gauze packet and patted the wound as dry as she could, the golden color of the iodine mixed with the blood still oozing from the incision made an awful color that would forever be enshrined in her mind; it was almost a greenish yellow with black. She inhaled sharply at each dab at the cut, and finally held the gauze in place as she picked up the coagulant pouch, trying to read the instructions. She held the packet out for her brother.

"Can you read this for me honey? My eyes are tired."

Dusty took the packet and read, "Not for use without a pres...prescr... description or professoral medicated assistants." He did his best and Carrie understood what he was saying.

She bit her lip. "Okay, go on."

"Pour grannies over open wound and apply gau...uze compass for three min...utes or more, clapping should oc...cur within five min...utes, minutes-seek emer...gency medicated atten...tion as soon as poss... poss... poss...ible."

"Thank you. You're getting to be so smart." She smiled and rubbed his head again with a bloody hand that smelled like iodine. He smiled.

Carrie took the packet back and tore the top off, again using her teeth and picked up the unused gauze from the kit and took a deep breath. She poured the powder on the wound, but there was little or no pain-extra pain-from the contents. She dropped the empty envelope to the ground and covered the area with the gauze and closed her eyes.

Jason was coming down the path from the mine, the sun shone behind him just like in the movies making his silhouette a dark shadow on the ground, along the sand that was already blood red and oozing something, and he was wearing that mask, the hockey mask, he was coming to kill them with a machete held high. He was stumbling around the clumps of sagebrush, but forward he pursued, down the hill, waving the long bladed knife like a circus performer…

"Cassie! Wake up!" Dusty cried.

Carrie shook the vision from her mind. She looked to where she saw her maniac husband in her hallucination, her nightmare daydream. He wasn't there. They had to get moving. Carrie looked down the hill towards Fallcast; it was at least ten miles and over very bumpy roads. She looked to her left; the Glowworm ranch was four miles and over the same washboard roads, but much less. She needed help fast, the Dickson's had a phone, and guns, just in case.

"Dusty? Can you drive? I know you can."

Dusty was silent for a moment and then said, "Cass, all the way to town? I'm scared I don't know the way."

"I'll navigate, just like when we were on the plane." She didn't know if the flying reference would help, if the mention of that bastar… bad husband of hers would upset Dusty, but she hoped her point was made.

He nodded.

Carrie used the side of the Jeep for leverage and guided herself to the passenger side, Dusty climbed in the driver's door. Once seated, the boy immediately put on his seat belt and waited for his sister to do the same. She smiled when she saw this and held up a finger.

"We'll need keys."

Another thing about being the daughter of a miner and knowing the ways of miners and mine policies; was where the hide-a-key was. She opened the glove box and reached up above the cardboard well. Just under the rim next to the light was a little black box with a drawing of a key on it. She slid the cover open and pulled the key out and gave it to her brother. He had driven several times with her and Jason, she hoped that was enough. It was going to be dark by the time they reached the ranch.

Dusty fired the engine, and after a confident breath, moved the gear lever to D and began turning the front end towards the road to the left, with his sister pointing and giving directions, he was almost standing to see over the dashboard, his eyes glued to the road ahead, his butt barely touching the upholstery. As the Jeep made the descent down the first hill, Carrie looked back. Something wasn't right. She couldn't put her finger on it, but there was something that was bothering her as soon as she came down the hill from the cave, she focused her attention back to the road ahead, hoping she was just hallucinating again.

It took nearly twenty minutes but the Jeep with its teenage driver and wounded passenger ground to a halt in the gravel driveway in front of the main house. The lights were on inside, but John Dickson was out in the barn when they came rambling down the road towards the house. He stepped from the shadows wiping his hands on a dirty rag as Carrie opened the door.

"Hey! Saw you comin'. You should have called…What in Holy Jesus' name!" John's eyes nearly bulged out of their sockets as Carrie slid out and fell to her knees.

"Need help John, (cough)son's the killer. He's killed Meg and tried to…" Her voice was blurry and she coughed again. Then she felt the world spin, the words she was trying to form wouldn't come, she pushed herself up as far as she could go then passed out, falling to the stone path with Dusty and John trying to hold her up.

CHAPTER TWENTY-THREE
An Hour Later...

It was dark. The wedding chapel at the church was full of
hundreds of well-wishers, mostly on the bride's side,
mainly all residents of Fallcast. The lights had gone out in
the chapel and some people we're using their cell phones to
light the walkway up the aisle for Carrie, who was dressed
in a well-deserved white lace and pearl satin gown.

Her father was there, but he looked like he was dead
tired, or at least dead. Her brother was sitting in the back
row, she noticed him just as she walked into the back from
the crying room, which doubled as the wedding party
dressing room. Carrie was still frustrated over the fact she
had to put her gown on with everyone watching. The huge
pane of glass that allowed mothers to watch Sunday
Services in the crying room with their unruly children
didn't have a curtain and the whole party was embarrassed
at having to expose themselves to the whole town as Meg,
who was the maid of honor, pulled her gown over her
exposed and shivering naked body, she had a choker band
of red satin around her neck. Carrie felt her body flush red
as she pulled the garter up her thigh and then settled the
strapless bodice into place holding her breasts in place.

Carrie walked up the aisle as Mendelssohn's
traditional Wedding March was played, her father
stumbling every now and again to readjust the knife
sticking out of his back. It took a full hour to get to the
pulpit, where the preacher stood. His hands were crossed in
front of him reverently; his right hand over the top of his
left, his index finger tapping impatiently at the time it took
to walk the twenty or so yards from the back of the church
to the stage.

It was a stage, more or less. Carrie was being put up
for auction. The most eligible bachelorette in town, the girl
who hadn't slept with anyone yet, the one who thought she

was purer that the driven snow that cap the mountains surrounding the town each winter.

As her father made his last step to the first step of the altar, he fell, the knife finishing its job. Those present clapped their hands in unison for his effort and then stood when the preacher raised his arms to his side, palms open. The music stopped. There was her love, the man who flew into town and swept her off her feet, the one who shoved the knife into her father's back, the man who was tapping his finely polished Air Force "Wing Walker" shoe in front of him as he waited for the slow moving bride and her mortally wounded father to arrive.

He had his back to her-rather his side. He was staring imperceptibly towards the crucifix on the wall behind the marble and wooden altar, the bloodied and tortured shape of a man that was hanging from this spot in front of them with his arms spread wide like he was welcoming her to suffer along with him. How fitting, Carrie thought to herself.

She paused at the side, one step behind and to the left of her future husband. The man of her dreams, the knight in shining armor. She knew her place. Jason tugged at his gold and red cufflinks at each sleeve and then crossed his arms in front of his chest. He was in a hurry; he wanted the service to be over so he could have the prize, the biggest prize in all of Fallcast, maybe even in Joshua County. The last virgin in all of Nevada, probably the only virgin in all of the United States. He wanted his prize now, so he could get on with his plans. His plans. What were his plans now? What would he do now that she and Dusty made it to...

The reverend told her and her soon to be forever-after to hold out their hands so he could bless them. Carrie held her hand out for the preacher and he rubbed his callused old wrinkly man hands all over them. He wants my gift too, Carrie thought to herself. She glanced up at the old man, the pillar of the community, the preacher that had told her of God and Jesus nearly every Sunday of her younger life, when she was a child, a prisoner of the Tradition Church of her grandfather's. The Father was wearing his normal church specials, black suit with tight collar, finely trimmed to match the thin curvy length of his body, the emaciated legs and right down to his loafers. Polished black loafers.

The priest asked Jason to join hands with his fiancée. Reluctantly, his came from the over and under he had made across his mid-section. He took his soon-to-be's hand. Carrie jumped a little; it was cold, ice cold. She tried moving her fingers a little to warm his hand up and that's when she felt the bone break. SNAP!

"I'll get you, you bitch!" He snarled at her. "You can run, but you can't hide!"

Jason pulled her close to him, his body smelled of sweat and the odor of that cave, the cave that was off limits because a bunch of teenagers got killed up there, years ago. She looked into his eyes, there was madness. He was mad with greed. He pulled her so tight to his body she couldn't move. He reached behind her and grabbed the hem of her satin and lace dress, the one her mother wore, or was wearing now. She was lying in the back of the church curled up in the corner with white candle wax all over her face and a similar wedding dress on, her leathery tanned skin exposed; her breasts sagging, like a sick puppy hangs its head, in the lace.

Jason ripped the dress off of Carrie. Again she was exposed to the whole town. He was going to take her now. Right here in front of God and everyone, he was going to get his well-deserved prize. Her gift to him. She felt his ice cold skin against her warm flesh, her exposed birthday suit, he felt as rigid as an icicle all over, she wasn't able to move, the cold was moving from his body to hers, she felt her feet freeze up first, then her thighs, her abdomen, her breasts, finally her face began to feel as if a weight of a hundred potato sacks were placed on her face. She breathed in and exhaled, but only icy frost escaped her lungs…

Carrie screamed and tried to move. A sharp pain drove her back onto the couch.

"Careful honey, you'll pull open that wound." It was a soft voice that spoke.

Carrie tried to open her eyelids slowly, but they had caught on the dried tears in the corners and flipped open under the increased pressure she put on them. The light was blinding. She saw three figures, one was sitting next to her, another was standing over her and the third paced restlessly further away. That person was holding something to its ear.

Slowly, very slowly, the room came into focus. Dusty was kneeling at her side, he was holding her hand. He seemed all grown up now; he would be thirteen in just months and he'd just helped his only sister escape the hillsides. He was smiling and the smile got bigger the more she opened her eyes.

"Careful." He said.

The other figure was that of Helen Dickson. She was holding a moist rag in her hand and had pulled it away from Carrie's face when she began screaming.

"You were having a bad dream honey. A terrible one from the way you were thrashing about. I was afraid you'd pull that nasty cut on your belly open again." Her voice was soft, reassuring.

Carrie turned her head to see the other figure, it was John, and he was pacing with the cordless phone to the side of his face. He was nodding as he was talking.

"Yeah, a terrible stab wound. The boy is alright, but he says Jason tried to kill them and the bastard killed Meg. Yep. That's what he said. Great… how long?"

John glanced at the now conscious Carrie and smiled. "Hurry." His voice became graven.

447

He pulled the phone from his face and pushed the OFF button then set the phone on the table behind Carrie's head. She was stretched out on the nicely covered sofa in the living area of the ranch house. The pain in her abdomen was still there, thundering every now and then, but as far as the ache that she felt the whole drive to the ranch, it had subsided.

"Jason…" She coughed.

"We know honey; Dusty told us everything he could." Helen nodded at Carrie's brother, there seemed to be a flash of pride on his face. "I'm so sorry."

"He's coming. He's on his way here!" She tried to sit up but the sharp pain in her side told her to slow down, so did Helen.

"Easy now Cass. He can't be on his way here, you took the Jeep, remember?"

"Meg's car. He's got Megan's Bronco. She had to have it, that's why we're up here. She was trying to help me and Dusty, she was trying to warn us…" Another phlegmy cough. "I didn't see it near the gully where the cave was, so she must have known some other way in and parked it there." Her voice was strained, it faded in and out and there was a hiss of fluid coming from her lungs as she spoke.

Helen looked to John and walked to the fireplace with his chin in his hand. He glanced up at the old double barrel side-by-side shotgun that was lodged in the huge rack of antlers on a stuffed elk's head. He turned to say something when he looked up above the folks in the room and a flash of light crossed his face. He saw a cloud of dust raised in the moonlight outside, the driver of the vehicle had shut lights off just as John spied it coming up the gravel road.

"She's right. He's here." John said with urgency. "Helen, go lock up the back, I'll get the rifle from upstai…"

There was a crash out in front of the house. The wall of the living room collapsed around the occupants, beams falling in and around what was then a window, now an opening the size of a Bronco SUV took its place as the vehicle violated the living room and came to a rest just a few feet from the occupants of the house. Glass sprayed everyone, John grabbed Helen and dove to the left to avoid large fragments of wood from hitting them, Carrie grabbed Dusty by instinct and not even the pain in her side stopped her from getting to cover.

There was a semi-silence as the debris fell all around them. Steam was hissing from the radiator of the Bronco, glass was tapping here and there as it fell from the large pane that gave a broad view of the valley out front. It was if a tornado had swept the house off its foundation and dropped it back in place, sans the front half.

John jumped up and grabbed the shotgun from the antlers, but Jason leapt from the open window of the Ford and scrambled over the broken glass to reach him at the same time. Jason used one arm and hand to grab the barrel of the gun and ran his other arm around the old man's neck. He had the man pinned standing up and with a wrenching twist, he tore the shotgun from John's hands and then shoved the man to the floor with his foot. Helen screamed.

Jason backed off and moved the open end of the 12 gauge, the business end, of the side by side to face his quarry. "Don't move!"

Carrie grabbed her brother and tried to slide him behind her.

"I said don't move!" Jason yelled again and this time kicked an electric lamp that was knocked to the floor when he made his entrance, the glass and cloth shade missed her head by an inch and shattered on the wall to her back.

"Jason…" Carrie sputtered as the pain surged in her abdomen.

"Shut up! This has gone way out of control now and it's all your fault. Damn you!"

He moved to where the Bronco was, reaching in and shutting the engine off by the ignition key and then concentrating the barrel on the Dickson's. "How many?"

John made himself a shield of his body in front of his wife. "What?"

"How many hands here?"

"None. It's Saturday. They're all in town."

There was a pause as Jason evaluated this and he took a step towards the older couple. He smiled and whispered over the still clacking of the cooling engine, "Don't move."

Jason stepped back to the Ford and made sure he could take any one of his charges out with a single shot. A shot? A look of panic crossed his face as he thumbed the lever to break the gun open. Two shells. Jason snapped it shut quickly and smiled.

"The most dangerous gun is the unloaded gun." Jason said matter of factly with a hint of sarcasm in his voice, a voice that was strained by near madness.

"That ammunition has been in there for nearly fifteen years…" John offered, his voice weak and startled.

"Shut up."

"And I had it for thirty years before that…" His tone grew with confidence.

Jason lunged forward and swung the butt end of the gun like a golf club, striking the old farmer in the side of the face. There was a sickening thuck! sound and the old man crumpled to the floor into his wife's lap.

"That'll shut you up."

Deputy Mike Tenner had his lights and siren on for about half a mile on the dirt road that ran from 201 towards the Dickson ranch. His adrenaline was pumping full; he had visions of shooting the bastard that stuck a knife into his

450

boss and nearly life-long friend's neck. He was seething, to hell with rules; this ass was going to die tonight. He had nearly four NHP cruisers ten minutes behind him, more force than he thought he would need. Problem with living out here in the sticks, there were hardly enough deputies in the area to get to where you needed them fast enough. Fortunately, the Nevada Highway Patrol was in force from just twenty miles in each direction of town.

Jason had forced Carrie and Dusty to sit on the couch, after they turned it back onto its legs, the force of the crash knocked it backward. Helen helped John onto the love seat, which their captor insisted they move next to the couch. John was groggy, but able to move on his own. The geologist turned killer paced slowly, he knew his time was limited.

"How many are coming?" He asked as he shoved the gun towards Helen.

"Don't know. Probably the whole town!" John shouted at him from behind his hand that was holding the lump on his forehead.

Jason pursed his lips and stepped back away from the older couple. "Doubt it. Maybe three or four." This didn't seem to ease his problem anyway.

"And a chopper from Vegas for Carrie." John finished.

Jason heard her name and looked at the woman on the couch, holding her brother. There was a band of white bandages around her waist like a cummerbund, "Nice." He sighed through his nose in contempt. "It's because of you this all went to hell."

"Jason, if you leave now we'll…" Helen began.

"Shut up!" He turned towards her with the barrels, "Talk again and it's over for you two." He focused his attention back to his wife, "Hurt?" His voice was almost sympathetic, almost, but there was a tinge of sarcasm and anger.

She shook her head. In her eyes was the look of death, cold, dark and accusing. "Why?"

"You should have known. We could've been together on this. We could've had it all."

"Why Parks? He wasn't a threat…"

"Sure he was. He told Ron at the Horseshoe that he was still in love with you. I wasn't in the mood for you to make a good guy-bad guy decision. He needed to go; he was poking around in my stuff, the laptop and the papers."

The adrenaline built in Jason's blood; he felt a wave of nausea and excitement coming at him at the same time, along with a surge of endorphins. He didn't know why he felt like talking, he just knew that it was coming out of his mouth faster than he could think. He knew they all were going to die-except the boy-so he decided to let Carrie in on everything, there was still a chance, but very slim.

"But…"

"No but's about it. Three million Mrs. Parmenter…" Jason began a sideways pace, not taking his eyes off his wife, but keeping the barrels of the shotgun pointed at the Dicksons. He felt they would be a bigger threat. "In the first year after the refit of the mine. That's how much we would've taken out of the ground. That's just my estimate based on the assays I did.

"Why do you think I started the fire in my hotel," He chuckled to himself a little, "well, other than the obvious?"

"You mean getting me to invite you to my place?" Carrie asked, glancing over his shoulder to see if she could see police lights yet.

"They're not coming just yet honey." Jason said. He noticed. "And, to answer my question further, to destroy all the work I had done prior to discovering the lithium. I had to get rid of everything that was important, written notes, laptop saves, everything. A fire cleanses, isn't that what you told me honey? Things just fell into place magically…"

His tone made Carrie want to throw up.

Jason didn't want an answer, he continued, "I burned my stuff to the ground so I could get a new laptop to fill it with misinformation. I wrote new notes that excluded my original findings. Then I used the assay office in Elko to do lab work. Bang! I found a goldmine, only it wasn't the gold your father and Marcus wanted, it was the lithium-the next standard.

"When I had to go out of town earlier this year, after our wedding, I had to make sure that certain areas of the mountains around here had the proper claims on them, and if they didn't I'd file the proper paperwork to ensure that the Dodson Mine and Mill had the mineral rights. I was brightening our future. Then your friends started to poke their damn noses in where they didn't belong."

"Meg? Steve? How could you?"

"Steve wasn't my fault, it was a convenient accident, but the whole brake thing fell right into my lap! Meg gets the blame for killing her husband for stalking you; she gets the whole blame for killing you and Parks later. To tell the truth, Steve was going to get it anyway. The first night at your place? My cell rang, and it was a friend calling to let me know that someone from Fallcast was looking into my background."

"Steven?" Carrie was stalling. "You killed him because he was poking into your background?"

Jason was on a roll, he was full of adrenaline and now grandstanding made him even higher. "Steve was the one who was sticking his nose in where it didn't belong. He was stalking you, he loved you and was going to divorce Meg and chase after you. He told your brother this and after he found out that I was your guest he went over the edge and began to do things only a real sociopath would do."

"Like you."

Jason smiled, "I've only killed once before…"

Carrie rubbed a tear that had dropped from her right eye and stopped at the tip of her nose. "Lindsay."

The smile got broader. "I told you my parents were killed in a car crash. That's true. Seven weeks before Christmas two thousand six, they were driving home from a party. A party in their honor, thrown to help release some of the pain they had."

Jason stepped back towards an end table and inspected an oil lamp as he spoke.

"You see, they had just lost nearly everything they owned. Their business was mining consulting, planning and investment. They had thrown it all on a small operation that was to be started in central Colorado, near the Pike National Forest. Everything was a go, permits even issued. But one week before the first shovel hit the dirt, an environmental group rode in on a bus and declared the mine a hazard for two reasons, first-the water table was not studied to the satisfaction of the group, they had a highly paid expert who told the federal government that the groundwater ran into the National Forest lands and that the mining would poison the area.

"Next another expert was brought in who claimed he had a picture of an animal that was thought to be gone from the area, only to show up on a hunting camera just three days before the ground was to be broken. Not a pair of animals, just one. When the fish and wildlife asked about where the photo was taken the animal activists stepped in and made a claim that if the location was made public, then someone would go out and kill the stupid thing."

"What has this got to do…"

"Shut up!"

Jason walked to a tall table near the knick-knack cabinet. With one hand he slid a box of kitchen matches open and drew three matches out, stuffing them into his front pocket. "Her tree-hugging boyfriend was the man responsible for the whole thing. My parents lost the investment because the state was forced to stop all mining permits in the area for at least one year, so the Department of the Interior could investigate. The company they were in the deal with folded six months later, they were counting on the mine to fill their bank account. Everyone lost except the group on the bus. Then they moved on to another site in another state.

"My parents never recovered. They drank day in and out, they went to parties their friends threw them from sympathy. My whole inheritance was lost on the deals. But they paid, Lindsay and her squeeze. They're together forever. She even had the gall to insist that it wasn't her fault this all happened before she met Mr. Forest Gnome."

Carrie wanted to hear the sirens before she quit asking questions, "You killed them?"

"Threw them out of my plane at fifteen thousand feet over the Rockies somewhere, after I shot them both." Jason relieved the moment in his mind, the sheer terror in his heart and chest as he drew the gun on the first love of his life, the rush of excitement as he pulled the trigger on Lindsay's boyfriend first, the look of surprise in his eyes, the shock, the flash of pain when the bullet entered his body, then the life faded from his eyes. Then Jason turned the gun on a shocked and screaming Lindsay. She was so surprised that her voice was lost, she couldn't bring much more than a simple yell before the gun went off again. Her eyes watered as the pain struck her; the bullet went into her chest just above her right breast and lodged in her heart. He smiled at the little trouble he had to go through; making sure that the ammunition he'd purchased, a special hollow-point, didn't have the capacity to go through his victims and out a window or something. He'd covered his seats with a heavy gauge plastic and then a cheap seat cover for a pickup truck the passenger and back seat. Lindsay and her beau didn't even question his motive.

Jason then took his plane as high as he could safely go, over the mountain range that had few visitors ever. At least not as high up as he was and within weeks after the spring thaw the remains would be fodder for animals and the bones scattered. It would take a lifetime to identify the bones-if they were ever found, and there would be no murder weapon. The couple and their friends had pissed off so many people in their exploits of shutting down businesses and mines; there would be a list of suspects a mile long. After he had killed them, he simply tossed the seat covers hundreds of miles away over another mountain.

Jason made sure there were no witnesses; he made sure that no one knew where they were going-they had told the troupe of troublemakers they called friends that they had hitched a ride on a bus; he made sure that they would not be missed. And he made sure that the gun was dropped a thousand miles away over another mountain range on his way back to Fallcast.

The thought of the neatness of his crime made him smile, Carrie flinched at this.

Jason spied the oil lamp that was on the table again. "My time's up. Dusty," He turned to the boy, who had said nothing since Jason had arrived, "Time to go."

"No!"

Carrie started to lift herself from the couch and Jason swung the shotgun into her face. She froze, but the look on her face was nothing but pure murder.

"I won't hurt him, I'm not an animal. But I need insurance."

"For what?"

Jason nodded at the boy. "Let's go and I won't hurt Cassie anymore."

Dusty looked at his sister and then he looked back at Jason, "Her name is Carrie!"

456

The room was silent for a moment; everyone knew that Dusty had not called his sister by her real name since his accident. Jason moved towards the boy and leveled the gun directly at Carrie's face again, this time pushing her chin with it back towards the couch.

"I mean it! Get in the Jeep or she dies!"

Tears formed in the boy's eyes and he moved towards Carrie, she reached for him but was cut off by Jason. The anger was growing on the man's face, he reached for Dusty's collar and yanked him backward, the gun barrels pointed up from her face, so Carrie leapt to her feet-pain and all-and grabbed for it. Jason saw her movement out of the corner of his eye and he tried to get the gun back on target, but she knocked the barrels to the side and reached for her husband's throat. Jason stepped back, kicked her in the side as she slid towards him.

The pain was excruciating, she fell to her butt on the floor and tried to slide behind the couch; Jason leveled the gun and pulled the trigger. The blast was deafening, smoke clouded the room and Helen screamed. John tried to get to his feet to grab the gun and he was kicked back to his position next to his wife.

When the smoke cleared, Carrie was holding her leg with the other hand, the hand that wasn't holding her side where the knife wound was. There were two holes in her jeans and blood was trickling out, but that was all. Jason fumed. His aim was off, he was too close and the shot didn't have time to disperse into a pattern large enough to do damage, he stepped back two paces and pushed Dusty towards the door, again leveling the gun towards his wife. He pulled the second trigger.

Helen screamed again, but instead of an eardrum shattering kaboom! there was a pop… A noise like a Lady Finger firecracker going off more or less and then a hiss; then a blue puff of smoke rose from the end of the barrel and nine lead balls of shot ran out and dropped to the ground like marbles out of a rain gutter's downspout.

"Your lucky god damned day honey!" Jason said as he pulled a knife he had found in Meg's glove compartment. He put the knife to the boy's neck and began to back out.

As he reached the opening of where he had made a drive-thru of the Dickson's living room, he picked up the oil lamp and threw it against the other one near the door to the kitchen, it shattered and oil splattered over the carpet and drapes. The smell of Neatsfoot oil filled the room then Jason produced a match from his pocket and slid it on his pants, the friction igniting the sulfur. The flame grabbed the eyes of everyone in the room, except Carrie, who was lying on her side holding her abdomen and leg and screaming, "Oh God no!" with her eyes closed so tight they hurt too.

Knowing that oil wouldn't catch, but the residue of it and the slick moistened carpet and curtains would act as a wick, he carefully sat the match at the hem of the heaviest drape that was knocked to the floor when he "entered". The flame grew slowly, just like it would have inside the flue of a lamp. The heat intensified as the flame licked at the curtain's base and then the carpet. The cloth and nylon fibers acted like a slow burning fuse, igniting everything it touched that could burn. In several seconds the whole living room just in front of where the last living occupants were sitting was on fire.

Jason stood at the opening of the burning pyre and waited till the flames covered the area enough to prevent his prisoners from escaping out the front, as he turned he saw that the exit through the kitchen was blocked by fire too. The only way out was through the fire or jumping from the second story window, a near impossible feat for two elderly folks plus a stabbed and gunshot woman. He turned with a smile and caught up with the boy, who was sitting on the ground crying, his head on his knees and face buried in between. Moments later the stairs caught and were now burning, no one was going to leap from the second story either.

"Dusty, Dusty…" Carrie was mumbling his name over and over. The pain in her side and leg was beyond her now.

John was struggling to get to his feet, the pain from the blows laid on by Jason had taken their toll, but he might have enough adrenaline left to… get… to…

The room was hot. Carrie felt her hair and clothes being soaked by sweat, but she didn't care. She was helpless; a glimpse over her shoulder made it clear-there was no escape unless you ran through the flames and hope you didn't catch. She was exhausted; her energy had been zapped by her previous wound, the new one that found a half-marble sized ball of lead in her thigh and her muscles ached from fighting to keep her brother out of the hands of the maniac she married. She had given up, her body had given up, there was nothing left to do but die and pray as she went that Jason would keep his word this time and let Dusty go when he had the chance.

A cold shiver ran down her spine when she thought of the man that had tricked her into marrying him. The lies had taken liberty with her good-naturedness, her sheer happiness to help another human being. She felt sleepy, her eyes were closed and there were dark shadows dancing across her lids in between the flicker of red flames surrounding her. Then she felt death grab her.

John, with the help of his wife Helen, had managed to get to Carrie who was now lying face down on the carpet at the edge of the firewall that separated them from the only doors on this level of the house, the only doors that Jason knew about….

John grabbed Carrie by the scruff of her neck and sweater. He began to drag her and she came around from her dreamy death fade. She screamed and swatted at the cold hand that had her by the neck.

"Carrie! It's me, it's John! Get up; help me get you up, now! We have to save Dusty!"

Carrie heard the voice, but her hair stood tall on the back of her neck when her brother's name was mentioned. She lifted her head, hard as it was from the pain and exhaustion, and looked into John's eyes, "The door..."

John tugged again and had drug her nearly five feet to the base of the burning staircase. He sat her on her butt and Helen grabbed the young dying woman before she fell back over. John reached under the bottom wooden step and pulled a short cord out. He gave it a hard tug and even over the roar of the fire, Carrie could hear a clicking noise and squeal.

The trap door under the first three steps opened up and a whoosh! of cold air wrapped her in comfort. "C'mon." John gasped as he scrambled onto his knees into the hole.

Helen pushed Carrie forward and John pulled at her hands until they were inside the wooden tunnel, on a floor that was made from concrete and it sloped downward to the underside of the house. John slammed the stair-door shut and the din of the flames died off quite a bit. John scooted on his knees for several more feet until the ramp-like floor had descended enough for him to stand. He reached back towards Helen and found a shelf with a number of flashlights on it as she helped Carrie to her feet.

"Don't know how good these'll be. Got them at an Army-Navy Store in Vegas, they work by shaking them, no batteries..." He stated to no one in particular. He raised the light to his face and shook the plastic tube several times to charge it. Then he turned the business end towards the wall and flipped the switch.

The room lit up with an eerie yellow-white glow. John glanced at Carrie and the sight of her face made him turn the light in another direction. She had the appearance of death warmed over-after several weeks in the ground. Her eyes were pouty and swollen from crying and squeezing them closed in pain. Mascara ran from under her lower lids to her cheeks on both sides giving her the look of some of the Goth girls that hung out at the smoker's corner John had seen in town a few times, by the high school.

On his glance down he saw her jeans were no longer blue, but dark blood red and soaking. Her left side was leaking again and soaked through the sweater they had pulled over her when she passed out on the driveway when Carrie and her brother first arrived. Small bits of pink and yellow flesh were protruding from the dime sized hole in her leg and John pulled his cotton over shirt off and stepped in front of his marred guest.

"Hold this flashlight, honey." He asked as he kneeled and began making a wrap around the wounded leg.

Carrie took the light and winced in pain when she felt the cloth contact her gunshot wound, the pain wasn't as bad as the ache the rest of her body felt, including a shooting migraine headache. She saw the amount of blood on her clothing and estimated she shouldn't have much left.

John cinched the shirt tight around the hole to make a good compress and stood. He took the light from Carrie who was holding her breath from the surge in pain the knot tying caused.

"Where… are… we?" She managed through her teeth.

"Old fallout shelter. My dad and uncles built it in 1962, after that Kennedy thing with Cuba. Big old kahunas that guy. Everyone figured the Reds were going to drop bombs everywhere."

"Oh." *Keep talking-you're dizzy*, she told herself. "Is there another way out?"

"Two more, one comes up under the equipment shed and the other under the barn, but you need to come with us, there's food and water plus emergency first aid for…"

"How do I get to the barn?"

Suddenly a large chunk of the stairwell above began to creak and the flames started leaking in, making the tunnel easier to see in, but the heat increased also.

"Gotta hurry honey, the wood under those steps are covered in asbestos, but it won't last long."

Carrie took a deep breath and grabbed a flashlight off the shelf, shook it and turned it on. She gave Helen a kiss on the cheek and took John by the hand.

"How do I get to the barn?"

John looked at Helen. Her blue-silver hair was matted and wiry, going off in different directions. Carrie knew once she was safe, she would grieve for her loss, the family heirlooms and photographs. The collectables and porcelain figurines that were just a dozen feet above them in an inferno, a fire that she brought to them. He followed her here, he lit the fire that was now destroying the Dickson's home but if it weren't for Carrie bringing him, this may have never happened.

"Helen, I'm sorry for all of this…" Carrie put her hand on the old woman's shoulder.

"It's not your fault. This town is full of prowling coyotes and it was time one got loose and wreaked havoc in the chicken coop. We all sat on the pain this town hid. This little Peyton Place has finally blown its protective cover. We'll all pay in the end I'm afraid." She took a small breath and showed a pained and hurtful smile, "Come with us…"

"Dusty, I need to get Dusty now!" Carrie began walking down the corridor of concrete towards the darkest of tunnels.

"Wait, I'll get a rifle from the bunker…"

Carrie was on a dead run, well as fast as a person with a knife wound to her belly and shotgun blast to her thigh could. John yelled after her, "The left, stay to the left! It's the ladder at the end of that tunnel!"

Carrie made her way along the black and creepy passage, the walls were made of concrete and she could see the lines along them where the plywood was used to make the forms. The path was still sloping downhill; she guessed she was about twenty feet below the ground now. It was cold and still, like the cavern and that gave her chills, just thinking about the cavern where this all had started, where Megan Cooke had ended.

Behind her she heard what sounded like a steel door slam; that would be Helen and John getting to safety, she thought. She gave a quick glance over her shoulder to see if there was a flashlight beam following her and it was just as dark back the way she came as it was in front of her. She was alone. Helen probably figured she'd lost enough to the fire and didn't want her husband to die too. That is what Carrie was going to do, she knew in her heart that she was dying; there was too much blood on her clothes, too much pain in her body, too much hurt in her mind and heart. He had already killed her heart.

A minute more and a thin metal rung ladder shone back in the meager light she carried in her hand. When she arrived at the base, her hopes were dashed. It was indeed a good thirty or more feet to the top. A metal door that looked rusted shut capped the small man tunnel at the top. Each advance to the top would bring a new experience in pain, her hands were slippery already with crimson body fluid from holding her wounds, but just out of habit she rubbed them on her jeans, her blood soaked jeans, and she smiled at her action. "Yeah, that'll help." She reached for the rung at her eye level and began her ascent. Behind her she could hear the staircase collapsing into the escape tunnel.

Jason got to the Jeep and dug his hand in to fish the keys out of his pocket. He laughed out loud at his stupidity; he'd dropped the keys back at the cave when he stabbed his wife, and the spare keys must be in the ignition, the keys that Carrie had used to escape the cave road. Dusty was in his grasp, the boy put up little resistance. He seemed to be sulking or at least the shock of his sister being trapped in the house as it was now falling in on itself. As the second story became the first in rush of wind and glowing embers shooting into the sky like a fireworks show on the Fourth of July, Jason had a pang of guilt and remorse. He did love her, ever so much. He felt like crying a little, he wanted so badly for them to be together, rich and powerful.

He truly loved Carrie, he did; he loved her as much as he had anybody in his life. He also loved Dusty as the child he always wanted, he began to question whether or not he was actually going to set the kid free as he had promised.

Another explosion rocked the ground around them. Dusty pulled free and ran to the Jeep. He opened the door and grabbed the key and threw it into the darkness. Jason was angry, but had no time to take his anger out on the boy; the cops would be close if John had called them as he said he did.

"Son of a bitch!" He shouted at no one in particular.

He ran after Dusty who was heading down the road, in the distance near the top of the hill three miles away, blue and red lights lit up the night sky. Jason almost slowed his pace, thinking about where he could hide from the incoming law. Then a smile blossomed across his smoke stressed, sweat and ash covered face.

Each rung took longer than the last. She had counted fifteen already, the tally being made to take her mind off of the hurt she was experiencing; she had to tuck the flashlight into her back pocket after the fourth step up for a firmer grip. The light danced a lazy swirl around her head on the hatch cover every foot she made upward, like some crazy drunk at a bar watching the lights on the stage, round and round. Carrie felt nauseous. She started humming to herself, just like Dusty did when he was nervous, she couldn't tell what tune it was, it could've been one she'd heard on the radio before the day began to unfold in bad way, in the sum of it as it was now.

The last five feet were the worst pain-wise, but the thought of her brother being held as a shield or hostage infuriated her no end. When she reached the last rung she had enough momentum and anger to nearly knock the door off of its hinges when she pushed it with her right shoulder, her head turned down to her left.

Dusty had made it to the cattle-guard at the main gate. He was tired and out of breath; he turned and saw the farmhouse falling in on itself. For just a few seconds he thought about running towards the police lights coming in the distance, in his simple math he figured it would be easier to get to the police if he ran. Then something stung his side.

It wasn't pain from an injury, it was inside. What was it? He'd had similar pangs when he was supposed to remember something, like when his sister asked him to take out the tra…

"Cassie, Ca… Carr Carrie!"

Dusty turned on a dime and headed back towards the inferno. He felt energy welling from inside he had never known before, an impulse to be faster and his legs made him faster, a feeling of urgency and his strength increased. He had no fear now.

Carrie almost dropped the flashlight when she pulled it from her pocket. She managed to pin it against the vertical concrete tube wall at the last second. She gave the place above her a quick shine and then back and forth around the large room the hatch had opened into. She was in the barn. Some of the energy she climbing the ladder eased, she had to fight to get her legs the last few inches out of the square manhole and onto the straw covered floor. She rolled to her back and tried to catch her breath. She closed her eyes in exhaustion and laughed out loud at something John had said a little earlier. "Kahunas." She giggled, "You meant cajones John!"

Dusty was back into the scarce darkness near the front of the bonfire that was once a home. His night vision was obscured by the flames as he searched the area surrounding the burning melee for signs of his sister.

"Carrie!" He called. "Come find me!" there was a niche of panic in his voice.

"Gotcha!"

Jason had been able to sneak up sideways on the boy as his attention was diverted to the fire. Dusty kicked and screamed; Jason had to hold the boy's arms to his chest and use a leg to keep the blows from landing anywhere important.

"Stop fighting me kid and you'll see your sister again."

"NO! CARRIE, HELP ME, PLEASE!"

She was now in and out of consciousness. She was hearing voices from the dead; Meg was lying next to her in that pool of ever expanding blood from her throat, the bright red blood-arterial blood-she had learned on TV from CSI, was bright red. Meg was calling to her.

"Help me Carrie…" Carrie took a breath sighed, "Can't honey. Been shot and stabbed, I'm done for."

Carrie, help me!

Carrie opened her eyes slightly and looked around the barns interior. The hay was lofted high for the summer

466

to keep moisture from soaking into it, the usual farm stuff was in here too; Carrie looked around to feel better about her surroundings, her mind was falling back into shock, or something like it. A tractor that was probably built in 1920, saddles on cross beams near the loft ladder. She shined the light around like a strobe in a disco, giggling. She could feel her life falling away, rest was coming and it would be easy, no more pain, no more…

The spot of light fell on the wall by the double barn doors. She saw many chinches between the boards she could see the glow of the fire, which was now beginning to flicker out in some areas, the fuel all but gone. It had consumed all the history of the Dickson family it could and now was living off the little things left that could possibly burn. But it wasn't the fire that caught her eye and made her stop swaying the light around. It was writing.

TWO BARRELS PLANE GAS FOR TWO BARRELS WHEN MINE GET TO THE MERCANTILE JASON PARMENTER.

Then it was signed by her husband Jason. Across the bottom of the makeshift contract was written in John's handwriting a week later:

PAID IN FULL

Paid in full.
Carrie heard Meg calling to her again. "Help me Carrie!" Her ears could hear a faint sound and her head stiffened then focused in the direction of wall. "Help me Carrie!" Her heart stopped beating.

"Dusty!" It wasn't Meg; it was her own brother calling for her. She tried to move onto the side to get on her feet. Her body fought back and she crumpled back to the dirty and hay covered floor.

Paid in full.

"I'm paid in full honey!" Jason was saying with a smile, that innocent smile of his, in her head.

Paid in full!

Then she heard again, "Carrie help me!"

Her lips curled under her nose. The pain disappeared from her mind, her limbs found animation from a source no one could have ever known. She rose like a curl of breeze lifts tumbleweed over a fence. She settled on her feet and hate beamed from her eye sockets.

"Paid in full, my ASS!"

Carrie bolted for the man-door that was in the middle of one of the larger barn doors, grabbing a pitchfork as she flew outside. Hell hath no fury.

Jason had managed to get Dusty to his feet and was now dragging him to the far side of the barn, where John kept his 172. Old as it was, Dickson kept the Cessna in good shape, the only thing that ticked at Jason's mind right now was how much fuel had actually been put into the tanks.

As he rounded the corner he saw the tarpaulin was still in place and he hoped that John was one of those guys who did everything with detail. When they strung a worm on a fishing line, they made sure that the squiggly little bugger couldn't squirm off by its own movement instead of just shoving the poor little thing over the barb and hoping for the best. Meticulous in daily routines would have meant that John did indeed fill the fuel tank to keep moisture from building up and that he had thrown the tarp back over the top of the aircraft and secured the corners back down. Jason's own grandfather was that way, not because he was trying to be perfect, but it was just the old man didn't have anything better to do.

Reaching for the knife to cut the tie-downs he had to wrestle with Dusty a little more, but he managed to get the blade out of the scabbard and when he held it out in front of him, the boy's struggles seem to subside a little. Jason hated scaring the little guy any more than he had to, but escape was paramount right now.

With a swish of the knife he had secured the lines on the right side of the plane and was moving around to the left when the house made its final gasp and the floor became the sub-floor. Debris and sparks shot into the air and hovered around in the slight breeze. Out of the corner of his eye and to the rear of him and his captive he saw movement, he turned but it was too late.

Carrie was coming at him full speed with the four ends of the pitchfork in front like bayonets on the end of Revolutionary War muskets. He stepped to his left just in time to take three of the tines in his thigh. It was his turn to scream in pain. He dropped the knife and Dusty wiggled from his grasp.

She let the handle of the hay bailer go and grabbed her brother by the arm. They began a dead run towards the open barn door. Jason let out a blood curdling yell as he pulled the pitchfork from his leg and tossed it to the side. He saw a glint of light coming off the blade of the knife in the firelight; he grabbed the butt end and gave it his best throw at his assailant. The blade sailed true and full of hate energy. It found its mark, Carrie collapsed to the ground, the handle of the knife wobbling like a top before it falls over. Dusty fell with her.

Jason managed to get into the plane and with luck, 'Ol trustin' farmer John left the keys in the ignition. Instead of making the check list a priority, he flipped the battery power on and turned the key. The Cessna sputtered a bit and finally caught on the fifth crank. Blue smoked puffed out the exhaust. He didn't have a second to lose.

Dusty was trying to get his sister to her feet, but this time no energy on the earth could mover her internally or externally. She had gotten Dusty away from her deranged husband. It was time, she knew it. She was destined to pass away; she squeezed her little brother's hand tight and whispered something. He had to lean in closer to hear what she was saying over the cacophony of the plane engine and prop whipping the air into a frenzy.

"I...love...you..." Her voice faded and a puff of air rushed from her lung, the one that wasn't punctured by Jason's knife throw.

Jason pulled the throttle out as far as it would go and before he had realized that John had chocked the wheels, the plane bumped over the top of them. It was at full power and little could stop it; that's when the maniacal side of Jason took over. He was going to be sure she was dead this time, no doubts about it. He pushed his left foot on the rudder pedal to the floor and the plane spun directly towards the downed siblings on the ground.

Dusty heard the approaching doom and tried to get his sister up enough to drag her, but because of her tall structure and big bones, he couldn't budge her against his own force. He stopped yelling her name and pulled her face close to his. He kissed her on the forehead, wiping her drying tears from her eyes. "I love you too. Wait for me..."

The subsonic thump of the tip of the propellers against the air drew even closer and closer. There was no fear in the boy's eyes, just relief that he and his sister, the only family he ever loved or could remember would be together. He knew what death meant, but he raised his head in pure defiance of the plane man, the geologist who stole his sister's heart and her life.

Jason saw the boy's head pop up and he shook his own, "If that's the way you want it to be..."

Suddenly the side window exploded into his face. Plexiglass shards scattered about the cockpit making clacking noises at they spattered against controls and glass dials. Jason looked to his left and saw John was standing outside of the barn aiming a deer rifle at him. He kicked his right foot down to turn the plane facing away from this new threat.

As the tail spun towards John, he had to cover his face from the dust kicked up by the prop-wash, but he kept firing blindly towards the plane when he had the chance. Bullets found a few areas of the plane's skin, but nothing vital. Especially the pilot.

When the dust cleared, John spied the young Dusty on knees holding his sister's head in his hands; he was leaning over crying and saying something John couldn't hear over the rumble of the plane that was now heading for the dirt road in front of the ranch house, the former ranch house, now just a smoldering collision of red ambers, sharp sparking small flickers of flame and smoke drifting into the half-moon lit sky.

A sound caught the farmer's attention and he turned to see a county sheriff's car rolling up the final mile of road to the scene of carnage and destruction, the vehicle bouncing high off the washboard. At the top of the hill a few miles back he could see flashing lights from several other police cars. He looked overhead to see if there was any sign of the helicopter yet.

This all took place in just milliseconds, the moment the danger of his Cessna running him over and making a break for the road, John was near running to be at his impromptu guest's side. He slowed to a trot when he came upon the young brother and what appeared to be a mortally wounded sister.

Her hair was matted and wet from blood, straw from the barn and dirt. The single sodium vapor light on this side of the barn made her skin look ghostly white. Her clothes were shreds of dark blood and dirt, mud and rust flakes from the tunnel hatch door covered everything else. Her legs were pulled up to her in a semi-fetal position, her arms at her side, her eyes closed.

Dusty was weeping, calling her name. On the road, the sound of the Cessna was drawing quieter as Jason was going to take-off. Sirens and the crackle of John's home dissolving into embers were faintly heard over the mourning boy.

John glanced over his shoulder and saw the unlit 172 bounce up and down a few times and then lift off into the darkness, the only light coming from the landing lights, the bastard had not even turned on his anti-collision lights or rotating beacon. Good riddance.

Deputy Mike Tenner rolled up with a wave of dust behind him. The prowler screeched to a stop at the front of where a beautiful farm house once stood. He jumped out of his car, Glock 17 drawn and sweeping the area for bad guys.

"Carrie! John! Helen!" His voice raised above the quiet.

"Over here…" John called almost silently, there was no need to shout, the world had silenced by the sobs of a boy and his dying sister.

Tenner ran for where he heard the faint call and was still scanning the area around them with his pistol.

"He's gone Mike." John's voice steady calm, his eyes never leaving the pair in front of him.

The deputy holstered his weapon and instinctively dropped to the ground to check the vitals of the girl who was four years older than him, but the town's raving beauty and until most recently eligible bachelorette-seemed gone from this world.

A thumping sound wavered in the distant dark night sky; the helicopter from the Las Vegas University Medical Center was on a fast approach. It circled the area for a few minutes, then the NHP units arrived, set up a perimeter landing zone with their headlights; Deputy Tenner giving them directions to do so on his Handi-Talkie.

The Mercy Air Agusta A-119 chopper touched down in another cloud of dust and a medic rushed from the opening door, the pilot staring at the scene with disbelieving eyes while the rotor swished at the air and the turbine engine whined its tune like a dying wind whistling through a stand of willows along a shoreline.

Carrie heard the fluttering of the helicopter blades coming in, but she couldn't open her eyes. She felt warm fingers touching her neck, holding her hands; a warm body embraced her cooling and broken one.

As the air ambulance noise got louder, the quieter things around her became. There was stillness in her mind, a relaxing state of endearment with what lie ahead. Although she felt her body shivering, she could sense as if she were in a pool of warm water-floating away towards a sunrise far off in the distance. An aura warm and inviting, so much so it called to her. She didn't know if it was using her name actually, but she was compelled to go. It was time, he said. "He" was the voice of reason, Carrie thought.

No more pain, no more worry, no more…

"She's going code blue!"

The air paramedic called into her helmet's boom mic as she arrived at the limp body of Mrs. Jason Parmenter. The pilot kept the turbine from shutting down, he knew they had to dust off immediately, as soon as the patient was strapped to an aircraft litter and secured aboard.

Carrie saw a bright light shining in her eyes and a voice asking her if she could hear them. Carrie tried to nod, but the warm air around her was lifting her, entrancing her to follow the sensation, to go with. The Staff of Caduceus on the nurse's helmet resembled a cross, a crucifix. The emblematic sign of death and life. The resurrection of the soul. He was here with her. Comfort flooded her veins; she felt a cold chill then nothing.

The flight nurse strapped Carrie's body to the litter as John pulled a crying Dusty back away so the medic could work. A Trooper from the NHP who was certified EMT helped the nurse, they seemed to know each other or at least each other's movements anyways and they danced around in a ballet of life saving techniques.

No one saw the smile that flickered off of the young patient's face. It was quick, lightning bolt fast, and then it was gone as fast as it came. Her face went sullen, then blank. Her eyes looked emptily towards the sky.

The nurse looked down to the cargo and gave a jerk to the litter, indicating that the deputy and trooper move faster to the helo, "We're losing her!"

Less than one minute and fifteen seconds later, the pilot pulled back nearly full on his collective and the Agusta lifted off in yet another cloud of dust and collecting ash from the house fire. He pushed the cyclic forward and the nose dipped on the bird as it lifted from the ground, the vibration from the rotors sending gut wrenching echoes throughout the stomachs of the onlookers below.

The pilot was calling McCarran Tower to inform of his return to the Metro airspace and Carrie just barely heard his final warning to them in her mind before it went blank, "…and make sure that that crazy bastard that almost clipped us in the Cessna on the way out is gone!"

John placed his hand on Dusty's shoulder just as Helen broached herself from the vault door by the equipment shed. Mike Tenner was still staring at the helicopter as its flashing A/C lights disappeared towards the big city beyond the next mountain range.

LAST

Darkness

A clap of thunder ravaged the still daytime air. Even
though there hadn't been a significant thunderstorm in
Joshua County and Soap Valley in the last dozen or so
years, the sky was threatening today. And why not? For the
first time since 1922 more than one person was being laid
to rest at the cemetery in Fallcast at the same time. Then, it
was an outbreak of polio and three children were cast down
under the white and brown soil, today it was four adults
who were needlessly sacrificed and being prepped for
eternity into the mineral rich ground of a desert town.
Nearly the whole town was present, crowding the small
black wrought iron fenced cemetery at the edge of town,
just a few yards from the rail line that went on through to
Vegas.

      Whitening stone mausoleums and ten foot tall
angels that looked down upon the brown and starving
grassed area looked even gloomier today, the eyes of the
marble cherubs wept with the oncoming and down pouring
rain, the areas of white dolomite gravesites of the poorer
individuals who could not afford marble or alabaster or
huge granite headstones-the ones marked with a simple
number or metal bracket with a name-all seemed less
destitute today. They ranked in and answered roll call of
death with the greatest of the tombs, in the ground and
above, they mourned the loss of the town, the loss of the
county and loss of the humans that had assembled here
today. Silently, the whole graveyard shuddered with the
breeze brought on by the thunderclouds overhead, as the
mourners collected for those to be buried today, the souls
of the ones who perished in the coldest winters or hottest
summers all gather around each other it seemed-to mourn
as one. The folk who entered the Fallcast Cemetery that
day, felt them.

A plot was being dug on the other side of the cemetery, next to one that was covered over several months back. Megan Cooke was being prepared for her internment here. Killed by her momentary lapse in jealousy of her friend, the only one who'd believe her, she believed that good would make things alright. She'd cried wolf, she let too many people know that she hated Carrie and would do anything for Jason, and the town thought she was capable of killing to get what she wanted. No one would believe her as she told them the truth.

Another hole was cut and already six feet deep, this was for Paul Davis. He had no family left in Fallcast, they had moved away years ago with the thought their son had run away; his bent and waxy body locked in a cheap coffin supplied by the county was to be buried with just a quick ceremony and a few words of peace from the preacher. A third was for Terrence Dodson, murdered for his reluctant generosity, even though he was on his way out, few suspected that Terrence Dodson had not taken a half dozen pain pills and drank half a bottle of scotch.

By his side, just to the left and soon to be under a huge granite stone was Marie Ann Dodson. Murdered by her own flesh and blood and cast into a cool dry cave to naturally mummify. Her remains were carefully placed inside an ornate coffin, with small angels adorning the seam. It was a fitting end to a horrible existence of her last few years. Hope was kept alive that she would someday return to Fallcast and in truth, she did.

The last grave next to Terrence and Marie was the hardest for the workers to dig; they all knew her by face and her big smile, her beauty and her obstinate opinion of her father's plan for Fallcast. They knew her as the last of the ones that could possibly turn this town around, they all wept as they dug the six foot deep hole for the nearly six foot woman.

"Souls of the earth, ashes to ashes and dust to dust…" The preacher from Fallcast Baptist Church ranted. He drew the short straw between the Presbyterians, the Lutherans and the scattered Catholics who wanted a priest brought in from Vegas. In the end it was settled by the town leaders-who picked up the tab for the funerals, burials and the ensuing wakes with the winter slush fund-that the Baptist was the best suited. Fact is, he charged the least and many of the mourners were from his side of the town.

Darrin Parker was leaning against a tree, his arm in a sling and neck was bandaged from the top of the sling to just under his left ear. He had a cervical collar on before the service, but took it off; he hated the way the thing looked on him and the heat made his neck sweat. Dry tears were evident in his eyes, sadness showed in his face in the form of wrinkles and dark shadows under his eyes. He had his right hand on Dusty Dodson's shoulder. Dusty was crying a little more openly than Parks, but he deserved to. He was here to watch nearly everyone in his world put to rest.

Another figure moved to Parks and stood to Dusty's right. Mike Tenner whispered over the sermon, "Any good word?"

Although he had heard rumors and quick facts, he had avoided talking the subject with anyone. Tenner had taken the job with the Highway Patrol in Vegas shortly after the night he helped put Carrie aboard the hospital-bound helicopter. Things had gone so bad in Fallcast he couldn't stand to look at the townsfolk any longer.

The cave was excavated for evidence, and then two hundred pounds of explosives closed the hole forever and left little room for an insect to roam the insides. A secret pit with deep dark secrets hidden behind false walls and false dreams of notoriety and power. A centerpiece of anger and hate, of death and more death, a murky hole that hid the darkness. The darkness that resided in the shadow.

Even though he was called in for testimony and to verify reports, he left the week after that night at the Dickson's. The mummies and the embalmed fresh bodies were kept on ice in the basement of the hospital until the investigation concluded and every family member from around the country could arrive at a date and time that was convenient for everyone. It had been one month since that night.

Dusty looked up to Parks, he flinched a little and Parks took his hand off of the boy's shoulder. Dusty shrugged his shoulders and began to wander towards where the service was taking place.

Parks whispered back to Mike while looking at the boy, "Tommy Dodson's on suicide watch. The M. E. sent a kid intern over to get a DNA sample and the kid told him they needed it to confirm one of the bodies we found in the cave was that of his mother's. Ten minutes after the stupid kid left, Tommy confessed to killing his mother. Said she was running away and he threw her to the ground to stop her and she hit her head. Said it was an accident."

"Good lord."

"They took a full confession and he signed it. The M. E. matched the details of the injuries on the mummy against Tommy's confession and verified it."

"So Tommy killed his mother."

"That's not all. In his confession, he also admitted to killing Paul Davis in a fit of rage over the honor of his sister." He began to make quotation marks in the air with his fingers, but in a flash in his mind stopped him short, he knew how much Carrie hated that gesture. "After one killing I guess it gets easier."

"Was for Parmenter."

Parks let a snarl creep across his face. Mike saw it and blinked an apology.

Tenner looked away towards the crowd, "And Terrence?"

Parks shook his head. "Nope. That one's on Parmenter. No one but he could testify if he'd put drugs in Terrence's booze bottle. The boys at the lab in Vegas said it was possible, but they couldn't prove it either; there was enough residue to indicate someone did." Tenner turned to look back at his friend.

"How's the neck?" Mike was looking at the bandage in the area where a yellow-red stain had formed, the spot the knife went in.

"Hurts like hell." Parks took a sharp deep breath and let go of s little smile, a sad smile like the ones seen on someone who had no idea of what to do with their face at times. "You can't imagine what I was thinking when I saw his face in the rearview mirror just before he... did this..." Parks took a shuddered breath and added, "I hope his plane ran out of gas and slammed hard enough into the ground that the bastard felt his body being torn apart." He sighed and gave a small smile to his former partner, and then he looked to the suddenly silenced preacher in front of the crowd.

Darrin had accidently raised his voice and the mourners had looked over to see what the commotion was about. Tenner smiled as he stared at each one of the tear reddened faces until they focused back to the service.

Mike put his hand on Darrin's uninjured arm and squeezed a little. Darrin continued with a reserved voice, "I'm going to be stuck behind the desk for months, maybe a year. I'm in the process of adopting Dusty, I need to keep the bills up and the Sheriff let me keep working. Boy was he pissed that you quit..." He smiled.

Mike just shivered a shrug.

"Kid's gonna be rich. You're going to be set for life with what that asswipe found on Dodson property. And..." Tenner continued as fast as he could as not to let Darrin interrupt him, he felt he had to say it, to get it all out, "...since the kid is the only heir to both the land from

Dodson and Parmenter's claims he made behind everybody's back, he'll need real good moral guidance when he gets older."

"Doesn't matter to me any. I'd trade it all in."

Tenner felt a sickness waving though his system, he changed the subject, "No sign of the plane huh?" He kicked at a dry piece of turf. "I heard the FBI checked every airport within the Cessna's fuel range."

Parks just shook his head. "Not every airport. There are hundreds of them. Private, farms, old worn out Army-Air Corps fields. He might've landed or dead-sticked it into a flat field somewhere and hitchhiked to another town. Probably screwing it up too…" Darrin took a deep breath and tried his best look of concern, "If he did crash they might never find him either. The FBI says he might have gone down anywhere. Remember Steve Fossett in '07?"

Tenner nodded slowly, slow enough though to indicate he wanted to hear what Parks was saying. Parks was on a roll to explain and it made Tenner think it made his old pal and partner happy to get this all off of his chest, he was going to need all the room he has to raise the young Dodson boy right.

"Took a year to find him, in the process searchers found eight other crash sites they had never mapped before, one even dated back to 1964. Some hiker found his remains and the parts of his plane near Mammoth Lakes; sixty miles east from where he was supposed to be."

"Nice." The sarcasm was very sour. Tenner cleared his throat quietly and looked around symbolically, "This town is a mess."

Park's voice cracked, "Would've been a lot nicer if he hadn't ever showed up."

Tenner looked his friend in the eyes. They were moist; he knew what Darrin Parker was thinking about, who he was thinking about and why. Mike knew that Darrin had fallen in love with Carrie so many years ago;

but because of his shyness, of his fear of Terrence Dodson-not the physical pain he could bring but the way Terry Dodson made people's lives miserable if they crossed him-he hadn't a chance. He knew Darrin's future was now made for him, the young boy that was once just a quiet kid with a traumatic injury was now going to be his responsibility. The added weight of taking care of a young boy with a mental problem that may or may not last a lifetime will strain his friend.

Even though Darrin didn't show it-and Tenner thought the better of the two of them was Parks-he should be emotionally drained. He should be angry and sick to his stomach for what was ahead of him, caring for Dusty was one thing, but caring for Dusty because the young girl he loved so much it hurt had left it to him to take care of her younger brother. And she wouldn't be around to help.

Parks said, "Don't take this wrong buddy, but he also unearthed a lot of truth. Truth that may have never been discovered before, truth about some people and he brought out the worst and best in others. But…" A lump filled his throat and tears burned the backs of his eyes, he felt as if he was going to lose it all, "…she had to pay too, and that isn't fair…"

Parks turned to keep his friend from seeing him break down.

END

From the Author

First I want to thank all the usual suspects, from my friends at *Radio Free Jericho*: John, Jess, Char, Denise, Debbie and dozens of others, who support me even though they get very tired of my theatrical diatribes on social networking sites. Grannie G, Aunt Char, Grandma Valda and my other extended family members who can't wait to read my next work deserve a special nod also.

For Catherine Gray my editor (yes I spelled it GRAY not *grey* which has everyone on my tail at all times to "spell it right", you're lucky I don't use *behaviour* and *harbour*. Actually I did use *Harbour* in *Follow*, but that's another story);

To Catherine Gray, my editor I say: a hundred thousand thank yous is not enough for the tireless pursuit in which you find my mistakes, and still are able to greet me with a straight face and baring no evidence of a nervous twitch caused by my butchering of the English language. If there are any errors in this novel, they are my fault and mine alone; she did her very best and made this work better than I could have.

Thank you to Paul Hinen my high school friend who helped me with his brilliant insight into the workings of modern law enforcement, since my days of the old bubble gum rotators and revolvers is long gone. Paul's advice and inspiration in our communications keep the cop blood in me flowing, though I'll never be able to spill it in the defense of others like he has. (He's also a Vet, so a double dog thank you for your service!)

To a real geologist: Rich, whose rambling about his love of the science over the pain in the ass paperwork and apprenticeship that kept him from doing what he loved most, I heard you. His stories from the small mining towns and the inner workings of politics that involved everyone from police chiefs to landowners and the way miners and mine workers get milked by locals and authorities inspired many scenarios within *Darkness*. I would like to add that although I didn't go deep into names and places, many situations were mostly from my imagination and the details were scrambled to protect anyone from retribution. Also, few details were used in the background of Jason Parmenter, his job, his science, the mineral industry, the mining industry and geology itself-so if you're going to write me to tell me that this isn't how it works, let me just say, I know. A brief overview from a geologist friend says that this was "pretty good fiction", including the way geology is broadly accepted. I won't represent myself here as having any knowledge of geology, even though my family grew up mining towns and even owned a few of them.

Fallcast does exist in a way. From Clifford, Ellendale, Tonopah, Silver Peak, Gerlach Nevada-those small mining towns that still inspire dreams for future stories, to Bodie California and Death Valley, Furnace Creek and other little bergs that had some influence one way or another on the basic description of Fallcast and its mapping out. To the rustic similarities of homes, businesses, cafes and other interiors described here. Somewhere, some places this stuff still is real.

To my family for sticking with me throughout the torturous nights and days of the final processes that cause my moods to shift, especially with the ending of this book. To my closest friend and sister-in-law Misty and my sister Deb for constant support battling the demons that haunt me daily and to them I say "Hey! Look! A nickel!"

To dad, ever vigilant to keep me on the right path and to his cousin Steve who was one of my first fans, I say thank you!

For those of you disappointed in the ending, I'm sorry. At the exact moment in time I was finishing this story, a macabre anniversary was taking place and it affected my writing as much as the frame of mind I was writing from. I couldn't finish the damn book! I looked deep within myself and for Mary, my friend from childhood whom I've missed very much for the last twenty-one years, I ended it the way I thought I should have. Honestly. Bad things happen and the way things turn out aren't always happy for everyone. If it helps, Carrie didn't die in the first ten versions. But then again, is she really dead? Better read it again! (I smell a sequel…)

This big thank you goes out to everyone who has read and will keep on reading what I write; it is for you that makes me who I am. It is for you that my hand moves, it is for you that makes me create. Thanks so very much for all your support all those dark and difficult years and the bright and (hopefully) bounteous ones.

And, as usual, if you see something that is out of place (spelling, grammar, etc.) let me know by e-mail or on my website. Sometimes during the conversion process; words, letters and sentences have disappeared, been moved or even find their way into another spot that makes things a frustrating mess. This is not the fault of the publishers, but I would like to hear about it so I can make changes. Thanks.

J JAY ROSS

Also from J Jay Ross:
Circle the Moon
Follow the Southern Cross
Glance Over My Shoulder
The Book of Asyla (Kindle series)
The Traditional Christmas Gift

An Australian Adventure: Follow the Southern Cross the Screenplay

J Jay Ross' Website

www.circlethemoon.net